Also by Jane Smiley

PRIVATE LIFE

PRIVATE LIFE

A NOVEL

Jane Smiley

ALFRED A. KNOPF · NEW YORK · 2010

THIS IS A BORZOI BOOK
PUBLISHED BY ALFRED A. KNOPF

Copyright © 2010 by Jane Smiley

Library of Congress Cataloging-in-Publication Data
Smiley, Jane.
Private life : a novel / by Jane Smiley. — 1st ed.
p.   cm.
ISBN 978-1-4000-4060-5
1. Officers' spouses—Fiction.   2. United States. Navy—Officers—Fiction.
3. Marriage—Fiction.   4. Psychological fiction.   I. Title.
PS3569.M39P75 2010
813'.54—dc22   2009037000

Manufactured in the United States of America
First Edition

In those days all stories ended with the wedding.

—ROSE WILDER LANE, *Old Home Town*

PROLOGUE

1942

S TELLA, who had been sleeping in her basket in the corner, leapt up barking and then slipped out the bedroom door. Margaret heard her race down the stairs. It was early; fog still pressed against the two bedroom windows.

Margaret sat up, but then she lay back on her pillow, dejected—she must have missed a telegram, and now her husband, Andrew, had returned. She woke up a bit more and listened for the opening of the front door. But, no, there hadn't been a telegram—she remembered that she'd looked for one. Had she not locked the front door? She stilled her breathing and listened. With the war on, all sorts of characters crammed Vallejo these days. Suddenly a little frightened, she slid out of bed and stealthily pulled on her robe, then opened the door of her room a bit wider and crept out far enough to peer over the banister. There was the top of a head, dark, not Andrew's, and by the dull light of the hall windows, a houndstooth jacket. A figure bent over to pet Stella, and Stella wagged her tail. This was reassuring. Margaret took a deep breath. Now the figure stood up, looked up, and smiled. He said, Put your clothes on, darling, we're going for a ride.

She was speechless with pleasure at seeing Pete, though he seemed to have walked right in—did that mean she had left the door unlocked, because how would he get a key? But getting ready took her no time, she made sure of that. She only brushed out her hair and redid her bun so that some of the gray was hidden, then got out her best blue suit with the white piqué collar and her last pair of hose and her nicest shoes. She put on the black straw hat with a half-veil, and she looked neat, she thought, though no better than that—at her age, you could not hope to look pretty, and she had never been beautiful. When she reached the bottom of the stairs, Pete smiled and kissed her on the cheek. She confined Stella in the kitchen and made sure the dog door to the backyard was unlocked. Then he led her to his car, which she hadn't seen, a Buick, prosperous gray and very clean. She said, Where are we going?

Somewhere you've been before. But that was all he would tell her.

Margaret had heard nothing from Pete in four months, not since their last agitated phone call two days after Pearl Harbor. Before that, she had seen him every couple of weeks. In the interim, either he had gotten old, or she had forgotten how old he was, because now, as they drove and she glanced at him, she saw that, yes, his hair was dark (that had never been natural), but his face was more wrinkled than hers, and spotted here and there. His teeth were yellow and a little crooked. It crossed her mind that maybe Cossacks weren't meant to live this long. Then she noticed her own hands, with their wrinkles and spots, and wondered what he must think of her. She would be sixty-four this year, and he would be—well, she didn't know for sure. But she adored him anyway, with a feeling that defied these meditations on the passage of time (did she adore him, or simply admire him, or how else would she describe her feelings was a question she often pondered). She looked at him again—square in the jaw, hawkish in the nose, kind, mysterious, not like any other man she had known. He didn't ask her about Andrew, and she didn't tell him that Andrew had gone to Washington or ask him where he himself had been all these months.

War again meant Vallejo was bursting, cars and trucks backed up and honking everywhere. When they got out of town—onto the 37, around the north shore of the bay—traffic was still slow, but the sun came out and the car warmed up. They made idle conversation— How was she feeling? When did he get the Buick? The weather had been sunny lately, hadn't it?—but she understood that important topics were to wait until the purpose of their trip was revealed. And the drive was especially pleasant because she had not been out of town, and hardly out of the house, since the attack. Everywhere, the grass was thick and green from the winter rains, and the air was extra bright because of the way that the sunlight shot through and was reflected off fluttering veils of fog. When they turned south, toward the city, the mountains seemed to almost impinge on the highway, they were so black and forbidding, but the waters of the bay seemed to sparkle, and then the fog receded, and they were on the Golden Gate Bridge. The sun shone on it; the cables swept upward to two peaks, and the road rose and curved between them. In the middle of the bridge, the waters of the Pacific spread away in two dazzling directions, deep dark blue, but ablaze with light. And then they were over, and the verges of the highway were green again until well into the city. Pete turned south on Van Ness and kept going. Houses and warehouses gave way to fields and marshes, and then houses and warehouses resumed. When he turned in at the entrance to Tanforan, she was pleased for a moment, and then she remembered that Tanforan was no longer a racetrack but a relocation center. It dawned on her. She said, Pete! You found them! She reached across the seat and took Pete's hand. He gave hers a squeeze.

In that moment, the racetrack vanished before her eyes. The orderly place it had been once, with horses passing here and there, and people walking purposefully or filling buckets or rolling bandages or raking walkways, gave way to high fences with guards outside them (armed), and milling groups of people inside them, not orderly or purposeful, but a melee—too many people, no horses, everything and everyone in a state of restlessness.

They were allowed through the entrance and directed to park to the left, in what was apparently a small visitors' section. This, too, was fenced off. Pete came around and opened her door. She said, I'm so glad you brought me here.

They asked for you.

Have you been coming here?

I found them last week. This is my third visit. Since I'm not a family member, it might have to be my last. I know one guy—one guy only—and he's not in the army, and the army runs things here.

He took her elbow. In his other hand, he carried a bag, but she couldn't tell what was in it.

The stalls had become makeshift rooms. All the doors were open, because the stalls had no other windows—if a door were closed, there would be no air, except, perhaps, through the cracks in the plank walls. She couldn't help staring as she went by (smiling, of course, in case anyone looked at her). The walls in the stalls had been whitewashed, but badly—nothing had been done underneath the whitewash to repair cracks or dents where the walls had been kicked—no doubt the stalls hadn't even been scrubbed down. But every stall was full—hanging clothes, suitcases, boxes, people, chairs, beds, little tables. They walked down one aisle, came to a cross-aisle, turned left, walked three more aisles, turned right at "Barn H." People looked at them as they passed, voices dropping, or falling silent altogether. Two children, little boys, shouted Hi! Hello! Howdy! in unison, and then went into a fit of giggles. She smiled at them, sorry she had nothing for them. Left again. Pete paused, looked around. Now they were at the far end of Barn G. He said, I thought they were here, and stepped back and looked up. Then he stepped forward and peeked over the half-door. Behind him, she peeked, too. There, on the back wall, was a painting of Mr. Kimura's that she recognized, a pair of finches, one perched on a railing and the other below, perched on the rim of a small bucket, drinking from it. The stall was neat, or as neat as it could be, but, like the others, it was full of things. The Kimuras had never lived grandly, and over the years the neighborhood in Vallejo where they had their shop had sometimes been quite wild, but the sight of the painting hanging here suddenly struck her in a way that the whole scene had not yet. She gave a little gasp and said, This is unbearable!

At least they have a whole one to themselves. Some families are crammed in two to a stall.

You lived in a stall.

As a lark. Or if I wanted to sleep later than four in the morning.

She felt the rebuke.

But neither Naoko Kimura nor her mother, Kiku, appeared. The people in the two neighboring stalls smiled but didn't speak. Pete opened the stall door and set the bag inside.

I don't like this.

Why not?

Because, when I was here two days ago, Kiku was quite ill. If she's up and walking around by now, I would be amazed.

Leaving her to assimilate this alarming news, he walked up the row three stalls and fell into conversation with a man who was standing there. He came back in a hurry.

We have to go to the infirmary, which is next to Barn V. That's across the compound. He says she went over there yesterday morning. They carried her on a stretcher.

But, Pete, what has been happening? Where have they been? Where have you been?

They've been in jail, but not in San Francisco. That was the thing that threw me for weeks. They were in San Francisco for a couple of nights, then they were sent to San Mateo, and then to Santa Cruz County. That's where they were until they were released and sent here. I couldn't have seen them there, even if I'd found them, since I'm not kin, but when I heard about this place, I got in touch with my friend and persuaded him to keep a lookout for them.

When did they get here?

About ten days ago.

Oh, Pete! This place!

It is one step better than jail. But Kiku got sick in jail, and she's only gotten worse here. He sighed. Now they were at Barn S, then T. She could see the training track, dusty and unused, with the practice starting gate sitting in the middle of the sand. They found the infirmary.

Pete opened the door and they peeked in. What they saw was not encouraging—a large, drafty space with a cocrete floor and cracked and partly boarded-over windows, in which fifteen or twenty beds had been hastily arranged at one end along with some cabinets. Most of the beds were full, and around most of them milled what looked like worried relatives, in jackets and sweaters (Tanforan was always chilly, given that it was in San Bruno), and nurses in white dresses, also wearing jackets. Two men who might have been doctors were talking together next to one of the beds.

Margaret peered at everyone, and finally recognized Naoko, whose hair had become truly gray. She was wearing a coat, sitting beside one of the beds, and leaning toward the patient, who must have been Kiku Kimura, who was heaped with covers against the chill. Naoko looked up and saw them, then rose and came toward them. Pete followed Margaret into the huge room. She felt her hat slip, and reached up to pin it, sorry now that she had worn such a ridiculous item, sorry that she had gazed into the mirror and indulged her vanity.

Naoko was full of smiles, but she looked drawn and anxious. She took each of their hands and thanked them for coming as if they had done her a great favor. She led them to the bed.

Margaret would not have recognized Mrs. Kimura. She lay flat on her back with her chin tilted upward and her mouth open. She did not have her teeth in, so her mouth looked sunken and pitiful. Her hair was smoothed back away from her forehead, and her eyes were closed. The covers were up to her chin, but one thin hand poked out to the side, and Naoko took it as soon as they got to the bed. It made Margaret shiver with cold just to look at her—she couldn't imagine that Kiku had enough body heat to keep herself warm even under such a pile. When she leaned down to say hello, she could hear that Mrs. Kimura's breath was labored. Pneumonia.

Naoko invited her to sit in the chair and perched herself on the edge of the bed. Pete stood nearby. Naoko took her mother's hand again. She said, She told me herself, when we were down in Santa Cruz and she got a cough there with a fever, that she would get pneumonia from it, and she would die, but that was a month ago. By the time we got here, I thought she would prove herself wrong, but the second night, she coughed all night, sitting up and disturbing our neighbors. There was nothing I could do for her. She glanced over at the doctors. They don't have anything for us. She smoothed her mother's forehead. If she were me and I were her, I know there would be some herbs she would gather or a tea she would make. Oh dear. I . . . The doctors were now going from bed to bed, but they didn't approach Mrs. Kimura.

Can they make her more comfortable at least? said Pete.

Naoko shook her head and said again, They have nothing.

Margaret looked around. At the end of the room opposite to the beds were tables and boxes. She saw that the "infirmary" was also being used as a storage shed. I was wondering so about you. I went to your apartment in San Francisco. It must have been the morning after you left. I can't imagine what you've been through.

Naoko lifted her chin and closed her eyes. The interrogations were the worst. Where were our notes on plans for sabotage? Was it my

mother, in her travels, who carried messages between various sabo-
teurs? Were we the ones who planted the tomato field that pointed
like an arrow at the airfield, or did the farmer himself think of that? We
had no idea what they were talking about, but they posed the questions
so that they were impossible to answer. How was Lester receiving
his information that he was then sending to Joe? Through whom
was Lester communicating his information to Joe? Had the Japanese
military been in contact with Joe before he went to Japan? Had I
ever met Mr. Masaoko? Was my mother the go-between? Was I the
go-between? Whose idea was it for Joe to move to Japan and enlist in
the army there? My mother was so nervous with these interrogations
that it made her sick, and then they asked if she was pretending to be
ill so that she could get to a hospital and communicate with her
contacts! All of this she said in a quiet voice with lowered eyes. Pete
kept looking at her, and tears started running down Margaret's
cheeks. And then they came to us one day and said that all the
Japs were going to camps and they were finished with us, so they sent
us here. They didn't charge us with anything, but they said they
retained the account books I was doing for my clients in Japantown, just in case there were coded messages in them. So I am still
under suspicion. It was only in that *"retained"* that Margaret sensed
the old, independent Naoko she had known now for thirty-some
years.

Pete said, What about Lester?

Naoko raised her hand, but gently, so as to not shake the bed. They
still have him. He's charged with illegal gambling. We knew he was
doing that. My mother tried to talk him out of that more than once, but
what else did he have in his life? The man he worked for was named
Rossi, Luca Rossi, and they haven't charged him with anything. He just
went out and found himself some other runners. He told Lester, You
Japs are going to lose all you got anyway, so you're not so good for business anymore.

Pete looked unsurprised.

Mrs. Kimura gave a strangled gasp, and her eyes fluttered but didn't
open. Margaret knew that it was Andrew, her own husband, who had
killed her, that Pete knew it, too, and that if Pete knew it Naoko knew
it. She said, I am so sorry.

Mrs. Kimura began to cough, weakly, and Naoko helped her sit up a little more. After the coughing subsided, she gave some harsh cries, and then her eyes opened. Her gaze fell on Pete, and then on Margaret. With great and visible effort she assembled her dignity, and finally she smiled. She whispered, You come.

I would have come much sooner if I'd known where you were.

We were in jail. Then, after a long pause, I didn't know. Margaret thought she must mean that she didn't know why.

You shouldn't have been.

Mrs. Kimura said, Lester . . . But her voice died. Margaret exchanged a glance with Pete, then she said, I'm sure Lester had nothing to do with it. Lester is a good man. He is. It was— But Pete's hand clamped down on her shoulder, forbidding her confession.

The doctors still did not come near. Margaret said to Naoko, Are you with her all day?

Naoko nodded.

All night?

I don't mind. But I can't keep warm in here. I go back to my place and warm up and then come here.

If they have nothing for her, then . . .

But she didn't go on. In fact, Margaret doubted whether Mrs. Kimura could survive being carried anywhere on the stretcher. She rubbed her hands together. When they were warm, and Naoko had gotten up to straighten her mother's covers, she took Mrs. Kimura's hand. It was small, thin, and cold. She tried to hold it as gently as she could and to impart a little warmth to it. After what seemed like a long time, she felt the dying woman squeeze her hand, just a bit. Then Mrs. Kimura gasped again and closed her eyes. Pete leaned down and kissed her gently, once on each cheek, his lips just brushing the skin, and then it was time to go. Naoko accompanied them to the door of the infirmary. Pete said, I brought you the things you asked for. I don't know if I can come back.

Naoko nodded.

THEY walked for a minute or two in silence. That was my barn, over there. Barn O. I enjoyed those days.

This is a terrible thing to do.

Yes, says the American in me.

What does the Russian in you say?

I hope they don't get shot.

What about you?

I won't get shot.

I don't know how to think about any of it, frankly, not any of it. If only the Japanese hadn't attacked Pearl Harbor! What do they want? What were they thinking?

Darling, they were thinking, Who do those Russians think they are? Why do you find those English fellows everywhere you turn? What makes the French act so superior? And look at the Americans! Such a bunch of primitives! A pack of apes in trousers, telling us what to do! That is what they were thinking.

They got to the car. One of the guards was staring at them. Pete smiled and waved at him. The man kept his weapon down. Pete unlocked and opened her door, then went around and got in the driver's side. It was now quite chilly, and they didn't open the windows. As he pressed the starter, she said, I put all my pictures away, I couldn't stand them anymore. I used to love them so, but now . . .

They backed out of their spot and turned down the line of cars.

Darling, there are whole categories of pictures that you never even looked at. Do you remember any of the scowling samurai we saw? With their teeth bared and their eyebrows lowered?

Yes, but—

Those are traditional Japanese pictures, too.

I didn't like those.

They drove out of the gate, waving innocently at the two guards in their little cabin, and then they made their way to Camino Real, and turned north. Pete said, What is the lesson to be learned?

Margaret flared up. It was Andrew—

But Pete stopped her again. I don't blame Andrew.

But he—

Pete raised her hand to his lips. It was clear he wouldn't talk about that.

She felt terribly cold inside her neat suit and her heavy tweed coat. Her hat was still on her head. She unpinned it and set it on the back seat, then shoved her hands in her pockets, but there was no way to get warm. She did not even shiver. Pressed down by her heavy blankets, Kiku Kimura would be too weak to shiver, Margaret thought.

They drove on in silence, this time crossing to the East Bay and pass-ing Berkeley and Oakland, where they were in the sunlight. San Fran-cisco, so beautiful in the morning, was now gray and invisible. They sat in the line of cars, waiting for the ferry at Benicia. Have I told you that I'm moving to Vancouver?

Pete, you've hardly told me anything. But Vancouver! Have you been interrogated, too? Her hand flew to her mouth, then she looked around, but no one, either on the wharf or in the other cars, was look-ing at them.

Pete laughed his old laugh, the easy, brave laugh that she found so irresistible now, the very laugh she had once distrusted. As he drove onto the ferry, he said, Not yet, but sometimes I do have the sense I'm being watched or followed, though when I look around I never see an extraordinarily tall, mustachioed man. No, darling, it's much simpler than that. I'm busted again.

The tall, mustachioed man would be Andrew.

She tried to adopt a bit of Pete's teasing tone, but she was alarmed. You always said armaments were a sure thing!

Not sure enough. Some innovations tempted me. I should have stuck to mere bullets. I don't know what I should have stuck to, per-haps. But I've found a position in Vancouver.

As what?

Now the ferry engine rumbled, and then they backed away from the wharf. The car shivered around them.

As a butler. It might be nice, just keeping order. I think I'll enjoy it. Do you remember my friend Bibikova, from St. Petersburg? She mar-ried a man named Yerchikovsky. It's their grandson I'll work for. I'll be an old family retainer. Vassily, they think I am.

He told her this as if she wouldn't care, as if nothing about it was of more than idle interest to her. The noise of the engine swelled again, and then the ferry docked with a bump, and they drove off it.

It was not quite three when they got to her house. As soon as they opened the door, she saw the telegram on the floor, where it had landed when the delivery boy pushed it through the slot. She picked it up. Stella was barking in the backyard.

Pete took one of her hands. Let's have a look at the pictures. I would like to see the ones Sei did for you. He meant Mr. Kimura. She took off her hat and set it on the hall table. The pictures were in the closet. She got them out, then went into the kitchen and turned on the gas under the kettle.

When she came back, Pete was standing in front of the rabbit. The animal looked nearly vaporous today, a rabbit made of mist crouched down beside stalks of luminous green bamboo. The bamboo reminded her more vividly of Mr. Kimura than the rabbit did—she remembered the exact way that his fingers held the brush and seemed to press the leaves of the bamboo out of it, one by one. That was decades ago now. Mr. Kimura had been dead for two years. They were all so old. Pete set aside the rabbit, and there were the coots. The rabbit was a sketch that Mr. Kimura had given her, but the coots she had commissioned. He had painted it on the north end of the island, not far from where they got on the 37 that very morning, though she hadn't been there in years. Now she gazed at the curve of the far edge of the pond against the higher curve of the hillside. Far to the left, a solitary chick swam so fast that he made ripples. To the right, the other chicks clustered together, picking bits of things off the surface of the water. Their lives had been so brief that they never even lost their red heads, but Mr. Kimura had caught their friskiness perfectly. Then she could hardly see the painting for the tears in her eyes. Pete, don't go away!

He put his arm around her, squeezed hard. He knew, of course, that she adored him, or admired him, or whatever it was. He was one of those sorts of men that women were wiser to stay away from, men who took an interest in women, and observed them, and knew what they were thinking.

Darling, I should have been a different person. But I'm not.

And Margaret felt herself almost say, Me, too. But she didn't know how to say it, because she hardly knew, even as old as she was, what person she had been.

The teakettle was whistling in the kitchen, but they wouldn't be drinking any tea. Pete, staring at the coots, leaned forward with an intent look on his face, and the whistle of the kettle rose in pitch, as if in desperation. She said, You take it. I want you to take it.

He stood straight up and looked at her, refusal written on his face, but then he relented. His smile came on slowly, and he kissed her on the forehead. She stepped forward, took the picture, and placed it in his hands. It wasn't terribly large, though it had always seemed to be. She said, The teakettle is going to burn up.

While she was in the kitchen, Stella entered through the dog door, her tail wagging, but Margaret went out without greeting her, and closed her in the kitchen. In the hall, Pete had his hat on, the picture under his arm. She walked him the step or two to the door and opened it. As he went out onto the porch, he pressed her hand.

Thank you, he said, then again, thank you.

She stood on her porch and watched him walk to his car, get in, and, with a wave, drive away.

PART ONE

1883

OR A WHILE, they lived in town. She had a particular and vivid memory of that time: she was running, as it seemed she always did, back and forth from one end of town to the other. She was fast and gloried in it. She wasn't racing against anyone or getting into trouble, she was just running and looking at things. She ran fast enough so that she could feel her heavy blond hair stream out behind her, subside across her back, stream out again. She passed one house after another.

At the far end of town, there was a pleasant large house where some ladies lived, though they never talked to her, nor she to them. She remembered how, one day, she came to a halt in front of this house and one of the ladies, a tall beauty, was standing on the porch, wearing an elegant white embroidered gown with a snowy eyelet skirt. Margaret stared at her, and the lady smiled. Margaret thought that she had never seen anything as beautiful as that dress in her life, which at the time seemed rather long. When the lady wafted back into the house, Margaret turned and pelted home, where she found her mother in the back parlor, sewing. As soon as Margaret entered the room, out of breath, she saw that her mother was sewing a copy of the dress she had seen on

the beautiful lady. She exclaimed, "I saw that! I saw that dress today!"
Then she went up and touched the eyelet. Her mother, Lavinia, didn't
reprimand her, but finished the seam she was sewing, and broke the
thread between her teeth. Then she said, "Perhaps you did. But don't
tell your father." It was years before Margaret realized that the pleasant
house at the far end of town was a brothel, and that, from time to time,
her mother sewed for the ladies, to make a little extra money. In Margaret's mind, these dresses were always white. When she was older,
though, and recalled this, Lavinia said that it hadn't happened, it
couldn't have happened; Margaret must have read it in a book.

What *had* happened, what Margaret should have remembered, was
that her brother Lawrence, who would have been thirteen then, had
left the house with her one day and taken her to a public hanging. No
one had stopped him, because Lavinia was giving birth—to Elizabeth—and her father, famous all over town as Dr. Mayfield (Margaret
thought of him as "Dr. Mayfield," too, he was that imposing), was
attending the birth. Lily, the housekeeper, was occupied with Beatrice,
who was two. It was said that Lawrence and Margaret left the house
and were gone for hours before anyone noticed. But no one suspected
that Lawrence, a studious boy, would have taken her to the hanging.
Ben, yes—Ben was rowdy and adventuresome, though two years
younger than Lawrence. The whole episode was a family legend, and
part of the legend was that Margaret didn't remember a thing about it.
"Margaret looks on the bright side," said Lavinia. "As well she should."
From time to time, though, Margaret had a ghostly recollection of this
bit or that bit—of her hand reaching up into Lawrence's hand, or of
him handing her a bit of a crab apple, or of her bonnet hanging over her
eyes so that she couldn't see anything except her feet. He might have sat
her on his shoulders—he sometimes did that when she was very young.
Nevertheless, it was a fugitive memory, however dramatic.

Margaret remembered other things that she would have preferred
to forget. She remembered that when Ben was thirteen he went with
some cronies down to the railyards. They found a blasting cap, which
one of the fellows attached to the end of a short length of iron rod that
they had also found. Employing this rod, they rubbed the blasting
cap against some brickwork to see what might happen. When it
exploded, the rod flew out of the boy's hand and entered Ben's skull
above the ear. He was killed instantly. None of the other boys was hurt,

and they carried the body home as best they could. Dr. Mayfield met them at the door, and this was the first news they had of the death of Ben.

That winter, Lawrence contracted measles, which led to an inflammation of the brain. The source of the original infection was what Lavinia had always feared, a child who was brought to see Dr. Mayfield. Elizabeth, Beatrice, and Margaret succumbed as well. But they were fairly young, and Lawrence was almost sixteen at the time. They lived and he did not.

And then, one evening about six months after the death of Lawrence, for reasons of his own that Lavinia later said had to do with melancholic propensities, Dr. Mayfield retrieved Ben's rifle from the storeroom behind the kitchen and shot himself in his office. Lavinia found him—she had thought he was still out with a patient, but, upon awakening very late, she heard the horse whinny out in the stable. She went to Dr. Mayfield's office to investigate and discovered the corpse. Margaret remembered that night—the sounds of running feet and doors slamming, the whinny of a horse, and a shout either half rousing her or weaving into her slumber. What she remembered most clearly was that when she and her sisters got up in the morning, there was once again a large closed coffin in the parlor. Their father was gone, and Lavinia, who had been sickly from so many pregnancies and so much grief, was a different person, one the girls had never known before. She was entirely dressed, her bed was made, and from that day forward, she never complained again of the headache or anything else. Margaret was eight; Beatrice had just turned six; Elizabeth was not quite three. On the day after the funeral, which Margaret also remembered, Lavinia moved the girls to her father's farm—it was the practical thing to do, and Lavinia said that they were lucky to be able to do so. She told Margaret, because she was the oldest, that death was the most essential part of life, and that they must make the best of it. Margaret always remembered that.

GENTRY FARM, not far from Darlington, down toward the Missouri River, was famous in the neighborhood, a beautiful expanse of fertile prairie that John Gentry and his own father had broken in 1828. Before the War Between the States, Lavinia's father and grandfather owned thirty-two slaves, quite a few more than was usual in Missouri—they raised hemp, tobacco, corn, and hogs. When Lavinia was twelve, John Gentry gave his oath to support the Union, unlike several of his neighbors. Two of his cousins went off to join the Confederacy. After the war, John Gentry's loyalties were questioned all around, and so he married his daughters to suitors of unimpeachable Union sympathies. Martha married a man from Iowa who fought with the Fourth Iowa Infantry; Harriet married an Irishman from Chicago; Louisa married one of those radical Germans from the Osage River Valley, who, though her grandfather never liked him, was a rich man and an accomplished farmer. And after the war, John Gentry managed to hold off the bushwhacking Rebel sympathizers by being well armed at all times and a notoriously excellent shot. They did burn down his corncrib once, and steal two of his horses. He knew them, of course. Boone County, Callaway County, and Cole County were wild patchworks of Union and Rebel sympathizers, and though blood didn't run as high there as it did out to the west, your neighbor could always tip his hat to you during the day and come to hang you that same night. John Gentry said that you would think that Lincoln, a man who knew both Illinois and Kentucky, would have given going to war lengthier consideration than he did, but those folks from Massachusetts and New York, who didn't have a thing to lose, got his ear, and that was that for a place like Missouri, which remained a stew of differing loyalties and long-standing resentments for many years.

Lavinia never expressed opinions about the war—for her, the three girls were occupation enough. She was frank—their assets were few—and as they grew into young ladies, her principal task was to cultivate them. John Gentry had a piano, and so Beatrice was put to learning how to play it. Lavinia had a sewing machine, and so Elizabeth was put to learning how to use it. Dr. Mayfield had left quite a few books, and so Margaret, never adept with her hands, was put to reading them. Quite often, she would read while Beatrice practiced her fingerings and Elizabeth and her mother sewed. Margaret liked to read Dickens best— *The Old Curiosity Shop* was a great favorite, and *A Tale of Two Cities*. Her grandfather, sitting in the circle smoking his pipe, enjoyed *Martin Chuzzlewit* for Dickens's faithful portrayal of the sad life of those folks who lived over by Cairo, Illinois, a spot on the map as different from the Kingdom of Callaway County, Missouri, as white was from black.

She also read *Ragged Dick* and *Marie Bertrand,* which were, of course, by her mother's favorite author, Mr. Alger. They were most excited to receive a copy of Mr. Alger's *Bob Burton, or, The Young Ranchman of the Missouri,* as a gift from Aunt Louisa, but though they did read it, John Gentry was dismayed to discover that the Missouri River in question was in Iowa, and was not their Missouri, the real Missouri, which was in the state of Missouri and, he always told everyone, the true main branch of the Mississippi, and therefore the longest river in the entire world. Another book that came to mean a good deal to Margaret was *Two Years Before the Mast,* by Mr. Dana. She read it to her sisters twice, all the while making bright pictures in her own mind of the wild and inaccessible coast of California. These pictures subsequently turned out to be entirely wrong.

Alice, her grandfather's cook, taught them how to make biscuits, coffee, doughnuts, flapjacks, and piecrust. Of farmwork, the girls did little, but they did pick apples, pears, plums, and peaches from their grandfather's trees, and blackberries and raspberries and gooseberries from his bushes. They were taught to make jams and cordials, and to think of Missouri as an earthly paradise.

Lavinia got pattern books and designed their dresses so as to minimize their disadvantages of appearance: With her blue eyes and fair hair, Margaret wore only shades of blue. Elizabeth, who was not fair, was allowed blue and green. Beatrice, dark like their father, wore deep reds, sometimes pink, and occasionally a faded and respectable violet. Beatrice grew tall; she had to wear wide sleeves. Elizabeth's frocks, with their buttons and tucks and insets, always drew the (ever-foreseen male) eye to her slender waist. Margaret's wrists were a bit thick, according to her mother, so she had to wear gloves into town. The girls trimmed hats. They knitted shawls. They crocheted collars and edgings. They bleached, trimmed, pressed, and set aside in their chests the household linens they would need one day. They embroidered.

For some months when Margaret was sixteen, there was a lengthy discussion of whether they should purchase a loom. Lavinia had heard that there was an enterprising woman in Osage County who made beautiful carpets. Lavinia wondered if this woman might take one of the girls, perhaps Elizabeth, as a student, or even adopt her outright— Lavinia felt that you never knew what an enterprising woman would do, anything was possible. But John Gentry put his foot down, and so the girls learned a humbler craft that winter, braiding rugs from rags. As the rugs grew beneath the fingers of her mother and sisters, Margaret read aloud, as a novelty, a book that had been written by a famous woman from St. Louis named Kate O'Flaherty Chopin. Her grandfather told them how he remembered the very day back in 1855, when Lavinia was still an infant, that the first train belonging to the Pacific Railroad brought down the bridge over the Gasconade River. Many were killed, including Mr. O'Flaherty, Kate Chopin's father. John Gentry was interested in everything about the railroad, for it had been a great boon to him. Nevertheless, he and Lavinia agreed that the fact that Mrs. Chopin wrote novels for remuneration was an unfortunate outcome of her trials. Beatrice, Elizabeth, and Margaret were encouraged to pity rather than admire her. But books were books—the hoped-for suitors would require an appealing degree of cultivation. Beatrice, with her talents (and good looks), and Elizabeth, with her skills (and her thick mane of chestnut hair), might get as far as Chicago or even New York (in Mr. Alger's books, the best place to find yourself ending up was New York), but even Margaret could get to St. Louis.

On the farm, talk of St. Louis was constant.

At first, St. Louis came to her as a fall, like a light snow, of names: Chouteau. Vandeventer. Eads. Gratiot. Laclede. St. Charles. Lafayette. Even Grand, which was a boulevard. Shenandoah, Gravois, Soulard. If there was a street name in St. Louis as dull as Oak or Fourth, Margaret never heard it. And every good thing was from there—shoes and boots, silks and nainsooks and Saxony woollens, books, pianos, books of piano music, candy, sugar, chewing tobacco, her mother's mouton capelet, pearl buttons. There was a vast emporium in St. Louis called Carleton's which carried goods sent specially from Paris, France, and London, England, and from Japan and China and India (if only tea—Lavinia drank tea). John Gentry seemed to take personal credit for the way St. Louis blossomed just over the eastern horizon of Gentry Farm, and the fact that they could get to St. Louis any day they wanted, on the train from McKittrick, was a source of eternal joy to him (they should have seen the roads, if that was what you wanted to call them, in the Missouri of his youth!). Even so, he went there not more than once in two years.

· · ·

AND then Beatrice was suddenly eighteen years old, a finished product. She could play any number of pieces on the piano, from "Jeanie with the Light Brown Hair" and "Camptown Races" to "Rosalie, the Prairie Flower," and some more complex pieces without lyrics, such as "Annie and I," which had three sharps. She could sing if the song in question fell into her range. Her tone was rich and melodious. The time had come to put her on display. A lady Lavinia knew in town had a very nice piano, much nicer than the Gentry piano, which she herself could not play, so, on days when John Gentry had to take a wagon into town anyway for business, he would carry Beatrice along and leave her at Mrs. Larimer's house on Pennsylvania Street, and Beatrice would play for her. Sometimes, with enough notice, Mrs. Larimer would invite a few friends in to have tea while Beatrice was playing.

The summer Beatrice was eighteen, the cousin of a friend of Mrs. Larimer, a man named Robert Bell, took over the town newspaper. He had money and credentials. What John Gentry knew about Robert Bell, within the first week, was that he was backed by some family capital, he was ambitious, and he had grown up in St. Louis in a big house on Kingshighway, a very wealthy and forward-looking neighborhood.

It was Robert Bell who decreed, young man though he was and new to town, that the Unionists would march at the front of the Fourth of July parade just behind the band; the farm-produce displays, the fire engine, the horse drill, and the mules would march in the middle; and the Rebels (numbering eight by now), dressed in their old Confederate uniforms, would march at the back, behind the Ladies' Aid Society and the German-American Betterment Society (which dressed in traditional Bavarian costume). He wrote about his plan in the newspaper, alternating discussions of the controversy with news of the war in Cuba, Guam, Puerto Rico, and then the Philippines, until everyone in town had had their say and gotten bored with the War Between the States, especially since the new war seemed to be going so well. According to John Gentry, this strategy of promoting patriotism over infighting was a mark of genius in such a young man, and he went by the office of the newspaper to tell Robert Bell as much. The young man thereupon invited John Gentry and his family to watch the parade from the windows of the newspaper office, which was closed for the afternoon.

To Margaret, Robert Bell was a disappointing sight. He had enormous muttonchop whiskers that only partly disguised his receding chin. His hair was thin and flyaway. His eyes were his best feature, rich blue and much more expressive than his words. He was nicely dressed. But he was considerably shorter than Beatrice—the top of his head came only to the middle of her ear. He made Margaret feel awkward just by standing next to her. He was attentive to them, though. He showed Lavinia to the best chair, which was pulled up right in front of a large open window looking out on Front Street, and then he showed Beatrice to the chair beside that one, and he brought her a cake and a cup of tea. Elizabeth and Margaret he left to fend for themselves, but he had gotten in nice cakes—light, with raspberry filling and marzipan icing, something Margaret had never seen before that day. He also had gotten in enough lemons for real lemonade, which he served with ice. He was comfortable with luxury, just what you would expect in a Bell from St. Louis—Margaret could see this thought passing from Lavinia to her grandfather when they caught each other's eye and raised an appreciative eyebrow.

The crowd outside the window undulated forward and then sepa- rated and backed toward the newspaper office as the band turned into the road. Margaret watched them for a few minutes, and then she did what she so frequently could not help doing, she glanced at a newspa- per on the table beside her, and began to read the articles. Since every- one around her was admiring the parade, she was free to read, but not, she thought, free to pick up the paper and open it in the midst of a cel- ebration. The dispatches related that American ships had landed preparatory to taking Santiago. As for Puerto Rico, victory belonged to the Americans, for General Miles had taken San Juan without resis- tance. Then there was an article about the fate of a two-headed bull-calf born in Montgomery County (died at three months), and an article about the extension of the MKT Railroad somewhere in Kansas. At the bottom of the page was another headline and part of an article, "County Man Returns from Mexico Expedition":

Little did Andrew Jackson Jefferson Early, of this county, suspect, when he was growing up on Franklin Street, that he would some- day travel the world and consort with famous and prominent men. Mr. Early is an astronomer. Before he journeyed to the mountains of central Mexico, the world was a different place. We had the sun, the moon, and the stars. We had Mr. Harriman and Commodore Vanderbilt, but we never had these last two gentlemen at the same time. Now, in effect, we do, for Dr. Early's expedition has discovered something we would not have suspected to be possible in God's grand Creation.

Beside the print was a photograph of a man that she thought she recognized, but perhaps it was only that he looked much like all the other young men she knew, the arching brow, the straight vertical of the nose, the square chin. He was wearing a hat in the Western style; his glance was direct and challenging. Unfortunately, she could not ascertain what his great discovery might be, because a man picked up the paper from the table beside her and carried it off. The Earlys were well known around town as Rebel sympathizers, too prominent and wealthy to end up as bushwhackers, but not the sort of people John Gentry socialized with. Margaret seemed to recall that there were many boys but no girls in the family, and that when the father had died (what was his name? Patrick?), the Rebel sympathizers had turned out in great numbers for the funeral, and John Gentry remarked, "There was another one who was never the same since the war."

Outside the window, the Union soldiers (numbering fourteen) had passed, and the brass band, and now came a row of wagons. The first of these bore a pile of hemp, upon which sat girls from the orphanage dressed in white and carrying bouquets of daylilies, black-eyed Susans, and a few late shrub roses. After these girls came Mr. Alexander's wagon that he got from a circus. It was pulled by a team of four grays with red ribbons braided into their manes, and into it he had loaded his best white sow and her squealing piglets. Then came the tobacco wagon that some of the local farmers kept in a barn somewhere. Margaret could smell the fragrance of the leaves as it went by.

She regarded Robert Bell and Beatrice. He was staring out at the tobacco wagon, but he had his hand on the back of Beatrice's chair. She was fanning herself. She glanced at him. Even sitting down, Beatrice could nearly look him in the eye. Then Margaret saw her mother look at the two of them and away, then shift in her seat and adjust her skirt to cover her feet. Lavinia's hair, which had once been so thick that she could hardly pin it up, was more manageable now, but she was the sort of woman who did not age, just as John Gentry, who was seventy-five, seemed closer to sixty. It was Lavinia's oft-repeated lament that the supply of men in the county was short. There were numerous grandfathers, but husbands, fathers, brothers, and sons were scarce.

Beside Margaret, Elizabeth leaned forward to watch the troop of horses go by. Whereas Beatrice was dark and tall, Elizabeth was brown-haired and small-boned, with a turned-up nose; Margaret thought she was beautiful. Beatrice had no dimples where they should have been, Cupid's-bow lips (her best feature), and large hands (and feet). But Beatrice had a way about her. Her smile was slow, her movements were slow—not as if she were lazy or sluggish, but more as if she had all the time in the world. Just now, Margaret saw her smooth her hand over the silk of her skirt, and heave a relaxed sigh. Robert Bell smiled down at her, perhaps in spite of himself. But he stepped back, and removed his hand from Beatrice's chair.

The horse drill passed. The riders wore bands across their chests and rosettes on their shoulders, and they waved their hats in unison as they went by, first to their left and then to their right. Every couple of minutes, they halted in formation, swept low over their horses' necks, then waved their hats over their heads and trotted forward. It occurred to Margaret to wonder again what Andrew Jackson Jefferson Early had discovered that changed the face of creation as the music faded into the distance when the brass band turned off Front Street four blocks down.

Elizabeth nodded toward John Gentry and said, "Look at Papa."

Their grandfather was sitting in his chair with his knees apart and his body squarely situated. His hat was pushed back on his head, and he was wiping his brow. Margaret said, "It's hot."

"His face is very red."

"Look at Mr. Bell. His cheeks are steaming."

Elizabeth murmured, "Proximity to Beatrice has given him a case of humidity," then laughed, and Margaret smiled. One of the great loves of her life was Elizabeth's low, rippling laugh, never girlish or coy, but always gay and sassy. Margaret said, "I think Papa likes Mr. Bell."

"It's true that he has made no disparaging references to Mr. Bell's nose, his height, his horse, his waistcoats, or his ancestry."

Margaret and Elizabeth exchanged a glance, and they nodded. They both knew that the task was to win Mr. Bell, not to approve him.

Lavinia was watching the procession of the German-American Betterment Society. Their uncle Anton was in the second rank, wearing his hat and his short pants and carrying his Bavarian walking stick. The entire association was singing a song Margaret didn't know, in German.

"Oh dear," said Elizabeth, standing up.

John Gentry had fallen off his chair, and the chair had fallen over. Lavinia at once knelt down beside him, and the man behind her moved the chair. Everyone turned to look. Mr. Bell bustled over, and Beatrice stood. Mr. Bell sent a young man out, and then her mother helped her grandfather to sit up. The young man returned with a cup of water; Lavinia administered a few sips. John Gentry took a deep sigh, put his hat on, removed it again, put it on again. His face was dreadfully red, Margaret thought. Outside the window, the Rebel soldiers passed, their rifles on their shoulders and their marching feet making the only noise. The crowd in the street was quiet—the Rebels' participation in the parade was more startling than anyone had anticipated. Who had seen those uniforms in thirty-three years?

Mr. Bell and another man helped John Gentry back into his chair, and he drank the rest of the water. He shook his head. He shook his head again, then he reached for Beatrice's hand. Mr. Bell moved Beatrice's chair so that she was sitting a bit closer, and Elizabeth resumed her seat next to Margaret. With her other hand, Beatrice gently smoothed her grandfather's hair back from his forehead, a kindly thing to do, and something Margaret would not have thought of. It was often remarked in her family that Margaret did not have a fine sensibility, or, even, a female sensibility. When she read aloud about the death of Little Nell, her voice was steady and her progress unremitting. When she read aloud Miss Alcott's book, which was sent to Lavinia by her aunt Harriet, it did not occur to her to weep at the passing of Beth. She thought that, for all of Jo's boyishness, she was a sentimental thing. Lavinia found her mysterious when Margaret shed no tears the day their cat Millie was caught in a raccoon trap or when Alice and Beatrice contracted the cholera and it seemed as though one or the other of them—or both—were set to pass on. But, apart from the fact that the first thing Margaret felt about these lamentable events was that they were *interesting* as well as *sad,* there was always also what she was feeling now, watching John Gentry, Beatrice, and Robert Bell, that a play had begun suddenly, perhaps when she wasn't looking. Now, Mr. Bell's leaning over Beatrice with a smile had something to do with Papa's collapse and something to do with the marching of the Rebels in the parade and something to do with the paper on the table, and these events were designed to go together. Her task seemed to her at these times to be not to leap into the action, but to observe it and discern a pattern, though what she would do once she had discerned it, she could not imagine. In all the times she had entertained this sensation, she had never in fact discerned a pattern. She didn't know what to make of herself, truly. She might have said that for ten years (and who could remember before that?) she had repeatedly pressed on, doing and thinking what she judged to be right and natural at the time, only to be told afterward that she had done just the wrong thing. It was as if she were plowing a furrow, intent upon the ground in front of her, only to stop and look around and discover that she was in the wrong field, and, indeed, the wrong country entirely. No, it would never have occurred to her to smooth her grandfather's brow.

When the parade was over, Lavinia and Mr. Bell helped Papa to his feet, and then out of the newspaper office and around the building, where they got into the wagon, Papa first, Beatrice and Lavinia after him. Margaret and Elizabeth were assisted into the back, and then Beatrice drove the pair of mules to the Fête. Mr. Bell followed on his own mount, a fine bay Missouri Trotter with a white blaze and a white front foot.

At the Fête, events returned to their customary state. The band played, the comestibles were served (including two of Lavinia's black-berry pies and almost a peck of John Gentry's cherries) and declared the best ever. The sun went down. No one would have known when they drove home that night (an hour in the moonlight, with Elizabeth sleeping against Margaret's shoulder, and Lavinia and John Gentry discussing something quietly in the front seat of the wagon, while John Gentry drove the team and Beatrice hummed in the evening air) that anything untoward had happened—Papa seemed hale and cheerful. Margaret's idle thought, as the moonlit road unwound between the fields, was that she had forgotten to find a copy of the paper, and so she knew it would be some time before she learned what it was that Mr. Early had done to modify the nature of creation itself.

THIS day, like the day her father shot himself, was the beginning of a new age—Mr. Bell became a regular visitor to Gentry Farm. He would appear in the morning, after breakfast, and drink coffee with them at the table, and then he would follow John Gentry into the fields, where he would be introduced to the mysteries of hemp, tobacco, corn, and mules. He even explored the hemp fields, which were down in the bottomlands, damp and dirty, teeming with snakes, the girls thought. John Gentry had a long, low building near the hemp fields, where, using a system of pulleys and hooks and mules and men with the hemp wrapped around their waists, he manufactured and tarred lengths of rope. But after he had explored the hemp fields, seen the workmen cut the plants off at the ground and then lay them in shallow clay ponds full of dank water, Mr. Bell suggested another plan for the hemp business. John Gentry, he said, should plant the seed differently—not so close together, but more in rows, so that the plants could mature and flower. The ultimate product of this sort of plantation was not rope but a medicinal cornucopia effective in the treatment of every ill. Robert Bell's favorite St. Louis practitioner, Dr. Caswell, made both powders and pills for the whole city. Robert Bell took the medicine—Madison County Cure-All, Dr. Caswell called it. It was even good for the cholera. Robert said, "Thank the Lord you stuck with the hemp." And John Gentry said, "You've got to make a mess of mule and cattle manure, and chicken litter, and till it in faithfully every fall. That's what you have to do, and if you have some fish meal, well, then, that's even better." They talked about it over and over, Robert Bell nodding, as if farming were in his blood.

Robert liked to look at the horses and the mules, and to go out with Beatrice in the gig. His Missouri Trotter was a sensible mare whom he sometimes rode and sometimes drove. He told John Gentry that he did not pretend to be a horseman but he knew some horsemen, and he knew that, among these horsemen, John Gentry had a good reputation for breeding both mules and horses. The upper part of the farm was rich pasture, and the hay fields were cultivated like the hemp fields, with plenty of manure tilled in.

Mr. Bell and Beatrice began to take lovely walks toward evening in these sections of the farm—sometimes Elizabeth and Margaret watched them out the back attic windows, but they never saw them do anything interesting. Beatrice strode along and Mr. Bell trotted to keep up with her. The sisters had been weighing the likelihood of a proposal for several weeks by that time. At night, in whispers, Elizabeth and Margaret figured the odds. They both agreed that the odds were two to one in favor of a proposal, so there was not much to discuss. When they brought this up with Beatrice, she resisted "counting my chickens." Even so, a proposal looked more and more like the favorite. The odds should realistically have been pegged closer to three to two, or even five to four, in favor of a proposal, especially since Margaret and Elizabeth knew that Beatrice was unlikely to do anything unusual that would throw the proposal into doubt. A book Margaret had read was *Jane Eyre*. In that book, the parents of Bertha—Rochester's wife, who lives in the attic and burns the house down—had been quite secretive before the marriage of Mr. Rochester and Bertha. There was none of that in Missouri. If you didn't divulge the skeletons in your closet to a stranger (should you be lucky enough to make acquaintance with a stranger), your neighbors and friends would divulge them for you. In short, what with the medicinal uses of hemp, the herd of equines, the flourishing hay crop, the tinkling of the piano, Alice's pork étouffé, and John Gentry's questionable state of health and lack of male heirs, Beatrice and Mr. Bell were betrothed not long after cessation of hostilities in the Spanish War. He rode out to inform them of that event as soon as the dispatch came in; because it was late, he stayed overnight at the farm and proposed to Beatrice the following morning.

In the books that Margaret read, the young lady in receipt of a proposal always found herself astonished and embarrassed—she blushed with happiness and could barely speak at the thought of marriage. Margaret would have been surprised if Beatrice had summoned up such a performance.

THE WEDDING was set for the fifteenth of December. Lavinia and Beatrice spent the autumn reconsidering every item that Beatrice had stowed away in her chest in light of her new circumstances. Yes, her new people lived on Kingshighway in St. Louis, but she and Robert would be living in their town. Yes, he owned and ran the newspaper, but she was the daughter of Gentry Farm, and everyone knew her perfectly well. They hemmed the tablecloths and monogrammed the bed linen, crocheted edgings around the napkins. Margaret helped with the laundering—they bleached and starched and pressed everything. Where there were pleats, she steamed them out and ironed them in until they were exactly right. Lavinia considered how the ladies in town would be looking for signs, signs that Beatrice was thinking too well

of herself, or that she did not think well enough of herself, signs that
their father's demise had taken a sharper toll on the family than Lavinia
had let on, signs that their father's demise had taken less of a toll
on his daughters than it should have. Signs that her grandfather was
failing, or that her mother was less fortunate and perspicacious than
she appeared. They did not actually talk of these things, but every
time Lavinia shook her head and decided that some napkin or pillow
slip or apron or collar had to be altered, Margaret knew what she was
thinking.

Beatrice and Lavinia went to St. Louis on the train with Robert to
meet his parents. They came home five days later with a bicycle of the
new style, with two wheels of equal diameter and a wide seat. It
belonged to Robert's only sister, a girl of sixteen named Dora. Robert
had prevailed upon Dora to loan it to Beatrice as a betrothal favor,
while Dora was visiting cousins in Springfield, Illinois. Margaret and
Elizabeth were to have the bicycle until Robert returned it when he
went for a last visit before the wedding. Beatrice did not care about the
bicycle, but described in detail the costume Dora had, solely devoted to
bicycle riding, made of blue serge, with gussets behind the shoulders
for leaning forward over the handlebars, and wide, skirtlike pantaloons. The girl also had special lace-up boots. Margaret and Elizabeth
had none of these things, but they could tie up their skirts well enough
to try riding, which they did.

The best place to ride this bicycle was in an area the mules had
pounded flat, around the biggest barn, and between the barn and the
tobacco shed. It was grassless and hard, and the three of them took
turns riding a figure-eight circuit one way round the barn and then the
other way round the tobacco shed. It was an unusual sensation, not like
anything Margaret had ever felt before. She took to it. She put on her
oldest skirt, without a petticoat, and then wrapped some strips of flannel around her legs like horse bandages, leaving room for her knees to
bend. Of course the spokes of the wheel could catch her skirts and
either rip them or topple her over, or both, but she got used to taking
care, and once she had figured out what to do, she went faster and
faster, even as the weather got colder and flakes of snow began to swirl
in the wind.

To be balanced so precariously, and to feel that balance become
steadier, even around the curves of their track, as she pedaled harder

and went faster, was exhilarating. Beatrice said that Dora was a hardy and determined bicyclist—that she belonged to a club of thirty members, both male and female, and they cycled all over St. Louis, which had many good roads. She could pedal up a long, steep hill and fly down the other side (this idea appealed to Margaret from the beginning). Once, Beatrice said, Dora had bicycled some twenty miles in one day, around the periphery of Forest Park, all by herself. No one had said a thing against it, because all the young people in St. Louis who didn't have bicycles were planning to get them, and, it seemed, a young lady bicycling alone was somewhat scandalous, but not wildly so.

This bicycle even impressed Lavinia and John Gentry, who did not try riding but enjoyed watching, as did all of the farm laborers and workmen. Bicycles were expensive. Beatrice told them that Dora had confided to her that the bicycle had cost almost a hundred dollars. When Beatrice quoted this sum, Elizabeth and Margaret were not horrified—they were impressed. Three boring months of wedding plans, and here, all of a sudden, was the casual wealth of the family Beatrice was marrying into palpably demonstrated. John Gentry was impressed, too—all of Gentry Farm, he said, though without the men and mules, was worth only 120 bicycles. Margaret rode the bicycle even as it got colder and colder, and every night she wiped it off and put it away in the barn.

As sometimes happened in Missouri, one of those days dawned bright, a fugitive remnant of Indian summer before the closing in of snow and gloom. On that day, Margaret was up the moment she saw the sunlight beneath the shade. It was not a Sunday. She could slip out of the house without getting breakfast, but also without arousing much of a fuss, and she did.

She went straight to the bicycle. The door of the barn was already open, and she walked the vehicle into the sunlight. Her plan was to ride it to town, some two miles off, and then, perhaps, beyond. The puzzle was which route to take. There were three possibilities. When they walked to town, they always cut across the upper pastures, petting the horses and mules and climbing the fences, thereby reducing the distance to about a mile and a half, but there was no question of that. When her grandfather drove the buggy, he took the western way around, which was more or less level and about three miles, in order to save the horses. That would have been her more sensible choice, but in fact she turned southeast, toward the bottomlands, because, after a flat stretch of some quarter of a mile, there was, first, a long curving hill around Old Saley's Bluff, then a long rise, and then the turn toward town. At this point, the road rose slightly again, and after that there was a set of steep dips and rises through Walker's Woods, followed by another flat stretch down Front Street (and right past the office of the newspaper). By this late in the year, the road had frosted and was pretty hard, though not icy. She congratulated herself on her good sense.

Pedaling straight forward was a new experience for her, and she understood at once how Dora had gotten all the way around the famous Forest Park in an afternoon. Covering distance in this solitary manner was marvelously intoxicating. The brown fields and the blue sky were all around; they seemed to dissipate crisply and evenly into all the distances—forward, backward, upward. The fields were darkly defined by the denuded brown trunks of hickories, black walnuts, and oaks. In Mr. Jones's pasture, across the fence from John Gentry's hay field, five or six white hogs were grunting and rooting for acorns; the noises they made had the clarity of gongs ringing in the air. And then she went down. She gripped the handlebars and felt the cold wind lift her hair and, it seemed, her cheeks and eyebrows. The brim of her hat folded back, and the hat itself threatened to fly off her head, but though she gave this a passing thought, she didn't, could not, stop. The wheels made a brushing, clicking noise in the dirt of the road, and she knew instinctively to keep going no matter how much such going now shocked her. Tears poured down her cheeks, and then she was halfway up the next slope—inertia—she knew what it was called. But she slowed again, and then she was stopped and the bicycle tilting to the side. Truly, riding a bicycle was living life at a much faster pace, and very stimulating. She dismounted and pushed the bicycle up the remaining expanse of the slope. She was now two farms away from Gentry Farm. She had forgotten this part of it—that she would be a solitary traveler for the first time in her life. She remounted the bicycle and pedaled for the next few furlongs, possibly as much as a mile. Everything about the effort was more difficult than she had expected, and fairly soon she was breathing hard. She rarely if ever had done that before in her whole life, given her lazy nature and her mother's views about proper female employments. She knew, of course, that she could turn the bicycle around and go back to the farm, but she also knew that she was more than halfway to town. The long slopes behind her seemed to grow longer, steeper, and more arduous with this thought, and then she was to the series of dips into Walker's Woods.

The pleasure of these dips, which she had happily foreseen, was that from this direction, south, they gradually diminished toward town. There were three of them. She pedaled hard into the first, and over the edge. She lifted her feet out to either side, and down she went, holding tight to the handlebars. She aimed, with some nervousness, for the bridge at the bottom of the hill and then was across it. After the bridge, the trees thickened and the light grew dimmer. Her momentum carried her fast up the first bit of the next hill, and she managed to resume pedaling more quickly than she had, and so pedaled to the top, back into the sunlight. The drop of the second dip was immediate; down she went. This time, she started pedaling as soon as she got to the lowest point of the road, and once again managed to get up the entire hill before exhausting herself. Fortunately, the third dip was quite long and shallow—pleasantly relaxing. Though her cheeks burned in the cold, she was warm with the exertion. Though her arms trembled with the effort, her legs felt strong. The seat of the bicycle was springy and comfortable. She had heard of bicycle clubs traveling vast distances—the Columbia cyclists had traveled to Kansas City and to St. Louis in a contest of some sort. She came over the rise at the top of the third hill, and the town lay before her, bright in the winter sunshine. She sat up straighter and began pedaling in what she considered to be her most dignified manner. And just then her skirt caught in the back wheel and brought her to a halt. She put her foot down as the bicycle tipped.

She dismounted carefully to the left, turning about and holding on to the seat of the bicycle. The lower hem of her skirt was well entangled; she squatted down, still holding the bicycle, and began to work the stuff out of the spokes. Her leg wrappings were collapsing all about her, and she saw that she had to pick those up, too. She was breathing harder than she had ever done.

A voice nearby, a male voice, said, "I haven't seen a bicycle in this town before," and she started violently, though she didn't jump up for fear of rending her skirt. There was a man, quite close by the side of the road, leaning against a leafless maple tree and peeling a staff. He stood up, and then bowed slightly. Margaret nodded, surprised—she hadn't noticed him on her way up the hill. He was tall and handsomely dressed, in a gray suit of clothes, with a soft gray hat sitting squarely on his head. Every man she knew wore a hat, and you could tell quite a bit about a man by the way he wore his hat—slouched forward, pushed back, rakishly tilted to the right or to the left. This hat was like the roof on a steeple—as square as if it had been positioned with instruments. With this thought, she recognized him as the young man in the paper, at the parade, who had changed the universe. Unfortunately, though, her skirt was still jammed between the spokes, and her fingers were too clumsy in her gloves to pull it out. She said (politely, thinking of how often Lavinia had criticized her manner with strangers), "I believe this is the first, but it won't be around much longer, as we must return it to its owner in St. Louis."

He seemed to peer at her, but did not lean forward. He looked as if leaning in any direction whatsoever was impossible for him.

He said, "We haven't been introduced, but may I be of assistance?"

Her skirt slipped from between the spokes, not terribly blackened after all. She stood up, then had to bend down and gather up the strips of flannel she had wrapped her legs with. She said, "No, we haven't been introduced, but I recognize you from the paper, Mr. Early. I'm Margaret Mayfield. Have you ridden a bicycle?"

"When I was studying in Berlin, I rode a bicycle quite often, but it was not nearly as nice as this one. I haven't had occasion to ride one, though, in some years."

"I understand it's the latest model." She looked around for a spot to sit down, a rock or a stump, so that she could rewrap her legs, but it appeared she would have to walk the bicycle to Mrs. Larimer's, at least half a mile, and reorganize her outfit there. Mr. Early said, "My bicycle in Germany had a roomy basket attached to the handlebars. Most convenient."

"That would be," she said. She paired her flannels and draped them over her shoulder, then wrapped them around her waist so they would be out of the way. She wheeled the bicycle forward, and he fell into step beside her. Though the bicycle was between them, she felt how tall he was, at least a head taller than she was, and on top of that there was the hat.

Margaret detested most company other than the company of books; however, she adjusted her own hat and walked on in as congenial a manner as she could. Mr. Early in the flesh looked younger than Mr.

Early in Robert's paper, but she recognized the eyes and the brow—not those of a conversationalist. It appeared that she was obliged to walk to Mrs. Larimer's with a man who would have to be chatted to, rather than one who was happy to do the chatting. Just then, out of what Lavinia would have called her "orneriness," she vowed not to do it, no matter how lengthy the silence. As an alternative, she reviewed her recent headlong progress on the bicycle, and found it as exhilarating in retrospect as it had been while she was enjoying and enduring it. She took a hand off the handlebars and touched her cheeks with the tips of her fingers. They were stiff with dried, or frozen, tears. She put her hand back on the handlebars. It made her smile to think of having gone so fast.

They walked on, and he said nothing. Undoubtedly, she could return home by this route, but she saw that there was the problem of the three dips, which had, as it were, poured her northward into town—if she were to turn around, they would present a barrier not unlike that of three walls rather than three dips, and then, of course, there would be the longer and less steep, but somehow even more disheartening, climb up the hill to Gentry Farm. But how tedious to go home the long way, and (she looked about) mostly into a westerly wind. She could certainly leave the bicycle at the newspaper office and walk home across the fields—there was no snow as yet, and if her grandfather had turned the sows out into his upper pasture and woodlot, she could use her hat to wave them off.

He spoke abruptly: "Do you have other leisure occupations?"

His ponderous and yet resonant voice scattered her thoughts and made it impossible for her to answer the question, or, in some way, even to consider it. Leisure occupations? What did that mean? They walked on. He tried again, "Perhaps our mothers know one another. My mother is Mrs. Jared Early."

She recalled thinking that his father was Patrick. Perhaps that was one of the brothers. She said, "Certainly, they do. My grandfather is John Gentry."

"You live at Gentry Farm."

"I do."

"When I was a boy, we had a pair of mules from Gentry Farm. Napoleon and Wellington."

"Did my grandfather name them?"

"No doubt he did, as our other mule was called Dick. But those two mules were old even then. They would have come to us before the war."

"I am sure that before the war Papa made use of a whole different set of generals. Since then, it's either Northerners or Southerners, but all West Pointers."

Mr. Early cleared his throat again. Margaret came to understand later that this represented a laugh.

She couldn't keep herself from saying, "Lee and Grant are the oldest, twenty-seven and twenty-five. My sister and I sometimes ride Zollicoff. The most stubborn one is Halleck, though I have to say he's very handsome for a mule."

Mr. Early cleared his throat again, which made her think he was going to say something. He didn't. After a few moments, she said, "What I like about the bicycle is that it has no mind of its own."

"Mules are very intelligent," Mr. Early declared, putting an end to that conversation. They walked along. As the aftereffects of her effort dissipated, she was coming to feel chilled. It was now past noon. The breeze had stiffened, and the air was colder than it looked in the sunshine. The steel of the handlebars communicated the chill into her hands, and her feet were growing numb. She could feel the ground right through her thin boots. He said, "Are you visiting anyone in town?"

"Mrs. Larimer, up here a ways. Though she doesn't realize it yet."

"Have you ever seen a telephone?"

"I don't think so." She wasn't sure whether she knew what a telephone was.

"The patents have been bitterly contested, or else they might already have telephones here. But they don't." He snorted disapprovingly. "With a telephone, you could let Mrs. Larimer know you were coming."

"From here, I could also shout."

He cleared his throat. This time, he also smiled a bit. He had even, healthy teeth. There was no evident reason why he would choose not to laugh or smile, but his smile quickly vanished, as if loaned rather than bestowed.

She shivered inside her jacket, and stopped to wrap her flannels more firmly about her waist, this time for warmth. The bicycle stuttered on the road, and Mr. Early glanced at her once, but mostly he gazed around in a discerning way, as if he were measuring the speed of the wind or gauging the likelihood of rain. She pressed on, feeling her cheeks beginning to freeze. Fingers, too. Discomfort was overwhelming that earlier sense of pleasure. She stopped suddenly, leaned the bicycle against her skirt, and cupped her cheeks in her hands, just to warm them. He said, "Are you in pain, Miss Mayfield?"

"I'm freezing."

"Indeed! I hadn't noticed a chill." He waited for her, but she saw through her fingers that he looked at her curiously, as if her behavior were simply a phenomenon and had nothing to do with him. And, indeed, it did have nothing to do with him. But she had the suspicion that, were she to fall over in a solid frozen block of ice and expire right there, he would be unmoved except by the novelty of the situation. She put her hands back on the handlebars and pressed on, this time hurrying as much as she could with her long and flapping skirts. She said, "I have to keep going. It's just there. We're almost to the Larimers'."

"Are we? I'll be sorry to give up your company." He neither smiled nor bent toward her in any way; she was so frantic by now that this remark seemed to her to have no meaning at all, to be launched onto the frigid air like a snowflake. But he exerted himself to keep up with her, and then they were at Mrs. Larimer's gate, and she was fumbling with the latch. He didn't help her, just held on to his staff and observed her. When she had gotten through the gate with the bicycle, he tipped his hat and said, "Well, it's been a pleasure to meet you, Miss Mayfield. I admire your fortitude."

She dropped the bicycle beside the path and ran up the steps to the porch. Charlotte, Mrs. Larimer's hired girl, opened the door at once, and then it was all frostbite and tears and warmth and concern. After that occasion, she didn't see Mr. Early (Captain Early, Dr. Early, she subsequently found out) for a very long time.

THE MARRIAGE took place—a morning wedding at Gentry Farm, with Beatrice in a dark-green velvet dress and Robert in a suit with a collar of the same dark-green velvet. Owing to the time of year, Lavinia and the Bells had decided that it would be better to have a small wedding in town followed by a larger party in St. Louis after the New Year, and their caution turned out to be justified—snow began falling during the afternoon reception at Mrs. Larimer's. It was so thick that if the guests hadn't left early it would have been impossible to get back to the farm. As it was, the horses pulling the carriage had to struggle the last quarter-mile, and Margaret and Elizabeth had to huddle down, covered over and suffocating with blankets, while John Gentry whipped the horses and urged them forward. Lavinia would not let the girls jump out and walk, because their dress boots were thin and the snow was already eight inches deep. Then they spent the days between the wedding and Christmas isolated at the farm, drinking tea and nursing John Gentry through a bout of catarrh. The weather continued cold and wet; only Lavinia went with Robert and Beatrice to the marriage celebration in St. Louis.

Margaret finally met Dora and the other Bells in the spring. Dora turned out to be a squat, plain girl with thin hair and nothing more to offer, Margaret thought at first, than a bicycle and a kind nature. But Dora seemed to take a great and flattering liking to Elizabeth and Margaret, incessantly seeking their advice and offering to take them places around town. She was far more sophisticated in her bringing up than they were, but, as Lavinia pointed out, she was the sort of unfortunate girl whose own mother never gets over her disappointment in what she has produced. There had been the nanny all the way from England, and now a boarding school in Des Peres. One night, while they were undressing for bed in the big house on Kingshighway, Lavinia remarked, "You girls can't know how short your lives have been. From the mother's point of view, first there is the infant, then, almost immediately, there's the young woman. That's how it seems." She lowered her voice, though they were sitting by the fireplace in their own set of rooms, the door shut and everyone else gone to bed. "When a lady's first concern is to preserve herself unchanged by the passage of time, it may be that the easier course is to simply forget the girl exists."

But Mrs. Bell was kind to Margaret and Elizabeth, inviting them to stay for a month in the winter, and taking a special interest in Elizabeth. She and Elizabeth were the same height and built in a similar way, and one of Mrs. Bell's fancies was to dress Elizabeth in her own old clothes, and to give certain pieces to her, on the understanding that Elizabeth would use her skills to remake these dresses and coats, preserving the fine goods but updating the style. John Gentry said, "Does she think the girl is going to have to sew for her living?" But Mrs. Bell acted more as if Elizabeth were her own sister than the sister of her son's wife. The goods were beautiful, and Mrs. Bell, as befitted a St. Louis society woman, had hardly put any wear into them.

JOHN GENTRY died in a condition of some satisfaction. He was almost seventy-six. At the funeral, the minister said, "John Gentry entered the state of Missouri riding in the back of a wagon. A son of the South, he proved himself a patriot to the larger nation, and he earned the respect of both sides." ("Well, he did that with his shotgun," whispered Lavinia.) "He took care of his slaves and, after that, his servants and his workmen, his mules, his acres and his horses and his daughters, and his granddaughters. He sustained his connections with friends and relations on both sides of the conflict, and the same cannot be said for every Missourian of those days. In doing all of these things, he took good care of his soul. And so"—the minister sucked in a deep breath and lifted his eyes above those assembled in the pews—"we plan to meet John Gentry up yonder, where no doubt he has already been put in charge of something." The congregation laughed and nodded, and afterward, many said of John Gentry that he was a generous man. To Margaret, his life seemed complete and all of a piece. The world had swirled around him, but he had done as he pleased and remained as evidently himself as a tree might, or a stone might. Lavinia and her sisters kept pronouncing his eulogy: "Well, Papa was always Papa, I'll say that for him."

Robert Bell took over the farm. What happened was entirely practical—Lavinia's sisters all had lives of their own, in Hermann, Chicago, and West Branch, Iowa. The farm would not be sold or broken up, everyone agreed (either land prices were low and certain to rise, or they were high and destined to go higher—Margaret didn't know which), and, furthermore, such a farm would virtually run itself, so efficient was the operation John Gentry had set in place. Therefore, Robert and Beatrice with their two little boys, Lawrence and Elliott, who had followed hard on the heels of the marriage, would live on the farm, being seen to by Alice. Lavinia, Elizabeth, and Margaret would move into the house in Darlington. Once installed there, Margaret understood without its being said that she was to parade herself, the blooming Elizabeth in tow, up and down Front Street, executing errands at the retail emporia and the better workshops. A single lady, especially an old maid, as she was getting to be, could not just stroll about uptown without calling her sense of propriety, or her actual virtue, into doubt; nevertheless, a subtle reminder to any unmarried or widowed and gainfully employed men, young or old, that a single lady had certain personal and social advantages was not out of order.

The house was small and cramped, not the spacious doctor's establishment where they had lived on Mackie Street, but an extremely modest appropriate-for-newlyweds house on Cranmer Street. Lavinia had been through the wringer of local gossip upon the occasion of the doctor's death, which, though it had been deemed understandable on the whole, was a topic of considerable vitality, given the additional bad fortune of the deaths of Ben and Lawrence. Lavinia was not ready to be batted about at local church suppers and quilting bees any more than she had to be, yet a reclusive life would certainly invite as much remark as a bold one. The key was to find a sociable but self-reliant middle ground.

It was a beautiful spring. Margaret enjoyed the succession of blooming trees planted everywhere—pussy willows followed by forsythia followed by dogwood followed by redbud, cherry, peach, apple, hawthorn, and lilacs white and purple. Some trees were fragrant, some merely foamingly rich and beautiful. She felt this unusual wealth of blooming to be a promise regarding the new century. As an old maid, she should have been sober and circumspect, but she didn't seem all that old to herself, not as old as Beatrice, who was becoming plump and harried and now wore her hair like Lavinia. Lavinia, of course, only had eyes for her new grandson, Lawrence, whom she considered the spitting image of Ben. He looked like a Bell to Margaret, however. She understood that Mrs. Bell agreed with her. Elizabeth confided that Mrs. Bell was disappointed in this offspring, and had said to Elizabeth more than once that she "couldn't understand how the Bell heritage proved so strong, considering that the Bells themselves are short and pale, though sturdy enough." Both the Branscomb heritage (hers) and the Gentry-Mayfield heritage had been overwhelmed—or "Perhaps the word is 'drowned' "—in the Bell heritage. Elizabeth and Margaret laughed and laughed. "What every mother needs is a nice cradle," opined Mrs. Bell, "so that she may rock her child and appreciate him, but not have to endure any suffocating personal contact." She supplied Beatrice not only with a beautiful hand-carved family cradle, but also with a nurse. In other words, she occupied herself by taking care of all of them according to her notions of kindness.

That summer, Mrs. Bell and Lavinia put their heads together and decided to do the easiest thing first, which was to take Elizabeth in hand, since she was almost nineteen. According to Mrs. Bell, there were plenty of up-and-coming young men in St. Louis, who, if not involved in manufacturing, were associated with the May Company, or perhaps the beer brewers, or were lawyers who had gone to school with the scions of wealthy St. Louis families and would be useful in some business or other. By the end of the summer, Elizabeth was betrothed to a man from New Jersey, a lawyer named Mercer Hart, who had come to St. Louis to assume a position with Mr. Danforth's livestock-feed company. Mrs. Danforth and Mrs. Bell belonged to a fashionable ladies' club, where once a month they listened to speeches about humane improvements to the lives of the lower orders, or other equally edifying topics. Margaret went along once. The speaker, a man from Wisconsin, discussed interior ceiling heights and their effect on the mind's tendency to think either in concrete particulars or in accordance with more transcendental spiritual ideas. Another one, which Mrs. Bell reported over the supper table, concerned the writings of Mr. Alfred Russel Wallace, which proposed that no modern person could be said, objectively, to be "fit enough" to reproduce and that, in fact, excessive human reproduction would certainly destroy the world as they knew it. Mrs. Bell talked about these ideas with approbation for several weeks.

Mercer Hart was a fairly young man, and had gone to Kenyon College. Dora and Margaret were eager for a look at him, but when they met him, they found him to be excessively polite—though, at least, taller than Elizabeth. They briefly perked up when Mrs. Bell reported that Mercer's grandfather had been a Jew, but (they fell again into indifference) the grandfather had converted, and upon coming to St. Louis, Mercer had joined her very own Methodist church. Anyway, the unusual and estimable thing about St. Louis, according to Mrs. Bell, was that people of all faiths lived there side by side, and many of the best families were Catholic—you couldn't avoid that, given that the city was founded by the French, with the Irish, the Italians, and the Germans "hot on their tail," as Mr. Bell said. All the best women's clubs had all types of women in them ("as long as they're rich," said Lavinia).

Mrs. Bell was a more lackadaisical chaperone than Lavinia. The streetcars had been the scene and occasion of a great strike only a year before—track had been blown up, electrical lines cut, and any number of men killed on both sides. Dora clung to the view that the policemen had committed tremendous crimes against the strikers. Whenever Mr. Bell fumed that the strikers had gotten off "scot-free," Dora's rejoinder was "Only a little starvation and destitution here and there," but she said it under her breath, and out of the hearing of her father. But no one stopped them when, one day, Margaret followed Dora out of the house on Kingshighway and they took the streetcar to Stix, Baer & Fuller. They ended up riding it to the end of the line and back, staying out for most of the day. Their excuse was that it was raining, and that they had to stay on the streetcar so as not to get their shoes wet, but no one asked them for an excuse.

As delightful as it was to go to Stix and look at the floors and the counters and the shelves of goods (lawns, organdies, mousselines, dimities, silks, velvets, laces of all kinds), Margaret enjoyed the streetcar itself more, for the power with which it surged away from every stop, for the airy breeze that blew her hair about and endangered her hat, for the swaying motion both lulling and exciting.

The very next day, they went out again, and got on another streetcar, and since it was not raining, they went to Mr. Shaw's garden, which was south on Kingshighway and past Tower Grove Park. They walked along the paths and looked at the trees, reading the labels beneath them, then wandered about the all-glass Linnean House for as long as they could stand the heat. The next day, they went out again.

Dora was most observant of the passersby, whether they were walking or riding the streetcar or wandering through the departments of Stix, Baer & Fuller. She would scrutinize them without seeming to, and then, when they weren't looking, she would produce some expression or gesture of perfect mimicry. Most of the people they saw were men, and so the effect was quite amusing. Her pencil might turn for an instant into a cigar, her parasol into a cane, her hat into a homburg, her smile into a supercilious smirk. The crowds they encountered were transformed into a gallery of types, all oblivious. For Margaret, there was the added pleasure of watching the eyes of these men pass indifferently over Dora just seconds before she put their idiosyncrasies—something as tiny as a gorge-clearing or an unconscious pull of an ear—on display. Margaret laughed aloud, drawing the attention of Dora's target, at which point Dora would pass effortlessly into her most maidenly demeanor.

One day, on the streetcar up to Fairground Park and Natural Bridge Road, which was a long, pleasant, breezy ride, Dora reached into her bag and handed Margaret some papers, a manuscript of some three or four pages, fairly but closely written. What it seemed to be was a transcription of the supper conversation of the evening before, written as a play. The dramatis personae were Father, Mother, E., D., M., and X. E. was Etheline, the serving girl. X. was Mrs. Bell's French bulldog, Xenia. M. was evidently Margaret, and so forth. Dora's handwriting was copybook—she could have earned her living in a law office.

No scene was set. The dialogue simply commenced:

> FATHER *Mrs. Bell, Dora is giving Xenia her lamb chop.*
> MOTHER *Of course not.*
> FATHER *Of course not what?*
> MOTHER *Of course she would not give Xenia her lamb chop. She would not do it, Mr. Bell.*
> FATHER *She is doing it.*
> MOTHER *She is not doing it. Dora, are you giving the dog your lamb chop?*
> DORA *No, Mama. Not exactly.*
> FATHER *What exactly are you doing, Dora?*
> DORA *I am giving her my parsnip.*

Margaret remembered this exchange. Reading it now made her laugh. When she laughed, Dora grinned.

She turned to the next page:

> FATHER *Etheline, why haven't you joined the union yet? They were around here just the other day, weren't they?*
> ETHELINE *Who was around here?*
> FATHER *The union organizers. She saw them. Did you join up, girl?*
> ETHELINE *No, sir.*
> FATHER *Did you give them any money?*
> ETHELINE *No, sir, I didn't.*
> MOTHER *To whom did Etheline give some money? Etheline, do you have any money?*

ETHELINE *No, ma'am. I ain't never got no money.*
FATHER *I told you.*
MOTHER *How would she get money? I don't give her money.*
DORA *Mama wouldn't give Etheline any money if her life*
   depended on it.

Just as Margaret was thinking that Dora was a remarkably observant girl, a man passed between the two of them and got off the streetcar at Cass Avenue. Margaret saw nothing except that he gave his nickel to the conductor, took off his bowler hat, smoothed the brim, and then replaced it on his head, but when she looked at Dora, the girl flared her nostrils and lifted her eyebrow, then straightened her shoulders as if they had been knocked to one side by the swaying of the car. Her head described the exact arc that the man's head had described when he put his hat on. Then the car jolted forward, and Dora laughed.

After this, Margaret could not take her eyes off Dora. When, in the course of a morning, she had occasion to mimic Elizabeth writing a note to Mr. Hart and absentmindedly putting a dot of ink on her nose, or to mimic Etheline sweeping behind the sofa as if she were stabbing an intruder to death, it was most uncanny, something like the effect of going to an arcade where she might pay a penny and watch a short film.

And this they did also. Dora was ready to do anything. The first film she took Margaret to was called *Another Job for the Undertaker,* and in it an ignorant fellow from the countryside went to sleep in his hotel room with the gas lamp on but not lit. Within a minute, he was carried out to a hearse and driven away, much mourned by his friends. It was shocking, really, until Dora told her that the whole incident was staged. Another of these films was about Kansas, and demonstrated what Missourians were always saying, that Kansans had a distressing propensity for violence. In this picture, Mrs. Carrie Nation entered a saloon with her disciples. They were all carrying axes, and they proceeded to smash the place to smithereens. Mrs. Nation was the victor, although she got a dose of beer in the face when she smashed the tap.

Mrs. Bell gave Elizabeth the wedding she must have wished for Dora—a breakfast at the big house on Kingshighway, with the Danforths and all of the members of the Ladies' Club in attendance, and the big staircase in the front hall strung with garlands of a yellow flower that Margaret didn't know. Elizabeth sewed her own gown, with the help of Mrs. Bell's sempstress, but the bodice was a piece of Branscomb family lace, Belgian and in perfect condition. The cake came from the best French pastry shop in St. Louis, and Margaret, Beatrice, and Lavinia all wore new hats from the May Company hat department. Elizabeth had seven new dresses, and her linen chest was full. Best of all, Margaret had had no hand in filling it. Mercer took his bride on a wedding trip to Hot Springs, down in Arkansas, a famous spa, and then they went to live in their new house in Kirkwood, which was two or three blocks from the railroad station. This meant that Elizabeth could come visit Margaret and Lavinia with hardly any trouble at all. Margaret herself rode the train back home after the wedding, and there were quite a few unaccompanied women on it, though, of course, they kept to themselves and did not go into cars where food or drink was being served.

MARGARET was twenty-three. Two girls her age, Mathilda Tierney and Martha Johnson, had gone out West to Idaho as itinerant teachers. They had found an abundance of eligible men and had married right away. It was exciting, it seemed, for a man or a woman to set out alone, not so exciting for them to set out as a couple. To Margaret, however, it seemed like a long trip, no matter how you made it. Lavinia said that she was a lazy thing, and that books had taught her to be more lazy. After you read a few of them, you had the feeling you knew all about wherever the book took place, so why take the long train ride? On top of all of this, according to many authors, dangers abounded in all of these locations. You had the dangers of train wrecks and gunshots and sinking ships and outlaws, but also the likelihood that you would be swindled. Inheritances would be stolen. Letters would go astray. The friendliest stranger would be the one that, long ago, purloined the deed to the family home. How much more preferable, it seemed to Margaret, in spite of the uncertainty of her future, to wake up in the warmth of the morning and look out the window at blooming honeysuckle, the skittering of squirrels, the cawing of crows and jays as they objected to the cats.

The natural thing would be that a bookish girl would teach school. There were schools around, both county schools and local academies, and plenty of the girls teaching in them knew less than she did. She might have talked her way into one of them, and perhaps she would have gone to a teacher-training institute—there was one held for three weeks each summer in the county seat. But the girls who taught school did not speak highly of the work—the big boys and the little girls and the firecrackers and the lost and damaged books and the evident indifference of one and all tested the teachers' patience unmercifully. The schoolhouses were drafty and chill or stuffy and hot. A schoolmistress had to dress with extra sobriety. A girl of twenty might look thirty or forty, and the older boys, who were almost her age, or, in some cases, older than she was, would tease her anyway. Lavinia felt that teaching was an occupation of last resort, to be attempted only when all matrimonial prospects were exhausted. Look at Martha Johnson—all the way across the country in Idaho, and what was her honeymoon, according to her aunt, but doing all the dishes her new husband and his brother had dirtied over four or six months, and carrying in and firing all the water herself—there were no servants in Idaho, even uncooperative ones, but she was married, safe and sound. As long as her mother could talk like this, Margaret knew, she wouldn't have to teach.

Margaret and Lavinia looked on the bright side every day. There was an apple tree (reliably pollinated by the tree next door, so that it bore every year), a pear tree, a rhubarb patch, a raspberry patch, and a strawberry bed. Their old horse Aurelius lived in the barn (replaced on the farm by a much younger and more elegant pair of black Morgan horses from up in Audrain County). A hired man who worked for all the families in the neighborhood took care of Aurelius in the mornings and the evenings, and Margaret gave him apples during the day. They sometimes took him out for a drive to the farm, where Lavinia and Beatrice consulted about Lawrence and the baby, Elliot.

Robert and Beatrice were thoroughly generous with them—every wagon from the farm into town brought them a ham or a sack of potatoes or a peck of apples that they didn't need. They had an account at every shop. This abundance became a burden to Lavinia—there was only so much apple butter that could be eaten, only so many articles of clothing they could wear, only so many shawls they could use to go out to the barn, only so many quilts they could pile up. And so they became very charitable: If a quilt had the least little fraying or a shawl had fallen into disfavor, they donated it to the church, just to unburden the cupboards a bit. They made rugs for the church, ripping up dresses that were only two or three years old. Every poor family in town became a judge of their pies and jams. If someone fell sick, Lavinia was the first to bring a hot dish to the family, or to offer to take a spell of nursing. Lavinia had been industrious for so many years that her industry had become redundant.

Margaret avoided these activities as best she could. She would wake up, read for an hour or so, eat a leisurely dinner, take a walk, read another chapter. But even though she set this example, still, they baked on Monday, washed on Tuesday, ironed on Wednesday, mended on Thursday, scrubbed on Friday, and blacked the stove on Saturday. They delivered pies and breads to every social event in town. There wasn't enough work for both of them. Maybe she should take up embroidery? Tatting? Crochet? Watercolor? Music? Lavinia racked her brain. Poetry? A lady was perfectly capable of writing elegant poems containing uplifting sentiments for the local newspaper if she wished. Over in Pettis County, there was a married woman who wrote a regular feature—every two weeks—about etiquette, and in Pike County, there was an old woman, much older than Lavinia, who published her memories of the early days from time to time. Gardening? Margaret helped mulch and bed at the end of the autumn, and started a few plants for the spring. By the end of the winter, Lavinia felt she had exhausted her ideas. Margaret teased her. She would say, "Ship me to Alaska." (Gold had been discovered in Alaska.) "It might take me a year to get there and a year to get back. Ship me to Cuba. Ship me to China." Lavinia would say only, "Oh, for goodness' sake." Several times a week, she sent Margaret to help Beatrice at the farm.

Unbeknownst to Lavinia, who would not have approved, Beatrice had taken up cardplaying, and was having afternoon parties, not in any way dissimilar to those Mrs. Larimer had once had. The first time Margaret was present at one of these, she watched a few hands and helped Marcie, Beatrice's new hired girl, serve the cakes and tea. They were playing poker.

She would have expected Beatrice to be a cautious player, as befitted someone who was fresh to the game and who also seemed to be preening herself on her matronly respectability, but her sister wasn't careful at all—she had been doing more at Mrs. Larimer's than playing the piano. She liked to raise the stakes and to bluff, and she smiled and laughed in frank enjoyment of the whole thing. After the ladies departed, she confided to Margaret in a comfortable way that she was up for the winter, thank goodness. She had been afraid, around the first of the year, to tell Robert about her gambling debts, but her luck had changed, and she had put some of her stake by. And, she said, it was not as though Robert didn't like to play—what do you think he did on those quiet days at the newspaper? If he weren't to play, and to play well, the businessmen around town would laugh at him.

Margaret sat in on a few hands, though she had no source of funds— she borrowed from Beatrice. She was lucky and cautious, and after a few parties—say, by the end of April—she was up by almost ten dollars, which she left in a jar at the farm.

It was about this time that Mrs. Jared Early began to join them. Here was a woman who was older than Lavinia, possibly sixty at that time, but she was active and healthy. Margaret watched her, thinking of that strange encounter she had had with Andrew Early—Captain? Dr.?— but Mrs. Early didn't notice Margaret. She seemed to like Beatrice, and she had a friend who came with her to games, Mrs. Hitchens, another widow, about fifty, who always wore beautiful hats. She had moved to town from Minneapolis—"for the fine weather," she said.

Margaret knew by now what Captain Andrew Jackson Jefferson Early had done to change the nature of the universe—he had gone with an expedition to Mexico and looked at the stars, and he had charted stars in the southern sky called doubles—two stars whirling in tandem. That spring, the spring of 1902, Captain Early was more famous than ever—everyone in town agreed that he was a wonderful example of what a town like theirs, full of enterprise and independent minds, could produce. Her memory of the man she had encountered on the bicycle, though, gave Margaret a chill; she thought he was nothing like anyone else she'd known.

Mrs. Early was a tall, generously built woman, sociable and good-humored. Margaret noticed that she often smiled quickly to herself, as if she was enjoying some thought that she dared not share with the other ladies. She had long, thick hair, still mostly dark, piled luxuriantly on her head. The ladies knew plenty about her—she had no daughters, but quite a few sons, of whom Andrew was the eldest (now thirty-five). They had come along all in a row—Andrew, Henry, Thomas, Daniel, and John, all named after famous men that Mr. Early was said to have known. Patrick had died as a boy of the cholera. Mrs. Early did not live in a mansion or have a big farm, but she had a nice two-story house on

Maple Street, painted bright white and surrounded by a picket fence, with lots of flowers in the garden and a nice orchard in the back. There had been a large farm, but that was lost after the war. Only John lived in Darlington. He was twenty-eight, worked in the bank, and had married a girl from Arkansas. He also had a big house, but even though Mr. Jared Early had been dead some eight or ten years by now (and quite solitary for years before that), Mrs. Early did not live with her son and daughter-in-law. Beatrice said that there was family money, though she wasn't quite clear about its source, but all the boys were enterprising. It was said that Mrs. Early and Mrs. Hitchens traveled together, and that they had not only visited Andrew in Germany but had gone to a famous spa there, and then to Paris. All the Earlys had gone to college for at least a year—Andrew, the brilliant one, had gone to college in Berlin, Germany (after he completed his studies up in Columbia, it was said, there was no college in the United States that could teach him anything he didn't already know). He was now teaching at the University of Chicago, which had been founded by the Rockefellers because the big universities in the East were too slow to enter modern times. It was very grand to be teaching at the University of Chicago and, as far as Margaret understood it, to be on the payroll of the Rockefellers, but, to her credit, Mrs. Early didn't talk about Andrew any more often than she talked about the other boys. Henry was in New York City, working on Wall Street; Thomas was in Texas; and Daniel was in England. Mrs. Early talked about their wanderings as if they were customary and entertaining, as if the strangest one among them was John, married and working in a bank in town. She did not have a habit that others did (Beatrice, for example) of topping some other lady's anecdote with something more impressive of her own, though they all knew she could have. She saved her competitive streak for the poker table.

Mrs. Early and Mrs. Hitchens sat at different tables. Every hand was five cards, and at first the ladies continued to chat while the hands were dealt and they were arranging their cards. Mrs. Early and Mrs. Hitchens chatted along with the rest of them, complimenting the cakes, or discussing the first strawberries, or comparing knitting patterns, but Mrs. Early and Mrs. Hitchens never picked up their cards as soon as they were dealt. They glanced about while the rest of the ladies were scanning what they had, then they picked up their cards, looked at them, and laid them down again, still genial. The betting rounds proceeded with lots of laughter and talk, as if each betting decision was a daring choice, and, indeed, it did seem to the other ladies to be so. Mrs. Early would urge them to be a little more bold—"Raise her two, Mrs. Landon. I'm sure you can stand it!" or "Surely, Miss Mayfield, you needn't fold just yet." Her voice was so friendly that Margaret felt as though Mrs. Early was helping her along, that she had Margaret's interests foremost in her mind. But Margaret never followed her advice, though some of the other ladies did. These ladies did not always come to grief, but often enough they did. Margaret understood Mrs. Early's purpose—to plump the pot a little before laying claim to it. At the other table, Mrs. Hitchens was doing the same thing, though in a different way—"I'm not sure I would lose hope, dear," or "It's so nice when the wagering is confident and straightforward." The stakes were low, but toward the end of the afternoon, after the losing players had dropped out, the value of the chips would metamorphose—nickel chips would be worth two bits, dime chips worth half a dollar, and two-bit chips worth a dollar. When the winning ladies consolidated at a single table, Mrs. Hitchens dropped out with a smile and an "Oh, I am a bit tired after all."

Mrs. Early's eyes were cheerful. Margaret never saw her scowl or lose her smile, nor did she fidget or sigh or touch her hair or move her shoulders, as many of the ladies did without seeming to know what they were doing. They all thought that their friends didn't actually mean to take their money, but Mrs. Early and Mrs. Hitchens did mean to take their money. They preferred it when the ladies all had to show their hands, and in order to promote this, Mrs. Early introduced high-low, in which both the high hand and the low hand split the pot. Once they started playing in this way, it seemed more fair and more fun, but Margaret saw that Mrs. Early also won more money. And she won more often at stud-horse poker than at draw poker. After a while, Margaret got wise to the fact that Mrs. Early was counting the cards, and that she never forgot that if there were three kings faceup on the table, the likelihood of her completing her flush was minimal. When they played draw poker, she paid close attention to how many cards each of them asked for, as if this told her something, as, indeed, it did. She and Mrs. Hitchens also liked to play vingt-et-un, and Margaret soon came to understand that Mrs. Early was keeping track of the cards that were laid.

One day that summer, when Margaret was sitting beside her at the table, Mrs. Early had just cut the cards. When she took the deck in her hand, she said, "There's a card missing." The missing card was under Mrs. Johnson's chair. This incident passed without remark, but to Margaret, the idea that a woman could be so familiar with the size and weight of a deck of cards that she would sense that a single card was missing was remarkable.

Lavinia had gone to Kirkwood to visit Elizabeth. The weather had been hot, but the heat had broken—it was late July. Margaret set out for the the farm just after dawn to bake a blackberry pie. Beatrice kept up John Gentry's special blackberry patch, and Lavinia and Margaret had already helped her pick and process many jars of jam, and this pie would be the last of the season. There was a fresh breeze, and the rolling fields were fragrant from the hay that had been cut and baled; down in the bottomland, the hemp was five or six feet tall. It would take her fifteen minutes to pick enough berries for a pie, and no time at all to make the pie—all you did with a blackberry pie was roll out the crust, pile in the berries, some sugar, and some flour. It had to be done early, though, before the heat of the day. Robert was still at breakfast when she came in. She saw at once that he and Beatrice were glowing with the pleasure of new and interesting gossip. Beatrice was saying, "So—is he coming here?"

Robert glanced up as Margaret entered the kitchen, then said, "They say he is. Where else would he go at such short notice?"

"Isn't there a brother in New York?"

She said, "Who are you talking about?"

"Andrew Early," said Robert. "Captain Early."

She knew who he meant, but said, "Mrs. Early's son?"

Robert nodded.

"He lied," said Beatrice. "It's a tremendous scandal."

Margaret closed the door behind her against the flies. She said, "People lie all the time."

"He misrepresented his observations," said Robert. "That's more than lying."

Margaret sat down and took Elliott on her lap. She handed him a rusk. She smoothed his hair and could feel the warm contours of his head through the silky strands. She said, "What observations?"

Robert looked at her. "I gather that he said he discovered that the sky is full of these double stars, except that it isn't. At any rate, he's been fired from the University of Chicago, whatever the reason."

"Dr. Early?"

"Dr. Early. Captain Early. I never do know what I'm supposed to call the man. No one calls him Andy, that's for sure."

She said, "I saw him once. When I was riding that bicycle of Dora's."

"You talked to him?" exclaimed Beatrice.

"I could hardly avoid it. He walked along with me for a piece, but I was so cold I had to run into Mrs. Larimer's to get warm. He was courteous, but in a stiff way. Not at all like his mother. And he didn't seem to feel the cold, even though I was freezing. He struck me as a strange man." Elliott struggled to get down, and she set him on his feet.

Beatrice sucked in her breath. "Was he quite frightening? I do think *she* is a bit frightening. She's up over fifty dollars." Robert scowled and she shrugged, then said, "I'm still up, Robert."

Margaret said, " 'Off-putting' is more the word."

Robert now looked at her. It was a fact that he didn't care about Beatrice's poker parties. He thought that they were fast, and that fast wasn't bad, at least for the wife of the editor of the newspaper. He nodded. "Captain Early is the most famous man this town ever produced, but not beloved. Though I never knew him myself."

"Who did?" said Beatrice. "He's very old."

"He's not more than thirty-five," said Robert. "He was born a couple of years after the war. He's something like five years older than I am. And his brother John is a personable fellow."

"John's wife never says 'boo,' " said Beatrice. "I always wonder," she added in a saucy manner, "if a wife looks and behaves like a rabbit, is the husband behaving like a wolf?"

Robert laughed.

Margaret said, "Where's the berry basket?"

"In the summer kitchen."

She went out. Robert left soon after, mounted on one of the pretty Morgans.

At the poker party, in the absence of Mrs. Early, all the ladies talked about the captain (So tall! So good-looking! No, not good-looking at all, rather glowering! He was coming inside of a week! No, he was going to New York City!), but none of them really knew anything. Margaret didn't relate her own experience, since she thought that the most appealing thing about Captain Early was his mother. The ladies went on. Was Mrs. Early embarrassed? Of course she was, given the transgression. Certainly she was not, given her nature. She *should* be embarrassed, though, they agreed on that. All Margaret said was "I can't imagine Mrs. Early being embarrassed about things."

"Isn't that true!" exclaimed Mrs. Landon, but Margaret had meant her remark as a compliment, and Mrs. Landon did not.

Four days later, Margaret left on the train for Kirkwood, and didn't hear another thing about Andrew Early for six months.

All the talk in St. Louis was of the coming fair, Olympic Games, and Louisiana Purchase Exposition, which was to begin on April 1, 1903, a hundred years to the day from the Louisiana Purchase (and wasn't it amazing that the city had been required to raise fifteen million dollars to put on the fair, the exact sum President Jefferson had spent on the whole of the Louisiana Purchase? If nothing else showed the progress humankind had made during the nineteenth century, that surely did). Among the Bells, on Kingshighway, near Forest Park, there was a blaze of chatter and news. There was absolutely no doubt there that St. Louis, Missouri, was the center of the universe, the coming city of the twentieth century, and certain to eclipse New York and Chicago, if not London, Paris, and Rome, as the greatest city the world had ever known. And why not? All the best Frenchmen, Italians, Englishmen, and Germans had decamped from those moldy old spots and set out for right where the Mighty Mississippi and the Big Muddy met and married. The twentieth century in St. Louis, Margaret was given to understand, was already vastly improved over the nineteenth century. In the nineteenth century, St. Louis was all cholera and typhoid fever, smallpox, and tornadoes and heat and damp air, a place where dead dogs and cats lay in the streets for weeks. Now St. Louis was shoes and shipping and flowers and ladies' dresses and coats and magazines and beer, not to mention plug tobacco and people from around the world meeting up in Forest Park to display their wealth. Would the capital of the United States be moved to St. Louis? It made perfect sense, even if it wasn't likely to happen. At least you could point out what a good idea it would be, the whole nation gathering right here in the natural middle of the country. And then, as if to ratify what everyone was saying, the imminent exhibition was put off for a year—until 1904—because so many nations wanted to come and display themselves that the facilities could not be built in time.

After Thanksgiving, Elizabeth had a baby—the child was named Lucy May, after Mercer Hart's mother (whose maiden name was Wilder—"not Jewish at all," said Mrs. Bell. "Very prominent out West somewhere. Where would that be, Mr. Bell? Where is it that the Wilders are prominent?"

"Big family," said Mr. Bell, "prominent everywhere," without looking up from his paper.

"Not here," said Mrs. Bell.)

Elizabeth and Mercer exuded the gravity of genuine parents from the first day of Lucy May's existence. Margaret got none of the feeling that she got with Robert and Beatrice, that the youth of the child was a mistake time would eventually correct. Although Elizabeth had little experience of children or infants, the nanny (actually a woman from southern Missouri named Agatha) had to show her how to do something just once for Elizabeth to understand and master it—bathing, dressing, nursing, changing, rocking, singing, carrying from room to room. Agatha said to Margaret, "Good Lord, I've seen some babies, you do exactly what is right to do, and it doesn't have any effect at all, they just go their own way as if you hadn't done a thing! This child is the kindest. Whatever you do for her makes her happy. Your sister is going to be spoiled, and go on and have another and then another, and then, one day, she'll get one of those unrewarding ones, and then she'll know how spoiled she is." She shook her head sadly at this thought.

Margaret found Agatha to be such a sympathetic person that she even told her about Lawrence and Ben and that hanging she couldn't remember she'd been taken to on the very day of Elizabeth's birth, so long ago now. Agatha shook her head again. She said, "Those days are gone, and it's a good thing. Down there, where I come from, near Sedalia, you were afraid to answer the door in case it might be someone bringing home a body, either dead or half alive—and which was worse, I want to know. If it wasn't snakebite, then it was gunshot, and if it wasn't gunshot, then it was a drowning or a tree falling or a horse that run off with the wagon and it tipped over. My own mother had herself fourteen babies, and toward the end of her life, she wouldn't answer the door at all." Agatha was forty-five, not twice as old as Margaret, but she looked seventy. She had no teeth, and she walked with a limp. Margaret was a little sad when, having taught Elizabeth everything she knew, the woman left.

Dora was now twenty, though no taller and no prettier. She wore mannish boots and coats. She never wore gloves or any kind of a hat that other women were wearing. "The only reason to wear a hat," she told Margaret, "is to keep your hair from falling in your face." And though her parents were wealthy and prominent, and Dora herself would have a considerable inheritance, everyone seemed to have given up utterly on the idea of getting her married. No one spoke to Margaret about her own future as an old maid, but if Dora didn't perennially hear about hers, it was simply because she was never present when everyone was talking about it. Mr. Bell's attitude was one of resignation. Mrs. Bell's attitude was one of grievance against Dora for, in the first place, having no feminine assets and, in the second place, making nothing of those she had. Elizabeth was more philosophical—maybe Dora would enjoy her condition, or else convert to Catholicism and become a nun. St. Louis had any number of convents, including one "where the nun takes a French name and lives in a tiny cell for her entire life, sometimes seventy years, and never sees a soul and gets her tray of food once a day through the wall and prays eternally." You could see this convent from the streetcar, when it went from Kirkwood north and then east into St. Louis. Dora was writing things, but no one knew what they were. She was sending them to magazines such as *McClure's,* but nothing, as far as anyone knew, had seen print yet.

Dora's behavior was attributed, by Mrs. Bell, to how famous St. Louis was. Even Lincoln Steffens, that terrifying man, was in St. Louis to report on the arrest of Boss Butler. Lincoln Steffens, said Mr. Bell, was trying to see to it that all the best people would have their money taken away from them and be sent in rags upon the streets to beg. That Dora would consort, even in the privacy of her own mind, with such an unprincipled man indicated to Mrs. Bell that Dora was some kind of changeling. The sum of all of this was that St. Louis was the world's most exciting and modern city, and such a thing could be either good or bad, morally, but there was no denying that the city was better to live in than it had been when Mrs. Bell was growing up as Miss Branscomb down near Tower Grove Park: you couldn't get really good silk foulard to save your life, and everyone ate catfish right out of the river. "And it's not so hot as it was, either. Is it, Mr. Bell?"

"Of course it is" (not looking up from his paper).

"He doesn't remember. Truly, Margaret, the weather has moderated in a very nice way. There hasn't been a typhoid epidemic in twenty-five years."

"Twenty-four," said Mr. Bell.

Shortly after this, Margaret happened to overhear Mercer and Elizabeth chatting. Elizabeth said, "It makes no sense. I think she's pretty." (This was where she divined that she was the subject.) "Prettier than Beatrice. And nice, too. But she's never had even a beau. She would have told me." Margaret smiled to herself even as she stilled her movements, instantly curious to hear her brother-in-law's reply. He said, "Pretty enough. But forbidding. You'll allow that, won't you, Lizzie?"

Elizabeth laughed. "That's silly."

"But she never looks at a fellow, and if she makes a mistake and lets him catch her eye, she glares like fury. I don't know anyone who can stand up to that sort of thing, at least at the beginning. I love her now, as your sister, and she's sweet as a peach with Lucy May. It's like she's a different person when you know her. But the average fellow doesn't get a chance to know her unless he happens to marry her sister."

"That can't be . . ."

"And then you don't know what she means half the time. I ask myself once a day, is she making a joke? The fellows can't take that. It makes them feel thick."

"She is making a joke," said Elizabeth. "I laugh all the time at what she says."

"But you know her. A fellow doesn't want to feel as though a girl is running rings around him, at least not till he marries her." Now they fell silent. This was, indeed, the first Margaret had ever heard about her demeanor. She had thought she was too old to have her feelings hurt, and now they were.

By Margaret's January return to the little house, Lavinia, Mrs. Early, and Mrs. Hitchens had become friends, almost a regular threesome. According to Lavinia, Mrs. Early had come up to her in Macomb's general store and spoken to her in a very friendly way about both Beatrice and Margaret, and then Mrs. Early had invited her to tea. The three of them turned out to have many interests in common, though none of those she listed was poker. When the two elegant ladies came visiting, they sat in the front room and knitted or crocheted. Or they trimmed hats. Or they talked about the exposition, and made plans to go to St. Louis and see everything, "even if it takes three or four trips to do it." Mrs. Early chatted genially about places she had been—yes, that spa in

Germany (Baden—the word itself meant "baths"), where you could see the excavations of the very spots where the Romans had taken their hot baths. She had also been to Paris and to London, of course, and taken hikes in the Lake District ("I love Wordsworth, don't you?") and the Scottish Highlands ("I grew up reading Scott, didn't everyone? I do believe it ruined me"), and she had been to Menton in France, and Amalfi and Rome in Italy (where, in fact, she had met Mrs. Hitchens and invited her to come to Missouri). And then she had been planning to go to Texas, to visit her son there, but when Captain Early returned to town, she didn't want to leave while he was here. She sprinkled references to Captain Early into her conversation—exactly enough so that they would know she had no worries about him. When Margaret asked about the scandal, Lavinia said, "Scandal?" and Margaret decided that Robert had not known what he was talking about. Margaret got used to hearing Mrs. Early talk about her son—he had installed a very nice telescope in one of the upstairs bedrooms, he was particular about his coffee, Mrs. Early was knitting him fingerless gloves because he wouldn't have a fire in the upstairs. All of these matters came up very naturally.

Mrs. Early made a point of conversing with Margaret about books. If she had read something Margaret liked, she would compliment her taste, and if she hadn't read it, she would frankly state that she wished she might someday. At last, after telling her for weeks about her extensive library, Mrs. Early invited her to come and choose a few things to read.

But by that time it was February, and there was no walking out, because of a tremendous cold snap. Lavinia kept a big fire in the kitchen stove, and they sat there most days and tended the fire. The cats sat with them. It was said that it was twenty or thirty or forty below, but Margaret didn't know. Supposedly, at forty below, if you threw a bucket of water into the air, the drops would freeze before hitting the ground. Old Paul, the hired man, shoveled a path between the house and the barn, and she went out, bundled up, several times during the day and made sure that Aurelius had plenty of hay to keep him warm, and that his blanket was properly adjusted. The cold made Lavinia feel old and lonely—she started talking a bit about Margaret's father. It was the death of Lawrence that "did him in," she said. What had happened to Ben hurt him, but that was the dangers of boys, dangers he well knew.

He had had no chance to save Ben when the boys brought him home from the railyard. Lawrence lingered for weeks, though, and Dr. Mayfield had thought that if he were only better educated, or more experienced, or more inventive, he might somehow preserve him. Afterward, he went to his patients as he always had, but with new self-doubts. "When someone died, he knew he had done something wrong, and when someone lived, he felt that nature had prevailed. Nature, I told him, is what kills them, but that's how it got to be. I dreaded that something would happen, and then it did." Lavinia sighed. Margaret listened and made her own sympathetic sighs, but her memories of her father were dim, and entirely overlaid by the cacophony of subsequent events. She remembered him more as a doctor than as a father, a tall, respected man who looked at her in a judicious, discerning way, to be sure that she was healthy and clean. When Lavinia chatted and reminisced about her childhood, and the boys, and her first years in town with Dr. Mayfield, how appealing Lawrence and Ben were, so healthy and active, and how she used to sit in the parlor and laugh at their antics when the doctor roughhoused with them, rolling them over and tickling them, turning them upside down in gales of laughter, making them run about and pretending to jump out and catch them, carrying them on his shoulders, it seemed to Margaret that she was peering through windows into bright, appealing rooms where everyone was merry and full of life. The people in the rooms of Lavinia's reminiscences were strangers to her, and Margaret could not get in. Anyway, it was painful to think of Lawrence, of her hand moving upward into his grasp, of herself sitting on his shoulders with her fingers twined in his hair, of his saying, "You hungry, baby?" Had he said that? She seemed to hear his voice, boyish but kind, saying that.

And then, the next day, the coldest day of all, Mrs. Early came in a sleigh she hired from the livery stable and took them off to her house for supper and to stay the night.

There was a fire in the kitchen, a fire in the parlor, and a stove in the library made, not of metal, but of stone of some sort. The library was warm in every corner, which seemed like a miracle to Margaret and Lavinia. With the gas lit everywhere, the rooms glowed, and Margaret's limbs seemed to warm and soften and stretch. Her very skirts lost their chill stiffness. Carpets and drapes seemed to envelop her, to give her the cozy comfort that a baby might feel when snug in his cradle. The library was two walls of books, floor to ceiling, in English, French, German, books Mrs. Early and Mrs. Hitchens had bought, but also books the sons had brought home or sent home. It seemed to Margaret that a door had opened, and rooms she thought she would never enter were hers to walk about in.

Mrs. Early held up a lamp, and they idled down the rows, looking at the titles: Mr. Verne in English and French (*Twenty Thousand Leagues Under the Sea, Le Tour du monde en quatre-vingt jours, Sans dessus dessous*), Mrs. Gaskell (*North and South*), Mr. Surtees (*Jorrocks' Jaunts and Jollities*). She was just taking down this last and opening the cover when a deep voice behind her said, "Try this one, Miss Mayfield."

"Oh dear," said Mrs. Early. "No telling what he's giving you." But she laughed.

Margaret hadn't realized that Captain Early had entered the room, but now he placed a tome in her hands. It was a book called *The Hound of the Baskervilles,* from England, and brand-new. She had heard of Mr. Conan Doyle, but never read anything by him. The book wasn't terribly long, and when she opened it, the first thing she saw was a picture of a large dog.

Mrs. Early said, "Is that some mathematical treatise, Andrew?"

Andrew said, "Certainly not," and went over and sat down in one of the chairs beside the stove. He at once picked up a book of his own. Margaret pretended to look at the one he had handed her, but really she looked at him. He was even taller than she remembered from that day with the bicycle, but his suit of clothes was neatly tailored and his face was attractive in its way (she thought of her own face and tried to compose it—not "glare," as Mercer said), with pale whiskers and a large but straight nose. He conformed himself a bit to the chair, and took on a quality of lengthy grace. His hair was fair, neatly cut and combed. Only Robert Bell and the president of the bank bothered to comb their hair. Every other man took his hat off and put his hat back on ten times a day, and that was that. Captain Early read calmly, then looked up and said, "Perhaps you haven't seen a stove like the one in this room, Miss Mayfield. It is of German design, and remarkably efficient. You may be familiar with the writings of Mr. Twain. He commented favorably on German stoves some years ago. We have had this one since I sent it home from Berlin."

"The door for putting in the wood is very small," said Lavinia.

"It uses very little wood, and it hardly has to be attended to at all," said Mrs. Early. "It is quite an innovation."

There was a moment of silence, then Mrs. Early said, "My son has an eye for innovation."

Captain Early nodded, looked at Lavinia and Margaret in a serious way, and then went back to his book.

He was like the person she had met bicycling, but he was unlike him, too. In her appreciation of the book, which she now opened, Margaret saw that perhaps she had taken an unreasoning dislike to the man. Even so, his presence had an odd effect on her—it was as if something around her, some field or edge, were impinged upon or dented by the same thing, but much more powerful, around him. It was a relief that he was sitting across the room.

The first line of the book he had handed her was "Mr. Sherlock Holmes, who was usually very late in the mornings, save upon those not infrequent occasions when he was up all night, was seated at the breakfast table." She felt a palpable pleasure upon reading this, compounded of the promise inherent in the everyday scene and the comfort of the room she was in, the gaslights on, the curtains drawn, the chairs and the carpet so rich and clean. There would be supper, and an entire night of respite from the exterior cold. She looked at Captain Early again. He was quiet and relaxed, and then he felt her gaze, and looked up and smiled. She dipped her head.

After a delicious supper, the captain and Margaret read a little longer while Lavinia knitted and Mrs. Early did embroidery. Mrs. Hitchens had coincidentally set off for Minnesota at just the wrong time, and was stranded in Chicago, but she was staying at the Palmer House Hotel.

Captain Early remarked, "The floor of the barbershop there is tiled in silver dollars, you know."

"My land!" exclaimed Lavinia. "How much could that possibly cost?"

"Thirty-six dollars per foot, or eighty-six hundred forty dollars, given the size of the room as I estimated it just by looking," said Captain Early promptly.

"Such an extravagance!" exclaimed Lavinia.

"It's a very elegant hotel," said Mrs. Early, complacently. "I'm quite certain that Helen will be comfortable there until they clear the snowdrifts from the lines."

That night, as they prepared for rest (three steaming hot-water bottles carried up ahead of time to warm the feather comforters piled on the bed), Lavinia said, "He seems to have quite a stock of information. And he's not bad-looking, all in all."

Margaret didn't say anything.

"He did smile at you, Margaret, dear."

"Was I glaring?"

"Why, no. You never glare."

"Mercer told Elizabeth that I glare and make jokes and so fellows are afraid of me."

"She repeated that?"

"I overheard it."

"We never overhear good of ourselves, and that's a fact."

"But maybe sometimes we overhear what we need to know?"

Lavinia didn't answer that, but said, "Of course, you are a quiet girl. Everyone knows that. But Captain Early looked at you several times. Four times. Once for quite a spell."

"As if he were calculating my dimensions?"

"Rather like that, yes. But that isn't necessarily unfavorable."

They didn't say anything after that, but each of them saw what the other was seeing also—that this third bedroom was furnished in the latest style, that the comforters were made of satin, and the sheets of linen, and the washstand of mahogany, and the draperies of velvet, and the carpet of thick wool, that the room was quiet and readily conducive to a peaceful rest. Heretofore, Lavinia had upheld the Bells' house on Kingshighway as the most elegant house she knew, and John Gentry's farmhouse as the most comfortable, but from this house, all questions of expense had been banished.

They had a pleasant breakfast in the morning, but Captain Early was not present—he had stayed up studying the heavens until almost dawn, taking advantage of the clear weather, and was still abed. They went home that afternoon.

They did see Captain Early one more time before he went away in the spring to take up a position at the Naval Observatory in Washington, D.C. Lavinia, a woman who did seasonal cleaning for them, Esther Malone, and Margaret were out in the side yard, washing all the sheets, towels, blankets, curtains, and petticoats from the winter. Margaret was stirring the clothes in the hot water, and Esther and Lavinia were feeding them through the wringer. They had already wrung out the less soiled items and hung them up to dry, when Captain Early, dressed informally in a floppy hat, light-colored loose trousers, and muddy boots, walked by, carrying a stick. He stopped and stood for a moment without speaking, then greeted them.

"I've been down to the river," he said.

The Missouri River was three miles and more from where they stood, so that qualified as an active morning's excursion, Margaret thought.

"It's somewhat higher than I expected it to be, but I understand that the snowpack upriver was greater than I had heard."

"Goodness," said Lavinia.

"Even so, there's no danger here," he went on. "That's my guess. But it's an educated guess. What will happen below St. Louis, though, I don't like to think of."

"That's always . . . ," began Lavinia.

"It's well known that the levee system is jerry-built below Cairo, but people in general, not just in Missouri, live with their heads in the sand. Not only officials. Officials aren't entirely to blame if the citizenry is itself indifferent or uneducated. I don't mind levees per se, but I've got my doubts about willow mats. And about dredging, too, I must say."

"They're dredging the river?" exclaimed Lavinia. "Around here?"

"No, ma'am. I was referring to the lower Mississippi." He fell silent, and seemed to watch them, passing his stick from hand to hand. Finally, as Margaret pressed the clothes down with her paddle, he said, "Did you know that the Romans cleaned their clothes by having slaves walk about upon them in vats of human urine? Urine was a rich source of ammonium salts and was sold and taxed in Roman times. I often think we moderns could take that as an example of how we could make better use of our own products."

Lavinia said, "No doubt that is generally true." She coughed, and maintained a personable smile. After a bit, Esther muttered, "Well, is he going to be helping us, now? What's he standing about for?"

Finally, he said, "Miss Mayfield. I hope you will feel at liberty to borrow more books from our family library. I can recommend two in particular. One is one I have been reading myself and have now finished, entitled *Visits to High Tartary, Yârkand and Kâshgar,* by Mr. Shaw. It has very nice drawings of Central Asia. I've set it out for you. And another is *Dracula,* by Mr. Bram Stoker, who is a friend of my brother in England. He runs a theater, and is a very able man. You enjoyed Mr. Holmes?"

She stopped pushing her paddle. "Yes, I did."

"Mr. Stoker is rather more daring than Mr. Conan Doyle, both in his formulation of the story and in his sensational effects. Good day." He tipped his hat and walked on.

Esther looked after him, then said, "You may say what you like, that he's a genius and all, but if I am asked, I will say that he's a strange one."

"But harmless, I'm sure," said Lavinia, with a glance at Margaret.

Margaret herself said, "There's nothing wrong with wanting to know things."

"Certainly not," said Lavinia. "The Mayfields have always been interested in knowing things. A man with some ambition, like your father, is much more eligible than a man who is content with what he has already."

It was perfectly clear to Margaret that Lavinia had made up her mind that Captain Early was not only an excellent prospect, but also a promising one. That he was neither attentive nor comfortable she put down to his eccentric education and his universe-altering occupation. Every so often, she would make some unexpected remark that indicated to Margaret that she was saying much less than she was thinking—one of these was "When all is said and done, my dear, a busy man leaves his wife considerable leeway to follow her own impulses." Another one was "I always thought a masculine presence in the house had a warming effect." Another: "Look at Robert! Not the most promising specimen at first, but thriving now."

Margaret began to have a fated feeling, as if accumulating experiences were precipitating her toward an already decided future. Once, shortly before Christmas, there was both a heavy snowfall and a long freeze, and Margaret took Lawrence to ice-skate. That fall, she had the boys with her quite often, because Beatrice was again with child and not feeling well ("The sure sign of a girl," said Lavinia). Everyone in town younger than sixty congregated on the ice, which was in a low-lying lot south of the town square and not far from the hotel. She saw Captain Early as soon as he arrived, and well before he saw her guiding Lawrence with two hands along the edge of the ice. She watched as Captain Early strapped on his skates, which made him even taller, and affixed his top hat more firmly on his head (still taller), and sailed among the other skaters like a schooner among sloops (she had yet to see, except in pictures, either a schooner or a sloop, but they were naval, he was naval—it was a good comparison). And then she felt a sort of pleasing dread as he skated toward her. He took off his hat, and his smile was as big as she had ever seen it. In order not to glare, she kept her gaze on Lawrence until she had made her own face welcoming. He said, "All factions foregather upon the glazed surface."

"You've returned."

"Time has stopped, indeed, Miss Mayfield."

She said, "Pardon me?"

"I was assaying a little joke. My responsibilities in Washington have to do with ascertaining the exact time, for naval purposes, by measuring the progress of the stars. While I am here, therefore—"

They smiled together. She said, "This is my nephew Lawrence. He's doing quite well today."

Captain Early clapped his hat back on his head and seemed to collapse, but in fact he was only squatting down to speak with Lawrence, who quailed, though he was normally a rowdy boy and not easily daunted. Captain Early's voice seemed to surround them. "Two plus two!" he demanded.

"Four," said Lawrence. His own age, thought Margaret.

"Three plus three!"

"Six." (A softer voice.)

"Four plus four!"

"Eight." (Very quiet.) This one Margaret was surprised the boy knew.

"Five plus five!"

Something inaudible emerged from Lawrence. She bent down and said, "What do you reply to Captain Early?"

Lawrence now yelled in the defiant manner she was more familiar with, "I said 'Enough!' "

Captain Early barked out a laugh and said, "Indeed, ten is often enough." He laughed again, and Lawrence laughed with him, his sassiness fully restored.

Then Captain Early shook her hand heartily, and skated away. She watched him in the crowd. Most people stared at him. He exchanged greetings with a few, but no lengthy conversations. One or two people looked from him to her and back again.

Later that week, Lavinia and Margaret were invited to the Earlys' for supper. The horse and the sleigh came for them. Once again the house was warm, and once again the supper was very good, and just a little more festive. Mrs. Hitchens nodded agreeably and said, "Yes. Oh, yes, indeed," every time Captain Early spoke. But this time Captain Early didn't speak much. He complimented his mother on the supper, told them that the exposition was still behindhand, and allowed as how some of the athletic performances scheduled to take place that summer, at the Olympic Games, which had been moved from Chicago to St. Louis, could well be "enlightening." Mrs. Hitchens asked what the Olympic Games were, and they were told that these were a competition between amateur athletes from all parts of the world.

"Don't you remember?" said Mrs. Early. "They had them in Greece several years ago, and then in Paris."

Lavinia and Mrs. Early discussed Christmas greenery and scarlet fever, and Margaret told how Aurelius had finally died—"a blessing not to go through the winter," said Lavinia, and possibly Beatrice would send them another horse, "but horses are such a bother," and everyone nodded, including Captain Early, who said, "Everyone will have an automobile soon enough," and Lavinia said, "Can you imagine?" Margaret could tell Lavinia was uncomfortable, because her tone of voice got suspiciously brighter each time she spoke, and then she said, suddenly, "You know, Margaret here once witnessed a hanging. A public hanging. But she doesn't remember a thing about it."

"Indeed!" said Mrs. Early, but gracefully, as if Lavinia were still talking about Aurelius.

"She was five, or almost. It was the day Elizabeth was born. Her brother Lawrence took her. I don't know what he was thinking."

"I remember that," said Mrs. Early. "It was quite an event. The last time in this town for such a thing, thank goodness."

Captain Early said nothing for a moment, then, "That was the week John and I went upstate to look for geodes. We took the train to Hannibal and then trekked up to Keokuk."

Mrs. Early said, "You should see the boxes of rocks in the cellar. I'm sure there are diamonds in there somewhere."

Captain Early said, "I sometimes feel as though I remember everything." He said this in such a somber voice that Lavinia immediately added, "Margaret has such a good habit of looking on the bright side of things."

This was when Mrs. Early, who was sitting catty-corner to her, momentarily put her hand over Margaret's and gave a squeeze. The older woman's hand was warm, and she said, "That is a personal quality that I've always appreciated."

But it was not a lively supper. Captain Early went back to Washington soon after, and Margaret had the distinct feeling of staring into her own future, the same feeling she had had so long ago, at the Fourth of July parade where John Gentry had fallen off his chair and Robert Bell had seen his possibilities expand. The play had begun. The customary ending was promised. Her own role was to say her lines sincerely and with appropriate feeling. At her age, she thought, she should know what those feelings were, but she did not.

As if to answer this question, Lavinia made sure Margaret was ever helpful that winter and spring. If people were down with any sort of fever or pleurisy or rheumatism and couldn't do for themselves, Margaret was the one who carried the baked beans to the house or did the extra housework or went uptown to the store for provisions, especially if the ill person was a maiden aunt or a widow or an impoverished woman of any sort. She quilted at the church with ladies who had time on their hands, making rough comforters to be handed out to those who couldn't afford their own. Lavinia's constant topic of conversation was the misfortunes of these women, and the greatest of these was finding themselves alone and unprotected in a world everyone acknowledged to be unsympathetic and even dangerous. Every time Margaret settled into a chair and opened a book, Lavinia wondered aloud whether Beatrice needed a hand, and maybe Margaret should walk over there ("The fields are quite hard with this frost") and stay for a few days, doing laundry. Margaret's future, as a result, seemed to narrow to a point, and the point was this room, where they were knitting in air so cold that they could see their breath by the lamplight.

Mrs. Early sent them things: dishes of brandied plums or a mincemeat pie. She sent them oranges once, and books, of course, and special tea from Ceylon or China. She came by and read them parts of the captain's letters, which they could see were lengthy and neatly written. He had a good command of language, and liked to walk, so she often read them his descriptions of his perambulations in Washington and Virginia—"Beloved Mother, Here in Washington, the winter is well advanced, and spring at hand. I went with Wilson Sunday into Rock Creek Park. The grass was up, in the tenderest threadlike shoots, and the air was fragrant with moisture rising from the earth as we strode across it. Wilson showed me where he uncovered a hand-ax and some spear points, demonstrating to all and sundry (or those willing to accept the truth) that America has been peopled for many thousands of years, just as Greece and Egypt have. The evidence is, of course, fascinating, but I could not keep my eyes or my mind off the dogwood, which is in flower, and the violets and toadflax." Margaret had to admit that there was something wonderfully elegant about such outings, something far, far away from the sighs and heavy fabrics of the quilting circle.

The Louisiana Purchase Exposition opened later in the spring, and everything in the world was changed by it, but Lavinia and Margaret did not make their first visit until the beginning of June.

Truly, it was not like anything Margaret ever saw before or afterward. It had been promised that they would get the whole world into one end of Forest Park, and it seemed as though they succeeded. Dora spent the entire summer at the exposition, supposedly writing about it for various papers near and far, but really, she told Margaret, she could not bear to leave, even when the weather was hot and the crowds were pressing and the roads (miles and miles of them) dusty. Mrs. Bell had a proprietary pride in the fair, and would hear nothing but praise for the beautiful trains in the Palace of Transportation, the astounding electrical display in the Palace of Electricity and Machinery, the thrilling pipe organ in the Festival Hall, or, for that matter, the contortionist outside of Mysterious Asia. The world was jumbled together, with the Irish Village right beside the Tyrolean Alps, but they got used to that. After three days, they went, dazzled and bewildered, back to stay with Elizabeth in Kirkwood, and then returned home, only to go back to the exposition in July, when it was much hotter but there was even more to look at. It was then that they met Captain Early, who was staying in St. Louis with his mother and Mrs. Hitchens, and "doing the whole thing."

The first day, they ate ice cream in the Tyrolean Alps; the day after that, they looked at the sculptures in the Colonnade; the day after that, they watched an athletic contest. Captain Early was in his element, and seemed eager to squire her about and show her every mechanical miracle on display. The contortionist and the pipe organ were not nearly so much to his taste as the *Moving Picture in Hardware,* or the ladies making corsets by machine, or even the enormous teapot. He was mildly diverted by the display in which criminals were measured, part by part, in order to demonstrate their criminal tendencies, and, indeed, he did take her to the Human Zoo, where all the races of man were shown off (and Geronimo was there, too). He was more animated than Margaret had ever seen him. He took her arm and hurried her here and there, but also was attentive to all of her possible desires—would she care for more ice cream, or for a sausage wrapped in a bun, or for some cherries? He seemed as unaffected by the heat as he had been unaffected by the cold on that strange winter day of their first meeting. Margaret saw now that he was not exactly like other mortals—he knew more, saw more. His mind worked more quickly and surveyed a broader landscape. Others stared at the three-thousand-horsepower steam turbine and the two-hundred-kilowatt alternator nearby, even removed their hats in awe, but Captain Early laughed aloud with delight at the two machines. He seemed positively joyful as dusk fell. He took Margaret's elbow, halting her on the path, and then he gestured with his arm, and electrical lights lit up all around the park, as if he himself were sparking them. Margaret gasped.

That was what won her in the end. Captain Early knew all about electricity, and it seemed to her, as he spread his arms and raised his hat off his head only to put it back on and laugh, that he was presenting her with a hidden and powerful force, asking her to observe and embrace it, while everyone else seemed capable only of gawking. And she did think, just then, that if it was meant for a man and a woman to share something with each other that they did not share with anyone else, then, somehow, for Captain Early and herself, this was it, the strange effervescence of the impending twentieth century, of bright light beginning in one place and instantly being in another place in a way that you did not sense with a candle or even a star.

As she felt this, they walked on. He was careful to anchor her hand on the sleeve of his jacket, and to pat it from time to time. But, as she told Lavinia that evening when Lavinia pressed her, he actually said nothing that was, as Lavinia put it, "to the point." Lavinia made her disappointment clear, but then she said, "Since there's always something to be made the best of, we will make the best of it."

In October, he returned again, but he did not make a proposal. As it turned out, he was finished in Washington, D.C. Lavinia said, impatiently, "If a woman's task is not to be patient, then I cannot for the life of me understand what her task is!" Margaret was patient. Mrs. Early stayed away. Christmas passed. Captain Early was understood to be in Flagstaff. Then he was understood to have gone to California. Spring came. Elizabeth had another baby, another girl. Captain Early returned from California. Shortly after he returned, he found her picking strawberries in Beatrice's strawberry patch, and got her to stand up, there in the morning sunshine, and, holding both of her hands, he asked her to marry him. She was twenty-seven. He was thirty-eight. The seriousness of his face as he asked her made her terribly nervous, but she made up her mind that this nervousness was love, a form of electricity.

Now Lavinia herself became very patient. There was a lot to do in the month before the wedding, especially since Margaret's linen chest was nothing like what Beatrice's had been, or Elizabeth's. What was there in it—three tablecloths, a dozen napkins, some unhemmed sheets and pillowcases, a quilt, neatly made, but old now, ten years old or older? And what dress did she have to be married in? Lavinia had overlooked that, and Margaret had overlooked it, too. Mrs. Bell had nothing suitable—Margaret was much too tall. It was Mrs. Early who took Margaret on the train to St. Louis, to Stix, Baer & Fuller and bought her a practical outfit, a blue shirtwaist with lovely lace over the shoulders and a flattering, bias-cut skirt, in a crisp wool, light but warm, and a coat to go with it, darker blue. They had tea at a French tearoom, and Mrs. Bell joined them. She had a hatbox with her, and she gave it to Margaret, and congratulated her, and gripped her shoulders and kissed her on both cheeks in that St. Louis way, but all of her conversation was about Lucy May and Eloise (named after Mrs. Bell), who was already smiling at two months old. After that outing, it was but two weeks until the wedding.

Andrew came over every afternoon. They were having a heat spell, so he would seat himself in the rocker on the porch. Margaret meant to sit and chat with him, but there were other things to be done—Lavinia would have her shelling peas for supper, or hemming, or even pruning the rosebushes in the bed by the steps. Andrew spoke in a pleasant way about what he had read in the papers that day, or what he had seen walking along the river, or the habits of bees versus the habits of wasps, or changing climate patterns in Equatorial Africa. He had a sonorous voice and a formal delivery. Lavinia never left them alone for very long, but Andrew didn't seem to mind. Every day, upon leaving, he stood beside her for a second and took her hand in both of his.

The wedding was quickly accomplished, in the parlor at the farm. Beatrice jiggled the baby, who was fussy with colic, and as Mr. Pine, the minister, asked Andrew if he took this woman, she passed her to Lavinia. The boys could hardly stay still—Robert had to grip them each by one shoulder and force them to stand. Only little Lucy May, now two, was smiling and excited in her smocked dress. She stood quietly holding Elizabeth's hand until Elizabeth whispered to her, and she walked solemnly over to Margaret and handed her the bouquet of lilacs. Mrs. Hitchens and Mrs. Early kept smiling through it all, and then, afterward, Mrs. Early said, "Active boys become adventurous young men, don't they, Andrew?" For breakfast, Alice served flapjacks, bacon, and her own blackberry-jam cake, frosted with seven-minute frosting. Margaret and Andrew caught the *Katy,* which was to connect to the *Missouri Pacific* at Jefferson City that very evening.

1905

PART TWO

1905

Lavinia told Margaret when she left Missouri, "You've always been a good girl, and now you've had a piece of luck, marrying at twenty-seven, but a wife only has to do as she's told for the first year." Since one of the things she was told to do was to have marital relations, when she and Andrew embarked upon the sleeper that carried them across the sere and enormous Western lands to California, she expected, as Beatrice had warned her, that marital relations would commence at once, but they did not—Andrew was too tall for the sleeper and too modest. He felt they should have separate berths. However, he gave her a chaste kiss every morning upon rising and every evening just before he retired.

Their progress from Missouri was, at first, a lesson in the effects of decreasing rainfall—the green fields paled from moist, rippling shoots of wheat, to grass, to straw, to brown earth, then abruptly thrust up in cliffs of granite against a hard blue sky like none she had ever seen before. What rain there was Andrew pointed out to her—a vaporous curtain in the deep distance that often didn't reach all the way from the cloud to the earth. The endless deserts of Nevada were succeeded by their opposite, the pine-clad Sierras by way of the Donner Pass, which were just as daunting. Andrew, in his sonorous way, spent the journey detailing the geology of every region, and then the various stages by which the Donner Party came to grief and later was rescued. Margaret had never heard of the Donner Party, but by the time they got to Sacramento, she knew more about them ("Almost all of the women survived. What do you make of that, my dear?") than she cared to. From Sacramento to Fairfield, while they sat in the dining car and shared a plate of chicken and potatoes, she thought unwillingly of the Donner Party and stared out at the darkness. California seemed forbidding and self-contained, just as Mr. Dana had described it. At Vallejo, it took them almost two hours to sort their baggage and then make their way, by wagon, from the station through the town and down to the bay, then by ferry across to the island. In the fog, she saw only dim shapes and sudden lights reflected back to her. When they got to their little house, brought in their baggage, and sat down for a rest, it turned out that Andrew had not yet purchased a bed large enough for both of them—it was as if, until he saw both of them in the room, the need for such a bed had not occurred to him. Thinking of Beatrice's warnings and advice, Margaret was relieved; thinking of Elizabeth's more reticent but entirely positive reports, she was disappointed.

It was only gradually that she came to realize that she was truly in California. First, there were the facts—Mare Island was the naval shipyard for the West Coast, an island and an entire world, self-contained and busy and dedicated to everything naval. Andrew was in charge of the small observatory on the base, where he maintained the chronometer. Every day, just before noon, a couple of sailors raised the time ball to the top of the mast on building 51, which was visible from all around the harbor. At precisely noon, upon orders from Andrew, the time ball was dropped, and officers in ships all around the harbor adjusted their clocks, which they called "chronometers." The shipbuilding factories ran in a long noisy row south along the harbor to the drydocks, where the parts of the ships built in the factories were, by means of huge cranes, joined together (or, in the case of decommissioned or salvaged ships, taken apart) and, eventually, floated (or not). Day and night, men were busy in these factories, which were breathlessly, ear-shatteringly noisy, but all around the noise, people bustled back and forth, laughing and giving orders and chatting about this and that.

West of the factories, their street of houses looked rather like any other street of houses, and their little house, Quarters P, was pleasant. She had seen similar houses back in Missouri, a single story with a front parlor and a bay window, a dining room, back kitchen, and two bed-rooms. The house to their north was yet smaller, but the house to their south (across a little side street) was the first in a row of houses that were as grand as any she had ever seen in St. Louis. There were four of them, and then another, even grander one, with fat columns and a deep awning, where the Commandant of the Base lived; after that, five more of the first type. Past those, at the end of the street, was a small brick chapel, nondenominational. West of this row of houses, but out of sight, were the barracks for the seamen. Not far away, there was a powder magazine. Margaret had never imagined such a busy place, so simul-taneously insulated and cosmopolitan, where everyone spoke of "Tan-giers" and "Buenos Aires" and "Lisbon" with less self-consciousness than people in Missouri spoke of St. Louis and Chicago.

Andrew's observatory, on Dublin Hill, had a five-inch telescope and a retractable roof. He took her there on their second night, once they had recovered from their train journey. It was a small brick building, chilly and crowded with books and papers, but the instruments he used to make his measurements (which he later explained to her, but not that night) were set out neatly. She didn't touch them, though she looked through the telescope and saw a few things she had never seen before— Mars, the craters of the moon, the rings of Saturn (which, he said, had been at their optimum visibility in 1901, and would be again in 1927), and Neptune, which, Andrew pointed out, was blue. He said, "My view is that Le Verrier discovered it, but Adams gets joint credit." He put his arm around her shoulders and spoke triumphantly: "They knew it was there! They expected to find it and they did! Bouvard and Adams did the calculations that showed it was there because it deformed the orbit of Uranus. That, to my mind, was the beginning of the modern world. Isn't it amusing? Six years after the Battle of Waterloo, and already they had begun." Then he kissed her on the cheek. Very late, they walked back to their house. Margaret was as impressed by the fragrance in the moist air—Andrew said it was from the alyssum—as she was by the solar system.

Since the only book she had read about California was Mr. Dana's, she had imagined it as a forbidding place—hard to get to by land or sea, protected by mountains, deserts, offshore winds, and an impenetrable coastline, but this California, the California pierced and conquered by the Southern Pacific Railroad, seemed to embrace her. The grass around her little house was green, and there were roses on the bushes. The breeze off the bay was sometimes damp and foggy and sometimes warm, but it was always redolent of the sea grasses that grew on the western side of the island. The sun shone, and as a result of this sunshine, of the observatory, of the factories, of the flowers, of the unending activity of all kinds—as a result of the constant, pressing presence of Andrew in their small house—she did not feel herself to be the same person that she had always been.

One of the first things that happened after she arrived was that the back of the powder magazine blew out in an explosion. They heard it, and saw the fire. By the time she and Andrew got outside, the boys next door, the Lear boys, were already walking around on the roof of their house. "It isn't like this all the time, by any manner of means," called out Mrs. Lear with a smile. She let the four boys walk around on the roof of the house all that day and did not make them go to school. The boys' names were Theodore, Martin, Hubert, and Dorsett. Mrs. Lear's name was Winnifred. Captain Lear commanded the *Leader* and would be at sea until Christmas.

The bed was delivered, and she and Andrew explored the fringes of marital relations. According to Beatrice, a woman was lucky not to conceive a child on her wedding night; with Andrew, this good fortune was not a matter of luck. Even so, they proceeded in what Margaret thought was a stately and warmly clothed manner to full marital relations. Since neither of her sisters had described with any exactitude what marital relations were, she found them unexpected, rather like the blue color of Neptune. But for Andrew, the lure of the observatory was strong. Their walks about the island and her visits to the observatory were what seemed to make him happiest and most affectionate. Any new variety of bird or detected movement of a star caused him to squeeze her hand, or even kiss her on the top of the head and tell her about all the other birds and stars he had seen over the years and around the world.

Margaret had no idea who she was anymore, since she was no longer an old maid in a small Missouri town where bitter cold was succeeded by dogwood, then lilacs, then breathless heat, then the bronze trees and gray skies of autumn, and at last snow again, so she kept her eye on Mrs. Lear.

Mrs. Lear was naval to the core. Her father was a retired admiral living in New York, also on an island (Long Island). He had known Admiral Farragut himself (a very famous man whom Margaret had never heard of) and had been present when Farragut shouted to his crew, "Damn the torpedoes! Full speed ahead!" ("Or maybe Papa was belowdecks just at that moment, but he was on the ship!") Mrs. Lear loved her house, she loved Mare Island, and she was as comfortable with the navy as most people were with their immediate families. When Margaret exclaimed at the row of enormous houses, with their porches and porticoes and assiduously tended gardens, she said, "What do you think the navy is for? It is for cheap labor!" And then she laughed. And it was true. Every time Margaret looked around, it seemed, something was being done for her by a young man—he was washing her windows or cutting her shrubs or mowing her grass or carting away her rubbish.

Mrs. Lear had lived all over the world and served strange things for tea—no cucumber sandwiches for her; rather, oranges, grapefruit, artichokes, oysters, tortillas, cheese made from goat's milk and sheep's milk that she had learned to like in Algiers and bought on her weekly trips by ferry to San Francisco. She would eat the egg of any bird, just to see what it tasted like. She enjoyed a certain sauce that was made of hot peppers, the hotter the better, and she had plants full of tiny, pointed, jewel-like red peppers that she showed Margaret but wouldn't let her touch. When the boys tumbled down the stairs, she laughed. When they ran in the front door and out the back, she laughed. When they rolled around on the grass, punching and fighting one another, she laughed. When they called out to her from the upper windows of the house, turning the heads of passersby, she laughed. There was nothing too strange or too lively for Mrs. Lear, which led Margaret to believe that a life in the navy was far more stimulating and less serious than life in Missouri.

Andrew very much liked the Lear boys, and took them up the hill after supper to look through the telescope at the observatory before they smoked their last cigarettes and went to bed. And the Lear boys were unfazed by Andrew. When Hubert or Martin came over, Andrew would instantly call out, "How many inches is four meters?" and then time the child until he worked it out. Or he would come out of his office into the parlor and say, "All right, boy, my wagon is being pulled by my horse at a walk. I'm taking a hundredweight of pears to Napa.

Each pear weighs four ounces. Every hundred yards, I throw a pear out of the wagon. It's fourteen miles to Napa. How many kilograms of pears do I have when I get there? And how many pears?" He would not let the poor child leave the house until he had done this problem.

He didn't mind that the Lear boys were allowed to run about, to jump on and off things, to swing on ropes from trees. Or that they walked the railings of the big porch as a matter of course (including up and down the stair railings), improving their balance—a boy with a naval future had to perch like a squirrel and climb like a monkey. They rolled their own firecrackers with newspaper and black powder. They wandered away and came back soaking wet from swimming in the bay, reminding him of swims in the Missouri River with his own brothers. And the Lear boys were never disrespectful. They "ma'am"ed and "sir"ed everyone as a matter of course, snapping upright and not quite saluting. More than once, Margaret was walking down the street and heard a greeting float out over her head—it was Hubert or Dorsett, balanced on the railing of one of the second-story balconies. As soon as the child saw her, he would shout, "Evening, ma'am!" and nod politely, no matter what he was doing. Andrew considered it ideal that the boys loved explosions of all sorts, which they called "ordnance." And that Theodore lived for the cranes in the shipyard. Marital relations, Margaret came to understand, were meant to reproduce this happy chaos, a return, for Andrew, to the boyhood he remembered, and for her, perhaps, the resurrection of a childhood she had missed.

One day, Mrs. Lear said, "You could have knocked me over with a feather this morning. I was in the nursery, looking at plants, and I heard Mr. Burgle speaking German to someone, who spoke right back to him, easy as you please, and who should I see but Captain Early! *Ja* and *nein* and *auf den Bergschrund* and I don't know what all."

"Didn't you know Captain Early was educated in Germany?"

"Whatever for, my dear?"

"For astronomy and physics. At the University of Berlin. I mean, after the University of Missouri."

"But why didn't he go to an American university, like Harvard?"

"I don't know." In fact, though he was always informative, Andrew hardly ever said a word about his past, or his feelings. It was as if his feelings were entirely accounted for by what there was to know. Nor did he delve into her feelings, seeming to think that, whatever they were, they were her business.

Another time, Mrs. Lear said to her, "Captain Early has very big feet, if you don't mind my saying so."

"He's a tall man."

"Goodness me, well over six feet—not made for a sailor, my dear, not at all. But do tell me, does he have his boots specially made?"

"I believe so."

"But where?"

That evening, when Andrew came in, she took a good look at his boots, which were a rich deep brown, and not really like any boots she'd seen in Missouri. She couldn't believe she had lived with these boots now for two months without noticing them. She asked him. He said, "German Street."

The next day, when she reported this to Mrs. Lear, the lady's eyebrows lifted.

"My dear, I'm sure he means Jermyn Street, with a 'J.' It's in London."

Margaret said, "I should ask him."

"You could," said Mrs. Lear, "but I find keeping a sharp eye out is more instructive. Captain Lear hates to be asked questions. My father was just the same way."

This conversation led her, the next afternoon, into his wardrobe, where she looked at his clothing for some minutes. He had five pairs of boots, four uniforms (he wore a uniform every day to the observatory), a stack of shirts and other linen, five hats in various styles, three summer suits, and three winter suits. He had two dressing gowns, of silk, which he wore about the house in the evening. She didn't know what was more surprising to her—that she had gone so long without investigating Andrew's wardrobe, or that its contents were so much finer than the contents of her own.

Spurred by this investigation into Andrew's wardrobe, she tried another—she looked at all the books in his library, which was a small room at the back of their house, to which the door was always closed. The shelves in their parlor were well stocked with Dickens and Verne and Conan Doyle and Rhoda Broughton. In his office the books were in German, French, English, Dutch, and what looked like Norwegian. She could not make out what any of them were about, even the English ones.

She ate with him, walked with him (it wasn't just birds he liked, but plants and snakes and rabbits), listened to him sing (he had a pleasant baritone, and sang lively songs in German), and watched him read (which he did, quite often, at meals, apologizing to her for not being able to break a lifelong habit). She cooked for him. He liked bacon fried in a skillet, then pushed to one side so that two eggs could be fried, sunny-side up, in the bacon grease until their edges were crispy and brown but their centers were still warm and a bit runny. At midday, he liked a steak, and in the evening, he liked a soup, especially a pea or bean soup cooked with a ham hock. He liked her to boil up the greens he brought home from walks—telling her they were nutritious and good for the digestion.

But there was nothing he loved more than new information. Their little house was a riot of books and papers. The first ferry of the morning (which arrived before 6 a.m.) brought all the current editions of the *San Francisco Call,* the *Chronicle,* and the *Examiner.* Of course there was the Vallejo paper also, and if you scoured Vallejo, you could get the *Sacramento Bee.* Dozens of copies of *Scientific American* sat by the kitchen door, where Andrew left them to go out to the rubbish or not, depending on whether he was offended by articles being run. The copies of *Nature,* another science journal, more respectable in Andrew's estimation, sat on a table in the front room for a long time, the stack growing taller and taller, but eventually that stack, too, wound up beside a door, its fate always in the balance, because it, too, ran articles that Andrew disagreed with. In addition, he had many correspondents, and received many letters every day, though not as many as he sent out.

Much of their conversation was about charlatans and idiots who held ridiculous notions. All these notions were much the same to her, since she didn't hold any scientific ideas at all beyond those of Jules Verne. For example, there was the metric system. Little did she know that, whereas in Missouri and even California people spoke of pints and pounds and rods and bushels and pecks, in France people spoke of grams and meters and centimeters, which were all scientifically related to the circumference of the earth. Germany had been a measurement madhouse before 1870, according to Andrew, with every town measuring its own ells, and the *Meile* different in Baden from what it was in Bavaria, and that didn't even begin to take into account the *Wegstunde,* the *Klafter,* and the *Zoll,* which was an inch, more or less. Andrew could not forgive the British Parliament for voting, in a "demented medieval manner," to decline to put the British Empire on the metric system. Margaret mentioned this to Mrs. Lear, who said, "Oh, my dear. That is marriage. As far as Captain Lear is concerned, the navy is riddled top to bottom with fools who were promoted for no apparent reason. But it could be worse—it could be the Royal Navy!" She laughed. "Better for them to air their complaints than take to drink over them!"

Andrew talked endlessly about the universe.

First, she had to be educated about everything that was known about the universe, such as the rate of acceleration for falling bodies, and laws of thermodynamics. Entropy was a concept that she grasped instantly. When he was explaining it to her, she imagined herself, first, busily cleaning house and cutting up a ham hock for baked beans, then, as a result of entropy, lying on a sofa and reading Rhoda Broughton. She didn't have too much trouble, either, with Newton's ideas about gravitation or his three laws of motion, except for the third one. Her life experience seemed to indicate that if you weren't careful, often the reaction was stronger than the original action, not equal to it. Against Mr. Newton's "equal and opposite reaction," she suggested "sow the wind, reap the whirlwind." Andrew laughed as if she were making a joke when she said this, and kissed her on the cheek.

Once he felt that she had a rudimentary understanding of the universe, he explained to her how he had changed its nature by identifying a multitude of double stars. These were two suns orbiting each other, rather like a couple spinning in the middle of a dance floor. However, *he* was not swinging *her* about—together, they were describing the circle. Andrew had found 246 of these doubles, of which 103 were confirmed by others and another thirteen were provisionally accepted. However, the remaining 130 were not accepted by certain men who were temporarily influential in the world of astronomy. The doubters would soon yield. "Herschel figured out that the solar system is moving through space, toward the constellation of Hercules, and it took fifty-four years for him to be proved correct." Andrew often spoke of Herschel, and with such fondness that it took Margaret several months to understand that Sir William had died in 1822, some forty-five years before Andrew himself was born. Andrew laughed his cheerful rumble. It was Herschel who discovered Uranus, along with the satellites Titania and Oberon; it was he who believed that Earth was not the only inhabited planet; it was he who named the asteroid; it was he who discovered the existence of infrared radiation; it was he who made many of the telescopes in use in England; it was he who would have ratified

Andrew's own discoveries, if only he had lived to see them. Double stars had once, Andrew told her, been hurtling about space as the sun does, solitary, accompanied only by random satellites, but these stars had exerted a pull on each other in passing and captured each other.

Margaret's letters to Lavinia were long and cheerful. She listed all the new things she was doing and thinking about. Lavinia usually wrote with her own news, but once she said, "Andrew is an unusual man. I, for one, never doubted that you would rise to the occasion. And in even the most ordinary marriages, Margaret, there are plenty of occasions to rise to."

Andrew did not bother to celebrate Christmas, so Mrs. Lear asked her if he believed in God; she had heard from someone on the base that he did not, and she had never observed Andrew and Margaret going even to the nondenominational chapel. At supper, Margaret asked him. He said, "Isaac Newton believed in God, my dear. He looked out into the stars, and he saw that they were fixed, and he made up his mind that God had set them there, just where they were, at the beginning of creation. He saw, too, that the stars were so far away from Earth that the average man could not imagine how far. And he could not help seeing that there were more stars in some parts of the sky than in others, and so, eventually, he had to admit that it was going to be fixity or gravity, and you could not have both. If the stars were not uniformly set into the sky, then they had to move toward one another or away, and eventually the universe would change, and, he thought, there might therefore be a universal collapse, as more and more stars gathered together in one spot. And so, because he did not think that God would allow this sort of thing, he decided that, from time to time, God puts the stars back where they should be, as an Almighty should be able to do. Of course, then they must ask the question why God set up the possibility of movement in the first place. Why not just make all the stars equidistant and equally large and dense, so that they don't move?"

"Why not?" she said.

"Does God want to keep himself occupied?" Andrew took a bite of his ham steak and shrugged. It was a rainy day, and their windows were shrouded with gray, but they could hear the clanging and booming of ships being built a few hundred yards away. Andrew shook his head, then said, "Simply because, not. Because that is a question not to be asked."

"I asked it."

"You may ask it, of course, my dear. I don't mean it is forbidden, as there are no forbidden questions. I simply mean it is not a question that I would ask. I am content to know that the stars do move, and to leave aside, for the moment, the purpose of their movement."

"So you don't believe in God?"

"I usually leave that question aside, too, but if you must have me respond to it, and, indeed, must fit your conception of me into the world of the naval base here, where Captain and Mrs. Lear and everyone else believe that God attends to their every thought and action, and judges them day by day, then I would say that, at this point in my life, I have come to understand God as a Being for whom it is my privilege to search, rather than as one for whom it is my obligation to perform."

They ate quietly for a while. Then Andrew said, "Am I to assume that you yourself believe in God, my dear?"

"My mother always said that the ways of God were not to be understood by mortals, and I do believe that anyone from Missouri can understand her sentiment."

He nodded. It seemed that, from their different perspectives, Andrew and she agreed on the subject, but when she spoke of this again to Mrs. Lear, Margaret said, "I think he would say that God is different from religion." Mrs. Lear disagreed with this sentiment, but their friendship was not affected.

One day, he borrowed a shotgun from Hubert Lear, and the two of them went off on a walk to the western part of the island. They were gone all day. When they came back, Andrew was as excited as she had ever seen him—he and Hubert Lear had taken plenty of ammunition, but they had shot no squirrels or rabbits, they had shot only mud. They had shot mud from many angles, including several times when Hubert climbed as far up a tall tree as he could go, carrying the shotgun in a sling and the shells in a separate sling, and from that height (some thirty feet, Andrew thought), Hubert had shot straight down into the mud. After each shot into the mud, Andrew would inspect the holes the shot made, and, he said, "Every single one of them looked like a crater on the moon, and so, my dear, I see that the moon is being bombarded by shot of all sizes, and craters have been formed, and many of them have remained pristine, just as when they were first introduced into the surface."

He was exceptionally excited by this idea, and had written it up by the next day, but he didn't send it to a journal that day, or the next day. It was still lying on his desk a week later. When she asked about it, he declared that it wasn't ready, that it required more thought. One evening, after he had gone to the observatory, she read it and replaced it on the desk, at just the angle he had left it. It was clearly written, and the idea seemed simple to her—beautiful, too, and fun, in its way, with Hubert up the tree shooting into the mud. Anyone, she thought, could appreciate this idea. Still he wouldn't send it. The papers sat on his desk just as she had left them, week after week.

FROM this, it was but a step to glancing into other papers that were lying around. Andrew saved everything. At first the stacks were daunting, full of numbers and equations and words that she didn't understand, like "parallax." But there were others as carelessly left about—for example, an old note from one of his professors to the president of the university in Columbia. It read, "Arrogant scoundrel. Stirs trouble among the students. A monster of self-seeking impudence." There was no name in the letter, no real indication of whom the professor was referring to, but of course, upon reading it, she searched more assiduously, and soon enough found a packet of letters from Andrew to his mother from those days.

In the first two years, he wrote only about his daily thoughts and occasional pleasures and successes, as a boy away from home would. His tone was affectionate and thoughtful, and Margaret was pleased at what she had found. In the spring of his second year, though, he wrote, "Dearest Mother, I know you will be disappointed in me, but I must report that I have done what it seemed proper for me to do at the time, and although the consequences are not what I would have wished (and I hasten to report this to you, as you will soon hear from others), I do not, as yet, regret my action, but I know that you have frequently counseled me to conduct myself with more caution. I am writing to say that I have failed to heed your advice, and will possibly be sent home from the college." It emerged in subsequent letters that Andrew had paid three other students to cede to him their allotted hours on the college telescope, a seven-and-a-half-inch model that he was eager to master, and in order to cover this up, he had helped them falsify their observations—letting them (or encouraging them to) copy his observations and present them as their own work. This arrangement had obtained for some three months, until the professor, growing suspicious of one and then another of the three students because of their inability to reproduce the observations they said they had made but didn't seem to remember, discovered it. Andrew then could not resist pointing out to the professor that the observations were his, and were all of the first order—accurate as well as numerous and "of better quality than the Professor's own work, which I of course would not have said had I not spoken in haste, but the remark was nevertheless true, and if he had not known it to be true, then he would not have offered to break my jaw for me." The other students received failing grades, but Andrew had to receive an A—his observations were indeed of the first quality. That professor, however, refused ever to work with Andrew again, because he had been "deceptive." Margaret guessed that it was this man who had written the original note. She could imagine their confrontation only too easily—Andrew would have loomed over the professor, employed his natural eloquence, said things he should not say, and in a deep and prideful voice. But Margaret was not entirely put off by the incident—she appreciated his honesty and his remorse. And anyway, in the intervening years, he had learned to govern his temper.

But her curiosity was piqued—after some days, she found herself rummaging in his desk again. She brought this up in an oblique way with Mrs. Lear as they enjoyed a bit of winter sunshine while sipping oolong tea on Mrs. Lear's porch. The boys were at school, and Captain Lear was expected home any day. Mrs. Lear knew what she was getting at as soon as she said the words "private papers." Mrs. Lear laughed. "Goodness me!" she exclaimed. "Why should a husband's affairs be private from his wife? He might easily find himself embroiled in more and more difficulties. I'm sure your mother would tell you the same thing. Do you know Mrs. Rudolph? Perhaps not. Captain Rudolph was"—she leaned forward and lowered her voice—"court-martialed. They lived in the third house down. Dorothy Rudolph kept finding objects about the house, bejeweled daggers and carved jade boxes and such, and she didn't have the sense to investigate their origins. She didn't even look into Captain Rudoph's bank book, just held out her hand once a week for household funds. He was stealing these things! Very strange. She might have stopped him, but she didn't understand her conjugal responsibilities. My goodness, Margaret! If there are papers to look into or drawers to open, then do it while you have the time."

And so she opened and looked into.

After Andrew graduated from college at Columbia, some fifty miles from their town, he went away to the University of Berlin, in Germany—everyone in town knew this, because it redounded to the credit of the entire county. Andrew wrote, "But, dearest Mother, if you think more deeply about the matter, you will see that there is nothing for me at an American institution. It almost doesn't matter what 'work rumor has done against' me—the resources your preferred institutions put into mathematics, or astronomy, or even the sciences, altogether, are laughable when not shameful." And then, from Berlin, he wrote, "They do think I am brilliant, dearest Mother. They do exclaim at how quickly I have picked up the language and the customs. They do admire the precision of my observations, but of course, they are hide-bound in their way, and very German and very Jewish, some of them. They stick together. I am endeavoring to remember, as you say, that all people stick with their own kind. And I am doing as you also bid me: I am NOT voicing everything I think, and I am not letting my temper get the best of me, even late at night, and I AM watching what I drink, because, as you say, it is evident that drink affects ANGLO-SAXONS somewhat differently than it affects GERMANS. Even so, they expected, they now say, to find once they got to know me, that I was ARMED at all times!"

The letters from Germany were not as numerous as those from Columbia—"Darling Mother, my studies so enthrall me that weeks go by without my realizing. Just to illustrate, I said to my friend Mauritz the other day, 'Isn't it about time for Easter?' And he laughed and explained that it was already three weeks since Easter, and had I not noticed that he was away visiting his family in Düsseldorf for five days around that time?"

Andrew was industrious about seeking out mentors—"I have been to England and met George Darwin! He was most kind to me, even after I told him (politely, dearest Mother!) that I question some of his findings, but he said to me, 'That is what young men do, Early! Question you must, and if the old men fume and fuss, you must not pay a bit of mind.' I consider our meeting to have been a great success, but though I have written three letters to him since, I have not received a reply." He made at least four trips about Europe, meeting or attempting to meet astronomers he admired.

Margaret had thought Darwin's first name was Charles; undoubtedly there was another one. She dared not ask, though.

There was one letter that he sent his mother not long after her famous trip to Baden, where he joined her for a month. In this letter he remarked that "Miss Maria Meyerhoff and Miss Meyerhoff seem to have gone away without a word of farewell," but there was nothing to indicate the extent of his relationship to either of the girls, and, indeed, whether they were German, English, or American. The Meyerhoff sisters were not mentioned again, nor was any other girl. She winced a little at how these encounters might have gone, with Andrew so big and intent and frank-spoken, but it was no business of hers, was it? None of this was any business of hers, no matter what Mrs. Lear said, but she read on.

The schooling in Berlin only put off the most pressing question, and by the time he was finished, Andrew was ready to find a place for himself in Europe—even in Russia. A return to the U.S. he seemed to view as a last resort. He wrote, "I have sent off the letter to Struve in Dorpat. Mauritz read the letter for me and complimented me on my felicitous German. I know I could learn Russian with perfect ease, if given the chance." An inquiry had been made at Yale, which resulted in the following remark: "Should I go to Yale (though I know this is a fond wish of yours, dear Mother), I would find myself teaching not only mathematics (and the highest level would be simple calculus), but also chemistry and geology (!), not to mention elementary biology. No astronomy, as there is no observatory! (Even Crete, Nebraska, now has a new observatory!) The great thing now, anyway, Mother, is to go south—to South America or South Africa. There is an observatory in Lima (PERU, not OHIO—I know Ohio would be preferable to you, Mother!) run by Harvard University. But we would be far away from my brothers, and so I hesitate. I will not hide from you that I am in a great quandary. For your sake, I've thought of BORDEAUX and BESANÇON, but the likelihood of the French accepting an American, especially one educated in Berlin, is altogether remote."

These letters were dated with Andrew's customary precision: "Operncafe, Unter den Linden, Berlin, April 2, 1894, 7:02 PM–7:22 PM." The dates and addresses did give her a strange feeling. Margaret imagined him sitting "under the linden trees," sipping an elegant cup of coffee and eating an apple tart of some kind in an impossibly fragrant world, surrounded not only by lindens, but by pots of geraniums and roses and daisies and other blooms of all kinds and colors, with mysterious notes of music floating among the various perfumes, and a horde of silent, graceful bicycles streaming by.

After she read this packet (and carefully replaced the letters where she had found them), she made up her mind that Andrew was not so different from other young men, after all. He had not left (many) implacable enemies behind him. He had gone to a different country and fit himself into it with some success. She said nothing in particular about her investigations to Mrs. Lear, but one day, after Captain Lear had been home for a month, and they were eating beef and mutton and potatoes every night and the boys were sitting up straight, speaking only when spoken to, and ending every sentence with "sir!," Mrs. Lear remarked to Margaret it was a wife's first duty not to be taken by surprise.

And it was true that now, when he said things like "People themselves are the problem," she thought she understood what he was getting at. "The lens looks at something. The mirror refracts it. These instruments are not perfect, but they are more perfect than the eye, and the eye is more perfect than the mind."

She asked him whether he planned to send his paper on the bullet holes in to a journal. He said, "Here is the paradox. It only takes one man to find out what is true, but he cannot live long enough or see widely enough to do it. Ten men see ten truths, and then they spend ten years arguing amongst themselves. A hundred men are ten times worse, and a thousand ten times worse than that. I've come to despair at how the truth is dissipated and distorted with every mind that turns upon it." He shook his head. They were walking to get the San Francisco papers and some vegetables and bread. He squeezed her hand.

She said, "I looked at the paper, Andrew. It makes perfect sense to me."

"My exile is the best thing that could have happened to me, after all. Here I am, out at the edge of the world." He stared down at her. "Even though the physical world has no edge, my dear, the scientific world does! And at this edge, I am relieved of the constant necessity of human intercourse, and so my mind becomes freer by the day." She nodded, and put her hand through his arm. He smiled and patted it in an affectionate manner. But the paper remained where it was.

Mrs. Lear guessed her condition before Margaret did, one day when she drank tea and then felt her stomach turn at the sight of some smoked eel. It was about time, said Mrs. Lear, and then she insisted ("for the sake of the child") on reviewing Margaret's recent history with an eye to ascertaining "the breeding date," and, "my dear, the *foaling* date." She said, "These things do not happen by themselves, as much as you might be led to believe that they do. My own mother told me that she did not understand how she came to have nine children until at least number seven, when some ladies in her sewing circle took pity on her and told her. But it's best to be well informed and not turn your modest gaze away from the whole subject, as so many are tempted to do." She estimated that Margaret was about six weeks along, which would make for an early-fall "foaling date"—"Not at all bad, though when the time comes to take the infant out for air, you'll have a bit of rain, but we shall consider that when we must."

Each day, she intended to tell Andrew what she suspected, but failed to do so. "Breedings," as she now thought of them, were neither frequent nor easy. Some days, she made the case to herself that the very rarity of these events was reason enough to tell him that an effort had been crowned with success. Was Andrew any more knowledgeable about "breeding" and "foaling" than Mrs. Lear reported her mother to have been? Possibly not. This was her excuse. What she didn't tell Mrs. Lear was that there seemed to be no way actually to produce the child she imagined, whose face came into her mind unbidden, simply a face, appealing but remote, with no maleness or femaleness attached to it.

"Goodness me!" exclaimed Mrs. Lear. "You look so shocked, my girl. Shocked every day. But of course you do! I cried my eyes out the first time. Captain Lear had me in Lima, Peru, and for a while it looked like China, if you can imagine that. But you do get used to it. It may take years and one child after another, but you do get used to it. I am not saying, into your ears only, that I don't sometimes find it a relief that Captain Lear is off to sea again next month, because I do, though of course he is a wonderful man, all things taken together."

Margaret walked about the island, and then about the town, staring at the children, boys and girls, young and old, being carried and walking by themselves, running, skipping, rolling hoops and playing marbles, fishing in the bay, and working, too, since the general population of Vallejo was enormously varied, and plenty of children were selling fruits and vegetables and eggs and newspapers and tobacco, or shining shoes or driving carts or riding horses or carrying things home wrapped in paper. She began to feel quite sanguine about the foaling, which would be followed by another breeding, and then another foaling, and then another breeding, and so on. Whatever Andrew's propensities with regard to marital relations, he clearly understood that marriages produced children, and, according to the evidence of his jovial pleasure in the Lear boys, he was bound to greet her news with pleasure, but still she didn't tell him.

It was almost March, her first in California. The rain poured down and the fog closed in. When the sound of the rain was not blocking out every other (except, of course, the constant clanging and roaring from the ship factories, but she had gotten used to that), the fog brought in a litany—ships calling to one another as they crossed the bay, ferry whistles and shouts of men, officers calling orders to sailors over in the quarters, bantering and laughing from the street. Once in a while, she heard someone singing. Even the calls of birds emerged from all the racket, especially at those fugitive moments when human sounds had suddenly fallen silent, and a crow would squawk or a heron would cluck or a goldfinch would carry on a conversation right outside her window.

She began to feel what Mrs. Lear referred to as "morning sickness," though these bouts did not take place in the morning. On the third or fourth evening of this, she was reading by the electric light, and she felt the strongest surge of nausea yet. Her first thought was that she should not have eaten, or, indeed, even cooked, the liver she'd made for supper. She had forced herself to eat a few bites—she decided while she cooked the liver (which Andrew had brought home) that she would tell him the next day, and then, perhaps, they would adopt a blander and more agreeable diet.

She went into the kitchen to fetch a piece of bread, and suddenly vomited into the slop bucket beside the table. Then she felt so tired, much more tired than she had ever felt in her life, that she staggered back into the front room and fell into a sleep, or into a stupor, right there in her chair, with the electric light on. In the morning, Andrew told her that he had come in very late and attempted to awaken her, but with no success—so little success that he was alarmed and took her pulse, but her pulse was strong and not quickened, so he turned out the electric light and went to bed.

When she awoke in the chair, stiff from her night's rest, the sun was shining and she felt much better after a few stretches—rested and not at all sick. She tested herself by eating some bites of bread and drinking some tea—both went down well. Andrew came out of the bedroom, and a few minutes later, he and she were laughing at his consternation at finding her "practically comatose," and afterward, when they ate lunch—sardines—she still felt perfectly fine. As soon as he went out, though, as soon as she sat down again to read, she found that she could not keep her eyes open, and she slept away the afternoon. Before she managed to awaken, Andrew had returned and found her, then gone next door to Mrs. Lear and elicited the whole story from her, including the probable "foaling date" and her bouts with morning sickness. When she awoke to make supper, she found that supper was made—a boiled chicken with slivers of carrot and parsnip and some baked beans, which were pleasantly sweet and easy to partake of. All of this Andrew had persuaded Mrs. Lear to provide—but, indeed, she was a kindly woman and needed no persuasion. They had a lovely evening, with Andrew staying at home and reading aloud the first chapter of *Belinda* in a sonorous, faintly Irish accent, and smiling, but pointedly refusing to allude to anything outside of the room—nothing in the past, nothing in the future, nothing in the world or the solar system or the universe. For that one night, it seemed, Andrew Jackson Jefferson Early allowed himself the luxury of a few hours of superstitious silence, where plans were not overconfidently expressed and hopes were left to mellow unsaid.

But such momentary measures did not work. By supper the next evening, it was clear that the little face she could not help conjuring was not the face of this child. Andrew, too, was disappointed, and stayed with her for the next two nights, but, truly, it was a small thing, Mrs. Lear told them, common as dirt, though sad enough, of course. Her own mother had miscarried at least three times, in addition to the nine children, and it was possible that Mrs. Lear herself had miscarried between Dorsett and Hubert, when she was down with something for three days late one spring. And as for her sisters, well, she had despaired of her sister Edith's ever having a child. She said, "I'm sure it's better not to know, but now you do." And she did. By the end of that week, that episode was finished—she looked at the children all around her in yet a different way, as a population of beings that she was cut off from, as if by a thin screen. And then that, too, passed.

As nosy as she had been, looking for Andrew's letters, checking the labels of his suits and shoes, peering into his books for clues to his life and his character, the next packet of letters was not one she found but one that fell into her possession, quite literally, as she was setting mousetraps in the linen wardrobe. She was brushing away dirt and what all, and bumped her head sharply against the upper shelf. As she then backed out of the wardrobe, it began to teeter, and when she pushed it back against the wall with both hands, one of the files that had been stored there, willy-nilly, fell out onto the floor and broke. There was the packet, this one not from Andrew to his mother but from Mrs. Early to Andrew. There were five of them.

She carried them to her bedroom, and sat down on the bed. The first one read:

January 14, 1901
Darlington, Missouri

Dear Andrew,
I was pleased to read in your last that you find the arrangements I made for your comfort in your new place in Chicago very much to your liking. I did consider a lighter stuff for the window draperies, but even in the short time that I was with you there, it was evident to me that you would have both a strong west wind, off the prairies (and straight from Minnesota, you can count on that) and, on other days, an equally punishing wind off the lake, and so, if you feel cozy and well insulated, you may thank my foresight.

I hasten to respond to your last, received today, because I sense in your dissatisfaction with Mr. C—— the ghost of the old difficulty, and this difficulty, son, resides in you, not in Mr. C——. I am going to be blunt with you, in the hopes that you will not allow your feelings to get the best of you. You must be patient. It is unfortunate that you and Mr. C—— crossed paths in Germany. He is certainly alert to your challenge to him. He is a short man, a younger man than you by at least a few years, and the only son of considerable wealth. He has not been given as much of a free rein as you have been given, to make the most of his abilities and to fly out of the paternal nest. He is undoubtedly sensitive to your claims and jealous of your abilities. This puts a strong onus upon you to be patient, forbearing, and, most of all, to drop old antipathies, even in the face of the fact that he outranks you at the observatory. I know you can do these things, and that you have, increasingly, shown yourself to possess a measure of tact. Your last disturbed me, it is true, but I have confidence in your discretion.

Love always,
Mother

The next one was dated in April:

Dearest Andrew,
Thank you for your last. Mrs. Hitchens and I did enjoy our visit to Hot Springs. Apparently, there is a great plan afoot to open a horseracing track, and I was telling Mrs. Hitchens about how much we enjoyed the racing at Saratoga two years ago, and of your luck at the windows, when you told me that a superior European education was good for more things than one. Your grandfather, though a respectable man in every way, would have been proud of such sentiments!

From your silence on the subject, I can only assume that you have laid aside your animus toward Mr. C——, and are prepared to take the long way round. THIS CAN ONLY BE GOOD. Son, you have not had the experience that other men have, which is to be part of an institution that works, and must work, in a certain way. Every institution has its own system, and woe betide those who rush in and attempt to change the system precipitously. Such efforts can only offend those to whom the ways of the institution seem just and appropriate, and those people will have their revenge, make no mistake about it. You have had things all your own way for all of your life (and for this, I must blame myself— your brothers are much more canny than you are about political issues). But I will leave it at that, and praise you for your continuing forbearance.

And then she went on with family news for a page and a half.

Given her new interest in motherhood, Margaret read these letters with respect for her mother-in-law's skill in finding words to address Andrew that were both straightforward and tactful. Andrew's mother was not like Lavinia, who kept her feelings and thoughts mostly to herself until they burst out in a surprising and sometimes hurtful way that she later had to apologize for. But when she turned to the next letter, she saw that, however tactfully and honestly (and wisely) Mrs. Early expressed herself, it had had no effect. She wrote:

June 2, 1902
St. Louis, the Chouteau Hotel,
Chouteau and South Broadway

Dearest Andrew:
John has forwarded your last to me here in St. Louis, where I am doing some business concerning the Gratiot Street property (and a thorny business it is, I must say, but too tedious to relate). I was dismayed to read that you have sent a list of objections and "suggestions" (which certainly read like ultimata) to your colleague Mr. C—— and also to your superior, Mr. D——. I cannot feature how you think this will help your case or promote your interests. I do realize that it is unfair for Mr. C—— to forbid to you use of the refracting telescope in Wisconsin, and I am sure, as you say, that his excuse for this—that you were not careful enough with it last summer—is simply patched together. But I am telling you that if you encourage him to repeat it too often, he will come to forget that it is a lie and a slander, and believe it as fervently as if it were God's own truth. One reason for "turning the other cheek" is that each time an enemy lands a blow, he is motivated to land another. Soon there is no way of stepping back from the most extreme possible positions. I know you know this, because you have enunciated all the right sentiments, but now, in the heat of battle, it is as if you have forgotten everything you've learned. You are thirty-five years old, Andrew, and must understand that if you spoil this opportunity at the University of Chicago, you will never get another like it, and all of your hopes and dreams, not to mention your work, will have been for nought. When you were enduring

the hardships of southern Mexico, it was for this very thing—the chance to work at such a place, with such men, at just such a time as this, when Americans have, as you say, thrown off provincialism in time for the new century. Yes, we have said that you were made for this position! You were! That the position requires something of you—some forbearance, some understanding, some CANNI-NESS—is not surprising to anyone who must make his or her way in the world. I urge you to step back now—to apologize to Mr. C——, to withdraw your complaints to Mr. D——, and to wait, simply to wait. If you can't do it there, on the scene, then come home to Darlington for the summer and cool your heels.

Your loving Mother

Margaret could not help reading this with growing alarm, even though it was dated years previously, and all these events were over and done with, and somehow they had resulted in their current, *her* current, situation with Andrew. She felt her heart quicken with suspense and anxiety while reading, and decided not to go on to the last one. She looked around the bedroom, then bundled the letters together and pushed them under the pillow. All that evening, she watched Andrew, but he seemed entirely himself—when Hubert Lear turned up, out on the front porch, smoking a cigarette, Andrew invited him in, and offered him a slice of apple pie. They talked about school, and Andrew showed him how to calculate compound interest.

The next morning, when Margaret opened the fourth letter, it was only because she made up her mind that it was irrelevant to her situation—she was happy, Andrew seemed in good spirits. The letter ran:

January 2, 1903
Darlington

Dearest Andrew,
I must admit that it was with considerable dread that I saw the thick envelope addressed to me, in your handwriting, in this morning's mail, and as I feared, the envelope contained a lengthy self-justification. As much as I love you, son, I cannot agree that you have done "the very thing that honor demanded" of you.

"Honor" has never demanded a thing of you in this sequence of events at the University of Chicago, but pride has goaded you at every turn since the day you arrived on the campus, knowing Mr. C—— was already there. As I said to you when you were considering whether or not to accept the position Mr. D—— was offering you, it was not that they were beseeching you to come, it was that they were extending an opportunity to you, and they knew it. You should have known it, too.

I believe you when you say that Mr. C—— is insufferable—to YOU. But he is not insufferable to Mr. D—— and to Mr. Rockefeller and to others who are powers in the University. He fits in with them, and they are comfortable with him. In addition to that (and I am disappointed that you are so unworldly that you do not understand this simple fact of life), his father donated the observatory and the telescope, and so he has a proprietary feeling about it. Is this so obscure an example of human nature that you cannot understand it? The disparities of wealth in Darlington are minor—the difference between sleeping in the front parlor and keeping the front parlor just for company. But the differences in wealth in Chicago or New York or San Francisco are considerable and ostentatious, and it is the job of every aspirant to simply ignore them, however grating they may be.

I understand from your letter that Mr. D—— is ready to accede to your demands in some degree, and to raise your position. My advice is to accept this with a strong expression of gratitude and withdraw the rest of your complaints (for that is what they are). If your work is important to you, then proceed with it.

But her advice made no difference, because a brief letter dated a month later said: "Of course you may come to Darlington and restore your health and equilibrium, and you may stay as long as you wish. I won't hide my disappointment in the outcome of this contretemps right now, but perhaps by the time you arrive things will look more just, or at least more inevitable. I remain, always, your loving Mother."

The letter was dated early February 1903, that period when Andrew was visiting his mother during the cold snap—when Mrs. Early was so kind to Margaret and Lavinia, and they were so grateful for and impressed by the warmth and beauty of her house. It did give her a chill, to read about the real torments Andrew and Mrs. Early had felt, which had swirled behind their courtesies. She blushed to think of herself and Lavinia, looking around that bedroom, so blindly impressed.

She put the packet away where she had found it, and decided to resist pursuing further investigations, and then a letter from Andrew's mother arrived—she wrote about once a month, always something addressed to the both of them, light and gossipy and never intrusive (Lavinia had begun asking in every letter when she might expect a grandson, and Margaret had only just mailed off the letter that described their recent disappointment). When Andrew handed the letter to her, she read it with a new appreciation of Mrs. Early's style and manner. It read:

Dear Andrew—
Here in Darlington, it is cold and gloomy and the windows are covered wth ice. As a result, Mrs. Hitchens and I are scheming about taking a great journey west, and, of course, your establishment, and you, yourself, and dear Margaret are first in our thoughts. I cannot imagine how it is that I have overlooked California in my travels! To think that I have visited Thomas in Texas, where the scorpions and the tarantulas hold sway, and yet I have not sojourned in the paradise of San Francisco! So—you and Margaret must prepare yourselves, Mrs. Hitchens and I are embarking for Vallejo in one week—on April 3, and we should be with you shortly thereafter, though I do anticipate that we will stop from time to time to gawk at the vista and stare at the natives (be they white or Indian—I understand that the two groups are equally intriguing). I will send to you by telegraph as we get closer. I don't expect to impose upon you and Margaret for more than a day or two, but to travel on in state to San Francisco, and there partake of every luxury!

Your loving and self-indulgent Mother

When she looked up after reading this, Margaret saw that Andrew was staring at her, and then at their little house, so jam-packed with papers, books, and assorted paraphernalia. She said, "Oh, I know Mrs. Lear will be happy to put them up—she has eight bedrooms, and she's always wishing her own relations would visit." And, of course, it would be the opportunity of a lifetime for her neighbor to divine something more about Andrew than what Margaret was able to come up with solely on her own—Mrs. Lear and Andrew's mother would surely get along famously.

The two ladies arrived late in the evening. Andrew and Margaret met the train and took them by wagon and ferry directly to Mrs. Lear's house, where the boys had put up a banner and, as they approached, set off a few homemade firecrackers for a welcome. Mrs. Lear had laid out a small but elegant buffet of lemon tarts, tea, and avocado-and-prawn sandwiches. By morning, after breakfast at the latest, Margaret knew, Mrs. Early would hear about her failed pregnancy, and probably about every other little observation Mrs. Lear had made of her life with Andrew. Margaret found this reassuring.

Andrew's mother and Mrs. Hitchens were far from fatigued by their journey. They had taken a private room on the sleeper and had been pleased by the provisions in the dining car—"as elegant as anything in Europe, and there is so much more time to enjoy everything. In Europe, as soon as you have settled in, well, now you are in Münster already, and must disembark! But here! Well, the train journey is a vacation in itself. I understood from the porter that there are some families that simply ride about, living on the railroads. The scenery passes and, rough as some of it is, it's quite all right with me to look at it and not to have to go out into it, or, God forbid, trek through it, don't you agree, Mrs. Hitchens?" Mrs. Hitchens nodded enthusiastically.

They had lovely weather. They tramped about the island while the ladies gave her news of home, which was welcome in several ways, one of which was that it did not cause her to miss their town, or anyone in it, other than her mother and Beatrice. Mrs. Early gave her a long letter from her mother, which Margaret read page by page but not all at once. This letter, mostly about the grandchildren, she found surprisingly painful, even taken in small doses. Of course Beatrice was pregnant again, and due in September ("very uncomfortable, I must say, and partly because she never denies herself a single indulgence and has had to have all of her dresses remade and pieced out"), and little Lucy May showed an amazing musical gift. ("Much superior to Beatrice's— perhaps the Hart side is musical, too? They say that Jewish families often are. At any rate, the darling child climbs up onto the piano bench and plays 'Twinkle, Twinkle' with two hands, and seems to understand harmony, though she is only three.") She had news of Dora: "Can you believe, Margaret, that Dora has gone to New York City, where she went to a lecture by Mrs. Tarbell? After the lecture, she walked right up to her and told her where she was from and then handed her a sheaf of articles she wrote, and Mrs. Tarbell took her out to tea, and the short version of the tale is that Dora might get a position at *McClure's*—'or something even better.' Mrs. Bell pretends to be frantic that Dora will certainly never marry now, but she seems happy enough, though Mr. Bell considers Ida Tarbell the 'Devil's own second cousin.' Robert, however, is quite proud of his sister." She could see that her mother wrote about the grandchildren and Dora partly to avoid writing about herself—her handwriting was not exactly shaky, but more spidery than it had been, and she who had, since the death of her husband, leapt out of bed at dawn and gone straight to work planting or pruning or harvesting or canning, now reported that she lay in bed until eight each morning ("although I hate for half the day to pass before I can get anything done").

On the second morning of her visit, Mrs. Early sat her down on their sofa and put her hand on Margaret's knee. She said, "My dear Margaret, I'm afraid you must think about what it might be like to do without your dear mother at some point. Though she is younger than I am by two years or more, I do think her health is fading."

"She says in her letter that she's easily tired."

"Twice I've dropped by to take her out for a little drive, and she's said she's just too tired to go." She sighed. "I sent my girl over to help her with the spring cleaning."

"She should go live with Beatrice."

"But she says that the boys are too wild, and give her a headache. And now with this baby . . ." She shook her head.

"Elizabeth is easier to get along with."

"I asked your mother three weeks ago whether she wanted to go with me to St. Louis, and make a visit to the spa at Meramec Highlands. This time of year, it's very restorative, and not terribly far from Elizabeth and the girls, but she told me she never liked St. Louis."

Margaret thanked her. Mrs. Early smiled at her in a kindly way and put her hand to her hair, which was grayer now, but still very thick. She replaced a comb and smoothed the front of her skirt, which was a rich piece of cut velvet, purple with a black shading. She had gotten more stout, but, as tall as she was, she could carry the weight. She went on:

"Did I show you the books I brought you, Margaret, dear? I remembered that you liked the Sherlock Holmes, so I brought you another book by Mr. Doyle, set during the Hundred Years' War. And Mrs. Hitchens thought you might like her book of ghost stories that she read in the train. I must say, I heard her gasp once or twice in the upper sleeper!" She smiled again, and all of a sudden, surprising even herself, Margaret leaned forward and put her arms around Mrs. Early, and Mrs. Early held her to her breast and, for a moment or two, stroked her hair, and Margaret couldn't help weeping. But then they stood up, and Andrew came in from his daily task of dropping the time ball.

The next day, the two ladies took a train to Napa to look about up there. Mrs. Lear filled them a picnic basket. It was a pleasure to cook for the two of them, of course, and Mrs. Early was very tactful about showing her some recipes she knew—pancakes in the French manner ("though the Germans love them, too, they are so thin and light, with a little confectioners' sugar and some rough-cut marmalade, and, you know, Margaret, it doesn't hurt a bit to warm up the marmalade and stir in a quarter-cup of rum. It's very bracing first thing in the morning, and there's absolutely no harm in it").

From Napa, she and Mrs. Hitchens brought two tennis rackets and some balls for the Lear boys, and by the time Margaret was up the next morning, the ladies had strung a rope between two trees in the backyard, and induced someone to cut the grass very close. She had Theodore and Martin out, laughing and hitting one of the balls back and forth over the rope, while Hubert and Dorsett awaited their turns by swinging in the trees. Mrs. Hitchens was sitting in a chair, fanning herself with the morning paper, but Andrew's mother was trotting back and forth, showing the boys how to grip their rackets and aim for the ball as it went by them. Martin seemed an apt pupil, already hitting the ball more than missing it; Hubert and Dorsett swung past her once or twice; then she saw Hubert perch himself up on the railing of the second-floor balcony and sit there, watching and rolling a cigarette, which he then smoked with a meditative air before swinging back to the tree. The whole scene was so lively and good-natured that Margaret thought of trying to persuade the two ladies to stay into the following week, just for her own enjoyment. Four days was hardly enough of them! And then, that afternoon, Mrs. Early enlisted both her and Mrs. Hitchens in teaching the boys "a nice game of Missouri poker, just a bit of five-card stud—which stands for 'studious,' boys, which is what you should be every day of school." They used the boys' stash of matches for chips, and she ensured that while they were learning they lost, but once they knew the principles of the game, they each won a bit, which she paid them out of her own bag, a half-dollar apiece.

When Margaret suggested that evening that the two ladies stay longer, Mrs. Early exclaimed, "Oh, goodness! You will have quite another dose of us after we have had our fill of the great city of San Francisco, and the famous Palace Hotel. Mr. Enrico Caruso is performing *Carmen,* which I have never seen, so we can't miss that. I assure you that, by the time we head east, you will be glad to see us go." Margaret laughed, but she couldn't imagine being glad to see them go.

With his mother, Andrew was much as he had been in Missouri, polite and even jovial, but taciturn by comparison with his customary manner. He told about the gunshots into the mud, which made his mother laugh, and she said, "My goodness, Andrew, that is clever! And you made drawings of the craters? What if you made photographic plates of them, wouldn't that be extraordinary? I wonder how you would do that." Andrew had not made photographic plates of the mud craters, but he instantly sat up and declared that he would do so, and that afternoon they tramped around Vallejo, looking for a photography studio and a photographer whom they might induce to make plates of the whole operation—Andrew and Hubert shooting from the tops of trees, and then the craters themselves. Even for Andrew, his mother was an invigorating presence. Then she said, "And that astronomy journal will certainly take it, it's so brilliant. Just put together an irresistible package, Andrew. You've done that before." Then she went over to the Lears' house and got Hubert to show her the gun they had used, and tell her all about his other exploits, which also made her laugh.

The following day, Mrs. Early and Mrs. Hitchens took the three o'clock ferry, the *General Frisbie,* which was a fast boat and Andrew's favorite (two hours to the city), quite luxurious and well appointed inside. You could buy any number of things on the boat, including drinks in the saloon. They waited on the dock, and they talked about how the ladies would arrive in San Francisco at five, and no doubt be in their hotel eating oysters by seven at the latest. They were dressed in their most stylish outfits—Mrs. Early in green, trimmed with white and edged with navy blue, and Mrs. Hitchens in dark gray with a high white collar and sleeves edged in a deep red. Her hat carried a tight bouquet of silk rosebuds just the same color as the edging on her dress, and Mrs.

Early's hat sported two curled egret feathers and a bunch of cherries. They embraced and kissed goodbye; then Margaret watched them board the ferry, looking about all the time, with the eager curiosity that both of them always seemed to display. As she and Andrew walked back from the ferry building, Margaret thought she understood more about him—she saw he had his mother's curiosity and energy. She found this reassuring, which was surprising—she had not realized she was in need of reassurance. She said, "They looked very elegant." Andrew laughed cheerfully and gave her a squeeze around the waist. They heard the *General Frisbie* blow her whistle just then.

They never saw Andrew's mother or Mrs. Hitchens again.

MARGARET had been in an earthquake before, back in Missouri, in 1895. They were sitting at the supper table when the water in their glasses began to slosh, and then some dishes on a railing over the fireplace rolled back and forth and one crashed to the floor. Lavinia jumped up from the table to look out the front window. Because it was dark, she could see very little, but it was a nice night—no wind or rain, only some of the fruit trees in their yard swaying. She said, "An earthquake! God preserve us!" and she told them about another famous earthquake that her own grandfather had heard of, down where Missouri, Arkansas, Tennessee, and Kentucky came together. The Mississippi ran backward and changed its bed; forests broke in two and toppled over; a noise such as no one ever heard before or after terrified the people and sent the cows and horses racing into the woods, some never to be found. That night, in bed, Margaret, Elizabeth, and Beatrice declared that they didn't see how they could ever stand to have such a thing happen to them. And then they forgot about it.

When Andrew and she awakened to the shaking of their little house and the falling of the lamp off the bedside table, he leapt out of bed before the first shake had ended. She stayed where she was, having that strange feeling that the play was commencing all around her, a feeling that immobilized her, until he grabbed her hand and pulled her out of the house. It was just getting light. They stood in the middle of the street—it was impossible to walk—looking first at their own chimney, which did not topple, and then down the street. The buildings and trees seemed to have a haze about them, or to be themselves rendered hazy. Andrew said that this was the effect of the shaking: the eye could not take in the object. The trees seemed not to go back and forth but around in little circles, which Andrew declared was akin to a needle on a piece of paper, and, if it could be measured, would show a great deal about the quake. In the last one, only seven or eight years before, he had been told, almost every building, or at least every brick building, had fallen down or sustained considerable damage—Andrew had read all about it in his voracious way. Since it was unsafe to go back in the house for more than a moment, they decided to pull on their clothes as quickly as they could and then go see what they could see. Andrew was sure that this earthquake, like the one seven years earlier, was a local one—important to Mare Island, and perhaps Vallejo and Benicia, but not much in the larger scheme of things. Naturally, he first checked on the observatory. The telescope was fine—it did not seem to have moved at all. Oddly, though, two picture frames were flipped face to the wall, yet no books or papers had fallen. At first this earthquake merely thrilled Andrew, as an example of what geological dynamics were capable of. It was a clear day, bright and fresh. Margaret was more frightened than Andrew, but still somewhat invigorated by the very novelty of the thing.

The navy already knew, however, because of wireless transmissions, that part of San Francisco had crumpled to the ground—all the buildings and tenements down near the Embarcadero and the wharf. Margaret was relieved, just at the very first, for the briefest interval, to hear this. Andrew exclaimed, "The Palace Hotel is at Third and Market, quite a ways from the water." And though buildings were down, not that many deaths had occurred, except maybe in Chinatown. Chinatown was ten blocks or more from the Palace Hotel, and the Palace, unlike the buildings in Chinatown, had been built to the highest standard. For about half an hour, they took comfort in that. They ran to the ferry landing, as yet somewhat optimistic, but at the ferry landing, they felt an aftershock, which was more unnerving, in a way, than earlier, stronger shocks. It was this aftershock that brought on the dread.

Each ferry was more jammed with men, women, and children than the one before it. Some people were carrying bundles, and some were carrying nothing at all. Almost everyone was dirty and disheveled, and all were telling of harrowing escapes. Many of them had no friends or relatives or business in Vallejo; they had just jumped on the first ferry they could. All the ferries were heading out—to Oakland, Alameda, anywhere away from the city. Through the afternoon, they expected to see Andrew's mother and Mrs. Hitchens, a little disarranged, perhaps, but full of energy and curiosity, thrilled to tell them all about it. Each traveler added to the general knowledge, and with each story they heard, Margaret was forced to picture the devastation creeping toward Third and Market, but no one knew for sure whether the Palace Hotel was down or not. And as bad as it was in San Francisco, it was rumored that conditions were worse to the northwest. Santa Rosa was flattened, they said. Just about then, with the aftershock and the tales told by the survivors, Andrew began to get frantic.

The earthquake was succeeded by fire, and the navy was sending three ships, including a hospital ship, across the bay. Andrew went straight to the Commandant and forced himself into a meeting—he begged to go on one ship or another, he was tall and strong, but the Commandant wouldn't hear of it. Then Andrew decided to take one of the returning ferries, but just then, news came in that the ferry terminal at the foot of Mission was already burned to the waterline. Mrs. Early and Mrs. Hitchens had not been on any returning ferry, and of course no one knew them. All Andrew and Margaret could do was mill about in the crowd and listen. There were miraculous escapes. A fellow from Vallejo had gone to San Francisco the day before, taken a hotel room, and been put on the fourth floor; when his hotel collapsed, he had dropped to the ground from his shattered window and run for his life. Andrew asked him which hotel—the Brunswick. Where was his hotel from the Palace? Sixth and Howard, four blocks, said Andrew, six at the most, half a mile as the crow flies. But people had helped this man—he wasn't even wearing his own clothes. The lesson Andrew took from this conversation was that Mrs. Early and Mrs. Hitchens could so easily be helped. Statistically, Andrew kept telling her, they were likely to be safe. The population of San Francisco was over four hundred thousand. By the end of the afternoon, they had still heard of only a few deaths. Even if four thousand people died, that was 1 percent. Nothing like four thousand people were going to die, Andrew thought, but even if they did, his mother and Mrs. Hitchens, separately, had ninety-nine-to-one odds of surviving, of returning, of having an amazing and astonishing tale to tell. "My mother," he said, "has never believed she would be struck by lightning. She doesn't hold out for the fourth ace or the fifty-to-one shot." He said this as if her predilections were a guarantee that she would eventually be counted among the safe majority.

They left the ferry building late in the afternoon, and he hurried Margaret out to the western edge of the island. From there, as dusk closed in, she could see the glow of the fire far to the southwest—was it twenty miles, or not even? They watched it, though it was only a glow and did not look like a fire. Even so, they also thought they could smell the smoke and sense a lurid haze between themselves and the setting sun. As the evening progressed, the glow became visible from the roof of the Lears' house, and they stood up there with the boys, gazing at it.

Andrew swore that he would get to the city the next day. Others had gone—Mr. Devlin, whom Mrs. Lear knew through friends in Vallejo— had gone to find his wife and child. From a distance, it seemed as if you could do just that. "Or they might have gotten out by train." Andrew kept saying this. "That would be more efficient. We don't know how far west the fires have run. They could be in Oakland, but they could also be in San Jose, or even Santa Cruz." Standing on the roof of the Lears' house, Margaret thought she heard explosions, distant rumbles, but perhaps she did not. Perhaps, since she knew that there were explosions (and many of them man-made, as they dynamited much of the city to make a firebreak), she only thought she heard them.

But every story demonstrated that really you could not go to the city and find a person, or two people, or entire families. Many stories were not only astonishing, they were wrenching and terrifying. One man had been out in the early morning, right down by the ferry building. He said that by ten o'clock Mission Street was an "inferno"—wagons left in the middle of the street burst into flames, and the flames roared and rolled overhead, as in a furnace. Hotels and boarding houses collapsed, with people inside screaming, and then burst into flames even as the rescuers were dragging people out. The hospitals themselves and the refuges had to be evacuated as the flames approached. What everyone reported as the most terrifying thing was that the rushing wind seemed to be made of flame, that the winds and the flames together seemed to be stoking themselves into a kind of whirlwind of fire.

Of course there were those, in the following days, who drew that customary analogy between the notoriously sinful ways of the people of San Francisco, most especially those denizens of the Barbary Coast, and those of the people of Sodom and Gomorrah, which people always draw. And the unnumbered deaths in Chinatown were, to these people, another piece of evidence for the wrath of God. But if someone dared to express such sentiments in front of Andrew, he would roar at them, and so even those so inclined kept these feelings to themselves around him.

On April 20, with the fires still burning, Andrew did manage to get to Sausalito, but he could get no farther: every boat and ship in the bay was engaged in evacuating people from the south end of Van Ness Avenue, not in carrying anyone into the city. When he came home late on the twenty-first, he was convinced that his mother and Mrs. Hitchens were in Golden Gate Park, or at the Presidio. "Thousands there. Thousands. Who is more enterprising than my mother, after all?" He sent reassuring telegrams to his brothers, not exactly saying that he had found the two women, but implying that he shortly would—though, of course, he knew nothing, had heard nothing. The Palace Hotel? Entirely gone. But perhaps they had not stayed there. Or not gone to the opera. They hadn't had tickets yet when they left Vallejo—maybe they had never gotten tickets. Maybe, upon arriving in San Francisco on the afternoon of the sixteenth, they had changed their minds entirely. Mrs. Early was a woman of strong impulses and good instincts. Equipped, Andrew said, to survive. Once, when he was a very little boy, but old enough to remember, he had been sitting in a wagon and the horses had bolted. At the very instant the horses lifted their heads and pricked their ears, before the wagon even started to move, Andrew's mother had stepped over to him and lifted him off the seat, easy as you please, then stepped backward as the wagon slid by her. It was a frightening thing when you thought of it—she could have been looking the other way, or not been quick enough and gone under the wheel, or been distracted by the thought of trying to stop the horses, but she had done just the rightest, safest thing, purely on intuition, so gracefully and quickly that no one had been afraid until later.

They did not sleep that night, or even go to bed. All there was to do, really, was to walk down to the ferry building and back to the house, talk to neighbors and sailors and officers, watch that glow on the southwestern horizon, and discuss whether it was brighter or dimmer, and all of these things they could no longer stand to do. At one point, Andrew, who was pacing from the front door to the back door, said, "I bet I could get to Oakland. They could well be in Oakland, and it's hard to get from Oakland to here right now. But Mother is enterprising. . . ." This for the hundredth time.

Margaret's manner with Andrew until this point had been agreeable and submissive—she was too shocked to behave in any other way, for one thing, and, for another, he had an answer for every doubt. She thought her own doubts—her own doubts that were shading into convictions—were best left unspoken. It was bad luck as well as unloving to say what she thought, especially what she thought when she found out that the Palace Hotel was down. But now, finally, she said, "Yes, Andrew, your mother is terrifically enterprising, which is why I think that she would have gotten a message to us now, somehow, if she—I mean, they did find Mr. Devlin's little girl yesterday, and she's only three and a half, and they did find that Mrs. Devlin was killed. Lots of news, one way or the other, has—"

She could see by looking at his face that this very doubt, the doubt that came from Mrs. Early's everlasting silence, wasn't far from his thoughts, even though he hadn't expressed it. He shook his head. "I'm sure it's something else."

"I am losing hope."

"But I am not." He walked out the front door. A minute later, he walked back in. His eyes were bright and his hair was standing on end, as if, while outside, he had torn his hands through it. He said, "It doesn't make sense. It doesn't make sense that they came out here to California on impulse and therefore died. It makes sense for us to have died, or people who have lived here for years and years to have died, but not this, this doesn't make sense."

"Life and death never make sense—"

"I know you think that."

"How can I think otherwise? My brother's friends found a blasting cap down at the railyard. What made sense about that? The universe makes no sense."

"It does!" He said this so pugnaciously that she nodded in spite of herself, then reached out and took his hand. She said, "Then I will just say that I don't know what sense the universe makes, though I might someday, I admit." He glared at her as if accusing her of making a joke. She said, "I want your mother to turn up somehow. I've offered all the bargains."

"What do you mean by that?"

"I've cried. I've prayed. I've stared down the street until I thought I could see her coming. I've opened the door to every room in the house just when I was most clearly picturing her on the other side. I've imagined a broken arm or a broken leg, if that's the price we would have to pay. I love your mother, especially now, after her visit."

"She could have lost her memory and her papers."

"Mrs. Hitchens—"

"Mrs. Hitchens might have died, which might be why she lost her memory. She could be wandering around."

"She could be."

"Someone could be taking care of her and have no idea of who she is or of who I am or how to find us."

"That could happen. But think about that, Andrew. Is that easier to think about than death? Is it? Even if it's just in your imagination, do you want to impose days of suffering on her rather than a simple and sudden death?"

"I don't want any of this."

"Of course not." He went out the front door again. As a rule, she didn't think of herself as adept at anything, but she saw that early practice had made her more adept than Andrew at recognizing death when it arrived.

A little while later, Andrew, who had come back in the house but not come into the bedroom, went out again. It was then, just then, sitting up in bed and listening to his steps approach and retreat, that she felt the old feeling come on, that of the spectacle unfolding around her and her own fascinated paralysis. She lay awake most of the night, remembering what he had said, what she had said, as if she were going over lines in a play and could not stop. It was strange and horrifying. She thought if he would come back and speak to her again she could break the spell, but he didn't come back that night. The next day, he told her that he had gone to the observatory and stared through the telescope, in spite of the fog and in spite of the smoke. He wasn't looking for anything, and he wrote down no findings or observations. He might even have slept—he didn't know—but the time had passed. Yes, she thought, the time had passed while seeming not to.

The fires had been burning for four days, but they began hearing some bits of good news, one of which was that, thanks to the efforts of their own Lieutenant Freeman (whom Mrs. Lear seemed to know), the contingent from Mare Island had, in fact, saved the ferry building and quite a few other buildings and docks on the water side of the Embarcadero, and also managed to keep order and prevent the locals from raiding the saloons, getting themselves drunk, and falling prey to the fires. With little water but much ingenuity, they had done a great deal of good for the city (though they had dynamited a few too many buildings as a precaution, but no one cared about that). That day, they heard that the fires were abating, turning back upon themselves, or failing to leap over dynamited areas west of Van Ness. That evening, Margaret was walking down their street, wondering what they could do, and Hubert Lear called out to her from the upper balcony of the Lear house. "Ma'am! Ma'am! Mrs. Margaret!" She turned, and he stubbed out his cigarette. He was standing on the railing, and he took off his cap and dipped his head. Then he shouted, "Oh, Mrs. Margaret, she was a very nice lady. We are all really sorry about what happened to her."

"Thank you for your thoughts, Hubert."

"We all prayed for her and the other one by name, every night. But I guess it didn't work."

"Maybe it still will."

He shook his head, began, "Mama says . . . ," then fell silent. After a moment, he said, "Anyway, we all liked her, and we thanked her for the tennis rackets. So she just . . ." But then he seemed embarrassed, and jumped down from the railing and went inside. She didn't say anything to Andrew about this when she got home, though it was a warm day, and the windows on that side of the house were open. He could easily have heard their exchange. But it was for herself that she was grateful to Hubert Lear: the interchange had woken her up again, reminded her that survival was a task, above all. Nothing more, really.

Andrew finally got himself to Golden Gate Park. He stayed overnight in one of the tents, then, starting at daybreak, walked all over the park and up to the Presidio, asking after, and looking for, the two ladies. When he came home, he was willing to admit that he had not found them. That afternoon, he telegraphed his brothers again, saying that he had searched for their mother and Mrs. Hitchens and "not found them." Margaret was with him as he wrote out the telegram. She saw him write "yet" on the form, then pause, look at it, cross it out, then look at it again. She didn't say anything. He sent the telegram that allowed his brothers to infer that the two ladies had perished. By this time, names of some of those whose remains were being discovered were coming out. There were not so many—a few hundred, for which the mayor declared himself relieved and proud. But there were more.

Everyone knew there were more. Everyone who had been there and escaped had seen more with his or her own eyes.

Andrew and Margaret could not stand talking about it anymore. She wrote a long letter to Lavinia, some sixteen pages, telling her as much about what had happened as she could, especially everything she knew, or suspected, about Mrs. Early and Mrs. Hitchens. It would be her mother's responsibility, after all, to fill in all the news and rumors. Even as she wrote this letter, she could imagine her words flying about the streets of Darlington and in and out of kitchens and parlors, alarming and electrifying everyone, including those who knew the Earlys only by sight. As for John Early and his wife, she told her mother to go to them first, share the letter with them first, so they would be prepared for the hail of gossip and well-wishing they would have to withstand. The letter took her two days to write. By the time she sent it off, it was eight days since the earthquake, or a year, or a lifetime. Then she began going to memorial services—for Mrs. Devlin, for other men who were lost, for everyone. Andrew went to the naval ones, but he wouldn't agree when Mrs. Lear asked him if he would like to hold a service for his mother, or to include her in one.

Margaret had been to many a funeral over the years. She had found, at least back in Missouri, that a funeral was much like a wedding, in that the display was as important as the occasion. Everyone knew with a funeral, as with a wedding, that there would be considerable gossip afterward about the real nature of the deceased and what the funeral showed about the family—the neighbors could get inside the house and look around while the family members were distracted. But it was not like this at the memorial services for the earthquake victims. At these memorial services, people reflected, not upon just deserts, but upon miracles and tricks of fate, the perfect example of this being the memorial service for Mrs. Devlin, where her three-and-a-half-year-old daughter sat in the first row, between her father and her aunt. The weather was beautiful, and the windows were open to the sounds of birds singing in the trees outside. Prayers were said. Eulogies were made. Father Nicoll didn't tell the story, but everyone knew what there was to know: Mr. Devlin, in his hasty trip to the city on the day of the quake, had had no luck, but later, there Mrs. Devlin was, in the middle of Beale Street, probably felled by bricks—her body was found next to a collapsed house. She was identified by the contents of her shopping bag, which lay underneath the body, unburned. The child, Emma, turned up in Folsom Street, many blocks away—almost to Ninth. She was shoeless, and her hair had been singed, but she was otherwise unhurt, walking about, crying. Had she been carried there by some kind person, then abandoned? Had she walked there? Every possibility seemed equally unlikely, and yet here she was, and she had no way of telling what had happened to her. How she was found was equally unlikely—two drunks, wandering from saloon to saloon in search of liquor, picked her up and took her with them. At their second or third stop, Mr. Devlin's cousin, who was a sailor on Lieutenant Freeman's ship, happened to be in that saloon, rounding up the drunken populace. He didn't recognize Emma, but she recognized him. The cousin was detailed to take a ferry and bring her home. It was the very next ferry to arrive after the one carrying a distraught and hopeless Mr. Devlin. Emma's father was wandering about the wharf, not knowing what to do next, when his cousin came running up to him and told him that Emma was found. The operation of larger forces, it seemed to Margaret as she sat at the memorial service, stripped them for the time being of their own pettiness, in a way that the steady and predictable stream of deaths she'd grown up with had never done. She had made a few friends at the memorial services and joined a knitting circle; then she met two other women who liked to read books.

Andrew did not accompany her to the memorial services, but he did reproduce his gunshot experiment with Hubert Lear, and he bought a camera and made some plates of the results. Then he sent it off to *The Astronomical Journal* with dispatch, as if he had never hesitated. Both Margaret and Andrew knew he was doing it for his mother, but they didn't speak about it. After that, he devoted himself to investigating the earthquake—he went to Benicia, he went all over Vallejo, he went up to Napa and overland to Santa Rosa. He went back to San Francisco and down to Oakland. He corresponded with men in San Jose and Santa Cruz and Sacramento. He gathered every fact and observation he could: How had the chimney fallen? Which bricks had toppled, which bricks had remained in place, which part of the road had sunk, and how far and what was the angle of the shear? He wanted to see every single thing that the earthquake had done, every change that it had wrought. He read all the papers and all the reports, but in fact he was not as interested in the casualties as he was in the killer itself, in its exact portrait. He walked right up to survivors and asked questions, not about how the survivor was feeling, but about what, exactly, fell off the shelf and what did not, and how wide the shelf was, and what it was made of. Which wall collapsed and which did not? What time, to the best of your estimation, did the fire reach your block, and where were you standing when you first noticed it, and were you looking toward Second Street or toward Harrison Street—that is, do you think the fire was coming straight toward you or doubling back upon itself? After the building collapsed, could you actually hear people screaming, and if so, for how long would you say the screaming lasted? There was a ghoul-ishness in the questions he asked (others did, too), but people wanted to answer, no matter what they had lost.

Later, Margaret thought that, in measuring this bit of subsidence and the cracks in that tower, and in estimating forces and keeping copious detailed notes, as he knew so well how to do ("Testimony of Mary Grif-fin, aged 27, who was residing at 306 Mission Street at the time of the quake. Miss Griffin was asleep in her bed on the first floor, in the north-east corner of the house"), Andrew performed the kindest act of his life. And he carried his camera about with him. He photographed mud-flats and rock faces and brick walls, usually with some easily recogniz-able object in the photo for scale. During these investigations, he did not talk much about his mother, but he did exclaim, from time to time, that now he understood what the earth had done, almost moment by moment. When the final report about the earthquake came out two years after the earthquake, Andrew put his copy on the shelf just below his mother's photograph, two thick volumes, her monument (more so, Margaret thought, than the stone his brothers had erected in the grave-yard, beside the grave of their father). But even the longest book, she now understood, was the merest reduction of any experience, or any life.

ONE DAY, after this work was finished, Andrew said, "My dear, do you ever think about the moon?" They were eating supper.

"You mean, about the craters?"

After the article had come out in *The Astronomical Journal,* he had written a more popular one for the *Examiner.* As a contributor to the investigation of the earthquake, he was given quite a bit of space to explain his theory. And there was also a picture of Hubert Lear with his shotgun, sitting nonchalantly on a high branch of a tree, with Andrew looking up at him from below. The article was a local success, and Mrs. Lear framed it and hung it beside her front door.

"No, no, no," he said. "Not that. Do you ever think about how the moon came to be just where it is?"

"Where it is in the sky?"

"More or less, but of course it's not in the sky. It's in space."

She had forgotten this. She considered him actually quite patient with her continuing, and apparently obdurate, astronomical ignorance.

"I gather that you don't ever wonder about how the moon came to be just where it is."

"I may have wondered that at some point, but I'm used to it now."

Andrew laughed.

"So, how did the moon get to be where it is now?"

"Well, you see, that's a question that is not so easy to answer, my dear. In fact, when I myself asked my astronomy professor that question in college, he told me that it wasn't worth asking."

"Why not?"

"Because most people think that it can't be answered."

She said, "It does seem like it *should* be answered."

"Yes, it does." But he fell silent, and it appeared that he didn't have the answer after all.

A few nights later, she was reading and decided to go to bed. She turned out the lamp above her chair. The room went dark, and the light through the window silvered over her book and her lap. She looked up, and there was the moon, just rising, large and round and friendly. She stood up and went to the door of Andrew's study. When he called out, "Come in!" she opened the door and said, "All right, where did the moon come from?"

He grinned and said, "What do you think of this idea—that, long, long ago, the Earth was not solid but was, instead, fluid and molten, hotter than red hot, more like a cauldron of molten iron without the cauldron?"

She thought about this. She said, "What would keep it all together if there were no cauldron?"

"A combination of gravity and centripetal force."

She imagined she understood this.

Then he said, "You know, the moon and the Earth don't remain the same distance apart. The moon gets farther away."

"It does?"

"A little bit every day, a very little bit. It's the effect of gravitation. The Earth's rotation is being slowed down by the moon, and so days are getting longer, while the moon is getting farther away from the Earth, and so it has to go farther to get around the Earth, and so the months are also getting longer. But, interestingly, the days are getting longer faster than the months are getting longer. A man I knew in Europe has shown this—George Darwin. He's the son of Charles Darwin."

She pretended that she didn't recognize the name.

"Eventually, a day and a month will be the same length, fifty-five days, and then all the forces will be in balance, and, supposedly, things will stay that way. Personally, I don't believe that, but—" He shrugged, stood up, and came around the desk. He was excited. "But, my dear, you are wondering what this means about the origin of the moon."

"Of course." Margaret had learned that there were many things that Andrew wondered about that would not cross the mind of anyone else. It was his greatest talent, wondering about things. He was two men, really. When he was wondering, he was a likable, congenial, and sociable person. When he had stopped wondering and was convinced that he knew the answer, he became stubborn and stern.

He guided her to the window. The moon certainly looked farther away now—not as huge and bright, but more its remote, normal self. "Darwin would say that we have entered the theater in the middle of the opera. If we had come in toward the beginning, the moon would be moving faster, it would be much closer and would fill the sky."

Margaret tried to imagine this while Andrew slipped his arm around her waist.

He said, "If the Earth was so hot it was molten, and it was spinning so fast that a day lasted five hours or so, then what shape might it have been?"

"Kind of an oval?"

"Yes, indeed, more on the order of a cucumber, a very hot, liquid, fiery cucumber. And what might happen?"

"An end might break off?"

He nodded.

"And that would be the moon?"

"Darwin said so."

She could tell by the way he pronounced "Darwin" that Early *didn't* say so. She said, "Why would only one end break off? Why not both?"

Now he kissed her on the forehead. "A very good question, my dear, and a perfect example of what is wrong with that theory. The fact is, the cucumber would not have been the final shape. The final shape of the rotating molten Earth would have been a pear. *But,*" he exclaimed, "no one has ever figured out a way to make that pear go fast enough to split off the moon, and they never will. Guess what has happened in the last ten years."

"What?"

"These ideas have been shot all to hell!" He laughed triumphantly. "Because the molten rock in the spinning cauldron isn't simple at all! It is not just iron and lead and gold and platinum and I don't know what all, mixed together and cooling down and solidifying bit by bit; there's something else in there."

"What is that?" Margaret actually felt herself get a little excited.

"There's uranium and there's radium."

"What are those?"

"Those are unstable elements that, even when they are just sitting there in the middle of the rock face, are giving off electrons and changing, moment by moment, into something else. All uranium, for example, will someday be lead." He gave her a satisfied look, then said, "All lead, they might then conclude, was at one time uranium."

"What does that mean about the moon?"

"Well, the moon has had a lot longer time to get into its present orbit than most men have thought. Billions of years rather than millions or hundreds of millions. Something else entirely could have happened. Time is of the essence, my dear, not so much when times are short, but very much when times are long, longer than anyone in the history of mankind has ever conceived of." He said this in a ringing voice, hugging her to him. She waited a moment, then said, "So—how did the moon get to be where it is?"

"The Earth captured it!"

"Has the Earth ever captured anything else?"

"Possibly. I don't know yet."

"Oh." It seemed as plausible that the Earth could capture something as it did that a person could claim a stray dog. Mutual attractions, she thought, were mutual attractions, whether you called them "gravity" or "affinity."

"I often think that I was born to think about the moon. The moon is that large object in the room that everyone stumbles over and no one thinks about."

He was jolly. He guided her into their bedchamber.

On his side of the bed lay a couple of books by an Englishman named Havelock Ellis, *The Sexual Impulse in Women* and then another one, *Sexual Selection in Man.* By happy coincidence, Dr. Ellis had also written a book entitled *A Study of British Genius.* Andrew kept the first two books to himself, but he read parts of this third book aloud to Margaret over supper, and in deference to the information in all of these books, he had shortened his hours at the observatory.

Andrew felt that, although he had not suffered from a delicate childhood, he fit perfectly into Dr. Ellis's model. "Delicate children were the ones who died in Missouri," which illustrated the equally exciting idea of natural selection. It was one thing to be a hereditary genius like his colleague George Darwin, coddled and cultivated from childhood in the easy circumstances of bourgeois English life, but to be a hereditary genius from a world where the easiest thing for any child to do was to succumb was all the more reason to value one's own genius.

The genius book revealed that genius could be inherited from either the father or the mother, which got Andrew fired up about their future child. According to Andrew's reading of Dr. Ellis, any child of theirs had a perfectly acceptable chance of being a genius. Indeed, if he and she had *both* been geniuses, it was all too possible that the physical and mental drawbacks of *too much* genius would outweigh the double inherited dose. Margaret asked him which of his own parents was the genius. All things considered, Andrew felt that it had been his mother, though it could also be true that her talents of method, application, and organization (and poker playing, Margaret thought) had been uniquely capable of meshing with those of his father, who had often played a game of sums with the boys in which he added up numbers they furnished him in rapid-fire shouting matches. His father was good at picking up languages. He could talk to the Germans in German and the French in French and the Spanish in Spanish. His father's various talents hadn't been well developed by education, according to Andrew, but "Look at my brothers and me. Only one tall poppy!" That was the right ratio, in the opinion of Havelock Ellis. Therefore, Andrew and Margaret were ideally matched—her lack of genius ("but there is a perfect balance between your womanly nature and your entirely acceptable level of intellect, my dear") was exactly the leavening their hypothetical son would require. Or sons. If the ratio in Andrew's own family was four to one, then that was probably a fairly representative ratio.

However, Dr. Ellis had led to no more interludes of marital relations until the moon intervened. The moon was a great facilitator of marital relations, since Andrew was so excited about his new theory that he was almost always in a good and affectionate mood. And so it was not long after their conversation about the Earth's capturing the moon that Margaret found herself pregnant again. Mrs. Lear was thrilled. Margaret was thrilled. Andrew was thrilled. He thought that the naval base was the perfect place to rear a squadron of boy geniuses—like the Lear boys, only more thoughtful and quieter, not only rolling firecrackers out of black powder and old newspapers but also reading books.

The first pregnancy, short as it was, had prepared her, and this one seemed all the more normal for that experience. She was not ill or uncomfortable; the days didn't slow to a soporific crawl. She pursued her rounds of cooking and shopping and walking and taking the ferry to San Francisco once a month. Andrew was busy in his office, turning his moon ideas into a book. It really was astonishing how the city had resurrected itself, though of course she never passed any of the streets she associated with Mrs. Early or the fire—Market, Third, Mission, Van Ness—without thinking about the two ladies so intensely that they seemed to inhabit the whole city at once. If, against Andrew's wishes, she produced a girl, she intended to name her Anna.

Soon enough, her condition was visible, and, more important, the child had quickened within, and as she felt every movement—first a fluttering, subsequently more strenuous but undifferentiated activity, then precisely identifiable kicks and punches—she allowed herself to make pictures in her mind, as well as baby clothes. In fact, she felt something that she didn't know how to talk about, especially to the very practical Mrs. Lear—a sense of awakening. As the child grew in her body and in her mind, there were other things that awakened with it. She dreamed of her brother Lawrence, holding her hand and preventing her from stepping in front of a trotting horse pulling a cart, but she didn't know if such a thing had ever happened. She dreamed that her father was in the next room, trying to talk to her, but she could barely make out his words, no matter how hard she tried. Scenes that Lavinia had described to her, of her father gaily roughhousing with her brothers, recurred to her vividly, as if she had seen them, though she could not have. This awakening was almost painful, considering, as her mother had always told her, that what was given could be snatched away—would be snatched away—but she let it happen. It came to seem the necessary prerequisite for giving birth.

Mrs. Lear made her go to a doctor in Vallejo. He was a young man, about her age, from Chicago, and his name was Dr. Bernstein. "He's a Jew, then," said Andrew.

"Of course he is," said Mrs. Lear. "Don't you want the best possible care by the best-educated doctor? Your other alternatives are Dr. Gray, who is nearly seventy; Dr. Howard, who is not very clean and who has"—she lowered her voice and whispered—"very fat fingers"— Andrew knew better than to ask what she was saying—"and Mrs. Kimura, the midwife." At first, Andrew accepted Dr. Bernstein as a necessary evil, but Margaret quite liked him—he was married to a beautiful French woman with her own healthy and quite stylish children, a boy and twin girls. Margaret saw their Jewishness as something desirable and cosmopolitan, and then Andrew was won over, because Dr. Bernstein addressed him as a colleague. They frequently discussed the works of Dr. Ellis, both about sex and about genius. Margaret was careful to tell Andrew whenever she went to see Dr. Bernstein, or encountered him anywhere, that he had asked after Andrew. Andrew agreed that it was good that they had gotten "a true man of science" to usher their young genius into the world.

It was soothing to talk to Andrew and Dr. Bernstein about the pregnancy and the birth; it made Margaret feel lifted into a higher, more knowledgeable realm. When women talked about birth, as they did in her knitting circle, it was always in the direst terms. Mrs. Tillotson would tell about a woman she knew who had seemed fine until she got a terrible infection and died within hours, then Mrs. Arness would top that with a story about a woman she knew who was in labor with her first baby for forty-nine hours, and the baby was born dead, and the doctor had to use an instrument to "scrape the remains out of her." And then Mrs. Jones, with a glance at her, would top this story with one about her cousin who had never gotten out of bed after the birth of her third child—it had been ten years now—"and the stink! Everything like a sieve in there now!" Mrs. Gess put a stop to such conversations when she found herself pregnant, too.

The main difficulty seemed to be that Dr. Bernstein was in Vallejo and they were on the island. Should labor commence, who would take the ferry to whom—she to Dr. Bernstein, or Dr. Bernstein to her? Privately, she imagined that, in a pinch, Mrs. Lear would run over and deliver the child, but she never said this to either man of science. She wavered, and wondered aloud to Mrs. Lear whether perhaps Dr. Howard, who lived on the island, might suffice. Mrs. Lear sat her down and exclaimed, "After all these months, Margaret, I cannot believe that you haven't gotten the point of my precautions. I do not want to scare you, I want to alert you. Your father, and Dr. Howard, and all the old-time doctors didn't truly understand about cleanliness. They said they did, but they didn't and they don't. Should you call him, he would come to your house by horse and buggy. He would harness the horse and drive him and tie him outside your house. No doubt he would pat the horse and give him a nosebag to occupy him during the birth. After that, he would pick up his dirty old satchel and carry it into the house. But from the moment he put the nosebag on the horse to the moment he birthed the baby, would he be absolutely perfect in his cleanliness? If your labor was not far advanced, would he eat something? Would he pick up the newspaper? Of course he would. Would he then thoroughly repeat his cleanliness procedures? Not the Dr. Howard that I know. Not the crusty old man who considers that a few dollars for the delivery of a child is not much to be earning in a day. No, my girl, you must figure out some method for ensuring the attendance of Dr. Bernstein."

The very next day, Andrew found her a pleasant room in a boarding house on Ohio Street, only half a block from Dr. Bernstein's office. He took it for six months, although they would need it at the most for two, and explained their plan to the landlady, Mrs. Wareham. Since it was winter, and boarders were scarce, Mrs. Wareham was only too happy to accommodate them, and since she was a kindly person with two children of her own, she bustled about, making sure that Dr. Bernstein would have everything he needed. Dr. Bernstein approved this arrangement, too.

By wagon and ferry, the room was about an hour and a half from their house, and farther from the observatory. When she was at Mrs. Wareham's, she felt lonely and wondered what was going on at her house. When she was at her house, she wondered what she would do if she went into a precipitate labor. Dr. Bernstein had calculated her due date—March 26—but everyone knew these calculations were more like wishes than guesses. Every letter from her mother told her what she had to watch out for. Lavinia's births had been either easy or terrifying, and as for Margaret's aunts, they were lucky to be alive. It didn't matter that Beatrice and Elizabeth had "birthed like cows calving in a field." Should Lavinia come out? She felt she should come out. If Margaret wanted her at all, she would come out—"I'm sure I can stand the trip. I hope you aren't going to depend on your neighbor Mrs. Lear for material assistance. She may be a charming and entertaining woman, but from what you tell me, her ideas are very unorthodox. And the landlady of a boarding house will not be able to give you the sort of help you need. I feel obliged to come out, and I'm sure I am strong enough to survive the trip."

Andrew read as many books about birthing as he could, and informed her that history was in her favor. His mother had never lost a child, her mother had never lost a child at birth, and neither of her sisters had ever lost a child. Every evening, an hour before the last ferry to Vallejo, he questioned her: How was she feeling? Any pains of any kind? Any waters of any kind? Unusual movements? Unusual lack of movements? He enlisted Hubert Lear to run to the observatory and find him at any time of the day or night. They had several practice sessions in which she threw open her bedroom window and shouted for Hubert, and then timed his appearance in the street and his speed to the observatory and back. All of this was fine with Mrs. Lear, because it made Hubert feel useful.

In the event, however, there were no difficulties. One day just before the due date, she did, as Dr. Bernstein told her she would, feel the baby drop, and Andrew was home, so he called a wagon, and they went to the ferry. She was ensconced in her room on Ohio Street before noon, and early in the afternoon, she felt the first pain. Andrew ran to Dr. Bernstein's office, and the doctor came half an hour later to examine her. Mrs. Wareham shooed the children out, and the boarders were excited but quiet. Because of Andrew, perhaps, Dr. Bernstein was on his mettle, and performed a perfect scientific delivery. Once he had boiled his instruments and washed his hands for ten minutes and disinfected them in mercury bichlorid, he stood with his hands uplifted and watched her as she progressed. He never touched a single thing before he touched the baby, he did not have to use forceps or chloroform, and the baby came shooting out onto a sterile rubber mat, was wrapped in sterile wrappings, and was a boy. The birth was so quick that Margaret was not daunted by the pains, especially after she saw the child. They named him Alexander Mayfield Early. He was extremely large.

It was about nine that evening when Dr. Bernstein left, and Andrew and she settled in for the night, with her in the bed (she didn't feel terribly exhausted) and Andrew in the armchair. Alexander was wrapped in a blanket, lying in the cradle Mrs. Lear had given them. Mrs. Wareham promised to look in on them every couple of hours, and said Andrew could call her at any time. Andrew fell asleep, stretched out with a quilt pulled up to his chin. The day had been fine, but the fog had moved in, and it was now chilly and damp. The moist air made the moon, which was full, look gauzy and pale as it shone into the room. Margaret ached all over, but she found the baby too interesting to admit of sleep. She sat up as best she could and stared into the cradle, which was beside the bed. She looked at his very round face, his hands, and the dark cap of hair on his head. The room was quiet. He was quiet. He had hardly cried at all, which she wondered about, but everyone else, even Dr. Bernstein, seemed mostly relieved at this. Mrs. Wareham had said, "Oh, he's just worn out. And he's going to be a good baby. I can just tell." Even so, she felt far away from Alexander, and she thought that if she could have him in her arms, if she could curl around him like a dog, she would feel closer. She was supposed to be sleeping, or resting, making good use of her time while she didn't have to nurse him or care for him. Andrew sighed in his sleep and shifted position.

Margaret slipped down under her quilts and stared up at the ceiling. Things were quiet for some time, and then Alexander gave a cry. A moment later, he started moving about and fussing. Andrew shifted in his sleep but did not awaken, and Margaret inched over toward the cradle and picked Alexander up. It was easy. He fit right into her arms, and it was a pleasure to look into his little countenance. Of course, she had held babies before. Beatrice, for one, didn't much like to hold her babies, so when they were fussy, if they were going to be held, others would be the ones to hold them. She was plenty adept at that little soft jiggle that babies seemed to like, and, sure enough, Alexander quieted at once, and the bundle that he was seemed to soften in her arms and conform to her.

She had nursed him already, under the guidance of both Dr. Bernstein and Andrew, and that seemed to have gone well enough, so when Alexander resumed fussing—really a sort of mewing—she tried again. It was not terribly comfortable in some ways, but it worked. And it was convenient. And it was silent and private. The last thing she wanted was for Andrew to wake up or Mrs. Wareham to come into the room.

The strange became familiar. Once he was in her arms, she was reminded that he had not "arrived." Maybe to Andrew and Dr. Bernstein there was an arrival, but for her he had been here a long time. He had now become visible, that was all. The movements he was making were exactly like movements he had made the day before, but visible. The face turned toward her now was the same face that had been invisible yesterday, but now she could peruse it. He was also a he. He had always been a he, only now she knew it. She felt a momentary, almost enjoyable pang—that girl, that Anna, that face vanished to the same distant world where that other face had gone, the face of the first baby. Alexander's face was here, turned toward her. His eyes were open. His lips, when he pulled away from her, formed a small triangle. As she looked at this face, she grew more and more interested in it, more and more curious about it, more and more drawn to it. She felt it change before her eyes from a strange face to a known face, and, more than that, a face she could not stop conning. She stroked his forehead and the crown of his head as gently as she could, and felt that new sensation against the skin of her hand, the smooth warmth—not of *a* baby, but of her baby. It was interesting to look at his head. Inside that head was also something new. Out of that head, things would blossom. That things blossomed out of her head or Andrew's head seemed utterly mundane, but that soon this would happen with this brand-new head struck her as astonishing.

Her love for Alexander developed right then, an almost physical sensation. Margaret was not a fanciful person, but she felt it as a kind of invisible swelling, infusing all her tissues, that she had never felt before. If she said she loved her mother or her sisters, what she was talking about was familiarity and habit. If she said she loved Mrs. Early, what she was talking about was delight and admiration. If she said she loved Andrew, what she was talking about were the necessary arrangements of her life, sometimes mysterious, sometimes pleasurable. But if she said she loved Alexander, what she was talking about was a bodily transformation. It was as if he were a dye and she was white wool. Looking at him and holding him dyed her through and through. As she was thinking this, she must have dropped off to sleep, progressing bit by bit from staring at him to dreaming of him, both states utterly peaceful.

Then came the shock. Here beside her was a female voice that was making an exclamation, and she woke up at once. Something had happened to Alexander, and it was her fault. But as she opened her eyes, she saw that it was very early morning—the room was hardly light—and Mrs. Wareham was standing beside her. Alexander was propped in the crook of her elbow. She was not lying on him, nor had he fallen out of the bed. Mrs. Wareham was now over beside the window, and she opened the shade. Having done so, she came back to the bed and bent down. She was peering at Alexander, and she involuntarily pulled him toward her, which caused Margaret to embrace him more tightly. When Mrs. Wareham stood up, Margaret saw her stare at her in alarm for a moment. Then she said, in a soft but urgent voice, "Dear, the baby is yeller. The baby is yeller as an egg yolk. You need to—"

Andrew was on his feet.

"The child is jaundiced?"

"Well, my land. He is. That's not so unusual, but . . ." She stood with her hands on her hips, staring up at Andrew, and he stared down at her. Mrs. Wareham said, "Now, Captain, you go on down to Dr. Bernstein's house. He's going to want to know about this, and I'll make Mama some tea and some nice dry toast. Go on, now." She said this lightly, with a shooing motion, as if she weren't saying anything frightening after all, and Andrew pulled on his boots and left the room instantly. She came over to Margaret and put her hand on Margaret's forehead. She said, "You're fine. No fever. You're just fine." She put her hand on Alexander's forehead, then his cheek. She said, "I don't know if you're a praying woman, but you might start."

Margaret had been staring at Mrs. Wareham, but now she looked at Alexander. His eyes were open, and the whites of them were indeed yellowish—she could see it more clearly by the moment as the room brightened. Mrs. Wareham sighed, and shook her head, then left the room. A few minutes later, she returned with a cup of tea and a plate. She said, "Now, you give me the child, dear, and I'll hold him while you take something. Just a little something."

She did what she was told, sipping the tea while she watched the other woman walk him back and forth between the bed and the window, humming and making kissing noises. She said, "You eat all the toast, Mama. You are going to need it." When Margaret had done so, Mrs. Wareham handed Alexander back to her. His eyes were still open, but he was making no sounds of any kind. Margaret tightened her grip a bit, as if to envelop him. Mrs. Wareham went out, only to return with some more coal for the fire. She opened the door of the stove, heaved the coal into it, and opened the damper, then went out again without saying anything more. For whatever reason, it was only then that Margaret began to feel real fear. Outside the window, the morning fog was thick. She could not even see the green wall of the house next door. When Andrew returned with Dr. Bernstein, they both paused a moment after they removed their coats and hats to rub their hands and cheeks. Mrs. Wareham brought in a basin of hot water, and after rolling up his sleeves, the doctor washed his hands very carefully, then held them up in the warm air to dry. Margaret stared at his face, but it was impassive, waiting. She looked at Andrew. Surely they had talked on the way and Andrew knew what Dr. Bernstein expected, if anything. But Andrew, too, looked blank.

Dr. Bernstein took Alexander away from her, laid him on the bed, then unwrapped him. He smoothed the infant fingers over his own forefinger, and stared at the tiny fingernails. He felt around Alexander's jaw. He lifted both his arms and gently set them against his little chest. He touched the chest with his forefinger several times, then ran his hands over Alexander's chest and belly. He lifted and spread his legs, then put them back together. He bent closer to the child and stared at him, or maybe he sniffed him. His look was as intent as she'd ever seen on anyone. He looked at the soles of his feet, put them down, looked at them again, then at the palms of his hands. Alexander was listless, even limp. She glanced at Andrew, but Andrew might never have seen a baby before, especially a squirmy, thrusting, active baby like Beatrice's boys. In fact, that's what her mother had said about her brothers, too: "They were like springs. You tried to hold them down for one instant, and they were up before you let them go." But possibly Andrew and his brothers had not been as active, and poor Alexander took after them. This was a fugitive thought—there was no reason to believe that any child of Mrs. Early was listless or limp. She bit her lip. No more than five minutes since Andrew and Dr. Bernstein had come into the room—their hair and whiskers still steaming—yet it seemed like an hour. Andrew, she saw, was not about to prompt the doctor. Observations, he would have been the first to tell you, often took quite a bit of time. She saw Mrs. Wareham peek in the door. Behind her was the girl who did the washing and the cleaning. She was Japanese. She looked about twelve, but Mrs. Wareham had told Margaret that she was almost sixteen. Her name was Naoko.

Finally, Dr. Bernstein said to Andrew, "You had better come look at this." Andrew clasped his hands behind his back, then stepped over to the bed and bent down. He was at least a head taller than Dr. Bernstein. Mrs. Wareham and Naoko stepped farther into the room. Dr. Bernstein said, "When you press on the skin of the chest, here, the color underneath the surface yellow is very pale. See that?" Andrew nodded. "But it's more than that. Here the belly is quite swollen. It wasn't this way right after birth. Here." He felt Alexander's belly. "The liver. The spleen. Very enlarged. Enlarged overnight. See how his limbs are stiffening up?" He lifted an arm. Then he shook his head. Andrew stood up straight and looked at her. Dr. Bernstein said, "I have seen worse."

Andrew said, "Have you seen worse that recovered?" His voice sounded scientific rather than fatherly. Margaret felt herself grow offended.

Dr. Bernstein sighed. "Once, I did." Then he added, "That child lived." He stressed the word "lived." Dr. Bernstein gently wrapped Alexander back up. All this time, he had made no cry, only a few quiet sounds. The doctor turned to her and said, "Mrs. Early, you might try to nurse the boy again. Whether he takes hold and seems eager for nourishment will tell a great deal about how he is going to grapple with his condition."

He put Alexander back in her arms, and the two men stared at her.

She wanted them to go out; she wanted all of them to go out, and herself and Alexander to be returned to that time in the night when they could do things on their own, without having to contend with this cacophony.

Andrew said, "What is his condition?"

"Jaundice. Icterus."

Now, she thought, Andrew was going to ask Dr. Bernstein to tell him everything that anyone had ever said about jaundice or icterus, but he didn't. The both of them simply looked at her, and she offered Alexander the breast.

He seemed indifferent, or more than indifferent—he turned his face away, as if trying to avoid it. It had been hours since the middle-of-the-night feeding, but he wasn't hungry, or, she should say, wasn't anything. But she touched herself to his lip, and all of a sudden he commenced sucking. As he went on, he sucked harder, as if sucking itself, the milk itself, reminded him of something good. He nursed for some ten minutes. Mrs. Wareham and Naoko left the doorway, and Dr. Bernstein looked on with evident satisfaction. When they were finished, he took Alexander away from her again, laid him on the bed again, unwrapped him. Alexander kicked his legs a few times and waved one of his arms. This was a good sign. She imagined herself fortifying her son, building him up like a little tower. She had never done much of anything, but, she felt, this she could do. Dr. Bernstein said, "That seems to have had an effect. Sometimes this resolves on its own. Depends on the child. I'm hopeful."

MARGARET settled in on Ohio Street and made herself stop thinking of the future. Andrew brought her a couple of books and more clothes and some knitting she had been doing for Alexander, but even after she was feeling well enough to get out of bed (some three days, a very short time, according to Mrs. Wareham, who told her she hadn't gotten out of bed after a childbirth in less than two weeks), the knitting looked to her like an abandoned artifact of a lost civilization. She had been knitting Alexander a little coat of red wool. Because of the color, she found she could not touch it. All day, whenever Mrs. Wareham was not in the room pressing sustenance upon her, she was staring at Alexander.

Yes, he was a strange boy, that much was evident. Not so bullish as the other boys she had known. He did not remind her of anyone, but he was no less interesting for that. Or, perhaps, he reminded her of her, of the strange lack she had of what her mother had always called, in admiration of her brothers, and also of Beatrice, "the life force." Of course, there was a lot to be said for the life force. People with plenty of the life force found the world falling away around them. They didn't feel the cold or the heat. They didn't hear what others said about them. If you were at the knitting circle, and you were talking about Mrs. Tillotson, for example, only to go quiet just before she entered the room, the woman would not even sense the enthusiasm with which all of her flaws had just been canvassed. She had so much life force that she never doubted her own welcome, and, indeed, whatever the women had been saying among themselves, when Mrs. Tillotson entered the room they smiled in spite of themselves to see her—her energetic walk, her healthy toss of the head, her pink dress with its green ruching, her lace parasol, her knitting that was always carelessly done. If you had the life force, your surroundings more or less escaped your notice, because you were too busy noticing yourself—your own ebbs and flows were strong the way a well-bred horse was strong, and if you didn't pay attention to them, they could throw you, the way such a horse could do.

But if, like Alexander, you didn't feel that, if the life force was nothing at all forceful, more a hope than an assertion, then the world was the vivid thing, the fascinating and compelling thing. A quiet room like her room at Mrs. Wareham's grew interesting, just in the way the sunlight shifted over the course of a day, or in the way the fogdamp seemed to enter invisibly through the very walls. If you didn't have much life force, then the mere weight of a blanket could tell on you, now just right, now too heavy, now too light. If you didn't have much life force, then sometimes the face of your mother looked one way, and sometimes it looked another way. Even though Alexander was far too young to see her, she sensed that her proximity sometimes troubled him, sometimes comforted him. When she sensed that it troubled him, she didn't stop holding him, though; rather, she shifted her thoughts consciously away from him and onto something else, but something not disturbing, something simple, like the rose-of-Sharon tree in her mother's yard. Mrs. Wareham had told her to pray, and this was what she did—she thought of flowers and leaves. As she did this, she imagined herself suspended, near Alexander but not uncomfortably close. She thought he might like that better.

And they nursed. She loved to nurse him. Every swallow bolstered him, carried him toward more life force—not so much of it that they might forget what they had learned here, but enough so he could survive.

That Andrew came into the room less and less was fine with her—she thought it was better, in fact. Andrew had more of the life force than Mrs. Tillotson or Beatrice or anyone else she had ever met. It was located in his curiosity. In most circles, curiosity was seen as polite, the opposite of talking only about oneself all the time, but curiosity flowed out of Andrew in a torrent, bowling over everything before it. He would ask a question, then another question, and the person of whom he was asking the question would answer, and then answer again. But Andrew's curiosity was beyond answers, and soon enough, he would be contradicting the person's answers and suggesting new ways of looking at the matter, possibly instituting some sort of investigation that would finally uncover the real truth. You had to admire how the life force operated in this way, and people did admire Andrew: Why was he stuck on the island, with such a tiny telescope? How could the island contain him (meaning his life force)? But his life force might be a danger to Alexander. If Alexander was lying in his cradle, Andrew would lean over and stare down at him with such intensity that she imagined suffocation. As a result, if she heard Andrew enter the house (he always came at odd times), she would hurry to pick Alexander up and hold him to her, half turned away from Andrew, using her shoulder for a shield.

And she knew that Andrew was disappointed in Alexander. Something in her resented this. All the time she worried about the baby, every time she lifted his little limp hands and felt his fingers droop over hers, each time she surveyed his flaccid chest and caught her breath, her next thought, or the thought after that, was "How dare . . . ?" How dare Andrew be disappointed? Who did he think he was? It was a strange feeling, like being suspended in midair, to know that Alexander's condition was disappointing and yet to hate Andrew's disappointment. She started thinking of Andrew in a whole new way, and sometimes when she was awake at night, if the night was clear, she would look at the moon in the window and feel relieved that the moon was distant enough from Andrew so as not to be affected or impinged upon by his life force, or his disappointment. The moon, at least, was safe.

But then she thought, doubting all her other thoughts, What if the life force is more like a contagion than a flood? What if Alexander needed measured doses of a healthy life force rather than protection from it? It was a difficult question, and involved two ways of thinking about the world, and life and death, that were more different than she could manage at that time, in that place, looking into his little face, looking at his little body, something so small that enclosed so profound a mystery. And, then, she appreciated the life force. Mrs. Wareham or Naoko or one of the children would come in, and they would seem so self-starting as to be miraculous. No effort at all was required with Naoko, who was quick and efficient. She opened the door and was across the room in a second, presenting Margaret with the sandwich or the cup of tea that she needed, laying a napkin across her lap, smiling in a kindly fashion, pouring out the tea, asking her how she was feeling, looking affectionately at the baby. Since she was small, she was less imposing than Mrs. Wareham, and so Margaret could appreciate her and yet never had to wonder how she was or if she would live or die. She embodied the life force at its best. Margaret encouraged Naoko to pick Alexander up and hold him. The girl's life force, she thought, could surround and warm him. Then, one day, Naoko said, "My mother would like to visit you and the baby."

"Your mother?"

"Yes. My mother is a midwife. She has birthed many babies."

Margaret stared at Naoko. She didn't know how to say no, so she nodded. Mrs. Kimura came the next morning. Mrs. Kimura was small, like Naoko, but smooth rather than quick. Naoko brought her to the door when Margaret was just finishing her breakfast, and Mrs. Kimura bowed slightly and smiled. She was wearing a simple blue coat and gray gloves, which she took off and gave to Naoko. Then she came over to Margaret and shook her hand with a smile. She said something in Japanese, and Naoko said, "My mother apologizes for her poor English, and asks that I translate for her."

Margaret nodded.

Naoko said, "My mother asks if she may pick up the baby."

"Yes," said Margaret.

Mrs. Kimura went to the cradle and lifted Alexander out of it, then rested him in the crook of her left arm in a practiced manner. She held her arm rather high, and stared for a long time into his face. Her own face was neither somber nor happy, merely unreadable, and after a while Margaret despaired of learning anything from it. She stared out the window at the green wall of the house next door. After a while,

Naoko said goodbye, and the two paused for a moment and then left. Margaret had nothing to say to them. Naoko did not seem to think this was rude of her, but continued to attend to Margaret's and Alexander's needs with quiet grace.

As for Alexander, sometimes his eyes were open, wide open and staring. Sometimes his body was stiff. Dr. Bernstein checked on him twice a day, not saying much, only asking if he was still nursing. More or less, he was still nursing.

On the morning of the eighteenth day, she unwrapped him and saw that his belly was hugely distended. She saw, moreover, that it had been hugely distended, but that she hadn't recognized it as hugely distended—she had only recognized it as Alexander. Alarm and guilt surged in her, burning upward from her feet, enveloping her head, her brain, her mind in a fever of knowledge. Her first thought was not to call Dr. Bernstein at all, but to hide this development from him and, for some reason, call Mrs. Kimura. Even as she thought this, Alexander started to make a noise, high-pitched and distressed, and to arch his back. It seemed to her that he was crying for help, so she picked him up and went to the door of the room and opened it. Naoko was in the hallway. She looked at her, and without Margaret's saying a thing, the girl ran out the front door. Margaret closed her door and carried Alexander over to the bed. She sat down and readied herself to nurse, but in that short moment, the moment between her sitting down and her putting him to the breast, he lost even that ability—Margaret felt it. It was a feeling of something dissolving. She looked at his face. She saw that he had but one thing left, which was that he could look back at her. She stroked the top of his head, moving the thin hairs this way and that, feeling the smoothness of his golden skin. She held him closer, as gently as she could. And then, in the way that you can feel with your baby but not see or sense with anyone else larger or more distantly related, she felt the life force go out of him entirely.

1909

PART THREE

1911

THE LEARS MOVED AWAY—off to Hawaii and then Anchorage ("A sad day for me," wrote Mrs. Lear, "but have you ever tasted moose? It is actually quite good salted and dried"). The big house was taken by an older couple, Captain Pritchard and Mrs. Pritchard, no children. Mrs. Pritchard was seventeen years older than Margaret, but she seemed to think they were two of a kind. Though she was an agreeable, mild person, she was afflicted with headaches and almost never emerged from her vast domicile. Margaret had her confidantes now, and everyone on the island was friendly, but she knew she had become the strange sort of lady that she remembered noticing as a child, the sort of lady who was always neat and kind, whose house was quiet because there were no children, who hosted the knitting circle and kept small treats around in case some child might be in need of a licorice whip or a shortbread cookie.

Then, in the summer of 1911, she got a letter from Dora, who was living in Europe. Dora's departure from St. Louis had been scandalous, but not unwelcome. Elizabeth had written Margaret, "Robert's mother has thrown up her hands and washed her hands at least ten thousand times, but it has had no effect at all. Now she says, 'We shall have to BUY someone for her on the black market!' " Dora wrote:

Darling,

I was sitting at a table at the restaurant at the new Goring Hotel with Ezra Pound, who is from Idaho, can you imagine, and in walks Hearst, my BOSS, I knew him instantly, and he sits down at the next table, and when he takes off his top hat, he puts it down on the floor beside Ezra. Without saying a word, or even pausing in his ingestion of his sausage and mashed potatoes, Ezra picks up his foot and puts it inside the hat. Hearst jumps up and says, "Young man! You have your shoe in my hat!" and Ezra says, "Old man! You have put your hat in my way!" And while they are glaring at each other, I say, "Mr. Hearst, Miss Dora Bell, *Cosmopolitan.* May I introduce you to Mr. Pound, Ezra Pound?" At which point, Ezra finished his sausages and exclaimed, "Pound the bell! Pound pound pound, /As Ronald her steed did tattoo the pavement / Hatching a flock of doors, a / barbed surreal randy will." He tossed this off in a resonant voice that caught the attention of all the people, who then clapped, though I doubt that they understood all of the puns he was making on our names. Then Ezra handed Mr. Hearst his top hat, and got up and walked out. Mr. Hearst invited me to his table, and he asked what sort of poetry that was, so I told him about Ezra and his friends. I can't say that he was impressed, except that he said that he had been to Idaho—"Full of jokers and freaks, Miss Bell." The result of all of this was that I have taken a position at the *San Francisco Examiner,* and I am to come and live there.

In Europe, Dora specialized in a certain type of article, in which she happened to find herself somewhere—walking down the road between Florence and Siena, or exploring the Fortress of Diocletian at Split. She would fall into conversations with people she met, and report them, as if word for word. Though she got interviews with important politicians from time to time, mostly her subjects were not important at all. They simply showed her how to gut a tuna or to make a pudding out of sheep stomachs or to hide in some rocks and keep the baby quiet while a bear ambled past. Were the articles reports or stories? Did Dora listen, or did she make it all up? Margaret didn't actually care. When Lavinia sent her a sheaf of articles that Beatrice had culled from the magazine, she read them avidly and felt as though she now knew the Adriatic per-

fectly. Andrew was more skeptical, but he read every article from beginning to end. He declared that he was glad Dora was coming, a breath of
fresh hot Missouri air in the California damp.

Dora arrived in Vallejo in the first-class car of the Overland Limited,
stayed at the best hotel in town. She was tiny still, but slender now
rather than square. She wore a medium-blue tiered coat over a lighter-
blue skirt, and her shoes were very neat, also in blue. After tea, they
went for a stroll. She walked and talked quite confidently, discoursing
on this and that as they tramped down the street. She scanned faces and
façades and perspectives, taking everything in. Every so often, she
would reach into her bag and take out a small notebook and a pen, saying only, "One little moment, darling," and then write something
down. When Margaret asked her what she was writing, she said,
"Goodness, I don't know. I never look into my notebook. But the habit
of writing it down keeps it in my mind. My mind is such a dustbin.
Don't you remember that in St. Louis you could hardly raise your eyes
from your shoes without offending someone? Darling, don't you enjoy
California? Do you ever get tired of it? I have never seen such a variety
of humanity all in one place." Her deep, satisfied breath was practically
a snort.

A week or so later, Dora asked her about Alexander. No, really, she
drew Margaret out in a practiced way. Margaret rarely if ever spoke
about Alexander—every lady in her knitting group had a tale to tell, if
not of her own misfortune, then of a sister's or a cousin's. After describing what happened as best she could, Margaret said, "Dr. Bernstein
told us about women whose children suffered from an icterus like
Alexander's, and then produced one child after another, each one
sicker than the last, though how a child could be sicker than Alexander,
I don't like to think. I took that to heart. Whatever the condition is, it
doesn't seem to be relieved by the passage of time or anything a doctor
can do." She put her finger to her lips, as if keeping a secret, and then
took it away, and said, "I hated Andrew for months afterward."

Dora nodded.

"I hated him for being disappointed in Alexander. Even though
Alexander was dying from the first moment he was born. I realize now
that I was beside myself, of course."

Dora took her hand. Margaret sighed, and then tried to be scientific.
"Andrew insisted that we test our blood, and our blood types are com-

patible. It's a mystery." She went on. "I did describe Alexander's symptoms in a letter to my mother." She sipped her tea, then said, "Of course, my mother was sympathetic, but Ben's and Lawrence's deaths were so much worse. And my father's, of course." Margaret didn't say that she supposed she had been cowardly not to keep at it, as Lavinia and every woman she knew had done. She had let the scientific speculations of Dr. Bernstein and Andrew make up her mind for her. The painful part was not so much the death of Alexander as it was that if she let herself dwell on thoughts of Alexander, then they would be followed inescapably by thoughts of her hand in Lawrence's, or her father bending down to say something to her. She turned these things over in her mind, and perhaps if Lavinia had lived down the street it would have come up one day when she found her mother in a meditative mood, and they would have talked it out. She never had the courage to write about it in a letter, though.

Then she said, as brightly as she could, "I thought of adopting. There was a boy I heard of, two years old, whose mother, father, and older brother died right in town. The boy survived all alone for three days. It was in the paper. I even went to the orphanage to look at him. Relatives in Texas took him in. But Andrew was interested in his own offspring, not someone else's. And he has gotten quite carried away with his book about the moon. No time for much else, really."

Dora said, "Oh, Margaret."

Margaret changed the subject back to Dora's adventures.

What Margaret didn't tell Dora was something larger and more nebulous—that it was Andrew himself who seemed dangerous. Not so much dangerous to her, Margaret, but dangerous to any child they might have. When she remembered those weeks with Alexander in the room at Mrs. Wareham's, what she remembered was not the fog of Vallejo, but the fog of Andrew, his voice booming like a horn, his breath filling the room, his body casting a cool shadow over the baby, his inquisitiveness a probe, draining Alexander's own small life force. Could any infant withstand such a thing? That Andrew, with the approval of Dr. Bernstein, stayed away from her—that he no longer read Havelock Ellis, or aspired to a houseful of youthful geniuses—was more than fine with her.

· · ·

AT the end of the summer, Dora happened to come on the ferry, intending to stay for the weekend and then take a horse up to Napa to explore. She put herself up at Mrs. Wareham's—in Margaret's room. Margaret had kept the room at Mrs. Wareham's, at first because she couldn't bear to give it up, and later because it gave them access to Vallejo when they didn't want to take the trouble to get the ferry to the island. She kept Alexander's cradle there until one of the ladies in her knitting circle asked if she could give it to her daughter for her grandson, and Margaret saw that she was right, and kind, in her intentions. As a result of her keeping the room, and using it, Mrs. Wareham had become her good friend. The two of them spent many evenings knitting and discussing, and lamenting, the wild habits of Mrs. Wareham's son, Angus. Andrew was as good with Angus as he had been with the Lear boys—since Andrew was up most nights, and was tall and strong, he didn't mind rousting Angus out of the bad neighborhoods, carting him home drunk, and putting him to bed without disturbing Mrs. Wareham. And it gave him the opportunity to exercise his curiosity about something other than the universe—he declared to Margaret that he could have mapped Vallejo if there were a call for that sort of thing. Angus had finally, in the last year, gone into the navy. He was now a sailor over at the island, about to embark upon his first mission, to the Bay of Fundy.

Dora stayed that night with Mrs. Wareham. By the next morning, when Margaret arrived for breakfast, the two women had settled it between them that Margaret's room was to pass to Dora. Dora fancied the idea of a retreat, not so much because she wished to rusticate herself and take a rest, as because she wished to have yet another place to explore and another group of friends.

While Mrs. Wareham's daughter, Cassandra, and Naoko served breakfast to the boarders in the dining room, the three of them sat down to a table in Mrs. Wareham's bedroom that was set with a selection of dishes: bacon, toast, some fried eggs, but also green tea and small bowls of a Japanese sort of savory soup that they all liked. Dora had never tried the soup or the tea before, but once she had imitated the way that they lifted the bowls to their lips with two hands and sipped it, she was enthusiastic.

Mrs. Wareham told her it was called miso.

"And you have it every day?"

"Well, sometimes we have flapjacks."

They laughed.

"Naoko has introduced me to quite a few things that I never knew existed. Or, let's say, that they didn't have in Red Rock, Ontario."

Dora said, "In France, we had crêpes, which are thin rolled-up flapjacks with stewed fruit. Stewed! Well, in St. Louis, they have stewed fruit. In France, they have white peaches simmered in brandy."

"Mrs. Early taught me to make those crêpes," said Margaret.

Dora said, rapturously, "If you have managed to stay up all night, and you find yourself on the Boulevard Saint-Germain very early in the morning, you may have white peaches simmered in brandy, or strawberries dipped in crème fraîche flavored with oil of violet." She sighed.

Mrs. Wareham said admiringly, "So lovely!"

Naoko came into the room to report that two new guests had arrived, looking for lodging. Mrs. Wareham pushed her chair back and stood up, while Dora's attention fell full upon Naoko.

Margaret viewed Naoko and Cassandra as a pair of young girls who were very well behaved and did what they were told—a testament to Mrs. Wareham's system and resolve as the proprietor of a respectable boarding house in a town that could be rowdy and even dangerous—but Dora was more curious. Possibly she had never seen a Japanese person before, or, at least, one who was trapped in the same room with her and obliged to talk.

Naoko had been born in Vallejo and spoke perfect English, but she had what Margaret thought of as a Japanese way about her—always retiring and graceful, always, apparently, yielding to Cassandra, but, according to Mrs. Wareham, getting her way in the end, "because Cassandra is so impulsive and inconsistent, I don't know that she remembers what she wants from one moment to the next!" The family had a shop on the edge of Chinatown, which in Vallejo was a small but wild place that Margaret had never dared to walk through. Though Margaret never forgot that it was Naoko who stoked her fire and kept the room warm while Margaret held Alexander in her arms and let her mind drift about, that it was Naoko who was silent while everyone else was chattering incessantly, the girl was too young for them to have achieved an actual friendship.

Dora said, "I read a book about Japan by Lafcadio Hearn. . . ."

Naoko smiled.

"I would like to go to Japan, and then cross China and Russia and visit Moscow and St. Petersburg. Most interesting place on earth. I would dress as a boy."

Margaret laughed. "Your mother—"

"She would be happy, because I would bring home a Cossack husband who had himself three other wives and was looking to import them all to St. Louis to go into the beer business." She turned to Naoko. "So, Naoko, where do you live? Does your father send home a lot of money to his parents?"

Naoko seemed a bit startled by this question, but still friendly. Margaret didn't step on Dora's toe to remind her of her manners—Dora had made a success of having no manners. Naoko said, "They live on Maine Street, near Marin Street. I, too, have thought that it would be interesting to go to Japan."

One for you, thought Margaret. Naoko pointed to the soup. "My father sells things. Miso. Rice. Rice noodles. Calligraphy brushes and paper. My mother is the *sanba* for the Japanese here."

Margaret said, "That's a midwife."

Naoko said, "My mother's mother was a midwife in their village in Japan. She rode a bicycle and was much respected because she could read and write. When my mother came here, she saw the same need in California."

"Do you like California?" said Dora, sounding idly curious, but with an underlying eagerness to her tone, which demonstrated to Margaret that she was planning to write something.

Naoko smiled politely and said, "I've never been anywhere else. But my mother says that life is very luxurious here compared to Manchuria."

"I thought they were from Japan."

"My parents came here because my father's parents lost two sons fighting with the Chinese. It appeared that my father would be next, so they found the money to send my parents here."

Mrs. Wareham, who had come in in time to hear this last remark, observed, "I always say, 'Don't go north unless they drive you there in a gang press, and even then, better to get shot for escaping than to end up in Red Rock.' "

"Very practical," said Dora. She looked at Naoko. "I want to meet them."

Of course she did, thought Margaret.

"I'll prepare them," said Naoko. She smiled and ducked her head. Mrs. Wareham said, "I suppose these new ones will be needing some linens, dear."

Naoko nodded and left the room.

"How old is she? She's not married," said Dora.

"She's planning to be a midwife as well," said Mrs. Wareham.

Dora's eyebrows lifted with glee.

When Margaret was accompanying her to the ferry a while later, she said, "I haven't met Naoko's parents, except that once, a few days before Alexander died, her mother came to see him."

"What did she do?"

"She held him and stared at him. I don't know what I thought. I thought she was going to perform some magic that doctors and astronomers would laugh to scorn, but that would work."

"And she didn't."

"No."

DORA was happy to gossip with Andrew, and he always sat longer at the supper table when she visited. When she interrupted him, he didn't mind. One evening, she stopped him mid-sentence and asked, "What about Tesla?"

"Ha!" exclaimed Andrew. "Nikola Tesla! There is some talent there, though he is Middle European to the core! Have you met him?"

Dora had.

"Very strange man. Very strange man. Talkative. Interrupts you all the time with ideas of his own. Never actually listens to anyone else, even when that person might perfectly well understand his ideas, and might even have a better idea himself. You know about Edison, don't you?"

"Hmm," said Dora encouragingly. "I've met him, too."

"That was a bit of a brouhaha."

Dora sat up. "Do tell," she said.

"You know that Edison hates Tesla and Tesla hates Edison, don't you? Tesla said that Edison promised him fifty thousand dollars if he solved a problem or two; then, when Tesla did the work, Edison said, Ah, it was just a joke! Americans talk big, didn't you know? Tesla ended up digging ditches for Edison Light there for a while. Adding insult to injury." Andrew shook his head.

"I interviewed Edison once," said Dora. "Down in Florida."

"The both of them always get talked up for the Nobel, but I can't see it. The Nobel Committee can't stand a fracas of any sort. That's why they always give the thing to the nice boys. Slow and steady wins the Nobel, you know. For example, my theory about the moon will be far too innovative for them. I already understand that."

He shook his head and leaned forward. He said, "But to my mind, that's not the interesting thing about Tesla. The newspapers always grab the stick by the wrong end. Inventors are a dime a dozen. You take a boy and you put him in a room with a stick and a ball of twine, a couple of rocks, and a piece of wire, and he'll invent something. But Tesla did something else, and the newspapers didn't touch it, and now it's ten-year-old news, but he got signals from Mars and Venus."

"Signals?" said Dora.

"Yup," said Andrew. "You know he had that lab in Colorado Springs for a few months around the turn of the century. Some Europeans funded it. A man of science is always having to go hat in hand to somebody with money. That's the real scandal, if you want to write about something." He pursed his lips. "Anyway, he was testing the transmission and reception of radio signals over long distances, and he was receiving a lot of them, as you may know. The universe is a noisy place. And when he pointed the receiver toward Venus and Mars, he got clicks. Clicks in twos and threes, sometimes fours. Never got that from anywhere else, either. Noise is noise. It's random. That's why it's noise. But clicks are clicks."

"Do you think there were communications from Mars and Venus?" exclaimed Dora.

"Well," said Andrew, "at the time, I wondered. It's a seductive idea. What else is God, really, but an extraterrestrial Being? But, finally, I decided not from both of them. That's the flaw in the whole idea. If you're getting signals from both, then it's the equipment. He's mad, of course. He told me one time, in Washington, that he was born at midnight in the middle of an electrical storm, and that lightning struck at the moment of his birth. Oh, I had a laugh over that, but Tesla was dead serious."

Dora and Margaret laughed, too.

Andrew smoothed down his mustache and chuckled. "Megalomania, I call it."

"How were you born, then?" said Dora.

"My dear, there are no legends to that effect, but perhaps, if I am to become famous, you could make one up for me."

"I might," said Dora.

"But he's never shy about Einstein. He shows Einstein up to be a fraud, and people listen to him, as they should." Andrew had begun talking about Einstein only that fall, but already the man was lodged in Andrew's head. "If Einstein's looked through a telescope, I'll eat my hat. It's all very well to imagine the universe was this way or that, but if you have never looked at the heavenly bodies, what good would such imaginings be?"

Though it was late when they finished gossiping, Andrew accompanied Dora to the Vallejo ferry on his way to the observatory. Dora felt comfortable anywhere, and at any time of the day or night. She needed little sleep, and she felt no fear of wandering the streets, either in San Francisco or in Vallejo, which was a lively, tough town, full of sailors and shipbuilders and foreigners. "Well, darling," she told Margaret, "I have a little something in my pocket. A last resort. Never had to try it except one night in Rome, with a gang of boys. They ran off in the end. If I need it, I will use it." Margaret was sure this was a pistol of some kind. A Missourian never minded a pistol, even a woman from St. Louis.

THE moon book had been a failure, according to Andrew. Yes, it had been published, and yes, it had been reviewed, mostly favorably, in *The Astronomical Journal* and *Scientific American,* and in *Science,* itself, as well as an obscure German journal and three newspapers. But the Attraction Theory had failed to displace the flaming-cucumber theory. "Drama is what they want, my dear," said Andrew. The Attraction Theory had not gotten him off the island and over to Berkeley or down to Pasadena or back to Chicago, and he was restless, day and night. Another thing Margaret did not say to Dora was that their grief, hers for Alexander and Andrew's for his moon book, did not make them more sympathetic to each other, but less. Their lives were mostly private now, lived side by side as necessary, but whatever there had been for them both—in the earthquake or the moon book or their hopes for Alexander—had dissipated the way certain qualities of light did. The reason she didn't mention it was that Dora would have said, as the ladies in her knitting group would have said, what did she expect? Did she not know what marriage was? But she didn't, did she? Except from listening to Lavinia's tales of those early days, when she had only sons and no daughters.

Andrew published another article in *The Astronomical Journal,* the first since the article about the craters. It was nothing about the moon—rather, he had rustled up his sets of double-star observations, made in Mexico so long ago, and he had attempted to coordinate these with observations made by other astronomers before and since, and to use the observations to propose a universe in which double stars were more common than single stars. The solar system, he thought, might be the remains of the sun's former double. Although the mass of all the planets and their moons and the debris between Mars and Jupiter that had been (Andrew was certain) a planet was less than the mass of a star that would have equaled and balanced the sun, the difference could be accounted for by time and attrition. All of this sounded plausible to Margaret. Everyone knew the sort of effort it took to maintain a stable partnership, and why should stars be different from married people?

On the whole, the reception of this article was positive, and two or three astronomers, plus a Mr. Akenbourn in South Africa, wrote him admiring letters.

Then, one day (it was July, because Margaret was in the kitchen making strawberry jam and thinking about Lavinia, who had died at Christmas, and whom Margaret had seen only once since leaving Missouri, when Elizabeth and the girls had brought her out for a month's visit; the visit hadn't been terribly easy, with the girls only seven and five and Lavinia visibly failing; it had, in fact, been a sad and difficult visit, but Margaret was thinking about how to persuade Elizabeth to come again, grueling trip though it was; Lucy May was nine already, and Eloise, seven), she heard the shattering of a window. She stood stock-still in surprise, then went to Andrew's door and knocked. No response. She opened the door.

Andrew was red in the face and breathing hard. After the article appeared, Andrew had spent some of his money on a typewriter, and begun another project, much more important than the moon book.

The typewriter was not easy to use, but it appealed to his pleasure in innovation. He attempted to master it off and on, though he railed against the arrangement of the keyboard, which had not been done according to any scientific principles that he could see. The typewriter had gone through the window and was lying out on the grass.

She said, "Did the—," but just then he picked up a copy of *The Astronomical Journal* and threw it down on the desk. She saw that he was not frustrated with the typewriter at all—the typewriter had simply been the nearest heavy object.

She picked up the journal.

The letter was right in the front, a long one, from a man named Dr. Martin Lovel, who worked at an observatory in Michigan. According to Dr. Lovel, he had worked with Andrew in Wisconsin, and knew, from both his own experience and his own inquiry into "the researches of Early," that Andrew had falsified data both in Wisconsin and in Mexico, and then had covered up this "fraud" when confronted by Dr. Lovel while Dr. Lovel was "a mere graduate student." Dr. Lovel had felt threatened by Andrew, who "was some nine or ten inches taller than I am" and "coldly angry." And although Andrew had given Dr. Lovel a good reference, there had been several interchanges between them that could have been (and were) construed (by Dr. Lovel) as threatening—"I was given to understand, in private, by Dr. Early, that recognition of my work would not be forthcoming if I didn't drop my accusations." Nevertheless, upon seeing Andrew's article in the spring, Dr. Lovel felt he had to protest—because Dr. Early's theory rested on bad data, and though plausible on the surface, it was "rotten beneath."

It took Margaret about thirty seconds to read this letter and understand the gist of it. She also understood its placement in the magazine, prominently positioned in the first section, just where someone would turn to begin reading the articles.

Andrew had dropped into his chair and was staring at the broken window. Margaret said, "Would you like me to go out and get the typewriter?"

He said nothing.

They were silent for a considerable time, while she wondered how to comfort her husband, and whether she should allude to the letters she had read all those years before. But he was red in the face and breathing hard, and she didn't have the courage for that, so she said, carefully, "An accusation isn't the same as proof, Andrew. You can defend yourself."

"I should not have to defend myself!"

"No, indeed. But maybe it would be a wise idea." Then she asked the most pressing question, which she later realized was not a question a wife who was truly in sympathy with her husband would have asked. She said, "Were the data falsified?"

He stared at her, but she didn't lower her eyes. The letters. Even though she couldn't mention them, she tried to keep in mind the straightforward but sympathetic approach that Mrs. Early had mastered.

"Not falsified, but there were some mistakes."

"Did you correct them?"

By his silence, she knew that he had not corrected them, but had allowed the issue to languish, probably out of pride. He said, "They aren't important to my theory. My theory doesn't depend on little mistakes, such as they were. There are plenty of other observations by other astronomers pointing in the same direction. The man was lying in wait to ambush me! He resented me then, even though I overcame my distrust of him and gave him a good reference. I see he's been harboring this grudge! I treated him perfectly well. I did him favors! Now he has ruined me."

"Well, it's not the first time someone has reacted to perceived favors with resentment, but I doubt that he has ruined you." That was exactly the sort of thing Mrs. Early would have said, she thought. "But how does this man know you?"

"He was my graduate student in Chicago. We got along well until he was set against me. By someone else."

"By whom?"

He stared at her, then exclaimed, "Look where they printed the letter! That's as good as a telegram from the editors that they will never publish my work again, and it's not just a telegram to me, but a telegram to every astronomer in the world."

"I understand that, but I don't see why you can't defend yourself."

"I should defend myself by going to Michigan and shooting the cur."

"Since it's a five-day trip to Michigan, thank goodness you're hot-headed rather than cold-blooded."

He gave her a little smile, sighed. At this very moment, she remembered her grandfather talking about mules and horses. He had said,

"It's harder to train a mule than a horse. You know why? When a horse sighs, you know he's giving up, but when a mule sighs, you know he's coming up with another plan." Andrew, she thought, had always been more a horse than a mule, but that didn't mean the mule wasn't in there. She went outside and got the typewriter. The frame was bent. She carried it into his office, heavy as it was, and set it on the desk, her demeanor as neutral as possible. A few minutes later, he went and got one of the sailors who worked around the base to come over and put a piece of wood over the window. A couple of days after that, another pair of sailors replaced the window while she was in San Francisco.

He said no more about the article or the letter, and both issues of *The Astronomical Journal* disappeared from among the papers that were stacked around the house. To others, Margaret thought, Andrew would not have seemed different from his usual self. He still stalked about the island in his brisk, upright fashion, smoothing his mustaches and filling out his uniform, speaking to everyone, and ordering the sailors about. Over meals, he was polite. But he avoided her. He spent all of his time in his study or at the observatory, working on his book, while she stayed in the kitchen or in her room. The effect of this was to make her more cool toward him, rather than less. When Dora urged her to meet at Mrs. Wareham's or invited her into San Francisco, she was happy to go.

Dora did not have a house but, rather, a lovely apartment in San Francisco's Cornell Hotel, with a large parlor, a bedchamber, and a bath, but no kitchen. "I hate a kitchen," said Dora. She ate only in restaurants, but they could be any sort of restaurant, from the Garden Court at the Palace Hotel to a nameless oyster bar on the wharf. Dora's friends, who seemed to walk in and out of her apartment at will, and could frequently be found in the mornings, slumped on the sofa or stretched out on the carpet, were not like anyone on the island. The ones who were friendly to Margaret were Mal Cohen, who wrote about crime for the *Call,* and George Roden, who covered labor news, along with the only other woman writer on the *Examiner,* Leonora Eliot (born Lena Priskov in Detroit, Michigan), who covered debutantes, society balls, and weddings. Leonora was even more fashionably attired than Dora, but every time Margaret complimented her on an outfit, Leonora would laugh and exclaim that she had gotten it for free— either Gump's or the White House had given "this thing" to her, or one of her society friends had cast it off. She put her arm across the back of the sofa in a boyish way, and said, "Darling Margaret, you know what I really like? Not polo, by any means, but rowing! The bay is so delightfully dangerous. I got all the way to Alcatraz last weekend, close enough that they drew their guns on me! The wind was blowing so hard I could not shout to them who I was."

Margaret said, "You could have been killed!" and Leonora laughed, as if this was a thrilling idea, and said, "The waves were so rough that I almost missed the livestock exposition I had to cover that evening."

Margaret said, "Livestock? I thought—"

"But that's what they are, these debutante balls. They are selling these girls. And I am terribly tired of champagne. George should exchange jobs with me." She gestured with her cigarette holder across the room.

The room was filled with painters and musicians and men with no daily occupation more pressing than finding a good cigar. Dora accompanied these men around the city, into shops and factories and livery stables and warehouses and brothels, or to garden lunches and society parties and masked balls, all the time eavesdropping and asking questions and writing up little pieces under the headline "In Another Part of the City." When Margaret came home from these visits, she chatted about these people to Andrew across the supper table, even though he was gloomy and preoccupied. She told him how Leonora Eliot had discovered that photos of herself had turned up in a gallery in Philadelphia, Pennsylvania, at the very time when Leonora's off-and-on suitor, a wealthy San Franciscan named Charles Coudray, happened to be visiting friends there. Coudray recognized Leonora's shoulder (which had a mole), and bought every print. When he confronted Leonora, she disdainfully returned all of the jewelry he had given her, and cut off communication. Andrew laughed and said, "These are odd specimens you are meeting, my dear."

In the fall, Dora had a little article in the *Examiner* entitled "Behind the Fence." Margaret read it with some surprise, because they had talked about visiting Naoko's family, the Kimuras, together, but had never done so. Dora had gone alone, though. In her article, she described the backyard:

The room seemed to flow outward toward the garden, which was small but intricate. The only flowers your correspondent recognized were some bronze-colored mums, and a trained elderberry shrub that was full of hummingbirds. Otherwise, there was a narrow path through a small thick lawn, and there were thick green shrubs neatly pruned to look like miniature trees. To the right of these was a group of graceful maples, their leaves now red and yellow. These reminded your correspondent suddenly of Missouri, in a way that caught her off-guard and made her throat catch, but truly there was no Missouri about it; possibly she had simply never seen anything like this garden, so small and perfect, hiding in a backyard in Vallejo.

The gentleman had started the shop, and planted the earliest parts of the garden as a welcome gift for the lady. He had built the fence with two brothers he knew, carrying in the dirt for the mountain. The rocks were from a hillside near Lincoln, where a friend of his had a vegetable farm. He found the pines not far away, in a stand over toward the coast. The maples came from Japan—a farmer he knew brought the seeds many years ago and planted them in his garden for seedlings. In the winter, when it is dark, the gentleman passes his time practicing calligraphy and poetry.

The couple have a daughter and two sons, who are at school. The boys were eager to demonstrate to your correspondent how well spoken they are in English.

Margaret had never imagined that such a quiet place could exist in that part of Vallejo, which was busy and rowdy, day and night. Nor could she envision Naoko making her way from that quiet place through the noisy streets to Mrs. Wareham's, but that was what the girl did, every day, twice a day. Once again, the curious thing was how strange and forceful the world was, how it battered and clanged and could not be withstood, and yet some individuals withstood it while others did not.

DORA began referring to one of the men she went about with, a man named Pete.

"He has plenty of money," said Dora. "He reads and he collects."

Given that Dora had never before taken seriously any of her idle connoisseurs of cigars and whiskey, Margaret was a little surprised. She said, "What does he collect?"

They were sitting in the Garden Court, having high tea. The feather in Dora's hat shivered as she breathed, and then bobbed when she sipped her tea. She said, "Whatever there is to collect. He was showing me some netsuke he brought with him from Japan."

"What are netsuke?"

"Tiny little sculptures. Rather like buttons, really. Most of his are made of ivory or jade, but one from the eighteenth century is carved from a tiger's tooth. It's carved into the shape of an attacking warrior. He has a valuable collection."

"He's a dealer."

"Darling, he's too impetuous to be a dealer. He likes something, he buys it without thinking of the market." She smiled brilliantly, as if this were a virtue.

Margaret leaned forward and caught Dora's eye, asking, as if she might report this to Mrs. Bell, "How long have you known him, really?"

Dora touched her mouth with her napkin, then set it in her lap. "Almost a year, to be honest. I met him through Mr. Kimura."

"I read that article."

"The editor cut most of it. Only flowers and plants. Nothing about, as he would say, 'all the Japs everywhere.' He held it for months."

"You have been very secretive!"

"Dear Margaret, you've known me since I was sixteen. When haven't I been *very secretive*?" She spoke with a satisfied smile. "Can you really be on my mother's side, waiting for me to get married? You? After all of these years with Andrew?" She stared into Margaret's face for a minute, no doubt gauging her reaction to this remark, then said, "Anyway, the question of whether Pete is that special Cossack I'd been planning to take home to St. Louis and shock my mother with was answered the first time he asked me to loan him a thousand dollars."

"I thought you said he has plenty of money."

"He does, but, he tells me, it isn't always available. Anyway, you know I am much more prudent with my money than I am with my affections."

"I didn't know that." Margaret tried to make her voice light.

MARGARET would have thought that, as a Cossack, Pete Krizenko would be a tall man, imposing and physical, but Andrew was taller than he was by a head, and had a fuller mustache, too—Pete favored something trimmer and more English-looking. Apart from his clothes, he was plain-looking—you would not pick him out in a crowd. Dora said he had grown up on horseback, but you couldn't tell that, either.

Andrew, so busy with his new book that he wouldn't leave their house except to go to the observatory, seemed fascinated by Pete—he came out of his study when he heard Dora's voice, and he took a chair rather than disappearing again. The four of them sat in the front room, drinking a bit of sherry and waiting for Margaret's baking chicken. Outside the bay window, the fog was so thick that it muffled the sounds of the factory.

Dora said, "Pete has made four fortunes and lost three of them, haven't you?"

Pete made a gesture that indicated to Margaret that he was rather proud of this. He addressed himself to Andrew, as if only a man could understand such adventures. He, his uncle, and his cousin drove a hundred Don horses to Kiev and offered them for sale to the Russian army. "I was sixteen," said Pete. "They were good horses, and we got a good price on them, because when the Russians made too low a bid my uncle turned them right there, and we headed southwest, as if we were taking them to Romania to sell them to the Turks. They let us go twenty verst. A verst is like a kilometer, in case you didn't know that, but then they came after us, because we went so fast with so many horses, and all beautiful chestnuts, like honey. They paid a hundred thousand for the lot."

"A hundred thousand what?" said Andrew.

"Call them dollars, I don't care," exclaimed Pete, good-naturedly. "They were as good as dollars to me. My uncle took half, and my cousin and I split the other half, and instead of going back with them to the village, I went to St. Petersburg and walked down the Nevsky Prospect and bought some nice clothes from the English Shop there, and I invested my money in a newspaper, and away it went, like a basinful of water running downhill."

Dora said, "No one loses money on a newspaper."

"Ah, but we were very principled. The editor was twenty-two. I thought he was a very worldly man." Pete smiled. His accent wasn't at all like that of Leonora Eliot, or any accent Margaret had heard around Vallejo. It came and went as he spoke.

"Did he steal from you?" Andrew asked.

"My goodness, no. He disdained advertisers, and his views were too depressing to attract customers." Pete threw his head back and laughed. "After that, I lived for a while like Raskolnikov in his room, and it almost drove me to murder, of course, but not quite."

Dora winked at her, and then Pete said, "I am a big talker and a show-off. Sometime Dora here will tell you which parts she believes and which parts she does not believe, but I am giving no clues myself!"

"Fortune number two?" prompted Andrew. Margaret could see he, at least, was believing every word.

Pete glanced at Dora. "Ah well. I will tell you only this. There was a woman in St. Petersburg named Bibikova. Her first name doesn't matter, you would not have heard of her, but she was from a well-known noble family. When I was about twenty, she took me up as her pet. Ach! She was a very ugly woman, even with her fortune and her family's house near the Winter Palace, she had not been able to find a husband, though possibly this was not her fault—everyone knew that her father, who controlled the money, was a miser and carried a pistol in the pocket of his dressing gown. But when her father and her uncle died, leaving her huge estates and houses in Petersburg, you can be sure that the handsomest men in Russia were lining up to marry her, and so she employed me as a spy."

Andrew was clearly enjoying himself, and Margaret was struck for a moment by the poignancy of such a thing.

"She dressed me nicely and sent me to parties to eavesdrop upon the gossip, or to bring up a certain name and then listen to what people said. In Moscow, I pretended to be just in from St. Petersburg, and in St. Petersburg, I pretended to be visiting from Moscow. I followed her suitors home at night, and peered into their windows. I was good at climbing up drainpipes and scrambling over roofs. Or I got their servants drunk, and discovered mistresses and bastards and God knows what. After my reports, she would get rid of one suitor or favor another in a way that seemed quite arbitrary and gave her for one time that experience of being courted. My reward was that every week or so she would take me out, and we would go look at things—pictures, china, silver, horses, carpets, old pieces of furniture, even jewels. If she liked something, and I liked it, too, she bought it for herself, but if there was something I liked that she didn't like, she bought it for me, and that was my fee for working hard. At the end of a year, she chose a boring fellow from Moscow named Yerchikovsky, who had large estates in the south, and I was dismissed with my treasures and my wardrobe. I sold it all to some fellows from France who knew enough but not too much, and that was my second fortune, four times the size of the first. Now I was homesick, because St. Petersburg is such a damp and gloomy city, so my plan was to go back to the Don and buy more horses, which would have been a sure bet, but I was too young to know any better, and so I . . ." He shook his head, but good-naturedly. Andrew was so intrigued, he shook his head, too.

"Do tell them," said Dora. "This is my favorite, because I would have done exactly the same thing."

"I invested in an expedition! Have you heard of Przhevalsky? Nikolai Mikhailovich?"

"I have! He went to Tibet!" Andrew nearly leapt out of his chair.

Pete said, "Well, I did not go with the great man himself."

Margaret stood up and went into the kitchen to tend to the chicken. A bit later, she heard Andrew's voice boom out, "Khara Khoto! Khara Khoto is in Mongolia! The Chinese destroyed it in the fourteenth century. There's no telling what's there! It's a lost world, like Troy, or Pompeii!"

When she returned to announce supper, Pete was saying, "Sinkiang is very interesting. I plan to return. In spite of the mosquitoes."

Dora laughed, then said, "I would go there."

"Yes, you would," said Pete. He seemed fond of her. They all got to their feet.

Once they were sitting down, Andrew pressed, "Now the third fortune."

"Ah," said Pete. "Well, by now I was an old man for those regions. I was twenty-three. Pushkin was already exiled by the Tsar before he was twenty-three. I saw that I had better hurry to make another fortune before infirmities would force my retirement. So—have you ever heard of Omsk?" Margaret went back into the kitchen for the beans. When she came back, Andrew was saying, "The latitude would make it more like one of the Canadian prairie towns. Or Scotland. Scotland is at the latitude of Omsk." Latitude and longitude were Andrew's daily fare.

"I imagined I would find a nice Cossack town and buy a horse or two, but the streets were crawling, yes, Dora always says this, the streets were *crawling* with Europeans, real Europeans, from Germany and Holland and France, which was good for me, because I spoke better French than English at that time. If you had a bit of capital, Omsk was the place to be. Those French fellows did. We bought some plots and built some elegant houses and named them 'Les Milandes' and 'Les Domes.' " Margaret passed him the platter. "White façades, you know, with mansard roofs and a dome every little bit. It will be a great city, Omsk. Up until the railway, it was an outpost, and Dostoevsky was there, did you know that? That's where he was sent to the prison camp after they didn't execute him. He wouldn't mind it there now. That railway is a great accomplishment, I am telling you."

Margaret passed him the bread and asked, "Is it finished?"

"The main lines have been finished for eight or ten years. As soon as I heard that the two ends had met, I got on it. It took me four months to get from St. Petersburg to Sinkiang, and three weeks to get from Sinkiang to Omsk, but only four days to get from Omsk to Vladivostok."

Andrew beamed as if he had built the railroad himself.

Over breakfast the following morning, Margaret said, "Did you believe all of that? I must say, he hardly has an accent."

Andrew shook his head. "Some people are naturally fluent, my dear. I do believe any native I might have known in Berlin would have mistaken me for a German."

"But there's something about him—"

"He's a brilliant fellow," said Andrew. "That's all. He's such a rare bird that we don't recognize his rarity."

Margaret turned this over in her mind, then said, "I asked Dora if he had ever been married."

"What did she say?"

"She said, 'I don't know, really. But if so, I'm sure the wife regretted it.' "

Andrew laughed outright for the first time in weeks.

Margaret would have said that Dora could not be duped, so she didn't understand her friend's delight in this Pete Krizenko. For herself, she didn't believe a word he said. He told his stories as if he had gotten them out of books, and she thought that it was perfectly possible that he was a small-time crook from Seattle, up to no good—Dora was something of an heiress, after all, and acted like one. But, of course, now Margaret sounded, even to herself, exactly like the Bells. It was also true that the man had had a magical effect on Andrew, and for the first time since his "denunciation," as he called it, Andrew seemed relaxed and even personable. Once when she was in San Francisco, Pete Krizenko appeared at the observatory and asked to be shown about the place. Andrew reported, with delight, that the fellow had looked through the telescope and listened to Andrew's theories. And Mrs. Wareham seemed to know him as well, and to like him—she complimented his manners. But Margaret remained suspicious.

ONE rainy day, Margaret and Dora were walking from Mrs. Wareham's house to the ferry when a horse-drawn cart passed them, then slowed and stopped. The cart was small, two wheels, freshly painted black with yellow trim. It had a bellows top, which had been pulled up against the weather. The horse was more of a pony—probably a pony crossed with a heavier, more lethargic breed, since it had a Roman nose—but it had an intelligent expression, and its ear tips pointed delicately at each other. A lady leaned forward and put her head around the top. Margaret recognized her instantly and with a start. Dora said, "Mrs. Kimura! How do you do, ma'am?" The midwife, wearing a brown wool coat and a man's trilby against the weather, smiled brightly and nodded. She said, "Miss Dora, you kind ladies must come out of bad weather!"

Dora was in the seat in a moment; Margaret clambered up more hesitantly. She could hardly stand to look at Mrs. Kimura, so strongly did her face remind Margaret of Alexander—but not of Alexander himself, more of that feeling she had had, horror and suspense that could not be acted on or even reacted to, only waited out. Once they had settled themselves, Mrs. Kimura stirred up the pony with the whip, and he trotted briskly away. As they bowled along, Mrs. Kimura put her shoulders back and held the reins in her gloved hands with a sense of dash, as if she had been born to do it. Margaret made herself look at the woman and think shallow thoughts about, for example, the distinct family resemblance between her and Naoko, so that that old feeling would be overlaid by something. Fortunately, they were going rather fast; Margaret had to grip the side railing with both hands. Mrs. Kimura said, all at once, "I have had successful delivery this morning!"

Dora shouted into the wind, "Boy or girl?"

"Oh, boy! And after three girl. Now mother no need bear any more baby!" She flicked the pony with the whip again. He freshened his trot. Soon they were out of town and in the countryside. A buggy ride was a rare treat. The rain on the bellows top was just a freshness, fragrant now with the scent of the spring grasses and the earth. In front of them, the hills (rough and ridged, not smooth like hills in Missouri) rose up east of the city. Even at this distance, Margaret could see a few human figures in the orchards that spread in a ragged, flowering cloud across their lower contours. She sensed her breathing evening out; she was not gasping any longer.

At the next turn back toward town, the pony went left. Soon he was walking along, calm, but with his ears pricked. When they arrived at the stable, a boy of about twelve greeted Mrs. Kimura and took the pony and the buggy. She patted the boy on the head and bowed to him, and he bowed to her, exactly imitating her. Then she put something in his hand. Dora said, "May we go to the shop, Mrs. Kimura? I'm sure my friend and cousin Mrs. Andrew Early would be honored to make the acquaintance of your husband."

"Please come," said Mrs. Kimura. Dora and Mrs. Kimura were the same height and looked, Margaret thought, like intimate friends, leaning toward each other and chatting with perfect familiarity about Naoko—was she accompanying Mrs. Kimura to births now? And Joe and Lester (who, Margaret thought, must be the two sons)—how were they doing in school? The midwife was of course polite to Margaret, asking her about fog on the island. She gave no indication that she remembered that visit to Alexander. By the time she opened the door of the shop and invited them in, the upright laughing driver of the pony cart had vanished, replaced by someone softer and more self-effacing. She was, Margaret thought, Japanese again.

It was late morning, and the room was light. Mr. Kimura was seated behind the counter with paper and brushes, and he and Mrs. Kimura greeted each other, then he greeted Margaret and Dora. He did not get up. On the counter were some stalks of bamboo growing in a tall green pot. He resumed stroking with the brush while Mrs. Kimura went through to the back, and Dora nudged Margaret over to a spot where they could see his paper.

The clump of bamboo on the page was thicker than the clump in the pot. He rendered each stalk with one stroke of the brush, tilting or pressing it here and there. After adding each stalk to the thicket on the page, he stippled in the leaves, youthful and transparent, seeming to glow in the sunlight that filtered through the stalks. As they continued to stand there, he finished with the bamboo, paused, laid down his brush and picked up another one. This he dipped into a different pot, and then he applied a nibbling rabbit to the lower third of the page. Without seeming to lift his brush, he shaded in what looked like fur. Only now did he glance at them.

When he stood up to assist them, his movement made Margaret feel a bit tall for the shop, so she backed awkwardly toward the door, but Dora happily pointed at some cups and a teapot in white porcelain. They were not in the Japanese style—they looked more as if a potter had used Japanese techniques to make an English tea set. Dora nodded, and he took the set off the shelf. He wrapped it and offered it to Dora, who counted out the money and laid it on the counter. They bowed. They shook hands. This exchange was accompanied by a lot of smiling. Dora began to put the teacups in her bag. Margaret divined that Mr. Kimura did not speak English, and covertly looked around the shop. For a moment, Mr. Kimura paused in front of her, and seemed to be waiting to serve her. She shook her head just the barest bit, and then he did a surprising thing—he went to the paper he had been working on, took it off his table, rolled it up, and offered it to her, Margaret, where she was standing beside the door. She must have looked startled, because he nodded. Dora muttered, "Darling, you must accept," and so Margaret smiled and held out her hands. He put the roll into them.

Just then, Mrs. Kimura emerged from the back, this time dressed in a gray kimono and looking entirely Japanese. Mr. Kimura resumed his seat, and Mrs. Kimura seemed to herd them toward the door, where she shook Dora's hand, then Margaret's, and bowed to them, saying, "Please, Miss Dora and Mrs. Margaret, you must come again." She held Margaret's gaze only a moment longer than she held Dora's, but that was enough.

"Oh, darling, of course we shall," said Dora, comfortable as always.

When Margaret got home and unrolled the picture, she saw how charming it was, as soft as the mist of the day, and as sweet, in its way, as the view she'd had of frothy, blossoming trees against the green hillsides. A dragonfly, which she hadn't noticed, drifted above the nibbling rabbit. Somehow this detail gave her special pleasure.

ANDREW and Dora had differing views of the war in Europe. Andrew was grateful for the pall that the war could, should, cast over silly European ideas about the universe. If cosmology was a race, then his rivals were suffering an inevitable and well-deserved setback, while American astronomers, equipped with the best telescopes in the world, were marshaling their observations and organizing them into worthwhile theories. "I have been in Berlin," he informed Dora. "I saw how they think. They are not pragmatists like we are, or, indeed, like the English and the Scots. The theoretical cart always before the empirical horse, always! It's an easy way of doing things. Well, now, just because they and their countrymen are so belligerent, they are discovering that the easy way is the hard way. I can't say that I feel sorry for them, really."

Few on the island did. The island had always been a place where ships were not only built, but repaired or refurbished and refitted, and if Margaret had thought that things were busy and noisy and crowded before, she soon learned what those terms actually meant. Dora was in favor of the war, too, because Dora considered any war a font of interesting stories.

As for Margaret, she was not at all sure how to pronounce "Ypres" when she saw it in the *Call*. When she read about the Christmas Truce, she fully believed that the truce could and would stretch into something more permanent. From California, the war seemed pointless except as a spur to economic activity. No one in California thought the U.S. would enter the war. If the Germans said that the English were shipping armaments on European passenger ships, the wisdom among the navy men was that they would be fools not to; that was why the *Lusitania* went down so quickly.

Stimulated by the war, Andrew's book was practically writing itself. Dr. Einstein's pre-war fame was a perfect example, Andrew claimed, of cronyism in science. Someone, a very young man, in fact, came up with some crazy ideas ("the younger the better, the crazier the better"), ideas that sounded plausible to those who didn't actually know anything. These ideas were picked up by a few dupes outside of the scientific world—industrious amateurs, society matrons, university students—and publicized around the world (an unfortunate effect of wireless and radio, though in principle, of course, Andrew was in favor of every invention), and then real scientists had to answer questions about these theories (a waste of time, really). Real scientists must talk in equivocal terms about everything, so the newspaper people didn't see the underlying disagreement in the remarks those scientists made. The ideas in his own book, he told Margaret, were much more systematic, better worked out, and they would be rapidly demonstrated soon after they were laid before the astronomical community, even if he had to bypass *The Astronomical Journal* to make his case. The crazy theory got a headline, and then the truth got nothing. Andrew wrote the *New York Times* a letter—not for the letters column, but privately, pointing out that their coverage of astronomy and physics was at best patchy and at worst "a scandal." He offered to serve as an independent expert for them, entirely free of charge. The *New York Times* did not respond. Even so, he maintained hope. "Soon," he said once, triumphantly, "they will agree with me."

Dora teased Andrew with some new theory of Einstein's that she had heard about, but he was so close to finishing his book that he didn't even get irritable, just waved his hand mildly. "Einstein is wrong, my dear. Obvious to anyone with the least astronomical training."

"Why is he wrong?" asked Dora.

Andrew leaned forward. Margaret could see that he was speaking to the *San Francisco Examiner,* not to their friend and relation Dora Bell. "The simplest thing to tell you is that what he says is the way the universe is can't be the way it is. Or, rather, it can't be *shown* to be that way. If it can't be shown to be that way, then it isn't that way—it is not the universe, but just a thought. Einstein's so-called theory takes something that we have measured, a force, and interprets it as something that is geographical—a slope, let's say. In his view, a ball runs down a slope because it is sloped, not because there is a force pulling it down. He ignores completely that the force has been measured and that the measurements show the force to be a powerful one. This thing is no different from any other story about the beginning of the universe. You know that myth, the myth of Ptah? It's the Egyptian myth. Ptah spoke, and as he spoke, everything he said was created. Who's to say that story isn't true? Except for the fact that it can't happen. Observations at Mount Wilson and the Lick will soon show that it can't happen."

"Einstein is a flash in the pan, then?" said Dora.

"A comet across the cosmological heavens, my dear." Margaret saw that Andrew had made a joke. And a few days after this conversation, he took time away from his book to write a letter to a journal in England, out of Oxford, in which he said more or less what he had said to Dora, though without the illustrative references to Egyptian myth, and they published it in the winter.

It was Leonora Eliot who told Margaret that Dora was lobbying her editor to be sent back to Europe—didn't she know? Everyone at the paper knew. It was almost a joke, the idea of little Dora wandering about the war zone with her pistol and her hat and her stylish shoes, scribbling about how to grow potatoes in the trenches.

Margaret said, "Dora's never written about potatoes."

"Survival is her subject," said Leonora.

Pete Krizenko was Margaret's only recourse. In the months since their supper, Margaret had seen Pete once, when he came upon Dora and her having tea in the Garden Court, and Dora, in spite of always pooh-poohing her affection for him, had outdone herself in smiles just to see him. At the time, Margaret had been both skeptical and disapproving. But as she lay awake in her bed the night after Leonora's remarks and imagined her life without Dora's vivaciousness (and money and shoals of friends), she decided that Pete was preferable, if the war in Europe was the alternative. The next day, she walked to Mrs. Wareham's, but when she turned into that block she hesitated—were she to ask Mrs. Wareham about Pete, Mrs. Wareham would certainly tell Dora, and Dora would laugh and tease, deftly turn her aside, and end up in Europe just out of pure contrariness—and so she directed her steps to the Kimuras' shop. She had no idea of the nature of the Kimuras' friendship with Dora, but she felt she could rely on their secretiveness, or perhaps upon what was merely an appropriate sense of discretion.

A customer came out as Margaret went in. She found Mrs. Kimura behind the counter, putting some things away, and although Mrs. Kimura gave her a friendly smile and a small bow, Margaret suddenly quailed at her errand and, instead of asking after Pete Krizenko, picked up first a packet of noodles, and then a pair of chopsticks, and then a newspaper with Japanese writing on it. While she was holding these things, her eye was caught by a picture—a heron, it was, standing beside a stone near some sort of overhanging tree, one leg bent—and she gazed at the picture without taking it in, but pretended to take it in. Another customer came through the door, bought something, went out again. Margaret continued to stare at the picture. Mrs. Kimura walked around the counter and stood beside her. The top of her head came to Margaret's chin. Mrs. Kimura said, "This painting from Japan. Mr. Pete gave to Mr. Kimura." She pointed to the red seal on the upper left corner. "Famous painter."

Margaret said, "I haven't seen Pete in a while."

"He come. He go."

"How do you contact him?"

"Mrs. Margaret send note?"

Margaret saw that she was being understood perhaps better than she wished to be. She said, "Yes." She turned away from the picture. Mrs. Kimura was looking up at her. She seemed amused, and so Margaret nodded. Mrs. Kimura handed her a pen and a small square of paper. She wrote her note. Mrs. Kimura held out her hand, and Margaret folded the note twice and gave it to her. Then there was the smiling and bowing, and Margaret set down the chopsticks and the noodles and the paper. Later, she thought she might have liked to buy the noodles. After that, she realized that in the shop she hadn't thought of Alexander. Pete did not answer her note.

In fact, Margaret was thankful for his silence, because it was impossible—you could not broach such a subject as marriage, and then, if you did, you were bound to say something rude or inappropriate, since you knew nothing other than what Dora had revealed, and all those revelations were jokes or half-truths. Pete himself was such a suspicious character that if you did promote something, and then that something came to pass, it would be on your conscience, whatever the outcome, and the outcome was so much more likely to be unfortunate than it was to be happy. Certainly he was married already—hadn't Dora hinted as much? There could be more wives than one, couldn't there? And children, too. What had been easy in Missouri—introducing a name into the conversation, walking past the family home, running into this friend or that friend, wondering aloud about an incident from years gone by, even looking in the newspaper, or watching a person from afar—was impossible here. But then she thought of what was now in the papers about Ypres again, about the unspeakable horrors that would draw Dora and her little pistol and her lovely shoes. Ypres was not far from Paris—Margaret didn't know the exact distance, but it was easy to imagine the rumbling boom of distant cannon. And no one guaranteed that Dora would stay in Paris once she was on her own.

Dora herself said nothing about going to Europe. Then she came for a weekend visit to Mrs. Wareham's. She had infiltrated a Wobbly meeting dressed as a young man and was very pleased with herself. She had worn canvas pants and broken shoes and used a string as a belt and spoken in "low, resentful monosyllables," saying that she was up from San Jose looking for a job. "But really," she told Margaret, "I'd heard that Lucy Parsons might be there, and I was hoping to get a word with her."

The Bells would have shivered in horror at the thought of Dora consorting with International Workers of the World and swooned at the thought of her sitting down with such a famous socialist and strike organizer as Lucy Parsons, but Margaret said, "You might write a book about her." Lucy Parsons was an old woman and would not be going to Europe.

"Too much time in Chicago," said Dora. She sighed. "The meeting was all Italian bakery-workers. And I could only understand about half of what they were saying. I was embarrassed at myself."

Nevertheless, she had written it up for the paper, and the article was appearing Sunday, which was why she was at Mrs. Wareham's for the weekend.

Margaret said, "I don't—"

"It's not as daring as it appears."

"How do you know?"

"Nothing ever happens, does it? I should have taken you to the meeting. It was all a lot of shouting. Nothing to be afraid of. No one was drunk, so it was safer than a saloon. They want to complain. They should complain."

"They work themselves up."

"Or they blow off steam. That's what I say in my little piece. They're happier afterward."

Dora was pleased with everything about her prank, from the way she learned about the meeting (eavesdropping) to her costume and her "acting" to her well-developed memory (she wrote the quotes down afterward, back at her apartment). The indignation about the article would come not from the Wobblies but from the industrialists, who would be upset that she had "defanged" their enemies, made them seem merely rowdy, almost good-natured.

Margaret stayed at Mrs. Wareham's most of the afternoon, even hauling out her knitting for a bit while Dora read, but she could not think of a way to broach the topic of marriage. It occurred to her that she might enlist Mrs. Wareham, but she knew full well that Mrs. Wareham's own marriage had not been a happy one, and as much as she loved her son, Angus, she pitied the girl he had married in Hawaii, and now there was a child, and Mrs. Wareham had sent the girl clothes and money. And Mrs. Wareham was not as set in her isolationist opinions as most people were.

Then Pete Krizenko appeared, when she had almost abandoned her plan, knocking at the front door of Quarters P while she was washing up after Andrew's dinner. The moment she opened the door, she knew that she had no idea how to ascertain his "intentions" or to suggest some "intentions" if he hadn't conceived any on his own. Dora was thirty-two. Pete was not as old as Andrew, but even by the way he walked into the room with his hat pushed back on his head and his hands in his pockets, she could tell he was long habituated to doing just as he pleased. Her project, she thought right then, was akin to harnessing cats. So what she said was "I'm so glad you've come! How can we prevent Dora from going to Europe?" And then she backed away from the door and let him in. Andrew was in his study, but the door stayed closed, because there was always so much uproar from the ship factories at this time of day; he would not know of Pete's coming unless she summoned him.

Pete sat down. He said, "Do we want her not to go to Europe? Not even to Spain? Things in Spain have never been better." Again, she noted, his accent could be from anywhere. She wondered if he had practiced it as he was standing outside the door, but then, remembering her purpose, she banished that thought. She said, "She wouldn't stay in Spain."

Pete settled back and crossed his legs at the ankles. He was holding his hat in his lap, and now he smoothed the brim. When he smiled, Margaret saw that he was amused at her. Normally, she didn't mind anyone's being amused at her, but now she felt a sense of offense take hold. He said, "Perhaps she needs a husband."

"I thought of that."

"*I* thought of that," said Pete.

"Did you really?"

"Indeed, I did."

He didn't add anything. The outcome of that thought was self-evident, wasn't it?

Margaret tried to gauge from Pete's demeanor how he felt about what appeared to be the failure of his hopes, then said, "Perhaps you could be more persistent."

He said, "What about my manly self-regard? Russian men especially—"

"It didn't seem to me from your stories that you have much manly self-regard." She shocked herself by saying this, but then said, "I mean to be giving you a compliment, you know." And she did.

He dipped his head. Compliment accepted, she decided. And then she felt herself relax a bit—not her distrust, but her discomfort. She asked him if he cared for any tea. The stove was still hot. He said, "May I prepare it?"

Margaret pointed to the kitchen.

Pete seemed perfectly at home in her kitchen, and perfectly at home making the tea, but he did it in a way she had not seen before—he boiled the water until it was rolling, then poured some into the teapot. After he had swirled it around inside the pot, he poured it out, and then added loose tea to the empty pot, and let it sit for some seconds. He invited her to look into the pot. She saw the tea leaves relax in the damp warmth into a dark, fragrant pile. Only then did he pour in the water, which, in the meantime, he had brought back to the boil. He looked around, picked up a shawl she had left hanging over the back of a chair, bunched it around the teapot, and cut a lemon into wedges. "Now," he said, "we have Russian tea. When I visit again, I will bring some salka pastries. They are good with tea and jam. Little buns."

He handed her the cups and saucers, and himself carried the teapot wrapped in her shawl into the front room.

The tea was dark and strong, and she liked the lemon. But they were no closer to securing Dora's presence in San Francisco. Margaret's task, she knew, was to extract information and then promises. Finally, she said, "Did Dora tell you my sister is married to her brother?"

"It is my impression that they have twelve or thirteen children."

"They have four children. Four boys."

"Dora does always seem to overestimate the negative effects of any number of children."

"Beatrice's boys are quite well behaved for Missouri boys. Not so"— she thought for a moment—"well armed as most."

Pete laughed.

"It's my other sister, Elizabeth, who has produced the prodigies." It was pleasant, after all, Margaret thought, the way Pete's willingness to be amused had infused her.

The door to Andrew's study opened, and Andrew came out, papers in one hand and a book in the other. He said, "My dear—" But then he saw Pete, tossed aside the book, and crossed the room in two strides. Pete stood up. They shook hands in a hearty way, and Andrew declared, "The thing is finished!"

He was talking about his manuscript.

Dora was forgotten, because the book he had tossed aside, which he now retrieved from the chair where it had landed, was a sample volume from a printer Andrew had unearthed in Oakland. The binding, green, was an excellent possibility. The title could, for only a small extra payment, be embossed in silver, and the front edge—Andrew stepped to the table and pushed the tea things aside. Margaret picked up her shawl and wrapped it around her shoulders. Later, she took the tea things back to the kitchen.

AFTER all, he chose deep ("navy") blue embossed covers with a silver title (*The Universe Explained,* by Captain Andrew Jackson Jefferson Early, Ph.D., United States Navy). The frontispiece was a picture of Andrew taken some years before, when his hair and his mustache were still dark. As Margaret held it in her hands, it seemed to her that it had arisen quite suddenly, popping into her presence as if from another world. The paper was glossy and the front edge gilded. The typeface, which Andrew chose on his own, was surprisingly appealing—upright and uncompromising, but friendly, just the way Andrew fancied himself to be. The pages of text were interspersed with ink drawings that Andrew had made. He had an elegant hand, as when he drew the impact craters from the shotgun experiment he had done with Hubert Lear. The endpapers were especially rich—swirls of blue and yellow that reminded her of the sky.

A thousand copies were printed. Andrew rented a room to store them, and paid a young man to send them out to every astronomical journal, geological journal, and physics journal in the world, also to twenty-five or so newspapers, from the *Times* of London to the *Sacramento Bee.* They were also sent to heads of observatories, and one, of course, to Mr. Akenbourn, in South Africa. One was sent, with

Andrew's compliments, to Oliver Lodge in England, another to Professor Russell at Princeton, another to Lord Rutherford at the University of Manchester. He sent them only to English speakers, and he sent these volumes as gifts, not as supplications. The rest he expected to sell to interested parties.

And that is that, thought Margaret with relief. He had gotten it off his chest.

"I have nothing to prove," he said to her one day at breakfast.

"Except your theory." She laughed, though he did not, so she added, "A man who is proposing a whole new way of looking at the universe has something to prove."

But he shook his head. "My task is to think through my theory as carefully as possible, working it out so that it is complete and self-contained. How can I prove it, with a five-inch telescope? Only those astronomers with expensive equipment can prove it, with mathematicians to back them up."

It was then that she saw how much he had to prove.

The first response was from Mr. Akenbourn, who congratulated Andrew on the "scope and depth of your analysis, and the pioneering genius of your ideas." But this letter was enclosed in the same envelope with another in a different handwriting, that of Mr. Akenbourn's daughter, who said that Mr. Akenbourn had died, but that he had been reading Andrew's book on his deathbed "and it seemed like he found it enjoyable, Captain Early, though his strength was waning very quickly. But he wanted to write you, and so he did. Yours in memory, Clara Akenbourn Maldon."

Oliver Lodge sent a card—"Many thanks. Very busy, all best, Lodge"—and *Science* noted it in the "Books Received" column. Andrew took this as a semi-promise that someone was even then busy reviewing it. It did receive an actual review from the *St. Louis Post-Dispatch* ("Missourian Sees the Big Picture") and the *Des Moines Register* ("Universe Like a Giant Net, Says Scientist"), and a few other, smaller papers, one in Australia. The editor of *Observatory,* which had published Andrew's letter on Einstein, sent a note—"Thanks for this, looks good." These acknowledgments dribbled in over the summer, to the swelling tune of Andrew's regrets.

Pete sent him a note asking for a copy of the book and offering to pay for it (Andrew sent it free, of course), and then, within a gratifyingly short time, Pete visited for the afternoon, just to discuss Andrew's theories. Andrew took this opportunity to walk Pete over to the observatory and show him the little telescope again. Over supper they talked about a happy subject, investments—Andrew's had flourished. He bragged a little that he had turned over his inheritance from his mother almost three times ("That's geometric, not arithmetic, you know"), and after a while Pete brought the conversation back around to the extraordinary way Andrew had managed to mesh "the *known* with the *unknown*." This conversation sustained Andrew's buoyant mood for days, and reconfirmed his sense of Pete's unusual talent. ("Not, perhaps, strictly speaking, genius, my dear, he's a bit too eclectic for that, but a rare understanding, at the very least. And it's no secret that Russians are easily distracted.")

DORA was one of several reporters assigned to cover the Preparedness Day parade—projected to be the biggest parade ever in San Francisco, and, everyone thought, a kind of ratification that San Francisco had resurrected itself, surpassed itself. Tens of thousands of people were to march, and fifty bands, ostensibly to show the Europeans where salvation was to be found, but really, Margaret gathered, to celebrate. Dora was assigned to ferret out interesting little moments, characteristic bits of San Francisco life. She persuaded Margaret to stay with her the night before, a Friday, and though she had not planned a party, the apartment was filled with friends and strangers who spilled into the hallway, down the stairs, and out into the park across the street, where Margaret saw Leonora and three women she didn't know gesturing with their glowing cigarettes in the late twilight.

By midnight, Margaret was sitting on the windowsill in one corner of the apartment, almost behind a drape, yawning, but enjoying the sparkly bustle in the street below, where four inebriates were singing "You Made Me Love You," and doing the harmonies quite nicely. Then Pete showed up, and he did not look happy. Margaret watched him make his way across the room to Dora, who was standing with Mal Cohen, and say something. Mal's eyebrows went up and Dora tossed her head, and Pete put his hands in his pockets. The three of them talked fairly earnestly for a while; then Pete wandered around the room. He had not taken off his hat. He spoke to this person and that person. Margaret tried to watch, and to gauge whether he was more interested in any other woman than he was in Dora, but her back kept crumpling against the window frame and her eyes kept closing. Perhaps he came up to her. Perhaps she heard his voice and felt a hand on her shoulder.

In the morning, Dora's attitude about the parade was slightly more subdued. She was ready to go, but not eager. At one point, she said to Margaret, "Darling, you could watch it perfectly well from here."

"No, I could not. I couldn't even see it!" exclaimed Margaret, pinning on her hat in front of Dora's big glass—bigger than any glass on the entire island, probably. Dora pursed her lips. They went down the staircase and out the front door, and turned toward the Embarcadero.

Margaret thought she was used to bustle, but she had never seen such a crowd before in her life, and it daunted her more than she expected. People were everywhere—on the sidewalks, on the streets, sitting in doorways, leaning out of windows. The parade was to march up Market Street, but it seemed that every street was full. She looked up. Boys were standing on roofs, and more than a few had shinnied up light poles. Hawkers peddled everything from umbrellas, to sardines wrapped in slices of bread, to apricot turnovers. Dora did not even look around as she snaked through the crowd. There were people tuning up their instruments and tightening their drums. Two ladies in uniforms marshaled a bunch of orphans into four straight lines, and two of the girls caught Margaret's eye as she passed. One of them, with blond braids to her waist, smiled. Margaret gazed at her, wondering how such a pretty girl had ended up at the orphanage.

That was when she lost Dora, who seemed to vanish like a fish through the surface of a pond. Margaret stopped and looked around. But it was impossible to stand, too, so she let the crowd move her along, only offering enough resistance so that she could keep the nearest corner—Battery and Market—in her sights. She and Dora had come down Bush Street, something of a hill—and it occurred to her that if the crowd got worse she could retreat back up the hill and still see at least part of the parade. She took a quarter out of her purse and gave it to a pushcart man. He handed her an appetizing-looking bun, sugar crystals sprinkled on top, but as she took it in her hand she had what could only be called a "turn," as Lavinia would say. The crowd closed around her and she began gasping. The man who had sold her the bun looked at her oddly, then said, "Hey, lady—" She remembered to do what she had thought to do so long before—she retreated up Bush Street. The effort was successful. Somehow, standing on the hill, seething though it was, calmed her nerves. She ate her bun.

When the flags and the first groups of horsemen came down the street, she could see them perfectly. Shouts went up. The ranks of the horsemen and then the first brass band were impressive—side by side, the trumpets, then the trombones and tubas stretched across the width of Market Street. Onlookers began to jump up and down, shouting and screaming. On the roof of the building across from the bottom of Bush Street, boys seemed to be firing their guns into the air. Margaret backed up a few steps, silly as that was, and looked upward. A bullet shot into the air, she knew, had to come down again. Suddenly, maybe at the sight of the boys on the roof, she remembered her father's saying that to her brother Ben.

The bomb went off right then. She heard it, faintly, and others around her did, too. Maybe she heard it because she was on the hill rather than down on Market Street. She didn't know it was a bomb— no one did, until the parade broke up and Market Street emptied. By that time, the news had circulated through the crowd. A bomb had gone off down by the Embarcadero, not far from the ferry building. The Wobblies had done it. They said they were going to and they did. Even as the rumor passed through the crowd and the crowd began to break apart, Margaret felt herself freeze up and disappear—yes, one bomb could be followed by others, but that had nothing to do with her. She climbed Bush Street, and she was hardly conscious of moving, even as she turned down Stockton toward Union Square. Crowds of people seemed to be pouring toward her from the east, and as time went on, their faces got more shocked. But they had nothing to do with her, she had disappeared. She asked two women what had happened, but they couldn't see or hear her—they didn't answer. Nevertheless, she came to know that the bomb had gone off on Steuart Street, at the bottom of Market, and there was blood everywhere. The bomb had been filled with lead sash-weights.

It took her two hours to get back to Dora's apartment, but she was not exactly frightened, she was too invisible for that, even as she stopped and waited at a Western Union office, sent Andrew a telegram saying she was fine and would be staying another night. Once inside Dora's place, she stood at the window, watching. It never occurred to her to worry about Dora—later, this confidence struck her as strange, but at the time, as she looked out the window, the havoc seemed to swirl below her, not touching her. It was Dora herself who brought it home and woke her up.

For something had taken off her hat—she had been standing that close. The flash and boom of the explosion, a rippling effect in the air, and then her hat flying off her head, followed by the screaming, the bodies, the dead, the wounded, the plunging horses, the running, pushing, pummeling people—she had hardly been able to keep her feet in the crush. But she had stayed there for an hour or more, her eyes peeled, and then slipped away to the *Examiner* building to write and file her story.

Margaret said, "I'm sorry I wasn't with you."

"I didn't want you with me, and I was right. What took off my hat was a lead weight of some kind that was packed into the bomb. It might have killed you. I was short enough to survive." Her tone was businesslike and direct.

After this, they were silent for a long period, sitting in the dark. Still Margaret wasn't afraid in a way that she recognized—now awake, she was thrilled in a physical sense, as if all her muscles had been suddenly struck and they were resonating. That bun she'd bought had frightened her more than the bomb, somehow. It was as if the bomb had fulfilled the prediction of the bun.

Dora said, "It was Mike Boda, not Sasha Berkman."

"What?"

"Did you see Pete last night? When he came over?"

"Maybe; I was very sleepy."

"He was upset, because he'd heard that Sasha Berkman is around. He shot Frick, remember that? But he's not a bomb-maker. I'm sure it was the Italians."

"You said the Italians are harmless."

"*Our* Italians are harmless. The Italians from Chicago are not harmless."

A long time after that, it occurred to Margaret to ask whether Pete knew Sasha Berkman—Sasha Berkman was a notorious anarchist. Dora said, "They are not friends by any means." Margaret saw again that Dora's life opened out like a funnel. She and Beatrice and Robert sat safely at the narrow tip, while people she would not have dared to know resided in the perilous and possibly malevolent distance. Still, she felt calm enough.

When the time came to retire, Dora insisted Margaret take the bed in the bedroom. She said, "I'm much too wrought up to be that far into the apartment. I might have to go out in the street and walk about a bit."

But she didn't go out. Margaret lay on her back and listened, a light cotton blanket pulled up to her chin. A clock struck one, and then another, more distant clock struck, and then she was dreaming of a crowd, of seeing a multitude of shoes and being unable to lift her head to look at the faces. One pair of shoes was her own, and another pair, a larger pair, kept pace with hers. They were walking through flattened grass and wild clover. Her voice asked where the bomb was, but no voice answered hers. It was the legs of the horses that made her nervous—she could only see them up to their knees. She asked again where the bomb was, but, though a hand pushed her from behind, no voice spoke. Now there was a dog, white with a black tail, and she reached out to touch it. The dog fell down and there was a gasp, as if all the people around her were watching the dog, and then she woke up.

The door had opened—she could see the glimmer of the gaslights from the hall, and, silhouetted in that light, a figure, or, rather (as she woke up more thoroughly), two figures made one, and then she heard Pete's voice as he said, "I told you not to go!"

Whatever Dora said in reply was muffled by his shoulder, because Margaret saw that he was holding her in a profound embrace, not even kissing her, but attempting to press her right into himself, as if in terror rather than in passion. Margaret sat up and leaned forward to get a better view, not abashed in the slightest, only as curious as she had ever been about anything. Dora seemed to rest in that embrace. Pete's hand came up and smoothed her hair. Then there was a sound, and Margaret realized that it was the sound of Dora weeping. Pete breathed out, "Ah, ah, ah." Margaret lay back down and turned away from the doorway. Moments passed, and then minutes. The sounds subsided, then the door was closed, footsteps crossed the room, and the sofa creaked. Sometime after that, Margaret fell back to sleep. When she got up at what seemed to be dawn, she could see Dora stretched out on the sofa, a pillow under her head, asleep. Pete was not there.

ANDREW began talking about how he should have written the book more clearly, he should have cut a lot of details—the big picture could have been easier for people to grasp. What if they were getting bogged down in chapter two or three, when the real meat of his theory was in chapter six and, especially, seven? And he should have put the equations in an appendix—he hadn't even thought of that, but it was the obvious thing. He could have written a sort of two-tiered book, with a text for "intelligent but nonspecialist" readers in one, larger typeface, and another text—essentially, an ongoing parade of footnotes, but linked, in a smaller typeface, for the ones who could truly understand what he was getting at ("as few as they may be"). Why had he been so impatient to get it printed? Another year of work would have enabled him to refine his theory, to demonstrate it more clearly, and the war over there might have ended, too, leaving room in the newspapers for a grand conception with long-term implications.

The book had been too advanced for a publisher, he accepted that, but the printer he'd used had kept throwing samples before him, tempting him to spend more and more money, taking advantage of his vanity. It wasn't the money wasted, because, thanks to investments, he was pulling money out of the air, but what would a scientist think when this heavy, deluxe publication arrived in the mail? It didn't look scientific. He had thought, another vanity, that his name alone would carry some weight, and maybe it did, but there was something about the book, he saw now, that was a kind of faux pas. And his haste in printing the thing had been matched by his haste in sending out copies, and now . . .

By October, he was literally tearing his hair and wringing his hands. He haunted their house, but then he began to range more widely—over to the observatory, then the Officers' Club, then into Vallejo. On one of these days, after she had cleaned the kitchen, she picked up one of the books and looked at it herself.

She managed to glean the gist of his argument, though it took considerable perseverance, many cups of tea, and a walk down the block to clear her head. It wasn't so much that she didn't recognize anything—

that moon-capture theory was there, set into the millions of years and millions and billions of what you would call cubic miles of space. What she understood seemed plausible. First there was gravity, which was a force exerted between masses, its strength dependent on their size. Then there was motion—those masses hurtling here and there, though not by any means quickly enough for someone such as herself to detect their movements with the naked eye. To gravity and motion, you added in the uneven population of space, empty here, full of galaxies there. When you combined that unevenness with the gravity and the motion, it was obvious (Andrew claimed) that the populous places were going to get more populous and the emptier places were going to get still emptier, because in the populous places, masses would come together and forces would get stronger and stronger until everything clumped together, and why not, given how long it was going to be? In the end, everything would clump together into one big mass, and then, within that mass, everything would change as the mass got hotter and hotter, and then the mass itself would get smaller but denser, and nothing could stop this from happening. The logical end to this process would be the disappearance of all mass, for once the mass had advanced to its logical conclusion, which was a dot that weighed as much as everything in the universe, the empty part would disappear also, though what constituted "disappearance" in this case she could not have told you. No doubt the problem was that words could not convey actual events, and, indeed, actual events were hardly imaginable. If you did find yourself, as she did, imagining something, then what you were imagining was wrong. But poor Andrew was more or less stuck with using words to describe their doom.

Except that, according to Andrew, his own researches showed that the universe, as big as it was, contained no empty space. This reminded her of something that Sherlock Holmes often did, which was to give the obvious solution, and then give the real solution, which relied on the one factor that only Holmes had discerned. The real story about the universe was that, although it appeared that gravitational force, mass, and motion would eventually produce collapse, the universe was actually filled with Something. Newton himself had known that the universe was filled with Something, and for convenience's sake, this Something was called Ether, or, to distinguish it from the chemical ether, Aether. This Something was the substance of the universe, some kind of thing that exerted a repulsive force insofar as it counteracted the tendency of the traveling masses to clump together in accordance with gravity and therefore eventually to contract to the size of a dot or a pinprick or an invisible point. The balance of these two processes (the Something filling the universe and pushing things away from one another, and gravity pulling things toward one another) resulted in a more or less even continuum of contracting and expanding. This process, Andrew seemed to be saying, was what was called Eternity.

She felt his presence while she was reading. When she was finished reading, she held the blue heavy book in her hand and contemplated it, not, now, as a miraculous object, but as evidence. There were people she knew who never once in their lives pondered the nature of the universe. Adam and Eve, the Garden of Eden, Noah's Ark, all of that was enough for them. Andrew was from her town. What in the world had set him on this path? A teacher? A book? Whatever it was, it was in some sense an argument against education—wouldn't he have been happier with smaller thoughts? As an investor, he was a whiz. As an observer of nature, such as after the earthquake, or out in the marshes, he was exact and careful. He could draw a bird or a flower or a diagram of a sewing machine. But day after day, year after year, he thought only of the universe, which he could not see.

Through the winter, Andrew pounded about the island on great walks which led him past the post office, and so he had to go in to see if some stray item of mail had been put, belatedly, into his box. When *Science* or some other journal came into the house, he tossed it on the table unread, and then circled around it for the rest of the day, eventually picking it up, leafing through it, and tossing it on the table again, with more vehemence. These magazines he didn't allow to stack up, as he had before—he threw them away in disgust after one perusal. His rage and dissatisfaction seemed to fill the place even when he was quiet. Margaret didn't dare engage him in discussion of these matters, because it seemed dangerous to her to give him a direction for venting his anger. She imagined him on his walks, his feelings flying out into the open air and exploding harmlessly, far from human habitation. Or, since the island was, if possible, even noisier than usual, she imagined his feelings diminished and subsumed in the general racket.

She distracted him, instead, with a safer topic—the war news. Did he really think, in December, that the Germans wanted peace? Was Wilson's letter about this sincere, in Andrew's opinion? Had his travels in Germany taken him to this area they were now calling "the Hindenburg Line"? And she did distract him: Andrew exclaimed that this line represented something about the Germans—it was mysteriously east of where many German outposts had been—but then the mystery was solved (vindicating him once again) when the Germans destroyed everything to the west of the line, stitched the blasted territory with land mines, and retreated into their impregnable fortress.

But, whatever the news, it did not keep his mind off Einstein for very long. He threw the scientific journals away, then retrieved them from the trash pile, read them, and saw that Einstein's silly theory was gaining adherents in spite of the war. He thought, though bitterly, that he had to write another book, a better one, refining and clarifying his theory, and incorporating the improvements to it that he had come up with. He stormed about the house (and the island), lamenting the injustice of having to write another book.

And his mood began to lift. On the one hand, he told her, he could easily let himself continue to indulge in vain regrets about how he should have written the book differently, or how he had been, in his enthusiasm, premature. On the other hand, he could revise his work, which would take two or three years but result in something more persuasive. Really, he said, he could see it quite clearly, and it was certainly true that every bitter pill contained within itself the sweet grain of a larger renewal. How often did he compare his situation to that of C—— now? The very five-inch telescope that he had looked upon with such chagrin the day he arrived on the island was now precious to him, while certainly C——, who then seemed so fortunate, must now feel enslaved by his monster. If he just explained himself a little more clearly, he would win in the end. Margaret found herself offering to type for him two hours every day—it seemed a small thing, a way of assuaging, or directing, or deflecting the energy coursing through the house. She had learned to do it, and it was easy for her—not that different from knitting.

WITHIN two days of the Zimmermann telegram, in which Germany tried to enlist Mexico against the U.S., and California turned out to be, at least in Margaret's imagination, very close to the front lines, Dora received permission to go to Europe—first England, then France, then who knew? Her column was to be called "In Another Part of the World." Margaret was shocked. For the entire autumn, Dora had talked to Margaret admiringly about Pete, and though she hadn't actually spoken the word "wedding" or the word "marriage," there was an intensity to her feelings for him—he had brought her an orchid in a pot made of a coconut, he had taken her to the Cliff House for oysters. Remember the way he had accompanied her to Fresno to interview that man in jail named Osmond Jacobs who had a powder burn on his cheek the day after the bombing and anarchist connections? At the jail, Pete had helped her conduct the interview in French.

When they came to the island for two suppers, they sat close together and finished each other's sentences. He took her to meet the editor of a famous poetry magazine, and the two women gossiped like old friends about Ezra Pound. Pete promised to introduce Dora to Emma Goldman, and Dora talked about writing a book.

But then she had her ticket—on the *Norfolk,* through the Panama Canal, thence to Southampton. She was to leave in ten days.

DORA made one last trip to the island, by herself. With her she brought some things of Pete's—a scroll and two screens, all wrapped in various layers of silk and paper. Pete had disappeared. Dora said she didn't know where to, but Margaret suspected that she did. Margaret was reluctant to take the artworks, because she was sure they were valuable, and Quarters P was a monument to disarray. But evidently she had to—there was nowhere else for them as safe as the island. More important, Dora herself looked to Margaret petite and easily damaged, all the while laughing and excited for her new adventures. And then, on the very Monday after she set sail, a letter arrived for Andrew from an editor at the *Examiner,* inviting him to serve as science correspondent for the paper. The editor said that he had heard that Andrew was "one of the foremost astronomers in the world" and "entirely up to date on every new scientific development" and "one of the smartest men in California" and "a prolific writer." He would be paid a penny a word.

It was a shock, but once war was declared, shocks came every day— one day they heard that the Germans blew up one of their own ships as it was being boarded by marines. Within a few days after that, San

Francisco Bay was being blockaded against enemy ships, a destroyer was attacked off Long Island, Field Marshal Haig, the British commander, was advancing first one mile and then another against the Hindenburg Line, and killing thousands of civilians while doing so. But even so, for the first while, Margaret could not help seeing the whole thing as the wreck of her own life and her own plans—she thought about Dora every day while she was out with the other naval wives who lived on the island, gathering provisions or charitable contributions, while she was sorting clothing and medical supplies to be sent to Europe, while she listened to herself talking about harvests and factories as she had never done before (although she could hardly imagine what it was they were talking about—wheat, barley, oats, workers, bosses, pig iron, output).

AND then spies blew up a powder magazine over by the bay one morning around breakfast time. The explosion was a body-shaking roar followed by a brilliant swoosh as that building and several others around it went up in flames. Margaret grabbed the edges of the table, the dishes jumped, her glass of water fell over, and Andrew's cup of coffee rattled in its saucer. It was much more frightening than the earthquake had been, or the small explosion that had welcomed her to the island so many years before.

Andrew leapt from the breakfast table and left the house. Margaret went out more slowly, first to the stoop, and then to the walk. Everyone on the island was outside, either running toward or staring at the biggest fire any of them had ever seen. She got her shawl and bag without giving Dora, or Pete, or their "marriage" a thought, and ran to the hospital. Her friends were there—they didn't know what they could do, but they thought something would present itself, if only fetching and carrying. At the hospital, she heard all the rumors—about the marine who had been knocked cold on patrol three nights before by an intruder, and about the men who had been seen around the island, and about how there were Germans all over the place whom the navy itself had charge of, and who was watching them? Five people were killed, including two children, and dozens injured. In the days after that, Margaret had her typing done by nine in the morning, and then went straight to the hospital. She hardly thought any longer of what now seemed like the utterly vanished life of not being at war.

But Andrew was unmoved by the war. Even though the entire knitting circle thought that the Germans had paid members of the IWW to get onto the island and blow up that magazine as a warning, he thought that the powder in the magazine had heated up overnight, and a rush of air into the building in the morning had set it off. Nor was he daunted, in his daily walks to the observatory, by what they saw around them— ash and rubble, death and burned-out buildings from the explosion, but also new buildings meant for the war effort seeming to shoot out of the ground. However, he allowed her to lock their doors, which they had never done.

Andrew did wonder aloud about Pete—he regretted not having him around as a sounding board for his expanded theories of the universe. Margaret had nothing to say about Pete. Like everything else, thinking of him reminded her only that fresh waves of men were getting shot every day, for either fighting or defending, spying or deserting.

Dora's pieces began to appear, the first entitled "My Woman Lorry Driver," about a trip she took between London and Southampton with a twenty-year-old girl who was transporting cabbages. Dora then got from England to France, made her way from Calais to Bordeaux, then over to Pau, Marseilles, and Genoa. She skirted the front lines, though not the war. Her tone was adventurous rather than fearful, and each time Margaret read one of Dora's pieces, she thought that her wish— her attempt—to keep Dora away from the war had been worse than futile and worse, even, than selfish. Surely Dora and Pete had known exactly what she was doing and laughed at her for trying to trim their adventurous lives to the dull pattern of her own. Her embarrassment lingered even when the dispatches from Italy began to sound worried—"Portrait of a Family That Has Lost Five Sons (Savona, Italy)," "A Russian Speaker Is Silenced by Doubt (Lucca, Italy)," "Children on the Beach (Portofino, Italy)," and "Opinionated in Parma." The pieces conformed to a pattern: Dora would set out to find a loaf of bread or to enjoy a patch of fine weather or to meet a long-lost friend, and she would encounter someone—in one case, children playing with a battered ball, whose father had been killed in the war and whose mother had disappeared a week before. Dora talked to them and gave them money, but when she returned with a local priest who promised to help, the children had vanished. The opinionated young woman in Parma was German. Her opinions concerned the catalogue of crimes committed against the Germans by the French, the English, the Russians, and the Americans. Dora quoted her without comment. She lingered in Parma for three weeks, then went east to Bologna, and farther east to Padua. She kept moving toward the war, recording the hardships that she saw, but with that same idle, wandering tone. In a piece called "Three Nights in the Mountains," she was driving from Padua to Perugia when her car broke down. She saw no one but deer, hawks, and a wildcat for three days. The village she walked to was abandoned. Then two men came along in a wagon. There was also "Hidden Treasures of Ravenna," in which she reflected on someone named Theodoric, who had previously conquered Italy from the north and was buried there. In "I Am Grazed by a Bullet," she related how the sleeve of her jacket was torn by a bullet outside of Trieste, which everyone seemed to be fleeing. But by the time the Italians lost the battle of Caporetto, Dora's dispatch was from Rome, and after that two weeks went by and she was in Spain, far from the fighting ("Toro!")—her Trieste experience seemed to have aroused a belated sense of caution. Beatrice wrote that the Bells did not read her articles, and put her letters away in a box, unopened. Bit by bit, Margaret forgave herself for trying to save Dora. Like everything else from before the war, she thought, the idea of "saving" things seemed the rankest delusion.

There was no word of Pete at all.

The two screens had been wrapped in blankets and tied with twine.

One day, she laid the first one on the rug and untied the wrappings. The screen consisted of four panels, each about two feet wide, depicting a mountainous scene. To the left and to the right, rugged slopes rose in the foreground, steeper than anything she had seen even in the Sierras. In the middle of the scene, more distant peaks were still more jagged, and on those slopes, several stunted pine trees were bunched together. The mountains were painted in a vaporous dark ink, so as to seem especially threatening, and the farthest ridges were partly hidden by clouds. A river flowed through a U-shaped cleft in the mountains, and in the river floated a long narrow boat with a rounded prow, carrying a man in a kimono. Her eye was drawn straight to the tiny face of the man, who was sitting quietly, looking upward, not, it seemed, in fear, but in curiosity and interest. The water flowed, the clouds drifted, the trees huddled, but the man seemed undaunted by his surroundings.

The second screen was smaller—only about four feet tall—also four panels, entirely painted on gold. The largest object was a black tree with rough bark, twisted and bending to the left. Willowlike fronds of leaves seemed to toss in a breeze. Turf, or perhaps moss, spread in irregular dark-green patches around the trunk of the tree, and colorful birds flew in and out among the blowing leaves, or perched on rocks sunk into the moss. Above the tree, golden clouds billowed in the golden sky. To the left, clouds of red flowers on long, frondlike stems also tossed about, and the branches and leaves of some other variety of tree, something like a plane tree, spread across the golden horizon. She stood this screen up beside the first one and stared from one to the other, taking in both effects—the startling and the soothing. She found herself breathing deeply, as if she could inhale their atmosphere or fragrance. She sat there for hours, it seemed, but possibly little more than a single hour. When Andrew came in, he stepped in front of her and surveyed the two, then said, "My dear, so this is what they look like. He offered them to me."

"To buy?"

"Why, of course, my dear. As an investment. But my mind was on other things, and the subject dropped, as I remember."

"They are beautiful."

"But not for display, my dear, in such humble surroundings as ours. I see that."

This seemed true. He helped her wrap them up again, and put them away. At supper, he said, "It has crossed my mind to wonder what we shall do with them."

So, Margaret thought, Andrew thinks Pete is dead, too.

Her daily round consisted of typing, cooking, knitting scarves, packing boxes, and discussing with the other naval wives the ins and outs of the million things that they did not understand, including what to think of the dead whose names they knew, among all of the dead whose names they did not know.

On the first anniversary of the U.S.'s entrance into the war, it seemed to Margaret to have lasted much longer than a year. The island was never silent at any time of the day or night. One thing happened that was amusing even to the knitting ladies—when the Secretary of the Navy had issued an edict saying that there could be no sales of liquor within five miles of a naval base, liquor and beer left town by the wagonload, and there was a funeral for "John Barleycorn" that passed down Sonoma Street. The corpse was a coffin-load of empty whiskey bottles. She remembered this because it was on this very day when Andrew commented on a disease outbreak in Kansas. "Strange thing, my dear. Very sudden, and it's not as if Fort Riley is at a crossroads. The Katy doesn't even pass through there." He shook his head; she felt her habitual inner clang of alarm, and then, in mid-May, he said, "Now, here, this Fort Riley thing, remember that, my dear? Very like this flu they've had in Spain." He wrote a column about it for the *Examiner,* but it was bumped from the paper by the Battle of the Marne. Things were so busy that she forgot about her fortieth birthday until three days after the date.

He went to the Base Commandant about it—one morning, he merely walked down their street and knocked on the Commandant's front door. The Commandant was in, and Andrew told him about what he considered to be the Fort Riley/Spain connection, though what that could be Margaret didn't understand. When Andrew got home half an hour later, all he said was "He listened." Then he went into his study and closed the door.

The news was about the Allies' advancing from one French city to another, and "the Bolsheviki" in Russia, who had slaughtered the Tsar and his family—nothing about the Spanish flu. But Andrew found out that the receiving ship at the Commonwealth Pier in Boston was overflowing with very ill sailors. Only a few days after that, Andrew heard that dozens were falling ill at Fort Devens, also in Massachusetts. He walked back up the street. Boston was far away. But, then, Kansas was far from Spain, too, and Spain was far from Boston. It was a mystery, but Andrew was determined that its mysteriousness would not lull the Commandant into apathy, even though the man had plenty of other matters to deal with. In early September, Andrew wrote about the Massachusetts outbreak in his *Examiner* column; the next day, the mayor declared that the influenza would never come to San Francisco and that to suggest that it would was irresponsible in the extreme. Andrew did not flinch, but said to her, "My dear, they may all *hope* that the influenza will not come, but I will nevertheless be vindicated."

The first case appeared toward the end of September. In two weeks, the base hospital was full. Cases cropped up in Vallejo. The Commandant issued face masks to everyone, and Andrew insisted she use one. About a week later, Margaret was standing on their walk, surveying her flowers, when she saw Evie Marquardt, who lived one door down from the Pritchards, come out of her house to the porch and sink to her knees. Margaret didn't know what to do, but then she pulled up her mask and went and helped Evie back into the house and onto her sofa. When she came home, Andrew made her wash her skin and hair with lye soap and leave her dress on the back stoop. He sent a passing sailor to the hospital to report Mrs. Marquardt's illness, and about an hour later, they came to get Evie in the ambulance wagon. She survived. Tales abounded—four women playing cards until midnight, three of them dead by morning. Roger Mattock, on the hospital ship, took water and food to all of the patients, but never got sick. Everyone on a certain block in Vallejo came down with it, except the ladies living at the brothel. Then the Commandant himself was near death, but he survived; Captain Asch, home on leave from China, never got ill but was killed by a motor truck late at night. It seemed death was all around them, especially every time Margaret was delegated to write the notification letter to the family of a victim.

Dear Mr. and Mrs. Smith,
The United States Navy regrets to inform you that your son, Evan Walter Smith, seaman third class, has succumbed to the Spanish flu during the recent outbreak. He reported to sick bay at 11:30 on the morning of October 6, 1918. The progress of the illness was rapid, and he succumbed to a catarrh of the lungs during the evening of October 8. Owing to the highly contagious nature of the disease, all victims at the naval base have been buried in the cemetery on the island. A service was held for your son and the other victims who died on October 8 in the nondenominational chapel on October 9. We regret that they have had to take these summary measures owing to the virulence of the disease. Your son's effects have been disinfected, and will be shipped to you in a separate parcel. All inquiries may be addressed to me, George McCracken, Commandant of the Base.

I am yours, regretfully

And Margaret, in her turn, lived in fear of letters. Beatrice's son Lawrence succumbed, but Beatrice and Robert lived. Elizabeth, Lucy May, and Eloise never came down with it, but Mercer almost died.

Dora lived, though she was in Cairo and Jerusalem. The Lears lived, but Hubert, in the navy off Jutland, died and was buried at sea. The sailor who washed their windows lived; his friend died. Mrs. Wareham and her daughter Cassandra lived, but Angus and his wife and child died. Mrs. Kimura lived, though she continued to visit every sort of patient, according to Mrs. Wareham. Naoko lived.

On Armistice Day, everyone Margaret knew or heard of was exhausted or changed by the Great War except for Andrew. In between the bookends of Andrew's two vindications, the powder-magazine explosion and the Spanish flu, every day had had its frightening news or its dire thought. The lesson of every incident was that forces were at work beyond their comprehension, and also that there were more people than one had ever imagined busily wrestling with those forces. Margaret didn't know where all these people came from. When the papers gave the toll of the dead on the European and Eastern fronts, it was almost impossible to believe that so many humans could have presented themselves to the bullet or the bomb, or, indeed, the poison gas, and yet there were still more left behind, and it was the same with the epidemic—the numbers of those who died were astonishing except in comparison with the numbers who survived. Like everyone she knew or read about, she agreed with the title of one of Dora's pieces, this one sent from Cairo, "My Life Didn't Prepare Me for This." Dora was writing about the mysteries of the Khan el-Khalili bazaar. Margaret was thinking about everything in the whole world.

ANDREW decided that, given the end of the war and his responsibilities writing his science column for the *Examiner,* Margaret should double her typing time—two hours in the morning and two hours in the afternoon, but not while he was sleeping, "as the tap-tap-tapping has a uniquely disturbing effect on my sleep, my dear." Margaret pointed out that she had other activities to occupy her time, but the only one that he would acknowledge was cleaning, which she should do quietly while he was sleeping. One night at the dinner table, she declared that she had her own projects, and Andrew said, with a rare flash of anger, "My dear, we both must put away idleness for the sake of the greater interests that draw us forward and outward. Am I enlisting you in a cause? Indeed, I am. I have a forum, and I am obligated to use it. Must I remind you . . . ?" He let this part die away, but she knew what he meant.

Soon she saw that he had still another project in mind.

You could buy a car for almost any amount of money, from five hundred dollars for a roadster with two seats, to six thousand or so for a limousine. For several months, Andrew took the ferry to San Francisco and explored the cars available while she typed her pages. At first he was drawn to the Locomobile. But they were expensive, and in the end he chose the Franklin five-passenger, which he said cost only fifty dollars more than the Franklin Roadster, though it was much bigger. Andrew thought this pricing practice was a sign of the intelligence of Mr. Franklin, who "can see that the real cost of the automobile is in the engine and the manufacturing process. The point of pricing is to draw customers of all types, not to penalize those who need a smaller or larger chassis." He felt that if Mr. Franklin were to become acquainted with him, he would appreciate Andrew (and would, no doubt, agree with his views about Dr. Einstein). But he did not plan to learn to drive the car. That was to be her job, like the typing.

Right about this time, the knitting group began to buzz with the news that Mrs. Tillotson had sued her husband for divorce, and Margaret said one thing: "Is it because she has to drive the car?" The ladies looked at her quizzically, and Mrs. Gess laughed out loud, as if she had made a successful joke, but the divorce had nothing to do with cars—it had to do with adultery. Mr. Tillotson had a mistress in Oakland, *with* a child. He had bought the woman a house, and it was the house that was the last straw for Mrs. Tillotson. The ladies then discussed what might make them divorce their husbands. Mrs. Jones said that you couldn't get a divorce for just anything—adultery was one thing; the others were conviction for a felony, fraud, drunkenness, "really bad beatings," or if the fellow ran away. All the ladies shook their heads as if they had never heard of such things. Mrs. Gess said, "Well, Henrietta Tillotson is brazen enough to do it." Margaret couldn't decide if her tone was admiring or disapproving, but she thought, yes, only Henrietta—she did have a surface, a kind of glaze, that was bold and worldly. The woman had always reminded her more of Andrew than even of Dora or Mrs. Bell. Mrs. Tillotson stopped coming to the knitting group.

But how she was to learn to drive she did not quite know. She explained her dilemma to Mrs. Wareham, Naoko, and Cassandra over tea one afternoon, without voicing her profound resentment of the whole thing. Naoko said, "My mother and I can teach you. My mother got rid of the horse and bought a Dodge Brothers Roadster for her rounds. Father won't go in it, but I ride with her all the time. We've driven to Napa and Benicia and once to Fairfield. Joe and Lester drive it, too."

Margaret said, "I hardly know your mother. Would she mind?"

"She loves driving," said Naoko. "I think she would enjoy it."

Naoko was not the girl she had been. Perhaps she was close to thirty now and still unmarried—her father did not want her to marry an American man, and she did not care for any of the Japanese men they knew. Naoko's opinion was that her brothers would marry, and when they did, would those wives take care of Mr. and Mrs. Kimura? Naoko doubted it very much. And so she was as free as a Japanese woman could be only in America, with indulgent parents, no husband, and no mother-in-law. "It's not as if she can't see the nose on her face," said Mrs. Wareham.

"Doesn't she want children?"

"Do you? Does anyone now?"

Margaret thought of Dora and Pete—her one and only matchmaking project—and then of all those letters she had written to bereaved mothers. Mrs. Wareham, no doubt, thought of her son, Angus. They sighed simultaneously. Alexander, if he had not died in this very house, would have had other chances to die. It was impossible not to be a realist.

The Kimuras' shop was still spic-and-span and jammed with many unidentifiable (at least to Margaret) packets, tins, and bottles. Mr. Kimura, who looked much the same also, only more precisely and dryly himself, welcomed her with a bow, and then went through the curtain to the back. Mrs. Kimura came out in her Japanese manner—though she was dressed in American clothes, her hands were folded together and her head dipped politely forward. Margaret bowed to her and then to her husband. The two women left the shop. Once again, though, as they walked toward where the car was kept, the midwife straightened up and her steps got longer; she looked around, too, as you would in a place like this, where there were people of all ages, types, and nationalities, doing all sorts of business. Margaret had to walk a little faster to keep up with her. By the time they were in the motorcar, driving toward the edge of town, Mrs. Kimura bore very little similarity to the woman in the shop. Looking at her, Margaret got her first inkling of the possibilities of driving an automobile.

But she also saw, as soon as she was seated behind the circle of wood that was the wheel, that realizing those possibilities was not going to be easy. A person had two hands and two feet. A car had three pedals and four levers, not to mention the steering wheel, and, unlike a horse, a car did not even begin to look where it was going. If it went. The hardest part for her was something called the "clutch," which seemed to have its own ideas about how far in you pushed it with your foot. The problem with this clutch was that when it popped out the car's motor died, and there you were, having to go through all those steps to start it up again. The clutch was under the left foot. Margaret had never before realized that her left foot was rather stupid. What it was most like, in its way, was sewing on a sewing machine operated by a foot pedal, but, then, she had always operated the foot pedal with her right foot.

Mrs. Kimura was sympathetic and good-natured, even after Margaret had stalled the engine what seemed like a dozen times. All Mrs. Kimura did was smile and say, "You must be pleased this is Dodge car, not Ford car. Very difficult, Ford car. No starter. You get out every time. But even though this car four year old, it has starter." Margaret thought going to the front of the car every time she killed the motor would be a lot of exercise.

At last, she managed to drive in a lurching loop around the pasture, arrive at her starting place, go forward again for a little bit, and then stop and turn the car off without feeling it more or less collapse underneath her. Mrs. Kimura came around to her side, and Margaret moved over. Mrs. Kimura took the wheel, and patted her on the wrist. She said, "We have plenty time." They drove smoothly back to the garage and put the car away—that was all. No one received it, groomed it, fed it. Mrs. Kimura turned it off with a tiny key called a "magneto" key, and they walked away from it.

Her freedom, on her driving days, was complete. She took the ferry to Vallejo, moseyed toward the Kimuras' shop, ate a bite, went into a few shops, and sensed Andrew diminishing in size to a distant point, as did the typewriter. Nor did he object to her being out for most of the day—they both knew that practice was essential. Soon she was bringing all sorts of gifts to the Kimuras, oranges and flowers and boxes of divinity. The gifts were accepted graciously, of course, and she therefore felt that she had to outdo herself, and so, one day, on the last day, she rustled Pete's old hand scroll out of the closet. She had never looked at it, and she thought perhaps Mr. and Mrs. Kimura would enjoy opening it with her.

She drove all through the streets of Vallejo that day, a fragrant, sunny spring day, a break from eight or nine days of fog and drizzle. She stopped and started, paused, turned left and right, used her clutch with amazing smoothness—amazing to her. Mrs. Kimura sat quietly, smiling pleasantly and occasionally waving to people they passed. They were back at the shop by about three, and instead of bowing, shaking Mrs. Kimura's hand, and departing, she bowed and opened her bag. She said, "I wish to show you what Pete Krizenko left in my keeping, and to learn from you and Mr. Kimura all about it."

When she saw what Margaret had, Mrs. Kimura hurried into the back of the shop. She said something Margaret could hear in Japanese, and Mr. Kimura appeared at once. Margaret offered him the scroll. He took it gently, and led her into the back. There was a long table there, and he set the scroll down. Mrs. Kimura picked up the flower arrangement that was on the table and took it into the front room.

Margaret had imagined that the scroll would be some sort of wide picture, like the screens (which she had looked at once again since the first time), but it was, rather, a tall picture, about twenty inches wide and about four feet high. As Mr. Kimura unrolled it, from top to bottom, nothing appeared except some gray coloring, shaped like the slope of a mountain seen through the mist—hardly a shape at all, and yet present. Then there was a light-colored, sharp outline that turned into a wide-brimmed hat. At last there was a face, and bright color— a blue collar, a green sash. When the picture was entirely flat, Mr. Kimura grinned. The picture was of three figures—a tall woman (the one wearing the hat), who was looking down at a child, whose hand she was holding; behind them was another figure, short and leaning to the side, which could have been either male or female—no doubt a servant. The servant was also looking at the child, who was looking up at the woman, presumably his mother. The servant was dressed in a rich bronze color, the child in a softer tan that echoed the color of the mother's hat. From their posture, it seemed as though the three were walking against a heavy breeze. At the bottom of the picture, she could see that they were treading through wavelets or puddles, carefully picked out in thin black curving lines—an everyday scene, two adults and a child making their way on a stormy day, but marvelously arresting.

Mr. Kimura said something in Japanese, and Mrs. Kimura said to her, "Is noble lady with son and servant. We have always honored Mr. Pete for discernment, but we never see picture before. Is very fine one." She bowed as if the picture reflected well on her. Margaret bowed back.

They conversed some more; then Mrs. Kimura said, "Might be hundred years old, according to fashion of lady, and worth much money."

Then again, "Mr. Kimura sorry that ignorance prohibits him from recognizing artist even though name here." She pointed to an ideogram.

They looked at the picture for a few more minutes, and then carefully rolled it up again, wrapping it. Now that she knew what it was, Margaret was rather frightened at having brought it out. She glanced out the window at the sky. All of these Japanese pictures seemed too fragile—merely paper. But some of them were hundreds of years old.

When she had put her picture away in her bag, Mr. Kimura went to a cabinet and brought out a picture of his own and opened it on the table. It was entirely different from Pete's, and yet also arresting and mysterious. Mrs. Kimura said, "Is not painting, but woodblock print. Is by Utagawa Hiroshige." She pointed to a column of writing in the lower right corner.

It was a small picture, possibly a foot high or a little more, and not ten inches wide—the size of an illustration in a book—a moonlit scene. In the dim distance, to the right, a pine-tree-covered hill rose out of a flat plain. The whole upper half of the picture was made up of a sky, the tiny stars picked out in varying intensities (this was a picture she thought that Andrew would like). In the foreground, to the left, was a sizable leafless tree. Looking at the branches, Margaret realized that the ground was covered with moonlit snow. Mr. Kimura waved his hand over the figures bunched at the base of the tree, and Mrs. Kimura said, "Foxes under moon." The foxes were pale yellow, their bodies merely outlined. There were fifteen or twenty of them, looking to the right, clearly on the alert for something. Though they did not look like any foxes she had ever seen, they had the demeanor of foxes.

What was remarkable to her about the print, like the painting, was the feel of the weather—so chill and still. Only the foxes, picked out by the light of the invisible moon, were animated. Mrs. Kimura said, "Utagawa Hiroshige very famous in Japan."

Margaret regarded the picture. The odd thing was that, even though she wanted it, or something like it, and even though Andrew had plenty of money, and even though she had learned to drive the car, and even though she went to San Francisco every couple of weeks, she could not imagine how to get such a thing for her own, such a grand and comforting thing.

THE FRANKLIN was a soothing sage green with black fenders, a tan top, and a black leather interior seat—indeed, the seat was thickly padded and sewn with deep tucks, like a luxurious sofa. The steering wheel was some rich golden wood. The front end of the car swept downward, giving it a birdlike quality. The top folded forward or back, as one wished. The man they bought it from parked it on the street in front of their little house, and Margaret watched through the front window as Andrew promenaded out of the house, marched down to the street, and then stopped and put his hands in the pockets of his navy-blue captain's jacket with the stripes on the sleeve. He pushed back his cap and lifted his chin and stared into the engine. Then he paraded around the car once or twice, opened up the hood, and stared at the air-cooled engine. If people stopped to look (and they did—navy men were always interested in machinery), he would tell them more about the air-cooled engine than they wanted to know—that it dispensed entirely with the problems of water-cooling, and that this famous person and that famous person would own only a Franklin. Margaret was ready to drive it—and she did drive it one time, over the causeway that now made Vallejo more accessible but had not replaced the ferry, and around the streets of Vallejo, to Mrs. Wareham's and then to the Kimuras', just to show them. But it took a week for Andrew to get in.

Then they did get in, Margaret in the driver's seat and Andrew enormous beside her. She let out the clutch and stepped on the starter, and they rolled away from the curb to the sound of the wheel spokes knocking. After that she saw him more in the car than in the house, and at closer quarters. It surprised her that he would leave his work, but it seemed that the feeling of rolling along, of being looked at and admired, of having to say nothing while knowing that the Franklin was saying something for him, was a feeling he could not get enough of. And then he was invited to give a speech, and instead of turning down the offer because he had too much writing to do, he went. She drove him all the way to Fairfield. His speech was not about the universe at all, but about the bubonic plague—his vindication with regard to the influenza gave him a great fondness for diseases of all kinds, so he read up on every infection in the news. He chose the bubonic plague as more dramatic than the influenza—the Yunnan outbreak in China in the 1850s and, once a war broke out there and thousands of people fled southward, outbreaks in Canton, Hong Kong, Taiwan, Bombay, Calcutta, and then on to Africa. Perhaps, Andrew exclaimed, perhaps the members of the audience recalled the plague outbreaks of 1899 in Egypt, or South Africa, or Hawaii, or, indeed, in San Francisco? San Francisco was the only city in America to host an outbreak of the plague. Did they remember (a few heads in the audience nodded) the first outbreak in 1900 and the second five years later, just before the earthquake? Did they shiver, as he did, not only at the gruesome symptoms, but also at what might have happened after the earthquake if Dr. Blue (a navy man) had not acted with such wisdom and dispatch? Of course they did! And did they know that, even as he was speaking to them here in Fairfield, the California countryside was full of plague-carrying rats that were crawling with fleas? Sixty thousand had died in Canton, a hundred thousand in Hong Kong alone! Where was the plague now? Who could say, except that it seemed to be in Russia, or, as they called it now, "the Union of Soviet Socialist Republics" (he said this with a snort).

The audience could hardly sit in their seats.

He went on to diphtheria, scarlet fever, cholera, typhus—describing symptoms and outbreaks, giving advice (washing hands, boiling drinking water, properly disposing of sewage and garbage). "We know how to stop these grave ills in their tracks, how to conquer them or keep them at bay! But we have to be alert! We have to attend to rather than ignore the living conditions of our fellow citizens, and the hygiene of our friends and family members!"

The talk was a sensation.

Through the fall and into the spring, he gave a version of this speech in Vallejo, Napa, Dixon, Benicia, as far south as Atherton and San Jose, as far north as Calistoga. They drove to all of these places, and Margaret was startled by the variety of the California landscape. Groups asked him back, and he returned, joyfully, with a presentation about the universe.

From his talk about the universe, you would have assumed that that fellow in Europe—what was his name?—Einstein, who was getting so much play in the papers (but really, as she looked around at the audience, more people looked blank at the name than otherwise), was a mere fabulist. For these lectures, Andrew carried a small thick book with a red leather cover, and right in the middle of the lecture, he would hold the book above his head and exclaim the word "Gravity!," then let go of the book, which would land with a smack on the stage. Then he would say, "The Earth has gravity! Gravity is a force. If the Earth did not have gravity, then this book would not drop to the boards here, but would flooooooat on the air. And the *book!*"—he would pick up the book—"the book has gravity, too! The book is drawing the Earth to itself, just as the Earth is drawing the book to itself! The sun exerts this force! The moon exerts this force! You exert this force! I exert this force!" Then he would turn, with his arms raised in a sweeping gesture, and say, "Do you see any hills on this stage? Do you see any slopes that might cause this book to *sl-l-l-ide* down toward the stage?" Long pause, a few shaking heads. "Do you?"

Some man always shouted, "No!"

"So gravity cannot be a slope, created by curvature. There is no curvature here. Remember this—you can't have one thing in one part of space and another thing in another part! You can't say that the universe is curved but this stage"—he stomped his feet—"isn't, so gravity works one way in one place and another way in another place. Gravity is a force!"

In a talk of an hour (including questions—he was great at answering questions), he demolished Einstein in about ten minutes and spent the rest of the time explaining what the universe was really like. After these talks, men buttonholed Andrew and gave him their own theories, while women patted Margaret on the hand and said, "So brilliant! How fortunate you are to be married to such an interesting man!"

When, much to Margaret's surprise, Einstein made a well-publicized trip to America, and then, according to Andrew, "went about hawking his crazy opinions everywhere," Andrew wasn't as offended as she expected him to be. He just shook his head, and said, "The ignorant and the enthusiastic are impressed, my dear, but see here—no invitation from Harvard, and Princeton has only let him in the back door. I am sure he expected much more, given his connections. My strategy must be to go on as I have begun and put my faith in the inherent good sense of our countrymen." The only other time he said anything about it was one day in the summer, after reading one of his long-delayed papers from the East. "Here. You see, Patne agrees with me. He maintains that Einstein partook of our American generosity, but now has spurned us. No great loss. No great loss indeed." At lectures, Margaret noticed that, while Andrew stuck to his usual script, his tone when discussing the fellow was more heavily and openly amused. When Einstein won the Nobel Prize at the end of that year for "The Photoelectric Effect" and not for his "silly theories," Andrew felt he had been vindicated. He mentioned the prize in one lecture, in Oakland. He said, in response to a question about it, "You see, he might have been an excellent scientist if he had focused his ideas. It is a very sad thing when an intelligent man compounds the demonstrable with the ridiculous."

At the same time, he dedicated himself to his correspondence. Many of his columns grew out of questions readers wrote in to him: How does ice form on a window? Does whiskey serve to disinfect the body? Did he foresee any imminent earthquakes? The scientific ignorance of the average newspaper reader came as an appalling shock to him, but only redoubled his sense that his newspaper and public-speaking work were important. He composed many more columns than the *Examiner* published—even without a war, the pages of the paper were filled, unaccountably to Andrew, with many other things besides science.

Little did these small-town lecture and Chautauqua committees who were directed to Andrew by the *Examiner* know that he would have gladly spoken to them for free. He took what they offered, and some of them were flush and offered as much as a hundred dollars. As she drove along the narrow gravel roads, grateful that they had a Franklin, so easy and reliable (Franklins were some of the first cars to drive coast to coast, Andrew told her), it hardly seemed possible that they would be stranded somewhere and left to die of exposure, and they weren't. When they got back to Vallejo, she felt, simultaneously, that they had done a very brave thing and a very easy thing.

But even as the lectures were his form of altruism, his absence from the book worried him. Each day, she typed up what he had written the day before—some two or three thousand words—and then he would go over it the next day and the next, changing his ideas and metaphorical illustrations. After he went over it, she retyped it and he went over it again. To have such flexibility—to go into print again and again—was a glory to him. Margaret typed forty and then sixty and then eighty words per minute, just like knitting row after row of garter stitch, and she really had no idea what she was typing. Her time was her own only when he was making his drawings of the universe, such as his drawing of the Aether—six-pointed shapes like stars with elongated arms that touched at the tips—but he liked her to stay within earshot. More than once, while he was drawing, he got up and came into the front room, where she might be reading a book. He noted her presence and nodded, then went back into his study. There was a chafing quality to his constant attention, and the days of Dora, when Margaret had thought nothing of leaving on the ferry whenever she wished, seemed gone without a trace, but what was her argument against his—the book was all-important! The lives of human beings were a kind of futile chaos, a chaos that preyed upon him every single day. To wrest a good idea, the right idea, from this chaos was a man's highest purpose and first obligation. Didn't she agree with that? He was nearly sixty, and though he was in exceptional health—

"You're fifty-five."

He looked at her but didn't answer.

She said, "I just think it's— Most people make themselves out to be younger than they are."

He went back into his office before she ever finished her remark.

ELIZABETH wrote her that Lucy May was proposing to travel to California, to Los Angeles, to visit some of Mercer Hart's relations, and wanted very dearly to visit Margaret on the island before going south.

The Lucy May that Margaret picked up at the railway station was someone she would not have recognized—tall, dark, nervous, eager. As soon as she saw the girl, Margaret understood why Elizabeth had written her three letters in three days, unable to stop detailing her worries about the long train trip, and ordering Margaret to send her a telegram as soon as Lucy May arrived. They went to the telegraph office.

Andrew came out of the house when they drove up, and peered at Lucy May. As they entered the front door, he said, "Can you type, miss?"

Lucy May shook her head and said, "Uncle Andrew, I can't do anything useful."

Andrew took her at her word and more or less overlooked her thereafter, but Margaret was wooed and won. The girl's clothes were beautiful—Margaret couldn't resist admiring them as she unpacked them and
hung them in the wardrobe of the spare room. Lucy May watched her,
not helping, but talking away ("Mother said to tell you everything,
which I do plan to do, Aunt Margaret"). She was so lively and grateful
for what Margaret provided that providing was a treat.

But Andrew filled the house. When Lucy May's gaze roved over the
piles of books and papers and journals, Margaret's did, too. When Lucy
May removed a stack of drafts from a chair to sit down, or pushed the
typewriter aside, or bumped into a box of "the first volume," as
Andrew now called it, Margaret registered the clutter and winced.
They had to go out, simply because the Franklin was comfortable and
clean. They drove around Vallejo and Napa, down as far as Oakland
and Danville. Listening to Lucy gave Margaret a view of the life she had
not had, set right beside the life she had had.

"All three of those boys are wild as can be, especially Elliott, who
was in the war. Lawrence was the only steady one, Mama says."

Margaret said, "He was a darling boy."

"Father was offered a job in Philadelphia. Ellie and I wanted to go,
too, just for a change, but Mama wouldn't hear of it, even though St.
Louis is so hot she has to lie in the back parlor with a wet rag on her
forehead to get through the afternoon."

Margaret said, "Oh, people have always prided themselves on living
in St. Louis."

"I think you were lucky to get out. We could at least move farther
west—all my friends live past Gore now. No one lives where we do."

Lucy May found old age astonishing, having never been sent on
charitable errands to witness it, as Margaret had been. "Everyone at
Mr. Bell's funeral was ancient, including Mrs. Bell. She has a nurse. All
they talk about is cats. Everyone tells her what her old cats are doing as
if they were still alive.

"Didn't you know? Uncle Robert is bald as a rock. Not even
eyebrows.

"Everyone says that you are a saint, Aunt Margaret. A pure saint.
And you seem like the youngest to me. Aunt Beatrice is so fat, she
doesn't go anywhere. She can't fit into Uncle Robert's automobile." She
said it again: "I think you had a lucky escape."

Margaret said, "But I miss all of them. I never got to know you until right now." Lucy May could not resist a tiny shrug, as if these were small prices to pay.

One morning, over breakfast, she sipped her coffee and asked, "Did you really see them hang Jesse James the day Mama was born?"

Margaret said, "Jesse James was shot in the head over by the Kansas border."

"But you did see a hanging?"

She said, "I don't know. I just don't remember. Your grandmother thought that was one of my signal virtues."

"Aunt Margaret! You must remember something."

Margaret thought about it as she drove them toward Napa for a picnic later in the day. The picture that came into her mind was muddy ground, flattened grass, and white clover. The restless murmur of a crowd and the creaking of wagons. An old-time Missouri voice saying, "Why, he's just a boy!" She said, "I think that hanging comes into my mind sometimes, but I don't know if what I think I remember is maybe something I read." She drove for another minute, then said, "I think his name was Claghorne." And she did—that was a name she knew but hadn't heard in decades. "I guess he robbed banks, or shot someone while robbing a bank. I don't know. I'll bet he was no older than you are now."

"How old were you?"

"Oh, I was five. Less than."

"What was Uncle Lawrence like?"

"He was a quiet boy. He liked books and bugs. That was why everyone was so astounded that he took me to the hanging. I'm sure Ben was there, too. He went everywhere there might be trouble."

"Do you remember when Ben died?"

"I remember when they carried him home. Beatrice and I were playing in the front room, and Mama looked out the window and gasped, and then she called out to our girl, Lily, and told her to take us upstairs. I remember how his feet looked as they were coming through the door, and then Lily stepped in front of me. I didn't see after that. Your mother must have been two."

"Oh, Aunt Margaret! I don't know how Gran stood it."

"But when you were born, Lucy May, your mother hired a nurse named Agatha from down around Rolla, and I gaped at what she told me, just the way you're doing now."

"I can't imagine it." As Margaret glanced at her niece staring out the window, she realized that what she couldn't imagine, though she had lived it, was never having gone back there, never having had the will to insist to Andrew that his work could be put off for a month or two, that a change of scene would be good for him. Then she realized that her mother had known that very thing—that Margaret's will could never match Andrew's—and, further, that her mother had accepted that as part of the price to be paid.

Margaret took Lucy May to Mrs. Wareham's boarding house, now called the Warrington Hotel, where the girl chatted with Mrs. Wareham and Cassandra and Naoko as if she had known them all her life.

On the ferry to San Francisco, they met Mrs. Kimura, who was going to Japantown. Because it was Lucy May's second-to-last day, Margaret had been planning to take her to Gump's and the White House and buy her an outfit for Los Angeles, but Lucy May chattered with Mrs. Kimura as if she were the child of Dora Bell, and they ended up on the cable car, heading out Geary Street. Eavesdropping, Margaret learned that both Joe and Lester would be moving to San Francisco—more opportunity as well as more to do. And Lester was already working at the Pacific Trading Company and living in a boarding house on Laguna Street, while Joe was finishing school in Vallejo and deciding whether to apprentice himself to a dentist on Sutter Street or to try to get more schooling. Mrs. Kimura herself came to Japantown two or three times every month. She was a member of two community-improvement societies and a church, but Mr. Kimura preferred to stay home and work in his garden. "How wonderful," said Lucy May. "How interesting!"

Margaret smiled to herself.

Margaret glanced about as tactfully as possible while Mrs. Kimura greeted several people. Most of the shops were the sort you would expect anywhere—cleaners, tailors, grocers, hotels—but full of Japanese people, the way the shops in Vallejo were not. The hotels, too, looked like hotels everywhere, except for the Japanese characters on the signs, above or below the English ones. Only the restaurants were decorated to look exotic. Lucy May peered in doors and windows—Margaret was glad that Mrs. Kimura did not seem embarrassed by the girl's curiosity. They went into a bookstore, a larger one than any in Vallejo (and Margaret had been to them all); the books were in Japanese. The only thing she could do with them was heft them in her hands and flip through, feeling the paper, but this turned out to be a pleasure, for the paper had a softer feel and rougher texture than the paper she was used to. The people in the bookstore watched her and Lucy May with curious politeness. Each time she put a book back on the shelf and picked out another one, they seemed to be wondering what on earth she could be looking for. In the meantime, Mrs. Kimura retrieved the proprietor from his office, and very soon he took Lucy May into a separate room, where he kept portfolios of prints. Margaret followed them.

After some discussion in Japanese with Mrs. Kimura, the man found two folders, then brought them over and laid them on a table beside a large window.

He opened the first one. The colors were brilliant and flat—curving fish, ferocious-looking men, women in brightly patterned kimonos, monsters, uplifted swords, corners of houses or doorways leading outdoors, with mountains or water in the background.

"Scene from drama or story," said Mrs. Kimura. "I like. Woman leaving house. Her child reaching for her. She halfway out door. But look." She pointed to the upper left-hand corner, where the translucent wall of the house was depicted. "Here is shadow of head. As she leave house, she change into fox." It was striking and clever, but it made Margaret uneasy. The proprietor kept turning, Lucy kept looking. There was a man with red stripes painted over his face, a cat sitting in a window, a stooped old man with a bare chest carrying a pack on his back.

The second portfolio was truly strange, and Mrs. Kimura said to her, "I do not think you like these, but Mr. Obata very proud of them."

Mr. Obata bowed toward her, and opened the portfolio. The first was of a viper of some sort, coiling itself down from a box, around what looked like a cup. Mr. Obata said something, and Mrs. Kimura said, "This is malicious gift—some nice present on top of box, and poisonous snake hidden inside."

Margaret said, "The snake is very realistic."

Lucy May reached out and traced the outline of the snake's head with her fingernail, then said, "When I was a child, my grandmother told me a story where the bones of all the animals slaughtered on a farm rise up and dance, then chase the farmer into the woods."

Margaret said, "My mother did tell that story."

Mrs. Kimura related this to the proprietor, and they smiled.

He closed the folder and glanced speculatively about the room. After a moment, he set another folder on the table, and opened the cover. The top print was in shades of green, orange, and yellow. It depicted three men passing a waterfall, which boomed over the whole left side of the picture. The men were very small figures, their faces hidden by wide hats as they looked up at the cascade. They stood on a bridge. Dark-blue water ran beneath them in a foaming torrent.

"This Hokusai," said Mrs. Kimura. "Very famous, and has made many, many prints. Some people say style show madness."

"I love that one," said Lucy May.

Margaret paid fifty dollars, about as much as she had spent on all of her clothing in the previous year. The proprietor of the bookshop wrapped it in heavy paper and Margaret handed it to Lucy May, who hugged her and kissed her on both cheeks, and then kissed the package. Then they went to a restaurant and drank tea and ate bowls of soup, noodles with pieces of shrimp and chicken in broth. Lucy May could not get over how delicious it was. When they left Mrs. Kimura in Japantown and got on the cable car to go back to the ferry building, Lucy May kissed Mrs. Kimura and embraced her, and Margaret didn't know how she was going to give up the girl when she left on the next part of her journey, and it was true—though she managed to put Lucy May on the train south with some dignity, as the train pulled out she found herself calling, "Come back! Don't forget to come back!" in a way that made the other people on the platform turn and look at her. That was why she returned to Japantown a week later and bought the snake print—thirty-two dollars. She didn't exactly like it, but she found herself staring at it, tracing the outline of the snake with her fingernail as Lucy May had done. It depicted, she thought, something that she had never seen in a picture before—that moment just before the recipient of the gift realizes the evil intentions of the sender.

ANDREW'S generosity in allowing her to spend so much time with Lucy May was much on his mind after the girl left. It seemed to Margaret as though she was typing or mailing things or cooking almost all of the day now, and into the evening. He even resented her weekly knitting group, but she put her foot down when he suggested once that she skip it. Her only breathing space was that, every morning after break-fast, she took the Franklin across the causeway for the newspapers, which took about forty-five minutes. Sometimes she found herself typing letters to the editors of these papers, especially the *New York Times,* and one morning, Andrew discovered that one of his letters was published. He had responded to a piece about a fellow named Dr. Harlow Shapley, whom the *Times* declared to have "newly revised estimates of the size of the universe upward by a thousand times." Andrew's letter contained a list of estimates of the diameter of the universe—including two million light-years by Herschel and four and a half million light-years by himself. Nothing about that young fellow Shapley was new, according to Andrew. "That's the thing that sticks in my craw the most," he exclaimed to her.

A similar letter to *Science* had been rejected, further proof of the conspiracy against him, but now, he felt, he had impressed a higher authority (with a much larger circulation). He said, "One scientist after another betrays the great ones to embrace the new and unproven. Who in our day can stand up with Herschel? Or Newton? And yet there's this insane rush to throw them over the side and try anything that is new. My dear, it has fallen to me to keep the lights burning as best I can. I appreciate how very much you contribute to that essential effort."

After that, a reporter from the *Times* came to the island and asked him about earthquakes. Earthquakes were caused by ocean water leaking downward into clefts in the ocean floor, the clefts in turn caused by the creation of new ranges of mountains under the sea. Since the earth was solid iron, Andrew had not worked out the mechanism by which new mountain ranges were being formed in the Pacific, but the evidence was incontrovertible that something literally earth-shaking was going on—now, with the telegraph, Andrew told the young man, reports of earthquakes came in all the time.

He went on to Einstein (Margaret peeked from the kitchen into the front room, and saw the reporter sitting in a chair like a rabbit in a trap, Andrew patrolling the front door). Up to now, Andrew had seen Einstein's German nationality as the telling flaw in his theory, but certain scientists at the observatory in Pasadena (he refused to name it aloud) declared that part of this relativity theory had been proved by their observations, and he—Einstein!—was allied with that very cabal who had always rejected Andrew's work and had spent so much of their time industriously demeaning and denying the truths of his own theories and had worked against him after he exposed their incompetence in the early days of their careers. That light from a star curved exactly in a certain direction and to a certain degree when it passed the sun during an eclipse was absurd, and their certainty about these findings ("They say that these results don't ever have to be tested again! Where is science *there*?") was enough to have him charging around the room in a fury. The *Times* reporter kept putting his hat on and having to take it off again.

When, a few days later, Andrew was quoted in a sidebar to a rather short article about these findings, he fired off a lengthy letter of elaboration.

For a few weeks, there was a modest flurry of correspondence about the issue. Some doctor from somewhere wrote in, attacking the very idea of relativity—Andrew was miffed that the mail from California was so slow as to prevent his letter from getting there first. Then came a "French fellow with a ridiculous name" who planned to combine relativity and Newtonian theory, who was interviewed by the *Times* correspondent in France. At last, Andrew's letter appeared, decisively and finally refuting Einstein on the grounds that (a) those in Germany who knew Einstein best didn't have one good thing to say about his theory, (b) Einstein himself didn't consider it proved, (c) you couldn't have a proper theory which didn't explain centrifugal force, a force as strong as "five million million steel cables each a foot thick," and (d) no account was made of the Aether, which could not simply be ignored!

As a corollary to this letter in the *Times,* he wrote a special column for the *Examiner* headlined "The Universe Is Filled with Aether and I Have Seen It." The paper gave him almost an entire page for this column, and he included careful drawings of particles of Aether—delicate six-pointed starlike motes, lightly touching at the tips of every arm.

Andrew's tone in his letter to the *Times* was very forceful (Andrew might have said "heroic") and, Margaret thought, a little condescending here and there, but understandably so, given his barely contained exasperation that these issues had to be gone over again and again. Einstein's theory was "the Gorgon's head, always having to be cut off again."

They were sitting at the table a week or so later when he opened the paper, not intending to read it while they were eating, precisely, but only to glance at it a bit, as he always did at supper. But of course, fatal to a tranquil meal, his gaze went directly to his own name, and traveled voraciously down the column of print even as his hand holding his fork holding his morsel of boiled potato was raised toward his mouth. His eyes got wide, and he grunted twice, and then groaned. He set his fork on his plate, read the column again, stood up from the table with the paper in his hand, and walked out of the house. She didn't see him until the next day—he slept at the observatory. When he did come home, at about 10 a.m., the only thing he said to her before going into his study was a despondent "Even when Einstein agrees with me, they attack."

It took her a while to find that letter in the *New York Times*. He had not saved it, either in his study or at the observatory, and that edition of the *Times* turned out to be missing from the library in Vallejo.

It was not easy to get to San Francisco—even in his unhappiness, they maintained his schedule of book composition and journalism, along with a talk in Santa Rosa (a long trip) and another in Sacramento.

But at last she told him she had been invited to a luncheon in San Francisco by the wife of the Base Commandant, and, flattered, he let her go—Margaret had heard about this luncheon by eavesdropping. Now she was in a library in San Francisco. Outside, it was raining. Her umbrella shed water next to the leg of the table. The room was quiet. The librarian left the room, and she couldn't help looking around once and over her shoulder for a large presence, but he truly was not there. It was one o'clock on a Tuesday afternoon. She laid the paper on the table.

The letter wasn't terribly long. Mr. "W. M. Malisoff" was no one she had heard of—not one of Andrew's old familiar enemies, or one of the obstreperous youths who occasionally cropped up in his conversation. Malisoff was no one, but he refuted Andrew's article point by point. Centrifugal force, he said, was merely a concept like any other; it was not five million million steel cables a foot thick pulling something toward it, it was a couple of words. Of the Aether, he said it doesn't exist. No purpose in contorting one's understanding of the universe to say that it does when it doesn't. She thought of Andrew's careful, star-like drawings of the Aether. She read the letter twice. It was not, properly, an attack but, rather, a dismissal. And although she would not have said that the principles in the letter were clear enough in her mind that she could have repeated them or defended them, they nevertheless seemed true to her, instinctively, exactly true. As she read Mr. Malisoff's words, she knew what had motivated him to write—Andrew's bluster-ing, grandiose claims, his circular reasoning. She knew that as well as if

God himself had whispered it in her ear. Just then, she saw Andrew as the world saw him, and she did it all at once, as if he had turned into a brick and fallen into her lap—who he was was that solid and permanent for her—he was a fool.

As she returned from San Francisco to Vallejo on the ferry, Margaret thought that if someone had asked her five days ago, or ten years ago, whether she "believed in" Andrew's work, she would have said, "Of course," without even thinking about it, but now she saw that "belief" was a kind of parasite that she had taken on by typing, by listening, by worrying about his reactions to the name "Einstein." She was infected with the "Aether" and with a vision of the universe that not only was alien to her, but was suddenly (in the middle of San Pablo Bay) terrifying in its vastness. Nothing worked as a charm against it, or a corrective, or a remedy. The book she had brought along to read dropped from her hands, ineffective against the images.

A few days later, she went to her knitting group. As she was taking off her overshoes and shaking out her umbrella in the front hall at Mrs. Tillotson's (Mrs. Tillotson, who still bore her married name, had returned to the knitting group bolder and more self-confident than ever), she heard the words "She is a saint!" When they stopped talking as soon as she entered the parlor (living room, Mrs. Tillotson called it), and everyone smiled at her, she knew that the saint was herself, and that they had been talking about her with some animation—their eyes were bright when they looked up to greet her. Lucy May had said the same thing. It was peculiarly painful all of a sudden to know that her friends and relatives valued her life not for anything she had done, but for what she had put up with. It was like being told she was a dolt, only in nicer language. The next week, she didn't go back, and when she saw Mrs. Tillotson on Marin Street one day a while later, she turned away from her, even though she knew Mrs. Tillotson had seen her.

But there was no defense against the typing. He was into volume two now. He projected another four years of hard work before he could even think about publication. He would not make the same mistake twice.

Except that, Margaret knew, he would.

1923

PART FOUR

1928

T HE ISLAND GOT QUIET, since everyone in the world agreed that there would be no more wars—civilization had learned its lesson. The navy made up its mind not to build many ships, and especially not large, expensive ones. The mishap with the *California,* a huge cruiser that upon launching had broken away from its restraints and skidded all the way across the strait, only to get stuck in the mud off Vallejo, was perhaps the reason that the island had begun to look awfully small and old-fashioned to a lot of people. Would it become an airfield? Would they build submarines? Was the future in airplanes landing on the decks of ships? Was Oakland more convenient for all of these operations? Why was the shipyard on the island, anyway? Why had anything happened the way it had? No one could remember, and starting anew seemed altogether more possible than sorting it all out. Andrew's job changed, too. Whereas he had once overseen the dropping of the time ball, now he sent out a set of time clicks by radio transmission. And time itself was different now, more a matter of counting something than observing the heavens. The navy kept asking Andrew when he thought he might retire. He kept not saying. He knew that when he was gone they would tear down the observatory, his nest and mole hole.

One day, Andrew brought Pete home for supper. Was it really ten years and more since they'd heard from him? But there he was, walking down Marin Street, in Vallejo, not dead after all. He looked down-and-out, but in his characteristic way—his clothes were classic and a little well taken care of, rather than flashy and new. Margaret put the short ribs on the table. Andrew said, "When you say that you lost all your money, do you really mean all?"

"My pockets were empty. But they aren't quite empty now. I have a job training horses." His travels had smoothed his accent still further—or else he wasn't bothering to maintain it. It was now unidentifiable.

She said, "What kind of horses?"

"Racehorses. At Tanforan." Tanforan was a racetrack somewhere south of San Francisco. Margaret had heard of it, but never been there. She said, "Racing is illegal in California, I thought."

"Betting is illegal, but not for long. Training isn't illegal. We just send them down to Caliente on the train when they're ready."

Andrew pressed him. "On your way to another fortune?"

He shrugged. But he grinned, too. "I'm living in a stall at the race-track for the moment."

Andrew said, "How is that?"

"Fragrant."

They laughed. Andrew really laughed. Perhaps, Margaret thought, Andrew considered Pete his best friend.

"No, truly. It's a fragrance I'm quite familiar with, and one that is very consoling to me. But I had to change my name to get a job as an assistant trainer."

"What's your name now?" said Andrew.

"Pete Moran. Irish is good at the racetrack—not so traceable as English, though I considered Peter Charles Cecil. I put on a bit of the Irish when I talk, and wrap those horses as if I larned the trick as a lad in Tipperary, and it works well enough. My chief is a fellow from Australia. Whatever I do is fine with him, as he's crooked as an elbow." Pete laughed this time.

Margaret said, "I think you've been Irish all along. Tipperary by way of Chicago."

Pete grinned.

Margaret said, "What have you seen of Dora? We've lost track since she quit the paper. Andrew's editor says she's writing a book."

"I did see her, twice. Just after the war, I saw her in Paris. I was walking down the Boulevard des Capucines, and there she was, dressed to go to the Opéra. She had on a nice hat with a peacock feather, and she was with a very famous man named Henri Bergson, who has made a whole career of books about laughing. They were laughing." Now Pete laughed. "It was contagious just to see them, even though I had been mooning about the city, wondering what was to become of me."

She waited for him to go on, and made herself not prompt him.

"The next day, I took her to lunch. She had spent all night interviewing prostitutes and hadn't slept in thirty-six hours."

"Interviewing prostitutes!"

"Yes, indeed. She interviewed them concerning their political opinions. She told me that no one ever asked them about those sorts of things, but they were happy to talk, because they had decided views and good ideas."

"For her book?"

Pete nodded.

"Then I saw her three or four years ago in Menton, each day for six days or a week. I'm telling you, she is the toast of the Riviera. She knows everyone, and wealthy American visitors go first to Dora to be spruced up. To have a few ruffles removed and a few pleats added, you might say."

"She was always very well dressed, even when she was sixteen and she looked a fright," Margaret said.

"Practicing," said Pete.

There was a pause, and then she said, "Were you ever going to marry her, Pete?"

"Dear Margaret," he said, "you were the only person in the world who considered it at all desirable."

The look he gave when he said this, though, told Margaret that there was one other person.

"How did you lose the last fortune, then?" Andrew insisted.

"I can barely remember, it was so long ago. Let me see. Of course, when I left here, I had a satchel full of dollars with me, which I should have left behind in a bank. My fatal mistake was that I thought I could do some good with it. I must have been thinking like an American! I thought I would help this friend in Petrograd and that relative in Moscow or Kiev. I should have remembered that what seems like a fortune when you embark here turns to nothing in Russia. My friends who were still in Petrograd were very deluded. They didn't want to flee in a third-class coach from St. Petersburg as they still called it, and find themselves a room in an outer *arrondissement* in Paris. The fellows who were prepared for that had already done so. These friends who had shilly-shallied, some of them very dear, I must say, could only abide first-class carriages, and porters to carry their bags, large apartments, and much idle time for grieving, helped by enormous portions of champagne." He smiled. "How could I deny them? And so I did not."

"But what about those Bolsheviks and the Mensheviks and the Tsarists and all?" said Andrew.

"They stole my money, too, but I expected them to. My old pal Joffe went so far as to have me beaten, so I gave him a thousand. 'My last thousand!' I kept saying, and perhaps he believed me, or perhaps he only told Lenin he did. Then there was my cousin, who when I last was in Russia was only a boy, and had since served in a Cossack regiment in the Tsar's army, and when I saw him in 1918 was back in their town. He swore up and down to me that he only wanted an up-to-date rifle, and he would then set about making his living off the land. He would kill birds for food, and he knew where all the best furs for trapping could be found. He showed me a list of his contacts—he was going to smuggle sables and ermines to the West. I procured the rifle for him, and the stock of ammunition, but the first thing he did was shoot his wife and her lover, and then himself. That had been his plan all along. And then the rifle was stolen by the police and disappeared, though I would not have wanted it back."

Andrew looked a bit shocked. Pete smiled and went on: "Who's to say that the three of them didn't get the best of it? They would have impressed him into the Red Army. Personal troubles, no matter how deadly they are, were small beer in Russia those days."

"You gave your fortune away," declared Andrew.

"Did I? When I left, I was thinking of something else entirely. Buying wheat or lamp oil. Wartime speculation can be very lucrative. Oats? I can barely remember. Something scruffy and venal. I recognized my mistake at once—contacting old friends! But it's hard on your pride to return from America with nothing to show for it, and so I did not. I returned from Russia with nothing to show for it!"

Margaret asked, "Did you starve?" She was conscious of the dishes of food on the table.

"Everyone starved. Starvation is a potent weapon, and the Bolsheviks are happy to wield it. The cheapest way to get rid of the opposition is to starve them. Lenin did it the expensive way, shooting them, but the Soviets can no longer afford that."

"Starving them on purpose?"

"Why not? Why not?" He shook his head, then said, "Americans will never understand Russians. Perhaps I don't understand them myself anymore."

There was a long silence while Margaret cleared the table. Really, she still didn't know what to make of Pete. Andrew said, "We looked at those things of yours while you were away. Didn't know what we would do with them."

They all understood that the end of this sentence was "if you died."

Margaret said, "We had one fright, when the powder magazine exploded at the beginning of our war. But I have to admit, I only thought of the screens after I'd already wondered if we were all going to be blown to bits."

"May I look at them?" said Pete.

He and Andrew carried them in, then unwrapped them.

Andrew said, "Mightn't you sell these, then? I mean, for funds."

Pete didn't answer.

First the gold one, then the man in the boat. She glanced at Pete. His face had a look she had never seen on it before—no skepticism, no bemusement, simply a smile of unconscious delight. He looked handsome for once. Margaret carried the platter into the kitchen.

When she came back, Andrew had started hmphing and knocking about. But Pete was still silent, entranced. "Well, you know, you did inspire someone," said Andrew. "My dear, you must show Pete what you've acquired."

She was instantly embarrassed, but said, "I've bought a few of my own now. Mrs. Kimura sometimes goes with me to Japantown. We got to be friends when she taught me to drive an automobile."

She brought them out and set them on the dining-room table. There were three of them. Pete looked at them for a long time without saying anything. Andrew had barely glanced at the prints, and was now marching about the room. Margaret knew he was tempted to go into his study and get to work, and she wished he would—his steps seemed to shake the house.

Pete pointed to a nighttime scene framed by a window. "See the lights of the boats on the river? The artist drew these boats one by one, just as they would look in daylight, then he printed on the pale yellow for the lights, and after that the black, for night. My guess is that this went through eighteen printings or more, and that was after the artist carved the block. They print books in the same way, carving each page by hand."

He went back to the snake. "This is very good. Though the horse, in this other one, is a very exuberant horse, and the fetlocks and hooves are correct. Very difficult to do. But the snake, the snake is a most discomforting one. The snake is almost lost in the wealth of detail, but then it asserts itself and cannot be wished away."

Andrew stopped stamping about, harrumphed, and said, "Are they valuable?"

Pete glanced at Margaret, caught her eye, and then said, "They are well chosen."

He left that night for the San Francisco ferry, and disappeared again. It was Margaret who wrapped the screens and the scroll and put them away. Of course he could not have them in a horse stall, but surely, she thought, he had other, closer friends who might take care of them.

ONE DAY, a young man showed up at the door. It was foggy, which made the man seem rather mysterious. The house was quiet—Andrew was at the observatory, and she had been putting off her typing. The fellow was almost inside the house as soon as she opened the door. Bespectacled. A black-and-white tweed suit, a vest, a pince-nez, and a nervous manner. He asked for "the captain."

"Captain Early is out. He should be back in half an hour."

"I'm Scanlan."

"Scanlan?"

"Len Scanlan? You were expecting me? Dr. Len Scanlan?" His valise was on the porch.

She shook her head. She had never heard of Dr. Scanlan, but when Andrew walked in, he was perfectly acquainted with him. Dr. Scanlan—or Len, as they called him thereafter—was writing a book entitled *The Amazing Discoveries of Captain Andrew Jackson Jefferson Early.* Dr. Scanlan was a graduate of the Iowa State College of Agriculture and Mechanic Arts (though in veterinary medicine, not physics or astronomy).

Len stayed with them, sleeping on the sofa, for two days, and he had a disturbing way about him—he was the sort of young man who always stood too close, always peered over her shoulder to see what she was doing, always seemed to have closed one of her drawers just before she entered the room. His fawning manner was meant to be reassuring and achieved the opposite. On the first morning, Len declared that he would do his own typing, which should have relieved her, but offended her instead. When he said, "I know shorthand. The Gregg system. Do you know it? I expect to get down everything Captain Early says, word for word," she felt an unreasoning dislike of the Gregg system and vowed never to learn it. He told her about himself. He was from Mankato, Minnesota. He had two sisters. His mother and father had passed. His father had been a pastor at the First Congregational Church of Mankato. His older brother had died in the influenza, over in Germany, after the war. His mother had never gotten over that, because his brother was the favorite, "tall, like my father, and very pre-possessing." One of his sisters was married to a man who owned a dry-goods store, and one of his sisters taught in a girls' school. He was a great admirer of Captain Early, and read everything he wrote. He had a special subscription to the *Examiner,* which was delivered all the way to Minnesota, and plenty late, but always "fascinating." He had copies of both Captain Early's books, and strongly disagreed with what Andrew now said about any failures of style and effectiveness; Len had been struck by both of them on the very first readings—"so lucid and self-evident; classics." He had then investigated Andrew's other writings, and had decided, as a hobby, to organize them chonologically, which, of course, had opened his eyes to the truth as well as the beauty of Andrew's system. He had humbly written to Andrew, to broach the topic of a few interviews by mail, and here he was. The project had mushroomed, and taken over his life. But he hated veterinary medicine, anyway. "A farmer might pay a man to save a cow, he *might,* but a pig, he'll give you a buck or two to slaughter the beast and haul it away—*if* you can persuade him not to throw it in the farm dump, which is always, believe me, right above the crick." He shook his head.

All Andrew said was "Dr. Scanlan is dedicated to truth in a way that few young men are."

Len found himself a boarding house, and he and Andrew quickly worked out a schedule. Andrew worked on his own book or articles in the morning, from eight until about eleven-thirty, handing pages to her, which she was to type. At around one-thirty or two, he walked up the hill to the observatory, where he met Len. He stayed there for three hours or so, then came home and organized his work for the evening. And he came home with an evident sense of well-being, was especially cordial over supper. Once a week, Len left him some pages, on which he noted questions and corrections. As the weeks went by, she began to wonder how many pages the two of them would accumulate. Certainly more rather than fewer. Len did not seem, on the surface, to be of an analytical or critical turn of mind. However, it was none of her business. Len declared that he would certainly find a publisher—two or three were interested already.

Len also attended a few of Andrew's talks and took industrious notes in the back of the room, then applauded loudly and once, in her hearing, shouted "Bravo!" No one had ever shouted "Bravo!" before, and Andrew responded with a tiny bow, which caused some of the audience to turn around and crane their necks, and Margaret to blush, but she had all sorts of strange symptoms now, breathlessness, headaches, even a kind of agoraphobia when she got up in the morning and the thought of leaving her room was repellent to her. As well as she knew that she would be fine in the kitchen, and that her own range and sink would look familiar to her, and that her own hands cooking and cleaning would draw her out of this strange mood, even so it took all her strength to put on her clothes and open the door. Andrew seemed to notice nothing.

And of course there was no help for it, except recalling bits of conversations she had overheard from time to time about marriage. That's what knitting groups and sewing groups were for, wasn't it? Commiserating about marriage. But through the years no one had said what she now thought, which was that marriage was relentless, and terrifying, and no wonder that when her father died her mother had risen from her bed and gone to work. Her father had been much like Andrew, hadn't he? Opinionated and energetic, loud and forbidding. What a dramatic and unnecessary thing to do, to kill yourself because you were a doctor and your son died of complications from the measles. Margaret knew she would always keep this thought to herself, but it was an oddly satisfying thought, and she had a right to think it—she was three years older than her father had been when he shot himself.

And so, one day when Andrew was due to give a talk in Saratoga, a

long drive, she said she had a headache. Andrew and Len came up with
the idea that Len would drive the Franklin. Franklins were easy to
drive—Len was experienced with a Hudson and a Packard. The
Franklin would be a new pleasure for him, Andrew said, air-cooled, the
best engineering by far. They went out the door, and a few moments
later, she heard the Franklin start up and roll away.

After they left, she lay there for a while with a cool, damp cloth
across her forehead. Really, in spite of his deficiencies, Len Scanlan was
a godsend, and it was purely a sign of her advancing age and narrowing
imagination that it had taken her so many weeks to realize this. She
decided to get up and go for a walk—not to Vallejo, but north, along
the coast of the island, which she hadn't done yet that spring. She put a
shawl over her shoulders and went out, not forgetting to unearth
Andrew's old field glasses as she did so.

The weather was beautiful. Her headache evaporated, but she had to
lament her newfound sluggishness. She had hardly gotten away from
the base (past the causeway) before she was looking for a place to sit
down, unhooking her collar, carrying her shawl over her arm, pushing
up her sleeves, wishing she had brought a hat. She sat on a rock for a
few minutes, remembering when she could walk across the fields
behind her grandfather's farm and get to Beatrice's house in town in a
little over an hour. She stood up, a bit rested, and walked on. At the
next resting spot, a rock set on a slight rise overlooking a small pond
just south of the marshes, she saw an amusing display. Two large-
bodied black birds with white beaks were making a racket in the water.
A mating pair, they looked familiar, though she couldn't have said what
they were. The female was using her large feet to run across the top
of the water, flapping her wings and stretching her head far forward,
and the male was hot after her, some ten feet to the rear. He did not
seem able to catch her, or perhaps he was not interested in catching her.
Rather, they seemed to enjoy their noisy game, and to splash as much
water into the air as they could. Then she noticed another of these birds
not too far away. When the first male saw it, he went straight for it and
began making aggressive feints and displays, to which the other male
responded in kind. At one point, the two males had a standoff, their
necks extended, their heads down, and their eyes on each other, looking for all the world like a pair of dogs. The first male succeeded in
chasing the other male away (that one pounded over the surface of the

pond, then took off and flew beyond the hill). The pair now proceeded to dine, diving under the water (and staying there for some time), plucking bits of things off the surface, and also stalking about on the edge of the pond, eating grasses and leaves. Margaret liked them. Unlike most birds, they were neither cute nor graceful, and they had no dignity, only energy. She watched them until the air began to grow quite chill and the afternoon light to dim.

When she described them to Andrew the next day, he said that they were "coots."

"Oh, mud hens," said Len. "Very common birds. Of no value at all, really. Though I'm told the meat isn't gamy, like duck."

"I was just watching them, not planning to hunt them." But by that time, they weren't listening, just repeating back and forth how important and successful the talk had been the evening before. Then Len brought up Teddy Roosevelt, whom he admired. Also. He glanced at Andrew. "In his own field, of course."

Andrew nodded slowly, as if acknowledging that being president was fine in its way. Then he said, "More recent specimens have not been comparable to him, that is indeed true."

Margaret felt a headache coming on and went into the kitchen.

She began shirking her typing and walking to that pond whenever it was fair weather. The coots were there the first two times, and then they were gone, apparently replaced by a pair of Canada geese, who busily built a nest right on the bank of the pond, out in the open. She went two more times to watch the geese, but they were rather dull in the way that elderly rich people are dull—too great a sense of propriety to do anything interesting. And then their nest was raided and the geese decamped. At the pond, she found, she didn't mull over the injustices of marriage, and so it was a relief.

In June, the coots reappeared; they must have been nesting out of sight. That day, it took her a while to understand what she was seeing. One of the coots was swimming about, ducking its head and plucking things off the surface of the water. It was putting these things somewhere, and then Margaret saw something like a dragonfly or a large insect fluttering. When she put the field glasses to her eyes, she saw that the fluttering thing was a very tiny bird, about as big as a walnut, bobbing and swimming in front of the large-bodied black coot, which she now decided was a female. Because the female's beak was white, she could see fairly distinctly how she held something out to the chick, and either stuck it in the chick's mouth, or allowed the chick to snatch it from her. Small and young as it was, the chick was an animated swimmer, as at home in the water as its mother. It paddled around in little circles and fluttered its tiny wings and bobbed. Margaret laughed just to look at it.

The weather was foggy and drizzling the next day, so she stayed home, catching up on her typing, but the day after that, she went to the pond again, and this time the coot had three chicks, all about the same size. Quite often, they would array themselves in front of the female in a half-circle, and she would plop insects into their mouths in turn. If she swam a foot or two in search of more food, they might swim after her. But the funniest thing was that the chicks were very independent, and it was quite usual for one or another of them to swim away entirely, the tiniest wayward infant in the world, industriously leaving all protection behind. At these moments, Margaret couldn't resist scanning the skies for hawks or an eagle. The female seemed not to notice—she continued to feed whomever she had with her until either that one swam away or the prodigal returned. Sometimes the whole troop walked up onto the shore, and the female yanked bits for them there. They followed her or they didn't. They were only birds, and just a few days old, but their size and behavior made them seem uniquely endowed with personality to Margaret. A stiff wind and the onset of evening drove her away.

When she got home that evening, she saw that Andrew and Len had been moving stacks of papers, some of which had been in one place for years. It was not even possible to sit down to supper, because stacks were arrayed around the edge of the table according to some system that she didn't care to inquire about. She knew that, were she to show the slightest interest, she would be enlisted to do something with the papers, and it would not be to throw them away. It was a nice evening, so they ate out on the porch, from plates on their laps. Andrew said little, and after ten minutes he was back in the house, fishing for something. Then, when she got up in the morning, she saw that he had been at work all night—the wardrobe in the front room was empty, and boxes that had been sitting on the hat shelf were emptied onto the floor. When he heard her in the kitchen, Andrew came out of his room and said, "We have found concrete evidence of the progress of my thinking.

It has been most gratifying." She didn't say anything. She hardly did say anything these days, and it didn't seem to matter, which was a relief.

Eventually, the chicks numbered seven. She walked to the pond three and sometimes four times a week. Andrew and Len never asked her where she was going, but she offered—she said, "Just running up to look at the birds!" They nodded and waved her away. It was so exhilarating that she leapt out of bed in the morning, all her former symptoms gone. Andrew's work on his own book tapered off—he didn't even notice what she was not typing, because he and Len were either in his study or up at the observatory most days. And then Andrew accepted a speaking engagement at a Chautauqua at Lake Berryessa. It was understood that Len would drive him and she would stay home. After they left, she fixed herself a lunch to take to the pond. She was humming.

The chicks had evolved from yellowish dots with a sometimes discernible bit of pink on the tops of their heads to fluffy, awkward, big-footed gray balls with ugly red heads and necks. They were bolder and more irresponsible. Quite often, the male and the female would be feeding three or four chicks on one side of the pond (which was probably fifty yards across), and the others would be on the other side of the pond, swimming energetically, or walking around on the bank. Their constant business made up for all of their awkwardnesses. Not for a coot the sort of graceful languor you saw in many birds, who rode a current of air and saved their energy for something important. To a coot, it seemed, everything was important.

Every time she mentioned the coots to someone, she was told again that they were common birds; she kept her observations to herself, but that night, alone in the quiet house, she found a sheet of paper and a pencil and attempted to draw what she remembered so clearly from the day. She closed her eyes, summoned the dark, plump figure of the harried parent into her mind, concentrated upon it, and then made a few strokes with the pencil. It was no use; she hadn't the gift. Just the beak? Just the curve over the back? It seemed as though her pencil was destroying the recollection rather than reproducing it. She looked across the room at the picture of the rabbit and the dragonfly. How quickly Mr. Kimura had given them life and personality! She got up early, knowing exactly what she would do, but then she was rushing about so, in order to make the ferry, that she knocked two stacks of papers off the table, and they slid across the floor. She looked at the clock. Andrew and Len had expected to be back by two. She stacked the papers willy-nilly and set them on the table in a way that more or less resembled the way they had been, then hurried to the ferry dock. At the Kimuras' shop, Naoko was wiping down the shelves, and she made her proposal. Within a few minutes, they had decided that Mrs. Kimura would drive Mr. Kimura across the causeway and up to the pond, if Margaret would meet them.

It was only ten-thirty by the time Margaret had done her business, and she was so pleased with herself that she went to Mrs. Wareham's for a late breakfast.

The mess she had left behind looked more forbidding when she opened the door on her return. Andrew and Len had clearly been rooting through years of papers, and she had no idea if they had left them organized in any way. After removing her wrap, she began going through the careless stacks she had made, trying to ascertain some principle of order. She thought of Anna Early as soon as she lifted one of the packets of letters, before she had noticed the writing on the topmost envelope, and then she had a turn. She untied the string around them. The letters had that look about them, crisp and cream-colored, the very stationery bespeaking the woman. Margaret put the packet to her nose, and the scent was still there beneath the dust. She felt herself smiling even before she realized that she had never seen these before. She took them into her room and closed the door.

The first dated from the fall of 1904, right after Andrew had taken her to the world's fair in St. Louis and then gone back to Washington, D.C. What was that now? Almost thirty years. How strange that was. Mrs. Early wrote:

Dearest Andrew,
I must tell you that most of the questions you ask in your letter are ones I cannot answer—not because I choose not to, but because I don't know how. You have gotten beyond me now, and I am thoroughly saddened and perplexed. I have, in fact, destroyed your letter, since I believe that your ravings in the letter were written in a passing moment, and I do not want to encourage you to ponder these things that cannot be addressed or resolved. You must think of torments like the ones you describe as ghosts or spirits that visit you in the night, but that leave sooner or later. Nor have I brought these questions up with Dr. Jacobs, or even Mrs. Hitchens. To address them, I feel, is to give them more life than they deserve.

However, I do think it is fair to tell you something. Not long before you were born, at the end of the War, your father was visited by demons that seem to me similar. He was not as old as you—not yet thirty—and, indeed, he was not alone in the mental disturbances he felt. Perhaps the despair of the War was compounded in Missouri by the peculiar events there. I can say now, forty years later, what I could not say then—many who had sympathized with the Cause saw not only that the Cause was lost, but also that it had not been worth the effort and pain that it had cost. Your father came to this conclusion without recourse to my feelings, since, as you know, I never quite sympathized with the Cause to the degree that your father and his brothers did. I sympathized with *him,* though. And I sympathize with you. A man of character is always in danger. He throws himself wholeheartedly into those things that inspire him, as your father did, who appeared on the surface to concede the battle in Missouri to the Northern-sympathizers, but in fact spent the War endangering himself by gathering and communicating information that he thought could help the Cause (and now you know his secret, son). He would certainly have been shot or hanged if he had been caught. And the great paradox was that he may have regretted in some way that he was not shot or hanged. The Confederacy's loss was not what played havoc with his sanity—it was what that loss revealed about the motives and intentions of the Confederacy itself. Recognizing that he had endangered himself in every way for such a thing was nearly his undoing. It seemed that all other men chose either the Union or the Confederacy and clung to their choices for the rest of their days. But perhaps to their wives they showed different sentiments. For several months the same sorts of torments as those you describe in your letter possessed your father, although with different origins. But, dear Andrew, I encourage you to think of yourself as requiring a bit of caution. Let these thoughts that you are having dissipate and vanish, leaving behind no trace.

Your loving Mother

The next letter was dated a week later, and was much longer. In part, she wrote:

On balance, my son, I do not think that isolation is your friend. You seem to be caught in a sort of mental vortex or downward spiral, where one thought leads inevitably to the next, larger, and more melancholy thought. As you go about your round of activities, thinking these thoughts over and over, they become wedded to every bit of the world around you, so that you cannot release yourself from them—if yesterday you stared out the window in despair, today when you look out the window, you are reminded of, and therefore precipitated into, despair. Your mental life is and has always been of a peculiar intensity, dear Andrew. Whatever mechanism works in an average mind like mine works doubly or trebly in a mind such as your own. Maybe you should take a few weeks in Warm Springs, and in every way break your routine and think of other things and meet with other people. Otherwise, I simply don't know what to tell you, except that I am, as always, your loving Mother

Within a week of that letter, Mrs. Early seemed to have visited Andrew in Washington. When she got home, she wrote the following:

Dearest Andrew,
I am both happier and sadder than I expected to be after seeing you. I am sadder because you seem unable to separate your thoughts from the anxieties and resentments that you feel toward your colleagues, but I am happy to see that what I had imagined— that you somehow would have lost track of your surroundings and your own person—has not happened. Is it only a mother who visits her unhappy child and checks that, though there are stacks of papers, they are neat stacks. The furniture is dusted, the clothes are not in disarray, and the shoes in the closet are straight. She breathes a sigh of relief. I fancy that any doctor might also be reassured.

Nevertheless, I am even more convinced that you need a change of scene. If you came here until Christmas, it might be the interval you need. Or you could go somewhere more festive and enjoyable than Missouri. Why not Europe? I fancy the thought of you hiking boldly through the mountainous landscape there, and with each step walking away from what bothers you. It would also be true that you would meet some other people who might appeal to you. Our thoughts about certain persons here in this town may not have come to anything (though the girl and her mother still seem receptive enough), but there are other girls and other mothers. My very least favorite thought is that of you solitary and alone, with no companion and no one to care for you.

It took Margaret a moment to comprehend that it was she herself who was being referred to, and then she found it so startling and yet so absolutely expected that she had to put down the letter for a few minutes. But of course they had discussed her and Lavinia. She and Lavinia had discussed them, too. Weren't all marriage negotiations, including unspoken ones, just that, negotiations? But the cool tone startled her and added a piece of knowledge to her memory of Mrs. Early that she was not quite ready to assimilate. In the years since her death, Margaret had gotten accustomed to thinking of Andrew's mother as a paragon, not only someone she seemed to have known better than she actually did, but also someone who had cared for her, Margaret, the woman who, as one of her last acts, had taken Margaret into her embrace, the rarest of rare things.

She picked up the letter and read on, knowing that she should not.

No, the girl is not educated nor evidently intelligent, *quiet* without being *mysterious* (though I think there is more to her than meets the eye), but what do you want in a wife at your age? Madame Curie? I do not, frankly, think that you could abide a rival or even a young woman who considered herself your equal and spoke her own ideas back to you with any sort of self-confidence. Possibly the other alternative, in your mind, is a beautiful young lady from a prominent family, but I shudder to think of you attempting that. This girl is a well-made young woman with proper instincts and reasonable connections. Her mother has trained her to take care of household matters. Most important—without even thinking of it, she understands the Missouri way of looking at things and doing things, that very pride that has gotten you into trouble so often (I do think Missourians are a separate species of human being, as you know). At your age, I think it is paramount that you avoid the sorts of divergences, and even, you might say, conflicts that your father and I suffered in our youth together. "Ohio!" as your grandmother often said. "Where is that?" "North of Kentucky." And then she would exclaim, "North! Hah!" and scowl into her tea. I tell you these things in hopes, my beloved son, of not only influencing your actions, but also of lightening your mood.

Margaret folded up the three letters she had read, and then held the packet in her lap for a few minutes. Sometime later, she heard Andrew and Len outside, coming noisily up the walk. In a moment they were inside. Through the open door, she saw that it was later than she thought. She got up to make supper. She gathered from Andrew and Len's conversation, overheard from the kitchen, that the speech had not been a success, but as she cooked, she heard them talk themselves out of any sense of mortification or disappointment. By supper, which Len was invited to partake of, they were planning future glories once again. Margaret watched them. Len goaded Andrew simply by agreeing with him and then adding a bit of his own. He never allowed Andrew to denigrate himself or his ideas the least bit. As she watched them, Margaret wondered what Len Scanlan could possibly be seeking—what profit could there be in this for him? He never asked for money, even for a loan, and Andrew wouldn't have given him one. Did he fancy himself Andrew's future heir? It was impossible to understand.

Before bed, she read the next letter.

Dear Andrew,

I was very sorry to receive the telegram from your Commander telling me of your removal to the hospital. He seemed to think that your misadventure with the gaslight in your room was exactly that, while, of course, I have different suspicions, with which I will not burden you. Whatever the circumstances of your being overcome, I pray you have been galvanized by the experience into some form of caution in the future. There are mental dangers as well as physical dangers that people of passionate temperaments must take care to avoid. It is in the interests of such avoidance that I have been urging you to connect yourself to a wife. The wages of solitude are that every mood is intensified. Yes, solitary happiness can be almost a form of delirium, but is that good? And, of course, the converse is true also—unhappiness can be almost a form of madness. You say that the tedium of marriage would irritate you beyond enduring, but that is precisely why I think that a certain someone is right for you. At the very least, she is an avid reader, and therefore would spend a good deal of time to herself. But I have pressed her virtues before this, and it is up to you to make your choice. I await some word from you or your doctor. Please do not run out of the hospital too quickly.

Margaret gathered from two subsequent letters that Andrew did stay in the hospital for about five weeks, at which point he came to their town. It was in the spring that he made his offer to her, and so, in the end, Mrs. Early carried her point—she had chosen the local old maid, harmless but useful, to marry and care for her darling son. Margaret sat there thinking of this, certain that Lavinia was in on the plot, and that things had been communicated back and forth between the two women that Lavinia did not communicate to her. Had they seen that she was not immune from that Missouri pride that Mrs. Early recognized in Andrew? Had their only choice been to lure her and trap her? She thought maybe it had been. Lavinia's view of marriage was never other than practical. Romance, she'd said, was always the first act of a tragedy. Lavinia had sent her around town with dishes and shawls for the solitary and dependent old women to show her what the life of an old maid was—in your earlier days, you were called upon to serve anyone and everyone, and in your later days, you waited patiently until someone thought of serving you.

But Andrew! Not only had he entertained doubts about her, he had tried her out, seen that he could have her, and then doubted and hesitated and suffered before taking her as the least of evils. And whatever anyone, including Andrew, might have said about the gas incident as alluded to in the letter, Margaret was convinced that an intention had been there, but it might not have been intention for actual death, only intention for relief. There was a distinction to be made, wasn't there? A doctor, her father, who is familiar with guns, knows what he is doing when he turns a gun upon himself, but not everyone who steps in front of a train imagines the enormity of death. Andrew's imagination might only have gotten as far as the yearned-for relief, not as far as his own nonbeing.

She tied up the letters and put them under her bed, behind some books.

THE much-anticipated day came about a week later. Margaret packed a hamper with fruit, bread, some sausages she had made, and some beers for Mr. Kimura. The Kimuras had provisions, too, in beautiful lacquered boxes, and Pete was with them. He got out of the car and walked on ahead with her. She told him that Andrew and Len had gone off to San Francisco for the day to look at sites from the 1906 earthquake. Andrew still considered himself an expert on that earthquake.

Three or four mallards floated on the pond; a couple of crows were pecking on the bank. An egret stood solitary at the edge of the water. After they had set out their blankets and the picnic, one of the adult coots came walking down the hill, followed by four of the chicks. Out of the water, the chicks, still gray and fluffy, were huge-looking, because of their feet and legs. She pointed them out to Pete and Mr. Kimura, and they watched them, while she and Naoko and Mrs. Kimura chatted among themselves. Not long after this, the other parent appeared, with the other three chicks in tow, and all of the chicks now swam busily all over the pond, into the rushes and out again, sometimes still getting a bite to eat from Mama or Papa, other times straying off. Mr. Kimura squatted on the hillside, watching, occasionally removing his straw hat and putting it right back on. She offered him her glasses, but he shook his head. When the rest of them gathered about the blanket for their picnic, he joined them for a bit, but then went back to the hillside. Naoko and her mother gossiped with Pete. They related a recent birth of twins, two girls, that Mrs. Kimura had overseen. She suspected that the two girls had two different fathers. Yes, she said, it was rare but possible. One of the twins was distinctly American-looking, and Mrs. Kimura was waiting to see if the Chinese husband would cause a scandal. Pete told them about a horse he was training, who could not be made to gallop past a certain spot on the track where the grandstand cast a dark shadow across the homestretch. "This morning, he stopped dead and reared up. The lad slid right down over his haunches, and it took ten minutes to catch him." Margaret described Len and his project. Pete said, "Fellow's after something."

"But what could that be?" exclaimed Margaret. "What does Andrew have that anyone wants?"

"Money," said Pete.

"If that's his game," said Margaret, "then he doesn't know Andrew."

Pete lifted an eyebrow.

All around them, the summer grasses waved in the breeze—golden but not yet dried out. A few retiring blossoms nestled in the grasses. The ground was dry. Mrs. Kimura said, "Have this bird in Japan. I think is called 'oo-ban.' But I never see picture of it."

One of the adults walked up on the bank, followed by three of the chicks. Suddenly the adult turned and pecked the third chick hard on the top of the head, and then picked it up by the back of the neck and shook it and dropped it. The chick flopped about in confusion, and the adult and the other two chicks headed out into the water to swim. The chick who had been attacked staggered about a bit, as if stunned, then shook its head a couple of times and fluttered its wings.

"That looked like exasperation," said Pete.

Margaret said, "It's been a long couple of months."

Pete laughed.

"You don't expect animals to be exasperated," said Naoko.

"I do," said Mrs. Kimura.

They took a walk around the pond, and Pete pointed out what he thought was the nest, a boatlike structure made of grasses, about a foot long and not quite so wide. Mr. Kimura pointed out small lizards and mice, a feral orange cat, a heron on the branch of a tree. Everything they did was simple, moment by moment. A breeze came up that was fragrant, though cool. The blanket had to be secured with stones. She had forgotten forks. But there was something about this picnic, some fleeting, perfect comfortableness, that impressed Margaret with the notion that it might be the high point of her life. In the instant she thought this, it didn't seem such a bad thought.

Three days later, Naoko came to the island bearing a small scroll painting, about fourteen inches wide and twelve inches tall. The expanse of the pond stretched across the paper, greenish gold, and the golden hill rose above it. On the surface of the pond, the adult coots were swimming. The larger of them turned toward the viewer, her eye bright and her white beak in the act of grabbing something off the water. Two chicks accompanied her. The other adult was closer to the bank; two chicks were on the bank. To the left, all the way across the water, another chick was larking about, swimming fast enough to make ripples. Perched on a tree branch that leaned over the pond was a crow, its beak pointing toward the coot chicks. It was beautiful and economical. The only bits of real color were the red heads of the chicks, a small butterfly, and the red seal that was Mr. Kimura's signature. She made Naoko take forty dollars.

It was that night that Margaret dreamed of Pete, of Pete and Dora, embracing, framed in light, but not, she realized when she woke, the light of a hallway or gas lamps, or even a doorway, but, rather, some sort of a forest light, dense tree cover giving way to a path. In the dream, she was happy and excited, but she also had the sense that she was not in the dream, except that Dora was wearing one of her dresses, her favorite gray crêpe de chine with a black belt and a black collar. Even so, in the dream, Dora was weeping as she had that night, the night of the bombing, weeping as though she knew what was coming and that she would not survive. Except that she had survived. It was a strange dream.

SHE had the picture framed. Both Andrew and Len noticed it and complimented it. Len said, "Did you paint this yourself, Mrs. Early?"

"No, I—"

"You know, I must say that Captain Early is a dab hand with a pen. His drawings are exquisite."

"Yes, he—"

"The layman can really get the sense of what he is going for, as far as his ideas. It's a rare thing in a physicist."

"An astronomer."

"Oh, madam, far more than that now. Far more."

"How is your book coming, then?"

"Well, of course, it has expanded. I knew that would happen when I proposed coming out here, but it has expanded *downward* and *backward*. When I think of what I had before, or what I was thinking, it seems literally flat to me. This is much more exciting."

"What has it been? Almost eight months now?"

"Oh yes. But I have nothing pressing drawing me back to Minnesota, and now, with the fall coming, it's very hard to leave California, isn't it? Very hard, indeed. Much bigger when you get here than you thought it was going to be."

"Isn't that true of every place?"

"Is it?" It was true that Len had expanded since his arrival, both in size and in self-importance. It was as if he and Andrew were inflating each other.

Andrew said, "This picture looks like California."

"It is."

"But in a Japanese style."

"I commissioned it. From Mr. Kimura, who did the rabbit." He glanced over at the rabbit. "I paid him forty dollars." He did not seem pleased. She said, "Pete was there. He said forty dollars was a fair price."

Andrew sniffed and put his hands in his pockets, but his expression lightened. He said, "Good investment, then?"

"Pete thinks so."

He stared at the picture for another moment, said, "Well, then," in a conciliatory way, and went back to his study. Pete's name worked like magic with Andrew. Len was a mere acolyte; Pete, an equal.

Then there were only five chicks. She counted them several times and walked about the pond, looking for the other two. She was surprised at how distressed she felt. That night, she even awakened thinking about it. But the next morning, all seven chicks were there, swimming and eating. She was reassured.

The next morning, she opened the door to Len and told him Andrew had already gone up to the observatory, but Len followed her into the kitchen and said, "Mrs. Early, I've noticed what a generous person you are."

"Thank you, Len."

"And you seem to be able to keep your own counsel."

"Do I?"

"Yes, ma'am."

She waited.

Len was looking at his shoes. "I wonder if you might help me with a little matter."

"Captain Early—"

"I suspect this matter would be disturbing to Captain Early, given his straitlaced views."

She wiped her hands with the dish towel and hung it up.

"My landlady says that she is going to sue me for breach of promise."

"Breach of promise! Did you make a promise?"

"Only in the sense that I was lonely and found her daughter a sympathetic listener. She is very interested in astronomy and physics, and everything about the universe. We talked only about that."

"Truly?"

"She's a—she's a—she's a plain girl. And possibly no man has heretofore talked to her about anything at all. One night, we talked until very late, and I, ahem, I kissed her. Could you come with me to the house and talk to her? She would respect you. Perhaps my side could get explained."

"What is your side?"

"Well, Mrs. Early, my side is that I'm already married."

She eyed him, the perfect example of the fact that almost any man could procure himself a wife, no matter how unprepossessing he happened to be. Len could have procured himself two had he been more daring. "You came here eight months ago. What is your wife doing?"

"She lives with her mother. I hadn't meant to stay so long—only for the winter. But Captain Early is very involving. Every time I say I'm finished with gathering material, he has a few more things that he simply must communicate. When I'm in his—orbit—I feel the—uh—gravitation of my other responsibilities fading."

"Didn't you tell me that you were unmarried? I mean, when you first got here."

"I don't believe I said anything about it. Our marriage has been . . . difficult." He looked her in the face. "Many are." Then he lowered his gaze and said, "I believe the separation has clarified . . ." His voice trailed off.

They went out to the Franklin. He moved toward the driver's door, but she stepped in front of him.

"Oh, goodness," he said, startled, "of course not." He went around the back end of the car.

Len's boarding house was on Carolina Street in Vallejo, up a steep hill. It was a nice enough bungalow-style house, large but a bit run-down, weeds beginning to claim parts of the front yard. The landlady was a Mrs. Branch, and the daughter, who looked about nineteen or twenty, was named Helen. She reminded Margaret a bit of herself at the same age. Mrs. Branch opened the door at their first knock. "You're Mrs. Early, then?"

"I am."

"Leonard works for your husband? I told Helen not to trust him, but she wouldn't listen, same as always."

"Len works *with* my husband, not *for* him. Len has his own project."

"I'll bet."

Mrs. Branch backed up reluctantly and allowed them in. Helen led them into the parlor. A couple of boarders could be heard scurrying up the stairs, and then running about the landing. She and Len sat down without being invited. Helen pushed her hair out of her face. The girl's skin was bad, but if she wore a pleasant expression, she could be attractive, Margaret thought, and a moment later, when the girl looked at Len, the look on her face did get more pleasant.

Margaret said, "I understand, Mrs. Branch, that Len hasn't been entirely forthcoming about his situation."

The woman's visage darkened.

"He does have something to tell you."

"What might that be?" said Mrs. Branch.

"Well, I'm married already, that's what," said Len. Helen gave a little gasp. Len glanced at her and went on, "And I never forget it, so I didn't make any promises, no matter what Helen has been telling you. I did kiss the girl, for which I apologize. But . . ." He trailed off. It occurred to Margaret not to believe him, but she chose to ignore that impulse.

"Isn't that a fine kettle of fish," said Mrs. Branch.

They all looked at Helen, whose eyes widened as her cheeks reddened.

Margaret understood right then that the girl was with child, though she didn't know what gave her that impression. She decided to ignore this intuition, too—whether Len was lying to her or Helen was lying to her mother was something she, at least, would never know. Len looked pettily triumphant, as if to say, Try and catch me.

"*Is* he married?" Mrs. Branch spoke pointedly to Margaret.

"Here's a picture of my wife," said Len. He reached into his breast pocket and pulled out a photograph. It showed him without his mustache, standing beside a round-faced young woman in a black hat. He had his arm about her waist. She wore a gardenia in her lapel. "We've been married for seven years."

He turned it over. On the back were the words "Mr. and Mrs. Leonard Scanlan, just married, May 4, 1921." The ink was a bit faded.

"Have you got any children?" said Mrs. Branch.

"I'm sorry to say that we haven't been that fortunate," said Len. His manner was utterly guileless, as if this fact was not quite Mrs. Branch's business but he was willing to answer. Now a bit of alarm began to replace the indignation in Mrs. Branch's face as she recognized the implications of this. She glanced at Helen, who was twisting her hand-kerchief in her lap. Len, Margaret discerned from the tilt of his chin, had no idea of the intelligence that was passing among the women in the room.

She said to Mrs. Branch, as if changing the subject and making small talk, "How long have you been in Vallejo?"

"About a year. I'll say this, it's dull here, but too many people at the same time." This was an idle remark, meant to cover her discomfort while she came up with a response to what she was figuring out. Helen coughed. Mrs. Branch said to her, "Well, you better get out to the scullery, miss. There's potatoes that need peeling."

Helen got up to leave the room—Len watched her out of the corner of his eye. She was an unlucky girl, Margaret thought, but not as unlucky as she might be, married to Len. Mrs. Branch said, "We hardly know a soul in town, really. I'm so busy with the boarders—"

"I think Vallejo's an interesting town. Lots of odd little shops to look at . . ."

"If you can get out."

"Well, if you do . . ." She took a bit of notepaper out of her bag and wrote Mrs. Kimura's name on it. Len watched her. She said, "This is a shop I like." She pressed the note into Mrs. Branch's hand. There was nothing else to say, so she and Len stood up.

With each step out of the boarding house, Len got perkier, and by the time they were sitting in the Franklin, he seemed almost giddy. She said, "You'll be finding another room after this, I imagine."

"Why should I? I like my room there, and it's cheap."

"Don't you think it would be the kinder thing to do?" She paused. "And your wife must miss you."

"Maybe."

He hummed a little tune as they drove back across the causeway.

She dropped Len off at the house and drove to the pond. She expected her spirits to lift at the sight of the coot chicks, who were get-ting quite large. She wondered when they were going to start learning to fly, for she had seen no signs of that.

The mist was heavier than it had been in town, and she didn't have a blanket to sit upon, so she simply walked toward the pond and then around it. One parent and four chicks were foraging along the edge, two of the chicks alternately walking and swimming in the shallows. Another chick was out in the middle, swimming in circles. She could not find the other chicks and the other adult. She walked around the pond until almost dark, looking as best she could into the shadows of cattails and damp grasses. A couple of times, she heard noises, as if some animal were rustling about in there, but she couldn't see anything. By the time she left, Margaret could only make out the adult and three of the chicks. As she drove home, she wondered if she had actually counted five chicks. She was no longer ready to say that she had.

Len was gone for the evening. Andrew, for once, was sitting in the front room, not even reading a book. When she walked in the door, he stood up and came over to her. She was shivering and looked around for her shawl. He loomed over her. "My dear, where have you been? You're all wet!"

"I was up at the pond, looking at the coots."

"Every time I want you, it seems you are gone."

"Does it? I thought you and Len were very busy." She slid out from under his shadow, but he followed her.

She envisioned the pond as if from above—a large target with bull's-eyes swimming about, getting bigger by the day. Andrew went on: "We are busy because our assault on ignorance, on the willful ignorance of my fellow scientists, is two-pronged. We must take them by storm, as we have not succeeded simply by being straightforward. My own preference would not be, I assure you, to have my name and accomplishments trumpeted about the way young Leonard proposes to do, but, as much as I need to present my ideas, I also need an advocate to set them in context."

"Is Len your best possible advocate, Andrew?"

"I have seen several pages of his writing, my dear, and it struck me as quite lucid and sufficiently detailed."

"But he's a veterinarian. He doesn't have a reputation in your field." She pushed these responses out, hardly noticing what she was saying, she was so cold and disinclined to have this conversation.

"He's quite as intelligent, though an autodidact, as some of, many of, those who purport to have degrees and monetary support. The substance of the ideas will carry the book."

"He isn't attached to any institution." She didn't think a bobcat would venture into the water, and the coots did stay in or close to the water. The nest she had seen was not ten feet from the water. A fox, though, or a coyote might swim. Foxes had been known to swim for prey. Even so, the real danger would be from hawks or eagles.

"That is a concern, I don't disagree with you. But he is my repository now! I have given myself over to him in a way I might not have done if . . ."

It was a terrible thing, the way the hawks and eagles allowed those infinitesimal just-hatched chicks to grow and put on bulk so that they would be worth eating. "If what?" she said, suddenly sounding exasperated even to herself. "I need my sh—"

"If I hadn't been so drawn in by his flattery. I admit that—that—"

The nest of the Canada geese recurred to her, now as an omen, the one egg broken in pieces and the nest ripped, flattened. She had thought the coots more careful, more deserving of survival, because they had built their nest in a secret spot.

"—that—that I am, or perhaps I seem, egotistical to some." He paused now, and looked at her, waiting for her to contradict this assertion. But she did not. "But it doesn't seem like ego, my dear, from the inside. I don't know what it does seem like, really." He said this in a pleading tone.

She had no reply, except that when he said "egotistical to some," she could not help thinking, "Egotistical to everyone." Everyone. Everyone. She felt the word rise to her lips and her whole body shift from cold to hot with the temptation to tell him the truth for once. She stepped away from him again, and he followed her again. She thought of her mother and Mrs. Early. The one so busy, the other so elegant. They had known what marriage was like. They had known what *Andrew* was like. That they had colluded in bringing this very moment about made her tremble with something unspeakable.

He stared at her. She was standing almost in the corner, and she had no idea what he wanted from her. He said, "I feel about Leonard that his mind is just a little common, you see. When we drive to my talks, he tells me all about the girls he has come to know in Vallejo, several girls, I can't keep their names straight, but he thinks that I will be impressed by such conquests. How can he think that, I ask you, having interviewed me for all these months, having listened to me reveal my, my thoughts to him about all those things that happened in Chicago and Berlin? How can he think that of me?"

She had a passing revelation that what Len Scanlan lingered in California for was nothing so simple as money or scientific innovation, but she said, "What happened in Chicago, Andrew?"

He blinked, and she realized that she had spat this out. Her hands were trembling, too. She grasped the left one with the right one. It seemed to her that if he said the word "universe," she really would scream. The universe, of course, was the very thing that circled around those chicks, vast and senseless.

Apparently, he decided to ignore this question, but his tone was conciliatory. "It's just that even in my new book, which you have so kindly typed over and over, I get lost in the versions. Did I say this already? Have I cut that? What is the best way of formulating a thought?" Then his voice rose and he put his hands in his hair. "The ideas simply come as a torrent! I can't describe it. When I spent time in Washington and Chicago, it was nearly— It was insupportable. I would be thinking one thing, and almost have it, almost understand it, some small thing, and then a thought, or even a word, dropped by a colleague, and that thing I was thinking simply lost shape utterly. It was a terrifying and frustrating feeling, I can't describe—"

What this conversation felt like, it occurred to her, was the ringing of many bells, their mouths yawning, their clappers hammering relentlessly. But finally, after a very long moment, she managed to say, "Andrew, you are sixty-one years old. You must have accepted that you have to accommodate—"

"Possibly that is what other men do, but I can't do that!"

"But what difference, in the end . . ." She trailed off, having said the most hurtful thing, but Andrew didn't register it. He exclaimed, "And I have! I have settled for less! I have settled for nothing! Can you not see that?"

What Margaret saw was that he would dispatch Len back to the East if she were to say anything right then about Helen Branch, or her own suspicions concerning Len's independent activities. All she had to do was confirm his doubts. Even a look might be enough. But she didn't say any word at all, didn't look at him.

Andrew said, "You will tell me that it's best to make of it what we can."

She remained silent, eyes down.

Now he sighed. Then, "If Leonard has been given me as the instrument, so be it."

So he was transformed once again. He said, "So many have died thinking their work had come to nought. Galileo. All of them, really." She lifted her eyes, no longer in danger. He smoothed down his mustache and then, almost jaunty, turned toward his study. He patted her arm. "Well, good night, my dear."

Margaret emerged from her corner and fell into her chair.

Later, she heard him leave for the observatory.

When she next got to the pond, she realized at once that the slaughter had progressed. In an hour of looking about, she saw only three of the chicks, two rather large and one smaller. The three went about together, pecking up leaves and seeds and insects, swimming, tramping along the edge of the water. They still had their fluff, or most of it; had neither molted to actual feathers nor learned, as far as she could tell, to fly. It was tormenting to her that everything she noticed about them endeared them to her, and yet proved to her that they were doomed.

Two days later, there was one left. The next day, that one was gone. She did weep tears. She did. She also took Mr. Kimura's picture off the wall and put it in a closet.

ON the way home from a talk in Salinas, Andrew and Len stopped at the racetrack and visited Pete at his stall. Len found the denizens of the racetrack "low," but Andrew was reminded of times he had enjoyed with his mother at Saratoga and somewhere in Europe. The visit made him jovial for a day or two, and he kept saying, "My dear, you should visit him. He asked for you. You would enjoy the equines a great deal." And again, "The air is quite bracing there, my dear. It would do you good." And again, "A change is always revivifying."

Margaret felt herself resist until he said, "And why don't you take those screens of his back to him? The scroll, too."

She said, "Surely he doesn't want to keep them in a horse stall at the racetrack."

"Then, my dear, he will find a place for them or sell them."

She loaded the artworks in the back of the Franklin and dropped Andrew and Len at the train station so they could go to Santa Barbara for Andrew's talk at the Club of Fifty. The Club of Fifty was giving them first-class tickets, overnight accommodations at the recently opened Biltmore in Montecito, and a fee of four hundred dollars. Andrew was very excited, and both of them had been looking forward to the date for two and a half months. His topic was to be "Are New Ideas in Science Inherently Different from Old Ones?" That answer, of course, was "no." His audience would be uniformly old, so he expected them to be receptive.

She circumnavigated the bay west of Oakland, then cut across by means of the Dumbarton Bridge, where she was stopped for quite a while when it lifted to allow a ship to pass, but the lifting itself was rather an interesting sight, and so she didn't mind. What was funny to her was how archaic the Franklin looked among all the other cars, but it was still beautiful, and it ran perfectly.

She drove through the gates at Tanforan, and heads turned and men in fedoras with cigars poking out of their faces and little books and pencils in their hands smiled at her. It was just after eight, and horses were still training. As Pete had told Andrew, there was as yet no racing. Most of the horses wore blankets over their haunches, and their riders leaned into themselves, keeping one hand on the reins and putting the other in their armpits. They all had their caps pulled down over their ears, breath pluming out of their mouths. The horses' shoes rang on the cold ground. Piles of soiled bedding seemed to smoke between the barns. And the fragrance did please her.

She found Pete walking from the track behind three of his animals. When he saw her, he said, "Goodness me, an apparition!" He kissed her on the cheek before he looked around, then he said, "Where is Andrew?"

"On the way to Santa Barbara with Len. I have your screens."

"I thought you might." He peeked in the window, then said, "Andrew has been warning me of their return." He didn't look disappointed.

"Show me a horse."

"My pleasure!" He was perfectly turned out, even in his horse-keeping clothes. He waited as she parked the Franklin, and then two of the grooms took the artworks and carried them away. He led her down the barn aisle. Grooms and trainers touched the bills of their caps and dipped their heads to her in a friendly manner. There was no sign of the crooked Australian. After she had appreciated how the horses arched their necks over the tops of the stall doors and put their noses out for lumps of sugar, Pete had his own four stripped of their blankets and led out for her appreciation. There were two bays, a chestnut, and a gray.

"This one is by Fair Play, goes back to Bend Or on both sides. Dam's by Tetratema, that's where he gets the gray color. This filly is by a nice French horse named Rose Prince, dam's by Son-in-Law. That's a very prepotent sire. All . . ."

She could make nothing of this patter, but it fell gloriously on the ear. When his voice ceased, she said, "You sound very expert."

"That's the first step."

"How is it you acquired these horses but live in a stall?"

"Unpaid bills, darling. The owners' unpaid bills," said Pete. "Chestnut is my nicest one, four wins already."

"Might I pet one of them?"

He pointed to the gray. "He's a friendly sort. I'm sure he would like it. Good racehorses often bite, but he never does—more's the pity for my pocketbook."

She stepped up to the horse, and he pressed his nose into her outstretched palm while she stroked along the roots of his mane. After a moment, she took off her glove. His coat was dappled and fluffy, perfectly clean. She put her cheek against his neck and took a deep breath.

Pete's stall quarters were neatly tricked out, with a cot and cases and trunks, and prints hanging on the walls, and a curled-up whip with a long lash, and a mirror in a gilt frame. She said, "You don't live here."

Pete smiled.

She dared to say, "I am sure you live with some rich woman in Atherton. Maybe she will like the screens."

Pete laughed.

She was glad she had come. The fragrance of the horses and the neat piles of horse clothing and equipment, the cold stables, the horses stamping and snorting—it was a change. Then he took her elbow. "I need some breakfast. Would you care for a pot of tea, madam? We can go to the canteen."

As they were making their way around puddles and piles of dirt, she said, "Pete, you do seem at home."

"You're never old at a racetrack. There's always someone older than you, who's been around since the Civil War and was actually there to see Kincsem run—or Eclipse, for that matter."

"You seem young to me."

"I'm two years younger than that pig Lenin, and he's been dead for five years now. So I'm old. In Russia, I would be dead. I'm older than you are."

"Then you must be old."

He said, "But see? Here you look especially elegant. I get on my pony named Ivan Grozny, who is the sleepiest, sweetest thing in the world, and I ride out to watch the boys train the horses and I feel very sprightly."

He didn't ask her about Andrew, and Margaret didn't say a word about him, either.

The canteen was a humble place, but it had eggs and toast and coffee and tea, and it was another nice change to sit at a rickety table among all the men with their bits of paper on which they were scribbling numbers or hotly comparing their bits with the bits others were scribbling on. She saw that the men greeted Pete sociably, as if expecting a witticism or a canny remark. After a bit, though, the canteen emptied out. She said, "Must you leave, too?"

He shook his head. "Mine are finished for the day. If they would allow gambling in California, you could see them run."

She nodded. Then, giddily emboldened by all these pleasures, she said, "Tell me something about you that I can't imagine."

He smiled. "I wore dresses until I was three years old."

"That's what boys did in those days. Something else."

"How about this? When I first came to the States, I worked in vaudeville. As a regurgitator."

"I don't believe that!"

"You see, there you go."

"What did you regurgitate?"

"I put out fires with sprays of regurgitated water." He was grinning. "Or I was supposed to. I hadn't quite perfected my act when I first went on in Vacaville, and the tube popped out from behind my ear. I got booed off the stage, and the theater manager fired me. Then I tried to join a circus, doing some horse vaulting, but they said they had Cossacks coming out of their ears, though most of the ones I saw were Mexicans or Italians. Now you tell me something."

"Nothing I have to tell is interesting."

"If I don't know it, it's interesting."

"When I was eight, my older brother went down to the railyards with some friends. They found a blasting cap and affixed it to a piece of iron they found, and then one of the boys rubbed it against some bricks. It exploded and drove the length of iron right into my brother's skull."

"That was a very unlucky thing."

"Yes, but unique. It seemed to me he couldn't possibly have died like that, so it took me a very long time to believe that he had. I'd think of what happened and I would start to laugh. I had two brothers and they both died as boys. But in Missouri after the War Between the States, you didn't expect boys to live, somehow."

"I had an uncle gored by a bull. My mother's brother."

"I saw a hanging, they say. But I have never been able to recall it. I was five. I recall earlier things, but of that I only remember fragments. Once I thought I remembered the boy's name, Claghorne. Such an odd name. Now I have no idea if that was really his name or not. He wore a red shirt. Maybe. My brother put me on his shoulders. Maybe! You'd think I would remember such a thing."

"Have you heard of Sigmund Freud?"

She said, "No."

There was a pause while he went to the counter for more coffee. She closed her eyes and made herself think of the hanging, but making herself think of it made it go away. When he sat down again, he said, "What were you like as a girl?"

"Oh, I don't know. I was the third sister even though I'm the oldest. There's always a beautiful sister and a smart sister, and then there's a sister that's not beautiful or smart."

"You kept out of trouble, then."

"Oh yes."

"So few do."

Now it was her turn to laugh. "But that's why I loved Dora so from the first time I saw her. She was always scouting for mischief, and she always dressed for it. When I first met her, she had a bicycle and a very strange costume, with pantaloons, but it was the newest thing."

"The first time I saw her, she had the shortest skirt in the restaurant, and you could almost see the swell of her calf. That was very daring then."

"I miss Dora."

"But she is returning! She should be here in a month."

This was news to Margaret. She sipped her tea in confusion. Pete said, "I haven't seen the painting."

"Mr. Kimura's painting?"

"I thought it would be good. He was very intent."

"It is good. But I put it away. I can't hang it."

His eyebrow lifted. "Andrew?"

"No, no. No! All the coots were slaughtered. Parents, chicks, all of them."

"Oh," said Pete.

"Did everyone expect that besides me? Is that why everyone was always saying what common birds they were?"

He leaned forward and looked her intently in the face. He said, "Tell me something about you that I don't know."

Tears sprang into her eyes. He said, "Tell me." He took her hand between his.

She said, "But you know it! Dora must have told you. Twenty years ago, my baby died," and in a moment she was really weeping, in spite of all the years and all the layers of "all for the best in the end." He did not grow restless in his chair. And he did not speak. He had seen a lot worse; wasn't that the first thing you knew about him? But he didn't mention any of those things, either. He waited for her to take her hands away from her face, and then he handed her his pink handkerchief. He said, "It was Kiku who told me."

Margaret steadied her breath, then said, "Oh yes. She came and held the baby. I never knew why."

"Well, she did tell me that, too."

Margaret waited. It was surprising how even now she couldn't ask the question. But Pete didn't need to be asked. He said, "She had some herbs with her, to offer you. But when she held the baby, she saw—"

"That nothing would do any good." But she was no longer weeping—she was again used to Alexander's fate.

Pete nodded. He looked like the soul of kindness. She blew her nose. She said, "But the coots were also coots. I hated the way the last three babies staggered about together, looking for bits to eat. I hated how doomed they were."

"Of course you did," said Pete. That was all, but it was enough, she thought.

They drank the last bit of tea. It was getting colder and windier outside, and she began to think she should get home. He walked her to the Franklin. He held the door. She got in and put down the window. Her gloved hand was on the door as he closed it, and he took it in his and kissed it. Then he bowed slightly and turned away. She pressed the starter with her foot, but she didn't drive off at once. She sat there until he disappeared through the gate, and even after that.

When she got home, she took out the picture. What she saw this time were the two curves—the steep rise of the hillside beyond the pond, and the answering flat line of the far edge of the pond itself. Beneath these two large shapes, almost lost among the waving grasses, were the cluster of coots in the right foreground, and the gay, foolhardy chick, swimming quickly (as demonstrated by the rivulets around him) to the left. His figure drew the eye, of course, and wasn't the eye that was drawn her eye, but also the eye of the hawk, unseen, floating on an air current high above? She thought it was a wonderful but terrible picture, like the picture of the snake, and she put it back in the closet.

When Andrew inquired after Pete, she said that he seemed to be prospering. Andrew was gratified at the success of his scheme for her welfare, and suggested, "Perhaps, my dear, you need a biweekly outing, if not all the way to the racetrack, then to some other place of recreation."

DORA finally came late in the winter, and what a winter it had been. The stock market had crashed, and the Bells had lost a lot of money. Margaret heard about it in every letter from Beatrice, who was in a panic, because Robert's partner had killed himself, and the reasons why were still locked in the books ("the second set," wrote Elizabeth, which could not be found). Andrew had lost some money, too, but not much. He was still planning to pay cash for the large Italianate house they were buying as a result of his retirement and his enforced move from the island to Vallejo. If he hadn't had so much work to do with Len, he would have liked to deliver her to the Palace Hotel himself, and welcome Dora back to the West Coast personally. As it was, he inspected and approved her outfit before she left the house and said that he would meet the dinnertime ferry just to hear all about Dora's recent adventures.

Dora maintained that the Crash would not affect her; her new paper (the *New York Herald Tribune,* much more fashionable than the *Exam-*

iner) was actually beginning to turn a profit, and her editor was so intimidating that the publisher didn't dare defy him. She was on a cross-country tour, interviewing victims of the Crash, high and low. Talking about the Crash took precedence in their conversation, as in every conversation Margaret had had in four months.

Dora said, "All the experts say this will be nothing truly fearsome."

"Do you believe them?"

"No."

"Why not?"

"Because the ones with the money don't have it anymore. It's gone, and they know it's gone. They don't believe the experts, even though they hired them."

"But Andrew says the stock market is going up again."

Dora shrugged.

"What is it like in Europe?"

"Well"—she shook her head—"Italy, of course, is terrifying—more so every day. England is okay, but you know they'll never recover from the Great War. I'm sure, if a real depression hits, they will blame the Americans somehow."

"What about France?"

Dora smiled. "You know France. It's nice there. When things start to go bad, for at least a while France freezes in place. You can go about your pleasures and say to yourself that disaster is coming, but this is a lovely peach and there are beautiful cows out in the field, and let's go find a two-room apartment in Biarritz and sit this out. Darling, I wonder and I wonder where I want to be for the next few years, and I can't come up with an answer. I just let the paper send me about, and count the places I don't want to be."

"Where don't you want to be the most?"

"Missouri."

"That's the safest place, maybe."

"Well, yes, darling. It's unprecedented."

When Dora probed Margaret, Margaret talked about the house—not up a steep hill, anyway—about the charitable work the ladies on the island were doing. Dora kept smiling, then said, "I love your life. When I would think about you in Europe, it was always such a comforting thought: Andrew like a big moving pillar, stalking down the street, never deviating from the path he had set, and you buzzing around him, his very own human being."

"Dora!"

"Oh, I wasn't thinking that you were enslaved or anything." She peeped at Margaret from under the brim of her hat. "Or, rather, while there are those women's rights advocates who think that marriage is a form of contract slavery at best, I wasn't thinking of you in that way. The thought just always made me give thanks for soundness and stability and the knowledge that, somewhere in the world, things were going on as they always do."

Margaret merely said, "You do talk like a woman who never got married."

She meant to be saying one thing, but Dora thought she was saying another. She tossed her head. "Don't you know? I was so short and plain and wayward, no amount of money could purchase me a husband."

"You haven't lived in St. Louis in thirty years. I'm sure there were candidates."

Dora looked around the tearoom as a hostess might, watching her guests take their leave. Then she looked at Margaret. She said, "What was the last book you read?"

"*So Big.* I'd like to read *Show Boat.*"

"Have you heard of *The Well of Loneliness*?"

"No."

"Gertrude Stein?"

"I know that name."

"I'm going to give you a copy of *The Well of Loneliness.*"

"But what about Pete?"

"I told you that years ago."

"That he asked you for money?"

"Did I say that? Didn't I tell you—"

"What?"

"Darling, he is married. He's always been married. He saw her when he was in Russia. She's a terrible Bolshie, and he likes to pretend that she's dead, but she isn't dead at all. I think that's why he changed his name, so she'll think *he* is dead."

"Do they have any children?"

"I don't know. If you ask him, he'll tell you that she strangled them in the cradle. I suppose that there's always the chance that a child will turn up to haunt him, but he's covered his tracks pretty well."

"We know him."

"But we don't know anyone else who does, do we?"

"The Kimuras."

"Secret-keepers extraordinaire, *n'est-ce pas?*"

"I hardly know them, but they're very nice to me."

"They don't gossip, do they?"

"No."

"There you go. Pete is safe with them."

"And with you."

"I don't know enough to be a danger to him—no names."

"But what did he do in the Revolution?"

"What did he tell you?"

"I got the impression that he escorted hapless aristocrats to Paris and rented apartments for them."

"He did do that. Three times. He was good at that. But that wasn't a full-time job."

"What was a full-time job?"

"Have you heard of Antonov?"

She shook her head.

"Well, there were more factions in Russia than just the Reds and the Whites. There was a faction called the 'SRs,' who splintered off the Bolsheviks after the October Revolution, mostly because the peasants didn't like Red grain seizures, and Antonov was their leader. All of Pete's relatives in Ukraine hated the Bolsheviks because they were city boys and had no respect for peasants. By 1920, Antonov's supporters were armed to the teeth. It was quite a popular and well-organized movement, and Antonov was a smart fellow."

"What happened?"

"Well, I'm not sure in which order this was, but the Bolsheviks rounded up the women and children and put them in starvation camps as hostages. In the meantime, they cleared out the forests where Antonov's army was hiding out, using gas. They just filled the forests with gas, and the Blacks, as they were called, died in droves."

"We never heard about this."

"Didn't you?"

"Poison gas?"

"That's the new way, I'm afraid. Pete says a million died, but I don't know. I'm sure it seemed like the end of the world. Anyway, Pete was there part of the time, and part of the time he was beating the bushes for money and guns. But they hadn't foreseen how ruthless the Bolsheviks were. Pete said to me, 'I knew them all along. I just didn't know *this* about them.' "

"The wife?"

"She must have been one of them. It's a wonder to me that he escaped, and, having escaped, that he can smile at all, but Russians are fatalists first and foremost. Antonov was killed in '22. After that, Pete was in Europe for a while. I don't think he dares go back to the Soviet Union, of course."

"Maybe he changed his name because of that."

"Maybe."

Margaret said, "I never believed he was Russian. I finally decided that he was an Irishman from Chicago pretending to be a Russian. His accent is so . . ."

"Fake?"

"Well, nonexistent now. But always uneven."

Dora stirred her tea thoughtfully, then said, "I believe the big parts. Most of the big parts. I don't mind the other parts. I don't know about the accent. Other people have said that, too. But he grew up speaking lots of languages, and he's a good mimic. I knew an actor in England who could speak in fifteen accents, including French, German, Italian, and Spanish, and if you heard him through a wall, you would think he was five or six men and women having a conversation."

When the weather was pleasant, she went back to Tanforan with Dora. The banter between Pete and Dora was the same as it had always been—affectionate but ironical. At one point, Dora said, "I want to ride one," and would not be denied. Pete said, "No, you may not, but if you come dressed properly, you may hack the pony." They went on about this for ten minutes, laughing. Margaret trotted behind them, overlooked. As they left, though, Pete squeezed her hand, and said, "I'm settled now, you know. I've found a house in Atherton. Here's the address. I was rather hoping that you could make the time to bring Andrew." He pressed a square of paper into her hand. It had a telephone number, too. Andrew was fond of the telephone. He called Len late at night when he changed his views on things.

LELIE SCANLAN appeared unannounced on a train from the east, and Len acted as if he were happy to see her. She was no longer quite the pale, retiring thing she had appeared to be in her wedding picture. She came for supper twice and talked incessantly—it was really rather remarkable, Margaret thought, that her voice could hold out. Len, no mean talker himself, remained silent. The woman even out-talked Andrew, who didn't say a word through dessert. Len had now completed his five-hundred-page manuscript entitled *The Genius of Captain Andrew Jackson Jefferson Early.* The publisher was in Kansas City. They planned to print a thousand copies. However, Len, they said, had to cut the manuscript to fifty thousand words. Andrew said, "They have told him, 'Folks are interested in Captain Early as a specimen of a certain era, but not *as interested as all that.*' "

Lelie was incensed at the time wasted. All Margaret said was "Goodness"—her surprise was that the publisher thought anyone at all was interested in any way.

For a day or two, Andrew and Len stormed about the new house, decrying the blindness of the publisher, but then they reconciled themselves. Now, as a result of the imminent publication of Len's book (he got busy with cutting and, newly emboldened, informed Andrew in no uncertain terms that he and only he, Len, was in charge of the final product), Andrew had to get his own volumes into shape, so that the books could be published at the same time and thus fulfill Andrew's dreams for a "one-two punch." Her typing time went up to five hours every day. At first she could barely stand it, and when she sat down at the typewriter, she felt a trembling, physical rage as she put her fingers on the keys. She thought of a sailor she had heard of on the island who learned to type very fast by putting a brown paper sack over his head, and then got so that he could only type with the sack over his head, and as she thought of this man, she was able to begin her typing. There were no teas with Dora at the Palace, no more trips to Tanforan.

The goal, Andrew said, was to get an absolutely clean thought, an uninterrupted idea of some six hundred pages (two volumes) that would unfold itself like a column of smoke rising into the clouds. The ideal would be that he would write and she would type from page one to page six hundred in one long session, but, of course, humanity was not made for ideals. The lower needs of humanity would always break up ideals with food and sleep and distraction. However, they did start at the beginning and go straight to the end, and Andrew did his best to remain on the subject. It took three months. In the last half of this period, Andrew simply dictated, usually from memory, and she took his dictation, invaded again by the universe, so thoroughly invaded after a while that the rest of her thoughts and memories and yearnings were scoured away. She cooked; she typed; she slept. They finished in the same week that Len sent off his manuscript to Kansas City. She dozed for three days.

But Andrew and Len needed no time to recuperate. They endlessly discussed the optimum season for publishing their books. They imagined themselves taking a cross-country trip and doing a set of joint lectures on the Chautauqua circuit, except that, for the most part, Chautauquas had fallen by the wayside. They envisioned a set of radio addresses, in which they would alternate lecturing with conversation about Andrew's great ideas—"an educational revolution" was the term they used. However, they found they had no access to the radio. They had worked for so many years on their books, and now that the nation was preoccupied with the aftermath of the Crash, fewer people than ever cared about the universe. They lamented what might have been if they had worked more quickly, if they had known then what they knew now, but, ultimately, they decided that the power of their ideas would carry the day.

All this time, Andrew talked a lot about his death, as if that, perhaps, were the one key to his ideas' prevailing. He was sixty-four now, and his father had died at fifty-four. Andrew had no sense of how quickly he might pass on—preferably of natural causes. Now that his book was to come out, the sooner the better was fine with him. He chatted over supper about the possibility of dying at just the right time with perfect equanimity, and also, Margaret thought, with no concept of what it would actually be like not to exist.

Dora was visiting for one of these suppers. She sat across from Andrew over the roasted chicken and talked first about a woman she had met who had given birth to her child by the side of the Lincoln Highway, just near Reno, and then set the baby in the middle of the road, "as the most merciful thing" she could think of, "since there was six others plus that one," then about Eleanor Roosevelt, while Andrew fell silent only to resume, as soon as Dora was finished talking, his catalogue of overlooked geniuses who died in despair. That evening, his favorite was Johannes Kepler. "His mother was tried for witchcraft," he said. Dora stared at him. "Of course, Kepler was a sociable man. One had to be, in those days." When he got up to go to his study, it occurred to Margaret to betray him, to betray him utterly, by taking Dora for a walk and asking for help. She could describe this feeling she had, that her marriage had become an intolerable torture, that the sight of his head ducking slightly as he went through doorways of the new house was repellent to her, that she felt warm, humid air press against her when he entered the room, that his voice made her want to scream, that she thought he was a fool and even a madman, and that she was going mad herself, that, from the outside, every marriage looked as bad to her, because she knew every house she passed was a claustrophobic cell where at least one of the partners never learned anything, but did the same things over and over, like an infernal machine, and the other partner had no recourse of any kind, no way out, no one to talk to about it, not even any way to look at it all that gave relief. The doorways of the new house were very high. It was mere habit to duck his head for them. She almost said it, but she could not.

Later that night, in bed, she wondered why she had simply gotten up from her seat with a smile and begun taking dishes off the table while Dora told her about a man she had met named Nucky Johnson who she was sure had ordered the execution of someone else—Margaret lost track of the rest. How could she so want to talk, and yet so much hate and fear talking? But what would be her recourse? When was it that Mrs. Tillotson had gained her divorce, ten years ago now? More? And what a nightmare that had been—since Henrietta had allowed the adultery to go on for years before he bought the girl the house, the judge had been quite skeptical. And Margaret could still remember what grounds for divorce were—abandonment, drunkenness, beatings, criminal behavior. Mere torment was not among them. In the morning, she walked out of the house before dawn and got into the Franklin. Soon she was heading across the causeway and then south around the bay.

Perhaps, she thought afterward, if she had used the telephone, it would have shown some doubt on her part about her destiny. Perhaps, she thought, using Andrew's telephone to call Pete would have been akin to asking Andrew to give Pete a message. And she didn't know Atherton, had never been there. But she drove as if directed, and when she arrived at Pete's door, he was standing in front of his house, his hands in his pockets. He recognized the Franklin instantly, of course, and burst out laughing.

Pete's house was long and low. The roof hung over the veranda like the roof of a bungalow, sheltering a line of windows and a modest black front door. There were chairs, as if a person could sit there.

Pete was at the door of the Franklin, opening it, and then he took her hand and helped her out, and then he kissed her, though only on the cheek, as if he were her brother or uncle, the most chaste of kisses, but still, indeed, a kiss. He took her elbow and guided her to the curb, then up the walk. She did feel wobbly, that was true enough, but it never crossed her mind to wonder at the fact that a man who worked miles away, who had calls upon his time and a profusion of associates, would be there to greet her, to take her through the gate to the back garden, to seat her at a neat little table inside a gazebo, and to bring her a cup of lemon tea. By the time he had set the pot in front of her, she was breathless and her hat had come unpinned. She took it off and set it on the chair beside her bag. Then she took off her gloves. Now it seemed to her that she was more or less unclothed.

But apparently Pete didn't see it that way. He chatted on, got up, went into the house, brought out a plate of shortbread cookies. She ate one, and the view cleared a bit. The backyard was a large garden—there were several lemon trees with lemons and blossoms, and daylilies along the fence, and a stand of bamboo between his yard and that of the neighbors. The gazebo itself was shaded by two large eucalyptus trees. It became possible to breathe.

Pete said, "Where is the captain this morning?"

"I don't know."

There was a long pause.

"Gone over to the island, I expect." It could be that he did not hear her, her voice was so weak.

Pete said, "You aren't used to this, are you?"

Margaret said, "Used to what?" But she also shook her head.

"You keep looking toward the neighbors, as if they might spy on us."

"Mightn't they?"

"They wouldn't dare." He lifted her bare hand and kissed it. She let him hold it. He did, stroking her fingers.

The interior of the house was clean and spare. The two screens were set to the back of the front room, out of the sunlight. There was another screen in the dining room, mounted on the wall, more modest but striking—in the picture, an old man was carrying something large and bronze, like a vase. Out of it a horse was bursting, its head up, its tail up, its knees tucked in front of its chest. Pete said, "That is a picture of unexpected good luck." He had not let go of her hand. The picture of the lady with her servant and child was hung across from the horse, much more colorful. There were other paintings, too, but they were European—harsh and bright, with strange shapes standing in for faces and bodies. She said, "Have you gone back to collecting?"

"Not art."

"What, then?"

"Armaments."

She laughed. There, in front of those pictures, while she was still laughing, he took her in that embrace she had seen, that tight thing, that deep, comforting, overwhelming, body-bending, mind-erasing enclosure. The rest, after that, was awkward and irresolute, hateful in the unzipping and the unbuttoning and the chill of his alien bedroom, but that thing that she had been thinking of for years, that was perfect.

LEN's book appeared in early January, right after one of the worst Christmases ever, in the midst of bad weather all over the country. Len told them that publication would be accompanied by advertisements in several Missouri papers, including the one in Columbia, and Robert's paper in Darlington, and one of the St. Louis papers. When these were sent to them, they turned out to be small boxes at the bottom of inside columns. The text of the ads ran, "Who is, perhaps, Missouri's GREATEST scientific genius? BUY *The Genius of Captain Andrew Jackson Jefferson Early* and FIND OUT how a HOME GROWN Missouri boy STUNNED the nation and the WORLD! Ask at your local bookstore TODAY!" After that, nothing.

Crates of Andrew's volumes arrived from San Francisco about a week later, very many of them, and once again, Andrew hired a young man to send them out, because Len declared in no uncertain terms that he was not a secretary, and that he had already begun his next book, which was about legendary ghosts of California—he had fifty pages and a publisher, this time in Los Angeles. Margaret didn't know whether this was a greater blow to Andrew's pride than the absolute silence that greeted his volumes, but the young man they hired did send them out assiduously to every scientific publication in the English-speaking world. There were no reviews, and it became clear, as the winter faded first to spring and then to summer, that Andrew's *New Theory of the*

Aether had met with either apathy or hostility, and, in the end, what was the difference?

What Andrew's theory was, precisely, she could not herself have said, though she partially understood the second half of the second volume, which was that if they could harness the power of the Aether, they would be as gods—space travel, time travel, *Alice in Wonderland*–like expansion and contraction, the idea of the universe as an idea, the expansion of a single person's inner life into the size of the universe, all would be possible. In other words, having been left to think and think and think, Andrew had made up his mind that thinking was everything.

Andrew invited Pete to supper and gave him all the volumes—his book and the biography. Pete came back again, at Andrew's insistence, and discussed them. He expressed surprise and delight at Andrew's ideas. He questioned him in some detail. And he was courteous to Margaret in exactly the way that he had always been. Margaret didn't know if she was hurt or disappointed or relieved. In fact, sitting across from him at the table seemed surprisingly routine. But didn't she know that he was practiced at exactly this? Hadn't he let her know that again and again over the years? She sat watching the two of them, not daring to do much more than pass the potatoes and maintain a pleasant expression. That she could do even this seemed astonishingly cool to her, as if she had turned into an entirely different woman—Dora, perhaps.

Andrew's position came to be "They have forgotten me. They have simply forgotten me." He stopped talking about his death, since he was healthier than ever.

It was when she was about to get on the streetcar in San Francisco that she picked up the *Chronicle*. On page three of the second section was the headline "The Strange Case of Captain Early." The feeling she had as she was sitting on that slippery bench seat, as the car tilted upward to climb California Street, was one she didn't think she had ever before had—something akin to being electrocuted, but not fatally. There was a picture of Andrew standing outside the observatory and a picture of his book, with the caption "An example of wholesale plagiarism?" And there was another picture, of a man she had never seen, who turned out to be Andrew's old student from Chicago, now a full professor, and possibly the only person to have read the books. His hair was gray, too. The gist of this man's accusations against Andrew was that where the ideas presented in "Early's two-volume monstrosity" were not laughable, they were stolen—from him. As evidence for this assertion, the writer of the article took two passages from books by each of them and compared the two side by side. Margaret read them as the streetcar lumbered along, and she judged that they were similar. One was from the first volume of Andrew's book, and that was slightly less similar. The other, from the second volume, was not word for word, but it was also not more than 15 percent different (she counted the words in both passages). The case, at least from these two examples, was a damning one. But the article was short—about a column. If she wanted to know more, she was directed to an article by this man in *The Astronomical Journal* to which Andrew had renewed his subscription in anticipation of his "one-two punch." There had also been, according to the *Chronicle,* a piece about this in the *New York Times. The Astronomical Journal* article, which she was sure was somewhere in her house, she had not seen. Had Andrew? It was impossible to tell. She read over the bit from the second volume again and put the paper in her bag.

On the way home that evening on the ferry, she could not help reconsidering the two passages. She decided, or possibly remembered, that the second passage was one that Andrew had dictated directly to her, without any sort of notes, just striding about the front room with his hands clasped behind his back (except for when he was smoothing down his mustache), holding forth. It was an odd way to commit plagiarism, except for one thing—Andrew's overcapacious memory. The terrible difficulty of writing the book had always been trimming and paring and pruning, not engendering. He had tried in every conceivable way over the years to clarify and straighten out the jungly growth of his ideas. He had written from notes. He had cut bits and pieces from early drafts. He had thrown away drafts and started over. He had made outlines and stuck to them. But the burden of his mind was that it *would* invent, it would proliferate, it would swarm and multiply. And it was horribly retentive. Andrew saw this as a sign of his own genius, as no doubt his mother had. That was the way it was when they were growing up—if you could memorize one poem, that was good; two was better, and four was best. Andrew said that he had excelled at memorizing and could still recite poems or speeches he had learned before he was ten years old. She saw it perfectly—even while he threw off the constraints of what he had already written and rewritten many times, he still thought in those very words that he had already composed, just as a high-speed locomotive races down the track that has been laid for it. For Andrew, plagiarism was not some laborious copying of someone else's words and ideas, but a wholesale and yet precise assimilation of them—the energy of the ideas as well as the particles of the individual words. As soon as she thought this, she knew that it was true, and that she herself was the only person to understand how it worked. As the ferry crossed the bay, making that peculiar deep groaning noise that was so familiar to her, she thought of him again and again, striding about, talking. And she thought, for the first time in her life, that he must be in agony, must have always been in agony. And once she thought that, she thought that as a kindness she might write to the *Chronicle,* or to *The Astronomical Journal,* defending him.

That night, at supper and after, she watched Andrew, trying to gauge whether he had read the *Chronicle* piece or *The Astronomical Journal* piece. She dared not ask, dared not precipitate a discovery. Indeed, could it be like what was said about vermin—if, purely by chance, you saw one article about your husband's plagiarizing as you were riding the streetcar, was that only the merest fraction of the number that were actually out there? Possibly, unbeknownst to her, he had a file of such articles stuck in a drawer in his study, and he mulled them over every day.

Over the next few days, she decided that the safest course was to pretend that she hadn't seen the article.

But Len had.

He was at their door, the paper in his hand. As soon as Margaret opened the door, he waved the paper and shouted, "I was up in Eureka! Where's Captain—"

"He's not here. He's—"

But Andrew came around the house—he had heard voices from the backyard. He saw that Len had a paper in his hand and said, suspiciously (but these days suspicion of Len, a believer in ghosts, was constant with him), "What's that?"

"Well you might ask," said Len.

Len turned to walk down the front steps, and Margaret let the door close. She went back into the house, first into the kitchen, and then upstairs. But she could hear much of what they said, because it was a warm day and the windows were open. She heard Len say, "If I had known this, if I had had any idea that such a thing was possible, I would never have devoted my life and my reputation to . . ." So, she thought, that was how it was going to go. No defense of Andrew by Len, either. She closed the window, and stayed in her room for about an hour.

When she came downstairs, Andrew was sitting quietly in a chair, look-ing out the window, but as soon as he saw her, he said, "I think, my dear, that I will go out for a walk. It is a beautiful day."

She could not resist. She said, "Andrew, just one question."

"What would that be, my dear?" Of course, he thought she was going to ask the plagiarism question, but she had answered that herself. The question she asked was "How has Len supported himself here for all of these years?"

His shoulders began to shrug, but she held up her hand. She said, "Did you pay for the publication of that book?"

"Well, I did. Yes."

"Does he know that?"

"Possibly the publisher let that slip at some point."

"Does anyone else know that?"

He didn't answer, and perhaps he didn't know.

After a moment, he said, "He was a stranger. Coming here was his idea."

"But it turned out that he couldn't find a publisher, and so . . ."

"We put years of work into his book."

She heaved a sigh, that was all. It was not in her to say, "Serves you right," or even to reflect more soberly that Andrew had reaped what he had sown, or received a just and fitting punishment. All she could do was wonder what there was in him that had to persist. And what came first, the persistence or the orphaned ideas? Astronomers all over the world, she gathered, had moved on, and been thrilled to do so. But this was what marriage was, wasn't it? A wife could know that her husband was thoroughly wrong, but the last thing on earth she could do was say so. Andrew got up and went out. About two weeks later, after sorting papers furiously, he did the only thing he knew how to do, which was start writing another book. When he showed her the first pages, when she saw the first mention of the Aether, she said, "You had better learn to type." She was firm. She thought that would slow him down, but he bought a more modern typewriter, and she could hear him every day, behind the door of his spacious study, tap-tap-tap.

1933

PART FIVE

1937

I T WAS TRUE, as Margaret remembered Lavinia saying, "Habit proves stronger than passion." What really happened, she came to believe, was that those nights when she lay awake wondering what it would be like to move back to Missouri (and would she live with Beatrice, whose letters were litanies of complaint or suffering, depending upon Margaret's mood, or Elizabeth, who had become so thoroughly reticent that Margaret had no idea at all of her true state of mind?) were remembered but no longer felt. Those mornings when she arose trembling with dread at the idea of hearing his first "my dear" came to be lived through—what seemed a horror was endured and then buried in the routine of daily activities. Andrew seemed to have learned a lesson, finally, and become merely himself—no larger than life-size. She took some deep breaths, planted a rose garden, did most of what was asked of her. Philosophy intruded—she looked around and compared her condition with the general run of things and was grateful for continuing good health. Most important, she became adept at the neutral smile, the moment of patient silence, the arrangements of the day and the night that kept order around the house (no stacks of papers in the front hall or the kitchen, the dining room neat). She remembered Lavinia saying that a wife only has to do what she's told for the first year, and wondered why she had forgotten that piece of wisdom. All of these efforts were small, and yet a balance was maintained—past episodes of imbalance became not present, and that was enough. It was akin to giving up a corset, perhaps, or buying a larger girdle, or forgetting notions of sin and retribution. Andrew, as far as she could tell, had learned the lesson of mortality, too—he was seventy-one now, and he knew he had missed many enjoyments over the years. Mostly, she had learned from watching Mrs. Tillotson that certain dramatic steps required an imperviousness of character that she did not possess; she came to be relieved that she hadn't taken them. She let it go at that. He had not committed adultery, or a felony, or abandonment. It was simple in its way.

One day, Margaret came home from a morning visit to Mrs. Wareham to find newspapers laid out on the dining-room table—the *Examiner* and the *Chronicle,* the Vallejo paper, and the *Sacramento Bee.* Andrew was proceeding around the table, reading every word about an unfortunate incident outside of Nanking. The incident looked quite straightforward to Margaret—the Japanese army had taken Nanking, which Chiang Kai-shek then had to abandon. In the course of this, Japanese planes sank an American boat because the pilots didn't see American flags. Though lots of men were wounded, only three were killed, and most of the sailors were rescued by nearby British boats. Roosevelt complained, and some admiral apologized. By the next day, the Japanese had offered to pay for the sinking of the boat, and the Foreign Minister himself apologized.

Andrew decided to go over to the island (he hadn't been there in months) and hear what they were saying in the Officers' Club and anywhere else he could manage to eavesdrop or to get someone into conversation. He was alight with investigative purpose. Margaret was glad to get him out of the house. At the end of a week, he even put in a call to Pete. Andrew wasn't the only person interested, of course—the ladies at the knitting group had talked about it for an hour. When he hung up, she reported what they had all agreed upon: "But, Andrew, when most governments make a mistake like that, they cover it up for weeks, and then go for more weeks insisting that there was provocation, and then wait to be sued for years after that. I think this incident speaks well of the Japanese."

"Perhaps it does. But it's a mystery. The sailors on the boat said that the flags were completely visible."

"And, anyway, it seems outside of your usual area."

"It is an interesting event, in and of itself." He paused. "And I have been feeling of late that I've let the world get away from me. What did I come across the other day? Oh yes, my bird list, from so long ago. Remember how we walked about the island and looked at gulls and hawks? I realized that I haven't always been a dull boy."

She thought, What harm can come from his getting out of the house and diverting himself with this? She said, "It's worth looking into, then."

She said reassuring things like this all the time now, while she was going about her own business, passing in and out of the rooms he was in on her way to shop or weed or visit someone or go knitting or work with the aid society she collected for. Though her happiness had taken a while to set in, she traced it directly to this house Andrew had purchased. It was pleasant to wake up in, convenient to all of Vallejo, and quite suitable for hosting her share of knitting circles and get-togethers. After a few days, she quietly put the newspapers away, and in fact forgot the whole thing until she ran into Mrs. Kimura around Christmas.

They talked about Naoko, Margaret asked after Mr. Kimura, and Mrs. Kimura asked after the captain; then Mrs. Kimura declared that she had just heard from Joe that morning. Joe had moved to Japan as a dentist, thinking there would be more opportunity there, but in the three years since going had never made up his mind whether to stay in Japan or to come home. Lester could not make up his mind whether to join his brother or to continue working for the Pacific Trading Company. Mrs. Kimura, Naoko, Cassandra, Mrs. Wareham, and Margaret had been over the pros and cons of all the choices—it was one of their standard topics of conversation. Now Mrs. Kimura reported that Joe and two of his friends were planning to go to the U.S. Embassy in Tokyo before Christmas, to leave off a letter of sympathy, and also a monetary contribution toward the medical and dental needs of those wounded aboard the boat in China.

Margaret exclaimed, "That's very kind!"

Mrs. Kimura said, "Many have done same thing, wealthy business-men down to simple schoolgirls. American ambassador wife doesn't have moment to herself from receiving wives of high families. I admit Joe not think of this, but two friends ask him."

"Even so—"

"They agree to donate two weeks from their employment to this." She gave Margaret a happy smile. "And Joe says he found bride from good family, twenty-six-year-old. She has business sewing Western-style dresses for wealthy Japanese wives."

"Two weeks' pay, though!"

"To me, I see because of this that Japanese people will prevail over the warriors of the army. Emperor is being pulled in two. He knows that Japanese people don't like war in China, but the army foils their wishes every time. Two weeks' pay for this is how much Japanese people want to live in peace."

Later, Margaret wished she had not mentioned this encounter at supper. Andrew was skeptical, and Margaret was rather sharp when she said, "They've been very forthcoming."

"Well, my dear, there is literally always more to everything than meets the eye. The eye is a very poor instrument for seeing anything. Over on the island, they are very, very suspicious."

"Of what, though?" Her voice was rising. She inhaled deeply. What did it matter, really? She adopted a neutral expression. It helped.

"Of some sleight of hand. The orange will be pulled out from behind the ear, big as life, and how did it get there when the magician was wearing short sleeves?"

She laughed. It wasn't very often that Andrew made her laugh, and he gave her a gratified smile.

And then the incident of the boat (the *Panay*) was resolved, and the papers completely stopped talking about it.

WITHOUT the universe, the big house was too small for him—the steep steps too shallow, the high ceilings too low, the spacious rooms only a stride or two long. Whatever she was doing, knitting or reading or cleaning or cooking, there was the constant drum of footsteps—boot steps, really—so she was happy when he went out, dressed nicely, always in a suit and well-shined shoes. He carried a walking stick and wore a hat to keep off the sun. He walked fast, and he was healthy for a man of his age. He would never be mistaken for a bum or a ne'er-do-well, she thought.

It was Officer Napolitano and Officer Kelley who stopped by one day and told her that once in a while he would flag down someone driving a car; once in a greater while, that person would stop, no doubt thinking that Andrew was an old man in distress. Andrew would open the passenger door and get in, telling the driver (almost always a woman) to drive him over the causeway to the island, or perhaps somewhere downtown. One poor girl took him about for an hour and a half, while he did various errands. The girl thought he was lost, and didn't want to "abandon" him. The girl didn't even know what the *Panay* was—she thought he was saying "Panama."

Margaret said, "I thought he had forgotten about the *Panay*. But is he in some sort of danger? Or is he a danger to others, stepping to the street suddenly? Is that the problem?"

"Ma'am, it is that he is relentless in engaging people in conversation. He won't let them turn away or refuse to answer, and when they do answer, he hooks his finger in their buttonholes and won't let them get away. Then they complain to us. Personally, ma'am, I'm afraid someone is going to pop him in the nose one day."

"Are his opinions that controversial?"

He said, "No, ma'am, it's not that. Here's an example. He flagged down Officers Lugano and Moore, who brought him here the other day—you were out, ma'am. He sat in the car with one foot in the street and the door open for forty-five minutes before they could get rid of him."

Margaret chuckled and said, "They should have taken him to jail."

"Would that frighten him, ma'am?" Officer Napolitano looked very earnest and young. She guessed he was about twenty-five or -six.

She shook her head, her tone still light. "From what you say, he would just engage everyone at the station in conversation and ask for rides here and there."

"I don't doubt it, ma'am. But—"

"Do these young women seem to feel threatened in any way?"

"No, ma'am. Not in the usual way. They seem to feel that it is rather like being with an elderly eccentric relative, but—"

"Captain Early has old-fashioned, courtly manners."

"All of the young ladies say that, ma'am. But one young woman had a job to get to, and he made her two hours late."

"Oh dear." They were smiling, but making it clear that this could not go on. She said, "Officer, I do apologize, but my husband is frustrated in his work."

"We know that, ma'am. We know that Albert Einstein has balked him at every turn and now comes to Vallejo to spy on him."

Actual alarm displaced the confusion she had been feeling. "Einstein!"

"Yes, ma'am. He told Officers Lugano and Moore that he saw Einstein on Capitol Street. He thought maybe Einstein had come to Vallejo to see him, but he wasn't able to make himself known to Einstein on that particular occasion."

They all three sighed at the same time. Finally, she said, "I see what you mean, Officer Kelley. I'll talk to him."

But first she called on Mrs. Wareham at the hotel. The Warrington was a good business and a respected establishment. Over the years, with her multitude of boarders and guests, many or most of whom were men, Margaret suspected Mrs. Wareham had seen a great many things.

Andrew, it turned out, came in there every day and had a cup of coffee. Mrs. Wareham said, "Margaret, I thought you were sending him to me. He's here promptly at nine-thirty. He gives me your best greetings, then drinks a cup of coffee with a lump of sugar and reads his paper. He stays about an hour, and then says goodbye and goes out. Rain or shine, really."

"But haven't you heard about his activities?"

"Not at all, dear."

She told her friend what the police had told her, then said, "Does he talk all the time and make people discuss the war in China?"

"He never says a word about anything. He just nurses his cup of coffee and then pays and goes. He always leaves the girl a nice tip, too."

"But what should I do?"

"Well, Margaret, first you must inform him in no uncertain terms that these girls aren't sailors, and he can't be commandeering their services as he once did those young men. They all did that. It was part of being a captain."

"That's true. I should have remembered that."

"And you must say that it looks very strange to the *police.* That will catch his attention. You and I know Captain Early. He is the most reticent of men, but he's very large also."

This thought made her nervous.

Mrs. Wareham leaned toward her and said, "I see you are shaking your head, as you always do."

Margaret hadn't realized that she was shaking her head. She made herself sit still.

"For once in your life, Margaret, you must take charge of the situation. Take charge of *him*, I have to say. I—"

In spite of her best efforts, Margaret must have continued to look dismayed.

"I mean this kindly, dear. You are who you are. . . ."

"Who is that? Who is that?" Margaret found herself saying.

There was a long pause; then Mrs. Wareham looked a little embarrassed. She said, "Everyone knows you're a good woman, Margaret. Everyone knows that."

It sounded like an insult, but it had the desired effect. That evening, she cooked Andrew's favorite supper dish and also made a pie, since there was some nice rhubarb in the market. Not quite sure how to broach her subject, she hemmed and hawed about the weather, but finally she said, "Andrew, I understand you have met Officers Lugano and Moore of the Vallejo Police Department."

"Indeed I have. They were most interested in my investigations."

"I didn't know you were pursuing any investigations, Andrew."

"Well, of course I am. Into the *Panay* incident. Surely you haven't forgotten that?" His tone was affable.

"You mean that boat that was sunk in China. The reparations were paid—"

He took a last bite of liver, set down his fork, and carefully wiped his mustache with his napkin. He shook his head. "Yes, they were. A clever gambit, and cheap in the long run."

"Do you think so? Mrs. Kimura told me how generous the Japanese people have been."

"Yes, yes. No denying that. But, my dear, I am now free to tell you that I have solved the mystery."

"You have?"

"Yes, I have. And I have informed the Vallejo Police of my views, and I have sent letters to the Commandant of the Base, to the Secretary of State, and, of course, to the *New York Times*. I mailed them yesterday. I feel that I can talk more freely about this, even to you, having committed my ideas to paper. And I certainly hope, though I have no assurance, that the *Times* will publish my conclusions. I believe that we would all be safer in the end were they to do so."

"What did you, did you . . . discover, Andrew?"

"Well, my dear, there has been a terrible massacre at Nanking, beginning the day after the *Panay* was attacked, and the *Panay* attack was cynically designed by authorities in the higher echelons of the Japanese military, and, I believe, the Foreign Service, to drive off the Americans and the British from the area, and to divert official American attention from the atrocities that the Japanese intended to commit. Not to mention, of course, the attention of the American public."

"But I read the paper every day, Andrew, and there hasn't been any mention of Nanking or anything—there's a war in China, but I don't quite understand what you mean."

"According to those I've talked to, many tens of thousands may have been killed by such methods as drowning and decapitation and bayoneting and, of course, shooting, and others have not been so lucky, I may say, especially the women and girls, thousands of whom have suffered the most terrible sorts of degradation before being murdered in cold blood." He said this with a grave and sorrowful demeanor, but his words were measured, as if he were giving a report. These phrases were the very ones that he must have used in his letters.

She said again, "But there hasn't been a thing about it in the paper."

"Precisely, my dear. Who is there to report it? Some missionaries and a reporter from England, but the Japanese control the mails and the cables, and very little has gotten out."

"How do you know about it?"

"Surely you remember that our former home across the causeway is a beehive of information and gossip? This man has a cousin on a ship who has heard things, and this other man has an aunt who is with the Presbyterian Mission in Shanghai, and this other man has a friend who works in the Japanese Embassy in Washington. A picture of events can be shadowed in."

"Mrs. Kimura has heard nothing about this. She hears from Joe, and Joe was terribly upset about that boat in China, and went to the embassy and gave the equivalent of two weeks' pay of his own money. His friends went with him. They had no link to America at all, except through him."

"I'm not entirely sure, my dear, that the populace in the home islands knows what the army has done in China."

"You're telling me that terrible crimes have been committed by the Japanese in China in a more or less wholesale way and no one knows about it other than you?" She tried to make her voice sound genuinely questioning, not merely skeptical. Andrew seemed fooled by her attempt. He said, "A massacre, my dear, and more than that, more than, let's say, thousands of people lined up and shot. I am not sure exactly what the term would be. Perhaps 'extermination.' " He sighed.

The word lingered in the air. Perhaps in order to chase it off, she said, "And the police also told me you've seen Einstein."

"Yes, indeed. Twice now." He seemed happy to talk about it. "He's surprisingly short. He wears glasses, and his suit was rumpled, but of good twill." He coughed and went on. "He does wear nice shoes. His feet are small. Looked to me like he has his shoes made in England. And his hair isn't as wild as it looks in pictures."

She said, "You noticed his shoes? Were you staring at him?"

"I am a naturally observant person."

"I've never seen him in glasses in the newspaper."

"That surprised me, too. He looks older than he is."

"He must be sixty."

"Looks seventy if a day."

"Maybe it wasn't Einstein."

"Maybe, indeed."

She ventured, "Why do you think he's here?"

"I had thought, the first time, that he was here to see me, and I was prepared to extend the olive branch, I must say. But I'm more suspicious now. I'm glad I did not reveal myself to him the first time, as I had thought to do."

She got up without saying anything and began to clear the dishes from the table. How to proceed was a mystery to her. He was evidently delusional, about both the Japanese and Einstein, but also, she thought, harmless. She took the dishes to the kitchen and set them beside the sink. When she came back into the dining room, fortifying herself with thoughts of Mrs. Wareham's very earnest instructions, she sat down, not across from Andrew, but beside him, and she put her hand on his knee. She leaned forward and said, "Andrew, I'm sure that those whom you contacted will read your letters with utmost interest and respect, and I hope that what you've concluded shows them what they must do. But at the same time, the policemen here today told me that you have been waving down automobiles, and then getting in and telling the drivers that they must take you here and there."

"Young people don't mind—"

"Maybe not, but if these young people are young girls, I am absolutely certain that their parents would object to you"—what was the phrase here?—"diverting them from their regular business. If you want to get around, you have to use the streetcar, or I will drive you myself."

"My dear, what I need to do is not always systematic or well organized. I am led here and there by my investigations."

"But your investigations seem to be over."

"In part."

"The *police* made it clear to me." Here she caught his gaze and held it. "You must not impose yourself upon any women. You must not. Doing so after the police have asked you to stop could seriously compromise your reputation in Vallejo and on the island."

He looked genuinely startled, and said, "I hadn't thought of that. I was only—"

"Yes, Andrew, I'm sure that you were only thinking of the next step in your investigation, but it looks different to others."

"People know I am enthusiastic."

"They do, but not everyone knows you in town the way they did on the island."

This he seemed to accept.

The next day, she went to the police station and talked to Officer Kelley's superior. She explained that her husband saw himself as a sort of detective, and that he wasn't meaning harm to anyone, and was, in fact, incapable of committing any sort of harm. The policeman seemed to agree with her, and he agreed that, since Captain Early was such a recognizable figure about town, the police would treat him more or less as a nuisance—keeping an eye upon him and sometimes guiding him in one direction or another, but not threatening him.

THE next time she had tea with Dora, Margaret told her the story—lightly, as if it were funny. Dora said, "Einstein does travel a lot."

"Why would he come to Vallejo?"

Dora shrugged.

Margaret said, "When Andrew's in the house, I can't wait for him to leave."

"He is very large, darling."

"Whenever something comes in the mail, even to me, he asks me who it's from, and then asks me if he can read it. When the telephone rings, he rushes to answer it, just to see who it is. And when we have a knitting circle, the first thing he asks afterward is whether anyone said anything about him."

"You daren't tell him that they didn't say a word?"

Margaret smiled. "I don't know what I dare tell him, other than 'They all asked after you.' But I don't know what to do with him. He doesn't know what to do with himself!"

"He's a grown man," said Dora. "He'll think of something."

Dora was being sent back to Europe over her own protestations. It was not, she told Margaret, that she was too old, it was that the events in Europe were too large, and as large as they looked from her perch on Sutter Street, they would be that much larger once she got to New York, and overwhelming once she got to London. But in fact she was too old, Margaret thought. She said, "Your usual snooping?"

"I don't snoop. I interview. People want to answer my questions, and I write down what they say."

"But you describe them. You say, 'He looks directly at me, but his left eye tracks toward the donkeys on the hillside.' "

Dora laughed. "That's not snooping. Snooping is reading their mail and listening to gossip about them."

"You've done a little of that."

"Well, I did, during my high-society period, but when someone looks at you surreptitiously while she's telling a juicy story about someone else, or just happens to leave her diary open at a certain page when she knows you might be alone in the room, you do what is expected of you. I haven't gone into high society in ten years."

"So why go back to Europe?"

"Believe me, I don't want to go. In 1916, I couldn't imagine anything more exciting than to have your ship attacked by a U-boat and write your last dispatch and stuff it in a bottle while you were drowning, knowing that an editor from the *New York Herald* would inevitably find it and put it on the front page."

"And now?"

"Now I know that it will be hard to find hot water for a nice bath, and there will be a constant stream of people in every city who will deserve to eat more than I deserve a new hat, and that friends from long ago who were once truly simpatico will now be disgorging the most impossible sentiments about Anglo-Saxon purity or the rights of Italians to a *'mare italiano'* or whatever they call it." It seemed to Margaret that Dora must be thinking of a particular person, but she didn't say anything. Dora leaned back and said, "My mother would say at last I am receiving my just deserts. You know, she used to say, 'Now, Margaret saw a hanging as a child and promptly forgot everything about it, as she should have. Dora never saw that hanging, and so she has always gone looking for one.' "

"I never heard that." Then Margaret said, "The truth is, I've never seen anything! I didn't even see that hanging, as far as memory serves. I should have just gone to Europe, and now it's too late."

"I should have taken you with me years ago, but now is not the time." Dora's tone was sympathetic, but idle, as careless of what she had enjoyed as of what Margaret had not enjoyed.

"Andrew wouldn't have stood for that, as there was typing to do. I have been such a fool!"

Dora's eyebrows lifted at this flash of anger, but she didn't respond other than to say, "He would have gotten used to it."

"I wish you'd said that fifteen years ago."

That night, in her bed, Margaret lay awake thinking of her conversation with Dora, how she had strayed into indiscretions that she had resisted for years, and how it had felt. There was the surprise that nothing she had said surprised Dora, and then there was the other surprise, that what she had said was still so emphatic, in spite of the equanimity she thought she had attained. No, she was almost sixty and she had not been to London or Paris or Rome, and there was no going there now. Yes, she was balanced, as she had gotten into the habit of congratulating herself for being. But, she saw, she was balanced on a very narrow perch.

POSSIBLY, over the years, she had hosted some ladies' circle or another two or three thousand times. Sewing, knitting, collecting toys and clothing for poor children, raising funds for soldiers, planning Christmas programs and Thanksgiving dinners and Easter-egg hunts. In every case, if Andrew was in the house, he would come to the doorway, bow to the ladies, greet the ones he knew by name, and then excuse himself to go off to other business more worthy of his attention. On this particular day, he came into the dining room with his hat already on and his jacket over his arm. He nodded to Mrs. Hermann and Mrs. Roberts. He greeted Mrs. Tillotson and Mrs. Jones, and Miss Jones, who was Mrs. Jones's unmarried sister-in-law. Margaret said goodbye to him with a wave and dealt out the cards, one down, one up. She heard him open the front door, and then she heard the front door close. As she was dealing the next round of cards to those who wanted them, though, he appeared again in the doorway. The ladies placed their bets. She dealt out a card to Mrs. Jones and one to Mrs. Roberts. Mrs. Roberts said, "I'm busted," and Mrs. Jones took the pot. Andrew said, "I thought you ladies were knitting, my dear."

Mrs. Jones said, "We've knitted enough mufflers to stock I. Magnin."

"You're playing blackjack?"

"Yes, Andrew."

To everyone in general he said, rather proudly, "My mother played blackjack all through my childhood. She called it 'vingt-et-un.' "

"Did you play with her?" said Miss Jones, evidently surprised that such a huge, gruff, gray-mustached man as Andrew had had a childhood.

"For a while there, we played every day. My father made a sketch of us one night. We were so intent upon the game that we didn't realize he was even in the room."

"How old were you, Captain Early?" said Mrs. Roberts.

"Oh, about seven, I guess. She started playing cooncan with me when I was five to keep me occupied, because I was a terribly restless child. I liked blackjack better."

Margaret shifted in her chair, ready for him to leave.

"What was cooncan?" asked Miss Jones.

"A type of rummy," said Andrew.

"You should play with us," said Miss Jones, and, lo and behold, he sat down with a thump in a chair and pulled it up to the table. Margaret felt disappointment set in, like a flu.

Miss Jones continued, "You should write your memoirs, Captain Early. I'm sure they're very interesting."

"Do you think so, Miss Jones? I don't need to do that. A young man once wrote my biography." He smiled in a dignified manner, and spread himself a bit.

Margaret was relieved that, before he could offer the girl a copy, Mrs. Roberts, on the other side of Andrew, gave a squeak that drew his attention. Mrs. Roberts was a retiring soul who played without any strategy at all, and her stack of chips was already noticeably smaller than everyone else's. Andrew glanced at her, and must have seen her hole card, because when she took a hit and was busted, he leaned over and whispered in her ear. She turned and said, "I don't know a thing about that, but you may show me, if you would like."

He sat with them then for about two hours, whispering first to one lady and then to another and another, until they stopped for tea, when he put on his hat and went out.

That night, over supper, he said, "Your lady friends have a deplorable feel for strategy. I wonder if Mrs. Roberts even knows that there are fifty-two cards in the deck."

"Possibly not. She only comes for the gossip."

"She is being robbed blind."

"Andrew, if she loses two dollars, it's a bad day. The stakes are low. Think of it as the price she has to pay for an afternoon's sociability."

"When are these ladies coming again?"

"They agreed on Monday." She saw that it was inevitable, but also that it kept him off the streets. That part was a relief.

On Monday morning, he put a leaf in the table, and over the course of the next few weeks, he installed himself as their tutor. His method was to help first one lady and then another with basic strategy. After that, he told them a bit about card counting, and then the higher mathematics of probability. He pitted the ladies against one another. Mrs. Roberts stopped losing all the time, and Miss Jones began losing a little more often. Margaret saw, possibly for the first time, just the palest shadow of Mrs. Early in the son who was now older than his mother had ever been. She was not as uncomfortable as she had expected to be—it was interesting to see him in the midst of so many ladies. He had a manner, stiff but gallant, right out of 1895.

In these games, Andrew never expounded upon any of his theories about the universe or the *Panay,* nor did he talk much in general—he was too busy whispering to his designated pupil to hold forth to the rest of them. Margaret felt fond of him, in a distant way.

Having succeeded with the cards, and still mindful of Mrs. Wareham's urging, she furnished him with a dog. Andrew was not opposed to a dog. For her, the idea of owning a dog had died with Alexander—at first it seemed like too much of a substitute child, and then it became a habit they had not developed. But one day she went to the pound, and she adopted Stella, whose previous owner had been transferred by the navy to South America. The animal was a terrier mix, housebroken. She walked nicely on a leash, and did not jump onto the furniture unless invited. Margaret was in the kitchen with the dog when Andrew came in. Stella walked over to him, sat down in front of him, and looked up into his face. Margaret said, "Her name is Stella."

He said, "Is it, indeed?" Of course her name was Stella—no other dog could be adopted by an astronomer. That evening, he invited Stella onto the sofa, and she sat quietly while he petted her on the head. That night, he made a bed for her in the corner of his bedroom by folding an old quilt, and the first thing Margaret heard in the morning, before she was quite awake and when it was still very gloomy with fog and darkness, was the sound of the kitchen door opening and closing. She sat up and went to the window. Down below, in the backyard, she could just make out Andrew, with Stella at his heels, opening the back gate and heading out for a walk.

Such a charming, bright-eyed, and well-behaved dog imparted her own respectability to Andrew. It was the perfect solution—he walked all over town and people engaged him in conversation, about Stella or about dogs in general. In his usual fashion, he exerted himself, and in short order, he had taught Stella to shake hands, sit up on her hind legs, roll over, jump a stick, and balance a piece of bread on her nose, then toss it in the air and catch it. When children stopped him to pet her, he took pieces of bread out of his pocket and showed off her tricks.

Then he took up movies, although she could have counted on one hand the number of movies they had seen. He had never liked silent movies; he had sat through Charlie Chaplin in *The Circus* without cracking a smile. As they went home, he said, "Tell me, my dear, why does he wear those shoes and turn his feet out in that way? Does he suffer from the aftereffects of some childhood illness?"

"No, Andrew, it's supposed to be funny."

"But funny in what way? Incongruous? Mechanical? Simply silly or ridiculous? I would have liked to enjoy it, I must say."

"You've enjoyed vaudeville. It's like that."

"But it goes on so long you can't stand it anymore. At a vaudeville show, at least if you didn't like the act, you knew it would soon give way to another."

After the talkies came in, he could not tolerate scenes of the sort where the two actors were driving in a car and a film of the passing landscape was playing behind them. He would say, aloud in the theater, "We saw that tree five seconds ago." However, after his interest in blackjack waned, Andrew discovered pictures. He was amazed that, while he had been ignoring them, they had become more sophisticated. The first one he came home and told her about was *Gunga Din,* which was playing at the Orpheum in downtown Vallejo. He had lots of questions: Who was this fellow Cary Grant? Was this movie based on Kipling's poem, and if so, how could you base a movie on a poem? Didn't the Khyber Pass look rather like the Sierras?

She said that Cary Grant was a big star, as was Douglas Fairbanks, Jr. (Andrew's response to this was "Why is that, my dear?"), that you could base a movie on anything, and that probably the film was made in the Sierras rather than in the real Khyber Pass.

A few days later, he went to see a movie about Jesse James. In this one, he liked "the fellow Henry Fronda," but, he said, "how do they not know that Jesse and Frank's mother wasn't killed? She lived to be eighty-five years old! And they had them robbing trains. They robbed banks. That was the point." He couldn't see how a movie that was so inaccurate could have been allowed to reach the screen. She said, "Andrew, did you talk to anyone during the movie?"

"Well, I did tell a few people around me that the story was all wrong."

He had brought Stella into the theater, but, he said, the proprietor didn't seem to mind even when she barked twice at the horses on the screen.

The local movies changed too infrequently—he hit upon the idea of taking the ferry to San Francisco. Soon he was going there four times a week. Stella went with him every time. Often he would watch the double feature, which meant that he left on the morning ferry and didn't return until fairly late. If he especially liked a picture, he would take Margaret to see it when it came to Vallejo. He came to have his preferred subjects—anything about St. Louis or Missouri (*St. Louis Blues; I'm from Missouri,* in which a man takes his prize mule to London; *The Adventures of Huckleberry Finn*), anything about the universe (*Buck Rogers*), anything about the West (*Stagecoach*). He did not like movies about scientists (*The Story of Dr. Jenner*). The first one he took her to ("for old times' sake, my dear") was *The Hound of the Baskervilles,* which she enjoyed very much.

Pete had become one of the outer planets, dim and blue like Neptune, visible with effort, but not exerting much force. His stability in this orbit, Margaret knew, depended on her remaining stable in her corner of space as well. But in the midst of Andrew's fervor, she had a letter from Dora that she wanted to show Pete, about how Dora wanted to get back to St. Louis and Missouri—not the St. Louis of today, which was, she said, an "outpost of Hyde Park and in the business of being told what to do," but the St. Louis of their youth, when "every man and woman went his or her own way, and the patterns they made as they crossed paths were as graceful and efficient as the migration routes of birds." Apparently, this was her new idea—that they should take wild birds as their models. "All summer long, every goose and duck eats and eats and eats, until his breast is glistening with fat and his liver is distended, only to foregather with his fellows and fly south, filling the sky with *intention,* but intention of a voluntary sort—no goose is ordered to fly, no goose is given a uniform, or chained to his or her fellow geese." Human society, by contrast, was akin to prison life. There were those in prison who knew it; everyone else was in prison and did not know it. Margaret thought it was a very strange letter. With Andrew spending several days a week in San Francisco, she told him, she was going to go along and have tea with Pete at the Palace Hotel.

"That will take two hours," said Andrew.

"At least."

"Can't stand that. Waste of time."

"You don't have to come. Though I imagine Pete will be disappointed."

"Can you get him to go for a walk instead? Nice day."

"I think he would rather have tea. You go to the picture, and join us afterward."

"Well, give him this, then. He'll like it." He handed her the notes he had written up about card counting in blackjack and gin rummy.

She wore her best hat, but that was all—no new dress, only a touch of lipstick, no powder. Pete was wearing a houndstooth jacket with a nipped waist, a rose-colored ascot, a silk-shantung shirt, and spectator shoes with rose-colored socks. After he kissed her on both cheeks and she took in his fragrance, he handed her a box with a gardenia in it. Her heart did not flutter. She was sufficiently immune now—she could appreciate these courtesies without putting any stock in them. He perused the menu and ordered for her.

When she took Dora's letter out of her bag, Pete smiled, then said, "Dora is no longer speaking to me."

"Why is that?"

"Because, when I saw her before she left, I would not agree that Americans are by nature incorruptible."

"I can't imagine her saying such a thing."

"She kept telling me that it is Americans who are truly free, and there must be absolute freedom and noninterference of any kind by such things as governments or benevolent people with benevolent schemes. And when I said that then the top dogs would simply accrue as much for themselves as they possibly could, in the style of Ivan the Terrible, she insisted that Americans would not, and could not, do such a thing."

"And you said?"

"And I said, 'Name one.' And she couldn't, and so she got quite annoyed with me, and told me that she intended to write a book that would show me the errors of my thinking."

"All of this seems so unlike Dora." But she was thinking how comfortable she was, exactly as if she and Pete were old and wise friends.

He shrugged. He said, "Dora fled her enemies at home, did she not?"

Margaret thought of Mrs. Bell and nodded.

"Compared with that, she felt she could handle anything."

"And she has handled everything!" Margaret exclaimed.

Pete shook his head. "The Europeans are in a pickle, and Dora is observant."

She said, "You are a fatalist," meaning to express her admiration. "It can't be that bad."

"Perhaps I'm a Darwinian. Each horror leaves survivors. Greater horrors leave fewer survivors, but those who do survive seem to assimilate the horror, and once they do, their imaginations are piqued. 'What could be worse?' they say, aghast, and then they think, Well, what could be worse? They start coming up with things, and there, in a nutshell, you have Russian history. Why shouldn't this be the history of the West, too? After all, Russians believe we are the saviors of the world, and whatever we do first, others will do subsequently."

"I thought that was Americans."

Pete laughed.

After their tea, she went to I. Magnin and walked about, looking at styles and catching her breath.

On the ferry, Andrew quizzed her: Did she really think Pete had lived the simple life of an Irish horse-trainer at the racetrack? How did she think he was occupying his time now? Was he traveling? Did they talk about Russia? Wasn't it odd that they'd known him for so long and yet they knew nothing, really, about him? She said, almost irritably, "If you're so curious, you should have joined us."

"Perhaps I will, next time." He didn't say anything about the double feature, so Margaret decided the pictures must not have been very good. Stella slept in her lap on the ferry, and Margaret wondered if she was ill—to be so tired after spending an afternoon in a movie theater.

The summer progressed: *Goodbye, Mr. Chips, Beau Geste,* and *The Adventures of Sherlock Holmes* (which was more suspenseful than *The Hound of the Baskervilles*), but Andrew also seemed to enjoy *Blondie Takes a Vacation, Each Dawn I Die, Stanley and Livingstone,* and even *The Five Little Peppers.* She told him that his tastes were getting quite eclectic. In the fall, after they saw a matinee called *The Day the Bookies Wept,* which had a horse in it, if not much else that was good, he went into his study for the first time in months, and when it came time to take Stella for her walk, he called through the door and asked her to do it. It was a pleasant day at the end of September, and she enjoyed it, though she could not help thinking of Dora. Since the invasion of Poland, England and most of Europe were at war, at least officially. The island was in an uproar, but their corner of Vallejo was quiet. Andrew didn't take as much interest in the war as she expected him to. He still read two or three papers, still went to the Warrington for his cup of coffee, still saw some movies, and still took Stella for most of her walks, but more and more he was preoccupied with whatever he was writing in his study—perhaps his memoirs. He was occupied, that was the important thing.

Or it was until the next day, when she suddenly took a fright and went into his office for a look around. He had gone to see *Drums Along the Mohawk* in a double feature with *Blondie Brings Up Baby.* But she recognized stacks she had known since they moved into this house, untouched and certainly unmoved. There were pens and blotters lying around, and pads of paper, but she could find no new material. She left things alone and relaxed again, certain that it was news of the war that was making her nervous.

·   ·   ·

THE day the black car drove up, she was out looking at her rosebuds. It was a pleasant afternoon, one of the first of the spring, and she was thinking of nothing more important than ham for supper. A man got out and walked up to the door—a short man, but upright, with an official look about him, as if he had been told what to wear (dark gray suit, dress shirt, black shoes, hat). He noticed her, but until he had gotten no answer at her front door, he didn't acknowledge her. When she said "Hello?" he said, "Mrs. Early?"

"Yes."

"Are you Margaret Early, Mrs. Andrew Early, the wife of Captain Andrew Jackson Jefferson Early?"

"Yes."

This was a very gloomy way to begin the week, she thought, the old dread creeping upon her.

He said, "Mrs. Early, my name is Marvin Keene, and I would like to talk to you." As he said this, he took her elbow and guided her toward her front steps.

She said, "Captain Early isn't here, he's—"

"Captain Early is in San Francisco, ma'am. We know where he is."

"We?"

"Step inside the house, please, ma'am. Thank you." He took off his hat. "The FBI knows where Captain Early is. He is currently at the Orpheum Theater, but earlier today he was walking across the Golden Gate Bridge. Do you mind if we sit down?"

As they sat down, he showed her a card in his wallet. He was indeed from the FBI.

"He was walking across the Golden Gate Bridge?"

Agent Keene squirmed on the sofa as he put the card away, then smiled.

"Yes, ma'am. He often walks across the bridge. At first, people seeing him on the bridge thought he was a jumper, but most jumpers don't take the dog with them. No, ma'am, not a jumper."

She asked Agent Keene if he wanted a cup of tea or a glass of water, just to put off the rest of this conversation. He took the glass of water. He seemed friendly. She hazarded, "Has my husband been buttonholing people or—or soliciting rides in automobiles?"

He said, "No, ma'am." Then, "Mrs. Early, do you remember the *Panay* incident?"

"That was more than two years ago."

"Sometime after the *Panay* incident, a handwritten letter crossed my desk which proposed an analysis of the incident that coincided in several particulars with my own analysis of the incident. These were, namely, that the Japanese knowingly attacked the American boat in order to distract and hamper Western observation of and aid to Chinese soldiers and civilians who were to be made examples of to the rest of the Chinese people." His tone was dry and direct.

"Andrew said that, but there wasn't anything in the paper that agreed with him."

"The paper doesn't report everything, ma'am."

"Yes, but—"

"And the Japanese were extremely successful at suppressing reports. I would say that, whatever we suspected, it wasn't until a year later that we got a fuller picture. But your husband's letter, which arrived in my office well before that, did in many ways anticipate the full picture. Did he ever talk to you about it?"

"Yes. Are you saying he was right all along?"

"Do you have any other reason to think he was mistaken?"

She wondered how she was going to answer this for a moment, then said, "Well, he says that he sees Einstein on the streets of Vallejo, over on Capitol Street. If you have reason to believe that Einstein comes to Vallejo, then you can draw your own conclusions."

"Captain Early is a physicist?"

"He's an astronomer who became a physicist. He has an interest in all types of science, and he used to have a column in the *Examiner*." She gave Agent Keene a long look. Finally, she said, "His ideas are now considered eccentric or old-fashioned. But he had a following in his day." Of only one, perhaps.

"How do you think that he came up with his information about the *Panay* incident?"

"He walked all over town and all over the island, and he got people to talk about it, and apparently they had information through gossip. This is a naval town, and a crowded one. People talk, even when they're told not to. The police came around and told me he was bothering people."

"That's all?"

"It's all they told me about."

Now it was Agent Keene's turn to stare at her, turning his half-empty glass in his hand. Finally, she said, "All I can tell you, Agent Keene, is that my husband has spent his whole life observing things and then putting two and two together. There are some people who would say that he doesn't come up with four very often, but he can't stop himself from putting two and two together." Her eye alighted on the snake emerging from the gift, and she thought for half a second of Lucy May, now mother of three. She said, "Maybe he was lucky."

"A stopped clock is right twice a day?"

"Yes, but—"

"Yes, but what?"

"That's not true in the navy."

Agent Keene laughed.

She said, "Should I mention to my husband that you've been here? That he has, uh, been vindicated?"

"Are you in the habit of confiding in Captain Early?"

"Not. Everything."

"Then I would suggest that you maintain your usual habits. We aren't investigating Captain Early. His putting of two and two together has been interesting, however."

"If that report crossed your desk so long ago, why are you visiting me now?"

"A lot of reports cross my desk, Mrs. Early. When it came to my attention that the man who sent that letter was the same man who has been repeatedly seen on the Golden Gate Bridge, I thought the coincidence was interesting enough to follow up on."

She thought about Andrew crossing the bridge, and, no doubt, criss-crossing San Francisco, pursuing some hobbyhorse. She said, "Do you want to be inundated with material?"

"We are inundated with material."

"My husband sees every vindication as a spur to greater efforts. How can I put this?" She pursed her lips. "Every atom is a star. Every hunch threatens to explode into a universe."

"I think I understand your meaning. We won't encourage him."

"Even though he's been vindicated?"

"Even though he's been vindicated."

"I think that's the best way."

She walked Agent Keene to the door, and watched him get in his car. The weather had turned cloudy, and it was raining by the time Andrew and Stella got home. Over supper, she made Andrew tell her the plot of the movie, with the leads and some of the bit players. He talked fluently, and seemed to have seen it. And enjoyed it, too.

NAOKO telephoned her one morning and said that her father expected to live about a week, and that he wanted to wish his friends farewell. Margaret had never known Mr. Kimura's exact age, but she supposed that he was older than Andrew. She hadn't seen any of the Kimuras for quite some time, though the rabbit by the door and the coots above the side table in the dining room fooled her into thinking that the artist was present in her house.

She said, "Dying?"

"I wouldn't have said that he is dying. He seems healthy enough, but he always said that he wouldn't live to see another war, and I think he is making good on his vow."

Margaret hesitated, but then she said, "Naoko, do you mean that he is committing suicide?"

"No, that he is omitting to recover from a bout of pneumonia. He won't let my mother try any remedies, and his breathing is getting worse."

"That must be terrifying for him."

"Maybe it will be at the end. But he's a stubborn man. I doubt he will change his mind."

"When would he like to see me?"

"This afternoon, if that is no trouble for you."

"Of course it's no trouble."

Over lunch, Andrew seemed surprised when she told him where she was going. He took a couple of spoonfuls of his soup and then a bite of bread and said, "I didn't know you were that close to Mr. Kimura. He doesn't even speak English, does he?"

"I'm not close to him at all, but I love the rabbit. And he painted the coots for me." She could see the picture through the kitchen doorway, from her seat at the table.

"And he wants you at his deathbed."

"I don't think they're calling it his deathbed right now. He might recover spontaneously, but I'm sure he's almost eighty, or even past eighty."

"I'm seventy-three."

She ignored this and was surprised when he offered to walk to the shop with her. She took the shears out and cut a nice bouquet of her roses, all white buds, more than a dozen. It was a fragrant bouquet, but she worried all the way to the Kimuras' (about twenty minutes) that perhaps it was too showy and mundane for them. Andrew walked at his normal pace; she made an effort to keep up. They left Stella locked in the kitchen, and all the way down the first block, they could hear her barking reminders that they had forgotten something. When they arrived at the shop, Andrew declared that he was going to do some errands, and "leave you to your friends, my dear." This was fine with Margaret, for she had imagined that Andrew would be awkward in every way—too big, too loud, too aware of himself. She watched him stride away down the street, and entered the door of the shop.

In spite of what she said to Andrew, she had been imagining some deathbed scene out of a Victorian novel—Mr. Kimura as Little Eva, for example—but it was not at all like that. There were several other guests, including Mrs. Wareham. Mr. Chang, it turned out, had a small restaurant three doors down. Mr. Lloyd sold stationery and art supplies on Napa Street, where Mr. Kimura had long purchased what he needed for his paintings. Miss Wolfe had a bookstore, and because she was close to Chinatown, she stocked a few books in Chinese and Japanese (as well as French, German, and Italian). She was an ample woman about Margaret's age.

It was a party. The reason Naoko had made it suddenly for today was that the weather was a little warm, which allowed Mr. Kimura to sit out in the garden. He sat in a low chair with a sturdy back, sunk inside his most elegant kimono—dark blue trimmed with white and gray. He seemed almost too weak to lift its sleeves, but he nodded and gestured to each of them, and Naoko showed them where to kneel or sit. After Mrs. Kimura brought around a basin and a cloth for washing their hands, Naoko gave them each a bowl of tea.

Margaret had been to the garden once, long before, but only briefly. Now she saw that the garden was Mr. Kimura's masterpiece, small though it was, and in a rather crowded part of town. There was a hillock, a pond, a raked gravel area. The trees were small and neatly trimmed. But, evidence of his advancing years, the fence was leaning here and there, and a few slats had slipped—she could see the dirty alley beyond the green paradise. And it was very green, though there were few flowers in bloom. When it was her turn to greet the old man, she stepped up to the low chair, bowed as well as she could manage, and laid the roses on a low table beside him, along with the other gifts.

Once they had had their tea, they were free to move about a little bit, first to approach Mr. Kimura and tell him, through Naoko, that the garden looked especially nice, and that he, too, looked well. In turn, he welcomed them and said that it had been far too long since he had seen them, and that he had thought of them many times with affectionate friendship. Then he gave each of them a small gift wrapped in paper and decorated with his personal stamp and an ideogram. The box Margaret received was about twelve inches long and four inches wide. The paper was yellow, and Naoko told her that the ideogram represented the word for "grace." She was quite moved by this; when she made her small bow, she suddenly had tears in her eyes. She backed away, as she saw others doing, and then went over to speak to Mrs. Wareham, who, as the oldest, had greeted Mr. Kimura first.

Mrs. Wareham asked her where Andrew was.

"He came with me, but he didn't come in."

"Andrew is well meaning, but he doesn't seem to fit here, does he?"

"Not really. I was a little afraid, myself, that he would crush everything that he sat on or touched. It would be very embarrassing for them."

"And you."

"Maybe. Though, if I found him embarrassing this late in the day, what would that signify?"

Mrs. Wareham smiled.

Margaret said, "Do you like my roses?"

"They're lovely."

There was no talk of the impending death. Mr. Chang invited her to his restaurant; Mr. Lloyd told her that, once he began carrying the papers that Mr. Kimura had wanted, he had learned more about paper than he ever thought possible. "I'm not even going to tell you how much he paid for the papers he wrapped our gifts in. You'd have thought they had gold threads. But he would have them."

"I'll remember that when I open mine."

"Goodness' sake, don't tear it. Frame it."

"I will."

She also struck up a conversation with Miss Wolfe, who said, "I only have the bookstore to supplement my income as a poet, but I am having to let some of the collections dwindle. It seems sad when you can't even put Dante on the shelves without raising a few eyebrows. Not to mention Goethe."

Margaret said, "What sort of poetry do you write?"

"Light verse. Sometimes I draw a cartoon or two."

"How long have you lived here?"

"Not quite a year. I moved up here from Los Angeles."

In honor of the serious occasion, Margaret dampened her interest in this very attractive person. The party was short, but even so, Mr. Kimura's evident exhaustion when Margaret stopped one last time to take his hand smote her, and as she stood outside the shop in the street, looking for Andrew, she felt lower than she had expected to feel.

Andrew came down the street from the west, the direction of the library. He was late because he had gotten tied up looking at maps. He asked if she had had a nice time, and whether Pete had been there. That was when she realized that Pete had not been there.

At home, she opened the package to discover one of Mr. Kimura's brushes—it still smelled faintly of what must have been ink. She showed it to Andrew, who said, "Most probably squirrel hair." She wrote her thank-you note at once, and walked down the street to mail it.

Mr. Kimura died two days later.

In the fall, Andrew said to her over supper, apropos of nothing, "I could have told Joe Kimura years ago not to go over there."

"Did you ever meet Joe Kimura?"

Andrew shook his head. "I should have. For his sake, I should have."

Margaret decided to ignore this remark, and said, "What was he to do here? Live in a room with his brother for the rest of his life, and never marry or have a family? Yes, he apprenticed to Dr. Matsumi in Japantown, but there weren't enough people in Japantown to support two dental practices. He did well in Japan for a while. Well enough to find a wife."

"How often do they hear from him?" He put a crumb of bread on the tip of his finger and held it out to Stella. She walked over to him in a dignified way and took it, then sat.

"I have no idea. I think Lester hears more often, since they've always been close. But it's true, Joe might be forced into the military and find himself stuck in Burma."

"Why do you say Burma?"

"I don't know. Naoko said her greatest fear was that he would be impressed into the army and find himself in the tropics."

"To my knowledge, China is far from tropical."

"Well, that's what she said. The geography is hazy to me."

He gave Stella another bit of bread. "You know, there are Japanese spies everywhere."

"We aren't at war with them, though."

"What they do is find these boys who are on the outs with the navy, or down and out, and they give them money, and these kids get them what they want."

"What do they want?"

"Codebooks. Operational manuals. Descriptions of ships. Almost anything, really."

"But we're neutral. They don't want to be at war with us."

"Do they not? They've signed the Tripartite Pact with the Germans and the Italians."

This had happened about four days before, and had been much talked about in the papers. Margaret thought, So this is what he's getting at. She said, "Even so, being at war with us would make no sense."

"Perhaps they think we will soon be at war with Germany, and then they can enter through the back door."

"Roosevelt knows—"

"We are the back door," interrupted Andrew.

She stared at him.

"My dear," he said, "I have something I would like you to read. It is of my own composition, a rough draft. I improved this version a bit before I sent it off, but the gist is the same. I'll get it." He stood up and went into his office. He came back with a sheaf of papers of the sort she recognized only too well—small handwriting (though readable), written from edge to edge and top to bottom, numbered in big slashing numbers in the top left corner, one to twenty-four. He handed them to her and turned on his heel, went to the coat rack, took his coat, and went out, leaving Stella with her. The papers were addressed to President Roosevelt, the Commandant of the Base, and the Secretary of the Navy.

In her hands was a diary of Andrew's activities for about two years— from the late winter of 1938, just after the *Panay* incident, through that year, and into January of 1940. What he had recorded were his observations from all sorts of vantage points around the bay and on the other side of San Francisco, as far west as Ocean Beach, along the shore of Golden Gate Park, and Lincoln Park, across the Golden Gate Bridge, and up into Marin County. He had been all around the bay: Oakland, Emeryville, San Pablo, Pinole, San Rafael, Corte Madera, Tiburon, Sausalito, San Mateo. In all of these places, he had stared out at the water with his binoculars. He had seen a number of suspicious things, like "Oriental-looking fishermen disembarking in a secluded spot, then huddling together and talking eagerly among themselves," or "the ripple on the surface of the water that could be evidence of a submarine beneath." He had observed a great deal of fishing activity around the shipbuilding yards on five occasions, and had observed that the fishermen in the boats "looked Oriental." He had seen others looking at the ships in the yard "too minutely and longer than tourists would do" on six occasions. He had seen a man writing things on a pad. When he approached the man, the man "hastily" put away his pad and "hurried off." On several occasions, when he was walking down the beach, cars above him on the side of the road "hurriedly drove away" as he scrutinized them. Everything was scrupulously dated, including time of day and weather conditions. Given his vindication about the *Panay* incident, she couldn't help feeling unsettled by his observations.

She turned the page. She read, "Other Matters." The first page of this section read:

> In addition, I have come to believe that my wife, Margaret Mayfield Early, has become the center, certainly unwitting, of a nest of spies that are cultivating her acquaintance (and have been for some time), as part of an effort to get access to me and to my papers. Primary among these foreign agents is a Russian man who goes by an Irish name, Peter Moran, and purports to be an investor. I believe that he was hired by the Japanese government when he was working and living at Tanforan Race Course. He speaks fluent Japanese and Russian, and semi-fluent Chinese. According to his own report, he also speaks fluent French and some German (not to mention his original language, which, I believe, is a Ukrainian dialect). Sometime about 1900, as a young man, Peter Krizenko (for that is his previous name, though

whether that is the name he was born with, I don't know) lived for a period in Japan. I have been unable to ascertain what sort of connections he made at the time. He may also be working for the Russians, but I doubt it, as I do not believe he is or ever has been a Bolshevist.

I believe that Mr. Krizenko's most important contact is a member of a family living in Vallejo who own a shop. Their name is "Kimura." Father—Sei, mother—Kiku, daughter—Naoko, son—Joseph, son—Lester. I have not made up my mind which of these is the agent. Mr. Kimura is very old. (Note—has now died.) Joseph moved to Japan in 1936 (not a time when any realistic young man would have chosen to seek his fortune there). Joseph is in constant communication with the boy Lester, who works on the wharf, but from what I have seen of Lester, Lester is not gathering the information—too busy and a bit dull. Both the daughter and the mother work as midwives, and therefore travel a great deal about the countryside. My guess is that one or the other or both of these women are gathering information about food, other crops, harvests, workers' movements, trucking, and other essentials of day-to-day American life on the West Coast. I have seen no evidence that they are observing the shipyard or have been seen on the island.

Margaret laughed out loud in disbelief, but could not have said whether the laugh was at the absurdity of Andrew's speculations or their cruelty.

On the second page of this section was a list of dates and times when Andrew knew she was meeting either Pete or one of the Kimuras, a list of dates and times when he knew that she had received or placed telephone calls to any of them, and a separate list of dates when he knew she had gone to Japantown "to eat in restaurants and look at galleries." He went on:

I believe that my wife's interest in Japantown is solely motivated by her love of Japanese art and artifacts, but it may be that she is serving as an unwitting courier for messages from these gallery owners to the Kimuras, as she usually shares her finds with them. Old Mr. Kimura is an artist. I have not been able to ascertain his reputation—whether these artistic efforts are part of a cover-up, or undertaken in a sincere pursuit of his craft.

After this, there was another section entitled "The Underlying Scheme." This was a relatively short section, because he had addressed the topic in some previous communication to the President, the Secretary of the Navy, and the Commandant of the Base. It went:

You will note that I have sent two previous reports to you. One of these concerned my investigations into the *Panay* incident and the contemporaneous slaughter of Chinese civilians in Nanking by the Japanese military, in December, 1937 and January, 1938. The second of these, which I believe is more germane to this nest of spies that I have discovered, concerns the activities of Dr. Albert Einstein in and around the naval base and in Vallejo. I have seen Dr. Einstein in Vallejo eight times. On four of these occasions, I had the opportunity to follow him about the town. It is my belief that he recognized me on three of these occasions, and so my investigation of his activities was aborted. Persons reading my previous report may know that Dr. Einstein is well aware of me, since I have been a persistent critic of his patently ridiculous theories about the nature of the universe for some twenty-five years or more. At any rate, on one occasion, owing to a very thick fog, I was able to follow Dr. Einstein for sixty-six minutes. My detailed report on that investigation is to be found in my earlier communication, dated February 5, 1940. The gist of what I had to say is this. I believe that Dr. Einstein is also serving as an agent for a foreign power (no doubt Germany) and that he is haunting the island in order to find out something. Given Dr. Einstein's interest in physical phenomena, my guess is that weapons systems are his goal—perhaps those carried on submarines. He may, indeed, be connecting with Pete Moran (Krizenko) and passing information to him.

Margaret threw down the papers with such vehemence that Stella jumped off her lap. Here he had evaded her attempts to control him, and very cleverly, too, by boning up on all those movies and manufacturing himself as a movie fan, while all the time doing surveillance of the city and the bay. She was angrily impressed by his enterprise in getting around—a man who could not drive! He must have used trains and streetcars, and of course walked considerable distances. She called Stella back to her and patted her. Through her coat she could feel that the dog was muscular and physically fit. And he had conjured the Kimuras and Pete into a "nest of spies." Poor Mr. Kimura, to have his artistic aspirations so cavalierly dismissed as a cover-up for espionage! And poor Mrs. Kimura, a woman who had witnessed as much daily horror as anyone! Andrew imagined that she was noting down harvest dates, and estimating crop sizes (peaches? cherries? roses?) as she was driving from delivery to delivery. Naoko had visited their house on the island, and come to several knitting circles. Did Andrew think that when the ladies weren't looking the girl was going into his office and rifling through papers for information on the Aether? Or, alternatively, sneaking about the ship factories, writing things down? Evidently, he did.

Yes, Pete was a shady character. All of Pete's attractions grew out of the fact that he was a shady character whose credentials were not in order, and whose stories could never be proved or disproved. The only things she knew about Pete were that he had in his possession some Japanese works of art, that he had shown her some horses at the racetrack that he said were his, and that, for now, she liked him. Very much. He was kind, observant, and enjoyable to talk to. Aah, Pete, she thought. Andrew was right to be suspicious of Pete, because Pete made a career of acting suspiciously, but the thought of his suspicions made her tingle with rage.

She got up from the chair, turned out the light, and went into Andrew's office. She laid the papers in the center of the desk, where he would be sure to see them, then she put a shawl over her shoulders and took Stella out into the yard. The dog did some investigating, and then they went back into the house. She left Stella in the kitchen, where he would find her, and went upstairs to her room, where she closed the door, changed into her nightgown, and got into bed. Sometime later, she heard Andrew come in, then come up the stairs. He did not knock on her door. He went into his room, then the bathroom, then his room again. After that, there was silence. She fell asleep.

In her dream, she didn't know whether she was frightened for Andrew or of him. Sometimes he was a figure stumbling through the sand, and sometimes he was a figure coming toward her, large and threatening, but overall what frightened her was the space around him, a vastness that seemed to indicate that anything could happen. She woke up from this dream and fell asleep again, into a different dream, in which the word "spy" itself was what frightened her. At first Andrew was the spy (as indeed he was), seeming to look at one thing but really looking at another. Then he was supplanted by other figures, none of whom she could recognize, who were also spying, though not, in particular, on her. Though they seemed innocent enough—rather like the figures of children running about—her dream self was filled with waves of horror that she could not escape or reduce, waves that might be tossing her about in the surf, just below the Golden Gate Bridge. At the end of this dream, just before she woke up, she thought the words "Agent Keene," and those words stayed with her and repeated themselves over and over through the next uneasy dream, which was about men coming to the house. In this dream, she kept going to the door and opening it, and seeing a figure on the doorstep. The roses like those she had cut and carried to Mr. Kimura also figured into this dream—she was afraid that the person on the doorstep would see her cut the roses and know whom they were for, and take them away from her. But she didn't actually dream about the Kimuras or Pete.

Toward morning, she woke thoroughly. The room was dark, the sky was lightening, so she lay there for a few minutes, breathless and with her pulse sounding in her ears. Her whole life seemed just then to be so unfamiliar as to induce a sense of vertigo. It was as if she were a child again, and had dreamed about everything that was to come, as if she knew to her very bones that she could not manage or handle what was to come. She had to remind herself several times that what seemed as though it was going to happen had in fact already happened, and she had managed it, or, at least, she had survived it. But she continued to tremble. And this feeling evolved into a more frightening one—she was herself, old, sixty-two, and her mind was so full of everything that she had seen and done and imagined that she didn't know what to make of any of it, how to think, what to do, how to live.

She heard Andrew stirring in his room and, after that, in the hallway, and she was seized with such fear and revulsion that she put her head under the covers and waited and waited for him first to go downstairs, and then to leave the house. She knew now that there was no telling what he was doing or where he was going, and that the least of her worries was that he would annoy someone and be brought home by the local police. She also realized that he wanted to talk to her about what he had written.

She did not want to talk to him about anything. She was a coward, and avoided him.

When the house was quiet, she got dressed and went to the police. She told the sergeant on duty that she had once been visited by an Agent Keene, from the FBI, and that she wanted to talk to him again. They gave her a telephone number in San Francisco. There had been a drunken brawl in downtown Vallejo the night before, and the police were too busy to ask her any questions, for which she was grateful.

But there was no Agent Keene. Agent Keene had been transferred to parts unknown (or, at least, parts not to be known by her), and she was eventually connected with Agent Greengrass, who was not familiar with Andrew and had never seen his "reports," although, he said, they sounded "interesting."

She said, "Well, Agent Greengrass, I don't think they are interesting. That's why I'm calling you. Captain Early's reports are a mishmash of crazy ideas, and I wanted to make sure that the people in your office understood that."

"Why did you want to make sure of that?"

"Because it's true."

Agent Greengrass was silent, then said, "Tell me your name again."

"Margaret Mayfield Early."

"And to whom did your husband send these reports?"

She thought of saying that she didn't know, but she couldn't bring herself to lie. She said, "Roosevelt, the Secretary of the Navy, and the Commandant of the Naval Base."

"Ma'am," said Agent Greengrass, "you wouldn't believe the pile of stuff that goes to the White House, for the eyes of the President only, that reports secret air attacks and webs of underground tunnels. But I will take down your name and address and let you know if I hear anything."

She thanked him and gave him the information, grateful that he seemed to think Andrew was simply a crackpot. It was only after they hung up that she began to wonder about that phrase "if I hear anything."

Andrew came in in the early afternoon, and she served him an apple and a liverwurst sandwich. He seemed a little abashed. Margaret knew she had to think carefully and move slowly in order not to waste her opportunity. She felt a wisp of that old temptation—curtain rising, play commencing—but she put it away and said, "I read the papers, Andrew, and put them back on your desk. Why did you show them to me?"

"Well, of course, I wondered what you think."

"What I think?"

"If you agree with me."

"About whether I am the unwitting center of a nest of spies who are using me to get to you?"

"Why, yes. I wanted to get your opinion."

"You say you've already sent everything in."

"I have."

"So what does my opinion matter?"

"Well, my dear, who else have I got to ask?"

She couldn't help acknowledging that, in other circumstances, this remark might strike her as poignant, or even funny, but now she said, soberly, "I do not think that I am the unwitting victim of a nest of spies."

"Well, of course, they would be sure to solicit your affections." He seemed to have no idea of how insulting this remark was. He finished his sandwich and picked up the apple.

She made her voice very firm. "My relationship with the Kimuras is almost purely a formal one. I've visited them a handful of times, and Naoko has come to the knitting circle. Did you also turn in reports on the other members of the knitting circle?"

He said, "Do you remember the party for Mr. Kimura?"

"Of course I do."

"I saw Pete back there, behind the garden, in the alley."

"Did you speak to him?"

"I only saw him from the back. He was taking things away, a box of things, like papers. When he saw me, he hurried away."

"I thought you only saw him from the back."

"But he saw me out of the corner of his eye. He took a large box out of the alley and turned left; then, moments later, a car drove away."

"Was he in it?"

"I couldn't tell. The man died two days later. *I* think Pete was taking his papers. I wonder what you think. You have good instincts. You could be unwitting but still have a sense that something is going on, and then, when someone suggests what it might be, it sounds right to you. It clicks."

"So—you're hoping that your theory will click with me?"

"I think it will, yes."

"You've already sent it in."

"I haven't said anything about Mr. Kimura's papers, or Pete carrying them off, but at least we know where they were last seen, and they could be picked up and perused."

"This is nonsense, Andrew." But she wanted to say "insanity." She should have started with the word "insanity," but she had done her usual thing, which was to be wifely and reasonable, which allowed him to weave a net of plausibility around her, and now they were discussing a piece of insanity as if it might be true.

"Then, my dear, I will just have to use my own judgment and draw my own conclusions. That boy went to Japan."

"He wanted to get married and live a normal life, which he couldn't live here!"

"That was a plausible excuse."

"It's a reason! I believe it."

He sat for a long time, looking first at his shoes and then at her. Stella jumped into his lap, received no attention, and jumped down again. Finally, he said, "My dear, perhaps it is that I can't get over your betrayal of me."

The guilty, Margaret thought, are always undone by the accusation. In her chest, the reaction began instantly, before she even pictured Pete, or their tryst in Atherton—it was a sense of being paralyzed and set on fire at the same time, accompanied by a casting about for evidence as to where the deception went wrong, and indecision as to whether to confess or to brazen it out. But it was not that she kept silent. It was that she couldn't speak.

Andrew took a very deep breath and smoothed down his mustache. At last, he said, "It was Len Scanlan who told me."

"Len Scanlan! Why would you believe a thing he said?"

"Because I sensed it was true. My own instincts were confirmed."

"Are you—"

But he didn't even seem to notice that her voice was strangled. He went on in an injured tone: "It was when we went to Saratoga. We were driving along, and he said—I'll never forget it—'I'm sure it's difficult for you, Captain Early, when even your wife doesn't believe you. When even your wife finds you a shade ridiculous.' And I saw at once it was true. The little secret smiles. The way you had about the typing. As if you were humoring me, or dandling me along like a child. As if my ideas were ridiculous to you."

There was a long pause, which felt like the insensate pause of lifting a heavy weight, as Margaret came to understand that he and she were not thinking of the same betrayal at all.

She finally said, "And, by contrast, of course, Leonard Scanlan believed every word you wrote and every word you uttered?"

"He did then. Not later, of course. Though I feel that he has always understood and appreciated my theories. Two scientists often agree on basics, and then fall out over details. The coming of his wife was not good for our partnership."

She exclaimed, "It was an evil thing, and entirely typical of Len Scanlan, that he should whisper such things in your ear. He was a flatterer and a sneak." Andrew seemed taken aback by the sharpness of her words, and did not meet her gaze. She took a deep breath and managed to say in a calmer tone, "I was not indulging myself in secret smiles."

"Perhaps not, my dear. But even so, you don't believe in my work, and you haven't for many years." He got up from the table and went into his study. Margaret sat looking at the apple core sitting on the plate and petting Stella. When she felt herself more composed, she got up, went to his study door, and knocked. He answered. She opened the door and said, quite smoothly, she thought, "Have you confronted Pete with your suspicions?"

"I don't think that's my job. I wouldn't know how. Others do that who are trained to read facial expressions and that sort of thing."

"You're afraid of him!"

Andrew said nothing to this for a moment, then, "I like Pete. I've always liked Pete."

"Why would you denounce him as a spy, then?"

"That has nothing to do with liking or disliking. He is or he is not."

"What would he be spying on?"

Now he sounded relieved as he entered upon this topic. "Well, my dear, I've turned that over in my mind. He was a man with many friends. When he left Russia, they stayed behind and were drawn into different camps. When he went back, in 1917, which camp did he enter and which camp did he betray, and how did those camps themselves betray one another? The ins and outs of this are perhaps imponderable for a Westerner. He spent several years in Japan, and he came to the U.S. with his tastes formed, in part by that experience. We don't know what he left behind in Japan, who claimed his loyalties there. He's been very quiet on that subject. And then he came here. Is his loyalty to this country? To our aims in the Pacific or elsewhere? Or is he tainted with that distrust of Western imperialism that seems to be motivating the Japanese and the Russians? Perhaps he thinks that those countries should throw off their chains. It could be as simple as that. You don't have to hate your tormentor in order to operate on the principle that the torment is unjust and must be rectified."

She leaned against the doorjamb and stared at him. Once again, as so often before, it all sounded so plausible that it seemed easy to be convinced. She could give in to Pete as a spy, and to the Aether, and to Einstein's investigations on the West Coast. Who was she to tell the difference between those things and the impact craters on the moon being like gunshots in the mud and the *Panay* incident and the Spanish flu turning up in Kansas? Who was she to say yes to one thing and no to another? That seemed to be the kernel of their conflict—if he couldn't convince her, his own wife, then who could he convince? If he couldn't convince her, then he was all the more at the mercy of people like Len Scanlan and, what was his name, his enemy in Michigan, and even strangers, like that fellow Malisoff. As she stared at him staring at her, she thought, What is at stake, really? What do I have to lose?

Andrew said, in his pushing, eager tone, "And then there is this. He has shown a suspicious degree of interest in my theories. He has questioned and probed me."

It popped out: "He was flattering you."

He looked hurt.

She felt her assurance enlarge, and said, "Aren't you afraid that you will be viewed by the—the—President as a crackpot?"

"No, my dear. I am not."

He spoke with such self-confidence that she said, "I have to tell you,

Andrew, that what you've done is . . . breathtakingly irresponsible, given the atmosphere we are living in. I cannot go along with this, or allow it to continue. Unless you write to your contacts and renounce these claims, I'll have to do something myself. I'll have to. It will be embarrassing for you, whatever I do, but I will do it anyway. Do you understand me?"

He was intimidated, at least for now. At least for now, he said, "Then what Len said . . ."

"It doesn't matter what Len said about how I view your ideas. That is beside the point." The snake picture was hanging on the wall, behind him and slightly to the left. She went on, "Andrew. Look at that picture. It's called *The Gift*. Look at it. It's a beautiful picture. It's a picture of Len Scanlan."

He turned around and looked at the picture. She walked out.

BUT she was not uninfected; her forceful denial gave way to uncertainty. She did not press him the next day or the day after that about withdrawing his reports. She told herself that she didn't press him because she had that same feeling that she'd had with Agent Greengrass—all references of any kind to these matters were damaging, and possibly denials were more damaging than assertions. What one wanted above all was to be forgotten. But she made an early date with Pete, with whom she lunched at the Palace Hotel with some frequency now. And the first thing she asked, almost before they sat down, was how Mrs. Kimura and Naoko, who had moved to Japantown after Mr. Kimura's death, were doing.

"They don't like it," said Pete.

"Why is that? I thought it would be a cocoon for them, with Vallejo so crowded. Down by their old shop, there's a racket night and day, with all the new workers and their saloons."

"Cocoons can be very constricting, and anyway, Japantown is not an enclave of kindly and well-meaning families going out for church picnics every chance they get. There are drunks everywhere, Margaret. Unhappy and nervous men make angry drunks."

"Surely they haven't been threatened."

"Surely everyone has been threatened, if only by roaming hoodlums. And Lester is hardly ever at home, and, of course, what he does during the day, on his job, is impossible to know."

"He's a bookkeeper. That should be quiet enough."

"It should be, but although Lester has a bookkeeper's skills, he doesn't have a bookkeeper's character. He's a little bit too inquisitive." He shook his head.

They picked off some of the leaves of the artichoke they were sharing, and Pete took a sip of his wine.

She spoke as if idly. "Of course, Andrew is sure he's a Japanese spy." How ridiculous it was to say this! Her pulse quickened.

Pete didn't smile. "Lester's not canny enough for that. He's more the patsy that spies buy drinks for and then get information out of. Naoko is sure he's involved with gangs or smuggling. He may be."

"You seem to know what you're talking about."

"Do I? I must have read *The Thirty-nine Steps*." Now he smiled.

"Andrew saw that movie."

"You see, then. Anyway, no American would tell a Japanese man anything, even a tall Japanese man with an American accent. They'd be more likely to beat him up, and Lester knows that. And discretion, thy name is not Lester Kimura. People who talk all the time have a much harder time being spies."

"Why is that?"

"Well, if you are a quiet, nondescript sort of person, pleasant in your way, but bland, and, say, a little plump, people talk in front of you, because they don't attribute any keenness to you. And if you seem a bit thick, they dismiss you out of hand. You find that, with plenty of application, you can introduce yourself almost anywhere, gather information, and disappear. Your life as a spy is a long and productive one." He smiled and added, "It especially helps to be an Englishman and have superior manners, but not everyone can manage that."

She wiped her fingers on her napkin and said, "You're teasing."

"I know what I'm talking about." He picked up the artichoke heart and scraped away the fibers, then cut it into four neat pieces.

"Are you a spy, then?" This was very bold, she thought.

"I've known a spy or two. But look at me."

She did. He was wearing a yellow tie, had a yellow square in his pocket, and his hat, she had seen when he checked it, had a yellow band.

"No one ever forgets me."

"Surely there are flamboyant spies."

"There are, but it's much more difficult for them. They have to keep so many things straight—not only separate *things* but the separate *stories* that make up their roles. Their lives are short."

"As spies?"

"That, too. Anyway, I'm too lazy to be a spy. And so I am not a spy."

"Now."

"Now."

"But."

"But, as I told you, when I was a young man in Petersburg, I did romantic spying for my friend Bibikova, and it was an invigorating exercise for a young man with an overabundance of daring. Spies, Margaret, are like all other sorts of criminals. They are either too smart for the job or too stupid for the job. I'm sure the Germans and the Japanese looking for American spies are gnashing their teeth in frustration at the poor material they have to work with." He laughed.

Then the wave came, the wave she thought she had worked herself away from, or talked herself out of, the wave of feeling toward him that was so painful and inconvenient. It was the stories, of course, that did it, himself as the foolish protagonist, making his merry way through a colorful landscape, always discovering too late where he had gone wrong. In his stories, suffering and death were hardly worth remembering—what was important were the telling details. The tiniest, most fleeting thing was preserved, while routine disaster was forgotten. The effect was to bathe him in a golden light—a light that shone from her eyes, a light that shone brightly and steadily even though she knew he was untrustworthy, mysterious, old, full of vanity, a failure in the larger scheme of respectable success. The golden light made him look utterly unique and therefore precious. She closed her eyes and felt the wave pass through her and, with a few breaths, ebb again. She said, "You'll never guess what Andrew has been doing all these years when I thought he was making himself an expert on the pictures."

"He has been guarding our shores."

"How did you know?"

"He told me. Or, rather, he sent me a letter."

"What did it say?"

"Well, there were three of them. One asked for my help in finding out what Albert Einstein is doing with that nest of Nazi physicists whom your husband has been onto for more than twenty-five years. I wrote back and said that I was not privy to any physicists' plots.

He wrote back and said that he considered all of German physics, which seems so theoretical, to be mere preparatory ground for their real goal, which is to construct an unprecedented weapon of some sort, to be used against Britain, though a submarine carrying the weapon and getting into New York Harbor or up the Potomac was, is, also a possibility. That letter I didn't answer. The third letter listed eleven suspicious sightings he had made around the bay, and asked what I thought about them. I was impressed at how active he is at his age."

"Andrew is very suspicious of everyone's loyalties, including mine. His, of course, are evident, because, although he's never been to sea, he's a retired captain of the navy."

"And he always thinks of such things in a very direct way. That's his nature. But this protracted commencement of the war means that other people's loyalties are still in suspension. He's right about that. Look at that fellow Mosley. He could play around a bit with Hitler, and do so in a public way, but he didn't do that after '39. When the war comes to us, loyalties will solidify." By his tone, they could have been talking about any old thing, but he gave her a glance, unhappy, naked, rare. She said, "I am so full of dread."

"We all are," said Pete.

Margaret stared at him, wondering if he was thinking of Stalin and Hitler, or of something more personal and tragic, but as always, she could not bring herself to pry. She glanced away, then said, "But when you talk to me about things, they make sense, and when Andrew talks to me about things, they make no sense. That's the terrifying part. I know what I think, and then he tells me something, and what I think collapses into bits and pieces. That's the kind of dread I mean."

Pete smiled at last. He said, "Not mere death, then."

Somehow, this was reassuring.

That evening, she asked to see Andrew's letter recanting his accusations. When he brought it out, she said, "Tomorrow morning, I am going to type this, and then we are going to walk to the post office and send it together."

He agreed, and they did. His letter read, in part: "I now believe that in the heat of present political and military circumstances, I have misinterpreted things I have seen around me as signs of something larger, when, actually, they are signs of nothing. I now believe that Mrs. Kiku Kimura and her daughter, Naoko Kimura, and her son, Lester Kimura, are not guilty of any activities that might be of interest to the military authorities, and I now believe that Mr. Pete Moran (or Krizenko) is an innocent party also." He apologized for his "overzealous patriotism" and admitted that he was an old man. It was Margaret who was left to wonder, though only about Pete, and only in the way that she had always wondered about him.

DORA returned from Europe, in trouble with her paper for being too outspoken. She was giving talks, and the gist of her talks was that Europe was no place for Americans, and that even the British weren't worth helping, because they were "mealy and corrupt to the core." As for the French, they had "swooned" without a fight, and now everyone was fleeing into the countryside, "and what will they find? The farmers and the villagers will have hidden their food and fuel, and they will simply cross their arms, keep their mouths shut, and watch their countrymen and -women die." Pouring money and aid into Europe was simply "flushing it away"—"How can you prop up those who refuse to stand?" All of Europe had been rotted from within by "recreational communism" on the part of the privileged classes. She was violently anticommunist when she wasn't violently anti-Nazi, and her tour gave her the pleasure of "breathing air unpolluted by ideology, sweetened by the practical effects of self-reliance." Her letters to Margaret went on and on in the same vein. She was slated to speak in Sacramento.

By the time Dora got to Sacramento, her farthest point west, the Luftwaffe had bombed Dublin, the Germans had invaded Russia, and American men were registering for the military draft. Margaret drove over there to see her in time for lunch on the day of her talk in a hall that had been rented by several ladies' organizations. She waited in the lobby of the hotel. Across the small rotunda, she saw the elevator doors open. Out stepped three people, a young man with a little girl by the hand, and a fusty old woman in what looked from a distance like a calico dress from fifty years ago—high neck, sleeves that were puffy around the shoulders, skirt with no drape at all, and very little waist. The skirt was long, and the woman had on low heels. Margaret thought of the song "Sweet Betsy from Pike" and realized that this throwback was Dora, costumed as an American pioneer. She laughed one laugh, but it was the dress, above all, that persuaded Margaret of Dora's sincere conversion—not only had the always trim Dora thickened, she had also gone back to her early habit of designing her own clothes. She was smiling. She hugged Margaret. Her hair was white. She said, "Recognize me, darling?"

"No."

"*Vanitas vanitatum.*"

"What does that mean?"

"It means, 'Vanity, thy name is Europe.' "

"It does?"

Dora took her elbow and propelled her into the restaurant. She may have gotten old, but her grip was as strong as ever. They sat down, and she ordered a T-bone steak with a baked potato, and a wedge of lettuce with Thousand Island dressing. Dora said, "Darling, you're gawking."

"It's—"

"Just a steak."

"But you've never been a big eater."

"I have a new plan. I am going to be a fat old lady living on my farm in Missouri—"

"In Missouri! You hate Missouri."

"Yes, right outside of Gumbo. I bought a hundred acres that back up onto the river. Lovely open country, and you can see the bluffs on the St. Charles side. Least of evils, in a way, but, darling, I'm so old now, all my local nemeses have passed on." She ate a big bite of her steak. "I closed the deal last week."

"What about the newspaper?"

Dora shook her head. "They're with Roosevelt all the way. He's going to force them into this war. Eleanor is behind it, her and her commie friends—"

"Mrs. Roosevelt isn't a communist!"

"—her and her commie friends. And so I am retiring to the middle of the country and writing my book and raising my chickens and hogs, and I'll walk around the place every day with my shotgun and kill rattlesnakes, and every time I get one, I'll shout, 'Take that, Ickes!' 'Take that, Hopkins!' " She laughed.

Margaret said, "You are joking, then."

"I'm laughing, but I'm not joking. How are you?"

Instead of telling her, Margaret said, "Everyone around here is convinced that the Germans and the Japanese are spying on our every move."

"But they are wrong. Hoover has been beating the bushes for spies for ten years, and the most they've come up with is two deadbeats who couldn't find jobs. They're going to talk about spies until they're blue in the face, just to get you suckers out here in California worked up and ready to fight." Dora waved her hand.

"Andrew thinks the Japanese want the Philippines and Hawaii."

"Maybe they should have them. And maybe the Germans should have Austria and the Italians should have the Balkans. What difference does it make? No one can answer *that* question, I'll tell you that."

"Dora!"

"Yes, if they decide they want Mexico, let's stop them. Or Alaska. But they aren't going to decide that." She leaned forward and stared at Margaret. "They are not going to decide they want Catalina Island."

"Of course not, but—"

"I've had a dose of Europe and Europeans to last me the rest of my life. You never saw so many people so quick to run to some squirmy little fellow and kneel at his feet and say, 'Tell me what to do, Duce! Tell me what to do, Führer! Tell me what to do, Comrade Stalin!' Gives Roosevelt goose bumps. You can see it in his eyes."

About every issue she had an opinion, and her opinions were expressed with some wit, but always a note of stridency, as if she knew she was losing the battle but she intended to fight it anyway, no matter what. When she got up to leave, Margaret felt that Dora barely noticed she was going, so wound up was she about what she intended to say to the ladies' groups at six that evening. The next day, Dora took the train to Reno, and after that to Arizona and then east.

ANDREW maintained that planning the attack on Pearl Harbor was what had brought Albert Einstein to the West Coast. But he insisted to Margaret that he had made no "report."

The day after the attack, she called Mrs. Kimura twice in the course of the day and Pete three times, but no one answered the phone. The next morning, she took the early ferry, and she was at the Kimuras' by eight o'clock. She had been there once before, in the summer, on the way back from a visit to the new botanical garden in San Francisco.

Always, with the Kimuras, she tried to be more polite than she was naturally, because they seemed more sensitive than most people— Naoko responded to a whisper the way her other friends responded to a declaration. So she stood quietly in their entryway for about ten minutes, occasionally knocking very lightly and one time ringing the bell. Finally, she awakened from her reverie and knocked three times quite briskly. The door opened. She stood there with both hands on her purse, and then she pushed it farther, and stepped into the room. She shouted, "Yoo-hoo! Yoo-hoo! Mrs. Kimura? Naoko?" But there was no answer.

The front room was not in disarray, but an envelope and two pieces of paper lay on the floor, a pair of shoes had been dropped willy-nilly in the middle of the room. She went out into the hall and saw that their newspaper from that morning had been kicked aside by someone passing through the entryway. She picked it up. She returned to the apartment, into the kitchen. Yesterday's paper was sitting on the kitchen table, unread. Beside it was a cup of tea, full, and next to that was a half-peeled orange. She went back out into the entry, then she went down the stairs and outside. She sat down on the front step and waited.

The street was empty. Every conversation, every radio broadcast, every newspaper article was now about the war, but on the front step of the Kimuras' apartment building, all was quiet. Up and down the street, the shops were closed and the lights were off. It was eerie, and moment by moment, her feeling that she was waiting for Naoko and her mother dissipated, and then she simply waited for something unknown that would tell her why the tea was not drunk and the orange was not peeled. After about half an hour, she got up and walked down the street and around the corner. The whole block was shut—the cleaners, the grocery, three restaurants, a doctor's office, a seamstress's shop. She had turned three corners and gotten almost to the fourth when she came to a small tobacconist, a shop only twice as wide as its own door. Inside, an old man sat behind a counter covered with cigarette displays. She greeted him and asked if he spoke English. At first, she had no idea whether he heard or understood her, so she said, "I am a friend of Mrs. Kiku Kimura, from Vallejo." Immediately he began shaking his head. Then he got up and went past her out the door. She was wondering what to do next when he came back with a young man. This young man smiled and dipped his head. She said, "I'm looking for my friend Mrs. Kimura. Maybe you remember that they came to—"

"I am so sorry tell you, ma'am, that your friends have been taken yesterday."

"Taken!"

"Yes, ma'am. All three. The boy, and then the lady, Miss Kimura, and then also the old mother." He dipped his head again. The older man said something, and the young man said, "My father hears they have been arrested."

She went to a telephone booth and called Pete. The phone rang ten, then eleven, then twelve times, and she had begun to fear that he had been arrested, too, but he picked it up. His voice was sleepy; he woke up when she told him about her morning. He said, "I did hear about a man being arrested down in San Jose, but he was a prominent businessman and a member of JACL. He'd bought a lot of land through his son, who was born here, and has been agitating for repeal of the Alien Land Acts. I can see how the local authorities down there would take this opportunity to silence that fellow, but—"

"Just to silence him?"

"And to get hold of his land. But I don't see how that operates in this case."

"But, Pete," she said, "Andrew denounced the Kimuras as spies. He sent letters to Roosevelt himself—top-secret, of course—and to the Secretary of the Navy and the Commandant of the Base. They were full of ridiculous claims, and he wrote them all out by hand so no one could doubt that he had composed them. I made him send a retraction, but, honestly, would anyone pay a bit of attention?"

Pete was silent. Aghast, she thought.

"He told me that Albert Einstein was coming to Vallejo repeatedly in order to meet up with Japanese agents and develop a weapon of some kind that would wipe Americans off the map and leave their natural resources to be developed by enslaved Chinese workers."

Pete's laugh at this was welcome, but it was not a guffaw, more of a chuckle. She told him about Agent Keene and Agent Greengrass. She said, "Agent Keene came by ages ago, and no one ever investigated after that."

"Why didn't you tell me?"

"Because it was so crazy. Talking about it made him sound so . . ." She paused. "I thought if he wrote a retraction . . ."

Pete gave a deep sigh.

She made herself say, "And he told them he thought you were a spy, too. He said that I was the unwitting center of a 'nest of spies' who were trying to get to him. When you weren't at Mr. Kimura's last gathering, right before he died, Andrew thought he saw you carry away a box of papers, down the alley behind the shop, and then drive off with them."

"Was he sure?"

"Is he ever not sure?"

"Is he ever not wrong?"

"He was right about the *Panay.*"

Pete said, "Well, go back up to the Kimuras' apartment and look around."

"I locked the door behind me so their things won't get stolen."

He said, "Darling, that was thoughtful of you, but I don't think that's going to do any good. I don't know what all of this means in the long term, but . . ."

"What does it mean in the short term?"

"Well, you know . . ." His voice trailed off.

"I don't know."

There was a silence, then he cleared his throat. He said, "Roosevelt would possibly not go as far as gassing them in the forests. He might stop at camps."

"Oh, Pete!" She was truly shocked, the way you are when a thing that has not occurred to you is suddenly present.

He said: "All-out war started Sunday, darling. The Japanese attacked Malaya, Hong Kong, Guam, the Philippines, and Midway, as well as Pearl Harbor. If they attacked Midway, that means they want to put a refueling base there so that they can get bombers all the way to here. The Germans have taken Kiev, Odessa, Kharkov, and Rostov. And I'm sure the Germans will declare war on the U.S. any day now." He fell silent, then said, more thoughtfully, "But I don't think they would have come and picked up Kiku and Naoko personally if Andrew's big arrow hadn't been pointing at them. . . ." His voice trailed off again, and then she ran out of nickels. When she had found some and got back to the phone booth, Pete did not answer. The next day, she tried to call Agent Greengrass, but he was long gone.

THE Tuesday after Pearl Harbor, Andrew decided to stay home. When he had finished his breakfast, he asked for another cup of coffee, and when she put on her hat to go to her knitting group, he said, "My dear, perhaps you would favor me by not going out today."

"I want to go out. I have things to do."

"Perhaps you would write me a list of those things."

She said, "No, Andrew. I am not going to—" But when she stepped toward the door, he was out of his seat in an instant, barring her way. She set her hat on the hall table and went up to her room. In the afternoon, she tried again, coming down to the foot of the stairs and saying, "Andrew, I am going to the store."

He came out of his office and said, "Let me get the leash for the dog. We can go with you." And then he stalked down the street beside her, carrying her shopping bag and leading Stella.

He did not come into her room, or even stand over her in the kitchen, but when she tried the back door, she saw that it was locked with the key and the key was missing. She didn't need to try the front door. Perhaps it was more disturbing not to see him. When she was in her room, his heavy footsteps walked from the front of the house to the back, and the back to the front, sometimes accompanied by the click of Stella's nails on the floorboards. Sometimes she heard a few steps that then stopped, and she would find herself concentrating on that sound, and when it would start up again. She could not read—even the books she had been saving for a free moment drew her in no way. Or she would start a task, like cleaning out drawers, and quickly abandon it.

When she went downstairs, she would find him reading one of his newspapers. As soon as he saw her, he would say, "My dear, you will be interested in this," and read something aloud. When an American oil tanker was torpedoed by a Japanese submarine off the coast somewhere (unidentified in the article), he said, "Here's something. What do you think of that? They saw the shelling from the town." When American forces surrendered Wake Island just before Christmas, he said, "You will want to read this, my dear." He stood up and handed her the paper, jabbing at the article with his forefinger. When Hong Kong surrendered, he said, "I suppose you will think it's for the best." When Manila was bombed, he suggested, mildly, that perhaps she wouldn't believe that the Japanese had "bombed mere civilians," but that, according to the newspapers, it was "indeed true. Their objectives, I would say, aren't purely military. I'm sure even you will have to agree." Her loyalties, she saw, were once more in question—her loyalties to him, to the navy, the U.S. In his mind, what was the difference, after all?

After the first day, she hated to go out with him, but he insisted they shop together and walk Stella together. He would not allow her to make or receive phone calls, but after a few days, there weren't any. He was unfailingly, frighteningly polite. He read to her about the arrival of the survivors from Wake Island as prisoners of war in Japan. He read to her about the loss of Singapore, and then the Philippines. When she simply refused to come out of her room, he brought her toast and cups of tea. One afternoon, he was sitting just off the entryway, where she could see him from the top of the stairs. He was reading a book and keeping his eye on the door. She descended the stairs and confronted him.

She said, "I want to go out, Andrew. If only for a walk. By myself."

"My considered opinion is that it isn't safe out there."

"What could happen?"

"There are those who believe that the Japanese are planning to execute a major attack on all the shipping, airfields, cities, and oilfields along the coast of California, which would result in the massive evacuation of millions of civilians to the east."

She felt a flutter in her throat at this idea, but she said, "Are there, really? What do you think?"

"I admit that it would be an unprecedented tactical undertaking."

"If it's not safe out there, then it's not safe in here."

He looked up at her. "But why go out, is my feeling. We would only use up more energy and require more calories to sustain ourselves."

"I'm going out."

"Well, I'm sure Stella would like a walk as well. Perhaps once or twice around the block would do us all some good."

"You are keeping me captive!"

"I don't think of it like that, my dear." He put down his book, got up, reached for his coat. She saw that he was obdurate in a way only he could be, in the way he had always been—like something large and insensate, a statue of himself. She went back upstairs.

She sat down on her bed and looked out the window, over the top of the many-trunked black-walnut tree in the side yard. The long dull-green leaves were well out, and the dangling ropes of buds were beginning to form. Margaret knew that if she stood up and looked down at the beds, she would see daffodils, but daffodils would remind her how long she had let him keep her here.

The terrifying thing, once again, was how plausible everything he said was. Hadn't this always been true—the very first time she met him, on that bicycle of Dora's, he had talked about telephones and she had believed him. And then, what was it, levees breaking or something on the Mississippi below St. Louis, and then double stars, and then his half-mad and permanently bitter former student and all the other resentful colleagues and unrelenting enemies, and then, of course, the universe itself, with its pillars of gravity, or was that iron cables? And vast spaces that he spoke about in a warm tone of voice, as if those spaces belonged to him above all other men. She had seen marriages from the outside, and even, a little, from the inside—it was utterly routine for women to talk about other women's marriages as Lavinia had talked about the Bells'—Mr. Bell staying out of the house as much as he could, and Mrs. Bell doing what she pleased, and everyone knew he thought she was a fool. Beatrice had gotten married and entered upon the same dissatisfied but workable course, and no one expected marriage to be anything different. All sorts of commonplaces covered it— "live and let live," "make the best of things," "it could be worse," "sauce for the goose." The ladies in her knitting group had dispatched one another's marriages every week or so for almost forty years.

Nor did they seem intimidated by Andrew. Even when they were not playing poker with him, they asked him questions and joked a bit and said goodbye and forgot about him. No doubt in her absence they dealt out a set of commonplaces about him, too—"thinks awfully well of himself," "too big for his britches," "barking mad." Even thinking of these bits of phrase was reassuring in its way.

But no. Marriage to Andrew was not that small. She could not make it small—not by parsing it out in daily tasks or making pleasant conversation or doing as she was told. He wanted something from her that all of these activities did not give him. Right then, she could feel what he wanted emanating from the floor below, mushrooming up the staircase, through floor vents, under the door—he wanted agreement, belief, even, possibly, worship. And he wanted that worship to be large and surrounding, something that he could feel, not the mere something that she, or anyone, could give. She had agreed with him more often than not over the years, hadn't she, and as soon as she agreed, he looked past her for a grander and more satisfying embrace. The hugeness of his ideas made her small, and then the smallness of her agreement goaded him to seek more. She enlarged in his mind only when she didn't agree with him—then he set himself to conquer her, and overwhelm her disbelief.

And yet—she lay down—his own developing smallness was what preoccupied him, wasn't it? He had been the most brilliant boy in their town, the best student at the university, that genius who changed the nature of the universe, that big fellow who bestrode the Rockefellers' university, until he was pushed here and shunted there, sent to an out-of-the-way island, only to be elbowed out of there, now confined to this ramshackle house and mostly (completely) forgotten unless he was recollected as a mere nuisance. She pitied him as a wife should, but that very pity, that wifely impulse, made her susceptible to ideas like Einstein blowing up London and the Kimuras spying and Pete not being Pete at all, but someone else—perhaps Einstein in disguise? If she listened to Andrew long enough, she would believe that anything was possible, and yet everything wasn't possible, and so there you were—at an impasse.

That day, she simply kept to herself except for two forays to the kitchen for tea. All Andrew said, looking up from his paper, was "Perhaps you will feel like cooking again tomorrow."

And then he was gone completely. When she came down toward midday for a cup of tea, Stella was confined to the kitchen. Andrew's empty coffee cup was sitting on the morning paper, and with it, he had secured a note. It read:

My dear,
You will be most surprised to learn that I have taken the train to Washington, D.C., on pressing business. For the last week, I have been torn as to my responsibilities as a navy captain. I understand what I must do here in Vallejo, but I have come to believe that my larger duty is to personally deliver my report to the Secretary of the Navy. It is urgent that the movements of certain persons be restricted. I have been unable to speak to Secretary Knox over the telephone, as I am not as well known to him as I have been to others in the past, and so I see with regret that I will have to return to my old haunts, and do what must be done. I am sure that, once I have spoken to Secretary Knox, the recommendations I intend to make will be speedily implemented. As for your own activities, my dear, it is my belief that they can make no further difference to our national security at this point.

She went upstairs, put on her clothes, and went out with a very happy Stella, though not before calling Pete, who didn't answer.

The knowledge that Andrew was somewhere between their street and Washington, D.C., and speeding away from her was thrilling. She suspected that his sense of mission would only grow more pressing as he acted on it—every step would reinforce every thought; every thought would motivate another step.

The weather, neither bad nor good, seemed glorious. The intervals of sunlight were dazzling, the intervals of fog invigorating. Daffodils were up, though not blooming. Pruned stubs of rosebushes had developed tiny shoots. There was a fragrance in the air of sweet grasses. Stella trotted in front of her, jaunty and alert. They walked toward the center of town.

In the period of her confinement, the crowds on the streets and in the shops and cafés had doubled. At the Warrington, she could hardly get in the door, so busy was it. She had to pick up Stella and carry her in. The lobby was crowded; every phone booth held a caller. More people were lined up, their nickels in their hands, waiting. Behind the desk, Cassandra and her daughter (now sixteen) were checking in guests, and there was another clerk busy, too. The customers lined up five deep. As she passed them, looking for Mrs. Wareham, she heard Cassandra say to one young man, "Sir, we are putting men four to a room. Otherwise, we have nothing for you. We are that full."

Then she saw Mrs. Wareham, sitting reliably in the parlor off the lobby. Mrs. Wareham was doing some embroidery, but stood up when she saw her. Margaret hugged her tightly.

"Margaret! Sit down right here." Mrs. Wareham patted the chair next to hers and poured her a cup of tea from the pot on the table beside her, but her face was alive with curiosity. "What has become of you? And Andrew? I haven't seen him in weeks."

Margaret sipped the tea and told her friend about their strange interlude of spousal imprisonment—in spite of herself, she made it sound more eccentric than frightening—then about his departure for Washington. Mrs. Wareham clucked with such comforting disapproval that Margaret felt a bit of horror set in. Yes, he had imprisoned her—that was not too strong a word—and so she said, vehemently, "I don't care about him! Good riddance! But where is Pete? And whatever happened to the Kimuras? The last I heard they'd been— He wouldn't let me even use the—"

Mrs. Wareham pursed her lips and started shaking her head. She had seen nothing of Pete in weeks, and as for the Kimuras, Lester had been charged in connection with an illegal gambling operation, and given no bail. That was as much as she knew. "Where Kiku and Naoko are, I cannot tell you. They are lost in the melee."

They both glanced through the door into the lobby. Even here, Margaret thought, the melee was frightening. She said, "But Lester's in jail?"

"I say this as a Canadian citizen, Margaret: the sheriff's department will make use of any excuse to keep a healthy young Japanese fellow behind bars." She leaned forward and said in a low voice, "Someone from the base who shall remain nameless told me that the very fact that there has been no sabotage is the clearest proof that some huge act of sabotage is in the works!"

"Was that Andrew?" The back of her neck prickled as she said this.

"No, Margaret, not Andrew."

Reprieve.

Mrs. Wareham put her hand on Margaret's knee. She said, "Time to be patient and hope for the best. We don't know what they are doing, or if they were picked up."

"I know they were picked up! I went to Japantown two days after the attack, and a neighbor told me they were picked up. They weren't doing anything." But she couldn't go on. The "melee" was too big, too chaotic. Her imagination could not follow the tiny figures of Mrs. Kimura and Naoko into it. She had that odd feeling again, that terror of her own life, as if she had not lived it yet and didn't know whether she would survive all the events she had already survived. All of the sense of freedom and pleasure that she had been feeling vanished, right then and there, no matter that Andrew was probably to Sacramento by then. She rearranged Stella on her lap, and felt that she might never speak again.

The letters from Andrew began about four days later. They came every two days. Other than hefting the envelopes, which were thick, and looking at the postmarks—Salt Lake City, Kansas City, Pittsburgh, Washington, D.C., Washington, D.C., Washington, D.C.—she didn't open them. She decided to follow the promptings of her heart and pitch them. She occupied her days by walking to the Warrington and doing as Mrs. Wareham did, working for the Red Cross. They knitted four nights a week, all in khaki yarn—vests, hats, socks, mufflers, even a child's one-piece suit or two (but in navy blue). During the days, they packed supplies to be sent off—surgical dressings, washed and mended articles of clothing from the Salvation Army, decks of cards, copies of books, stationery, envelopes, pens, and other items wounded soldiers and dispossessed civilians might find useful or entertaining. When the ladies asked after Andrew, Margaret said that he was doing secret war-work in Washington. Since everyone seemed to be doing secret war-work, no one probed any further.

One day, when she was walking to the Red Cross center, she saw in the *Examiner,* "Ouster of All Japs in California Near!" She walked right past. In the next few days, she found she could follow the story entirely by means of headlines and gossip—internment camps, relocation centers. Once again, Pete had been prescient, but she had had no word from him, either. Fortunately, there was a lull in Andrew's letters, but then a thick one arrived. She held it in her hand and stared at it. He had been gone for weeks now, the only pleasure of her existence. She almost opened the letter, but then she put it in the drawer of her bedside stand. Two nights later, though, when she came home from the knitting, after she changed and got into bed and turned out the light, she began to sense Andrew's letter. It chilled the room, an ice cube, a black dot in space, infinitely cold. She turned on the lamp, opened the drawer, took it out, carried it down the staircase and into the kitchen, where she opened the back door and tossed it into the yard.

1942

1942

ONCE PETE PULLED AWAY from the curb, she couldn't help stepping out on the porch and watching his car for a few moments—he turned north on Marin Street and disappeared. How long did she stand there then, staring blankly across the street at the front door of the Rutherfords' house? As long as it took for Lydia Rutherford to open the door and shout, Margaret? You okay?

Margaret summoned up a smile and waved her hand, then turned and went back inside. She closed the door. She locked the door.

It was almost four.

She went into the kitchen and let Stella out, then fixed a bowl of food for her—some leftover rice and some small scraps of pot roast and boiled carrots. I have, she thought, no reason to be alive. Thinking this was a sort of pleasure, so decidedly did it contrast with every thought that Andrew had ever entertained. Through the window she could see his last letter. In eighteen hours it had turned into a wet white rectangle in the lily bed.

She was in bed but not asleep when Andrew stepped onto the porch. Stella, who was downstairs, barked twice—her bark that said, Someone is here; I know who it is. The door to Margaret's room was open, and she went out into the dark hall without making a sound, but not down the stairs. She had locked the front door; he had a key. The door opened and closed. He set down his bag and greeted the dog. Not having read the telegram, she hadn't kept the light on—he stumbled on the hall rug, knocked against something, then found the light. Margaret shrank back into the shadow. After a moment that was punctuated by his sighs, he went into the kitchen. The kitchen light flooded into the hall. Now she heard him open cabinet doors, pull out a chair. She untied and retied the belt of her wrapper, then twisted back her hair, which was falling in her face. She went back to bed.

But she could not stay away after all. When she at last entered the kitchen, he was turned so that his back was to the door. His elbow was on the table and his head was propped on his hand. Stella, in her basket by the stove, lifted her head but didn't get up. Margaret's first sensation was resentment at the renewed tedium of it all. Her second was of the cold, now that she was out of her warm bed and in the clammy kitchen. It would be colder at the racetrack, in that immense building, of course.

When she sat down at the table, Andrew lifted his head as if its weight was almost too much for him, and turned to her. He sighed. She knew he wanted her to ask him how he was, or how his train trip had been, but she didn't say a word. After a very long time, he said, My dear, you are up. May I offer you a cup of tea?

She shook her head. Andrew, you should know that I didn't read any of your letters, and so I have no idea about your trip. I don't even know for sure why you went.

Well, Einstein . . .

I was afraid of that. You went to report Albert Einstein's activities in Vallejo to the navy. How did they take it? She couldn't keep an edge of mockery out of her voice.

They . . . He paused but then soldiered on. Every agency is overwhelmed by the war effort. At first I couldn't get in. . . . He shifted in his chair. No one in Knox's office knew who . . . Then he coughed and said, Well, my dear, they asked me . . .

Just then she was genuinely curious. Go on.

They asked me to stay away. They . . . He began clearing his throat over and over.

Well?

Someone gave an order that no guard should admit me to any secure building in the capital, and if I tried to gain admission, I was to be arrested. He fell silent, trying to leave it at this.

Did you get arrested?

More silence, then, One time.

Andrew!

I didn't mean to argue with the young man, but he was very disrespectful.

What happened then?

I spent a night in jail. In the drunk tank, because they seem not to have had anywhere else to put me. It was rather interesting. My theory is that drunkenness is actually a sort of allergic reaction—

She said, Stop.

He took a deep breath. I paid a fine. Five hundred dollars. But then he fell silent again.

She stared at him. You should know that they did act on the one report, and they threw Mrs. Kimura in jail and interrogated her and now she's dying of pneumonia she contracted there. The whole thing makes me both angry and sick.

Oh dear.

Oh dear?

I didn't mean for that to happen.

What did you mean to happen?

I thought maybe they would be sent to live with relatives in Japan. You said that the older boy had gotten married—

Andrew, they weren't spies.

He smoothed his mustache and took a sip of his tea. He said, No, of course, they weren't spies.

Einstein isn't a spy.

No one seems to think that he is, no. No one seems to think that he's been to Vallejo, either. You did express doubts, my dear. I admit that. I don't remember what you said in so many words. . . .

She said, Andrew, you are so perennially certain of your own innocence. You have . . . But even now she didn't know how to accuse him. Finally, she said, Pete doesn't blame you. I saw him today.

How is—

But I do. I blame you for . . . But she stopped. He was looking at her, and she saw that he had no way of knowing what he didn't know. She said, I should have stopped you.

Could you have? He seemed genuinely perplexed.

I don't know.

SHE got a note from Naoko that Mrs. Kimura had died and that Naoko and two friends from Japantown were being sent to a relocation camp in Arizona. Margaret sent her a box of warm clothes and some books, hoping she would be allowed to keep them. In her note, Margaret said that they would send her whatever she needed, no matter what. She didn't know what else to offer.

She never again heard from Pete. She wondered why she hadn't begged him to take her to Vancouver. And she knew it was because he thought she was going to.

When the knitting ladies asked her how Andrew's trip to Washington had gone, she said that it had been a failure.

Mrs. Jones said, Well, I'm sure it was well intentioned, and we should be grateful for that.

It was not well intentioned. She kept on knitting for a few moments, then put her work in her lap and looked around. Even Miss Jones, now Mrs. Milligan, looked exhausted. Her husband was stationed in North Carolina for the time being, then would be off to Germany. Mrs. Roberts had a grandson in the navy and a granddaughter in the WAC. Mrs. Jones's husband had died in the winter. Mrs. Tillotson's youngest son was on a submarine in the Pacific. Everyone looked as old as the hills, Margaret thought. I told Andrew that I am going to write a book.

Are you really!

What about?

I know you love reading.

Didn't you say your cousin wrote a book? Was it your cousin, dear?

Did you know I once saw a hanging?

Good heavens!

Back in Missouri. I was five. It would start with that.

Hangings weren't uncommon then, said Mrs. Roberts.

My brother Lawrence took me. He was thirteen. I can't imagine why he took a five-year-old to a public hanging. It must have been May, so I wasn't even five, actually. There were people everywhere. I remember sitting down on the step of the gallows and refusing to go another step. She did remember this—her back to the gallows.

You poor child!

They unshackled the outlaw right beside me, before Lawrence thought to pick me up. The sole of one of his boots had split away, and as he went up the steps, the flapping made him stumble. It formed in her mind as she spoke, the whole scene.

What was your mother thinking?

She was home having a baby. They always said they didn't know where we had gotten to. I think my brother gave me a couple of crab apples and a roll of bread. When the outlaw got to the top of the steps, they took him to the center of the gallows. I think Lawrence said, That one stinks. My bonnet must have been put on my head, because for a while I could only see boots and white clover flattened in the grass. Then Lawrence put me on his shoulders with his hands around my waist.

The outlaw wore a red shirt. A man beside him shouted, Son, what's your name? It was like a play.

You remember all the details?

In a way. In a dreamlike way.

You were five?

My birthday would have been a month later. The outlaw stood himself up a little and said, Jefferson Davis Claghorne. Don't ask me how I remember the name.

A woman next to me said, Why, he's just a boy hisself.

The accent came out of her mouth like a voice from far away.

Son, you have been sentenced by the court of this county to hang for the murder of Ezra Salley, and of Daniel Lackland. Do you understand why you are being hanged?

Our part of Missouri was heavy Rebel territory.

You have also robbed banks in Callaway County, this county, and Audrain County.

Maybe he fancied himself a member of the James gang, said Mrs. Roberts.

Son, do you have any words to say before you meet your just and fitting punishment?

Now the outlaw looked away from the other man and out at us, in the crowd. Right at me, I thought, a little girl on her brother's shoulders. He gripped a Bible in his hand, then dropped it, then bent to pick it up again. He looked at the Bible for a moment, then at me again. It was like the little girl was the only one he could see in the crowd. I was. I was the only one. But I could see everything. Two men came up behind him and lifted the noose over his head. One of them held his shoulders, and the other one tightened the noose so that it made his head cock to one side.

Mrs. Roberts said, I sometimes think people had no sense at all in those days.

Do they have any sense now? said Mrs. Jones.

Another man came up and said something to the outlaw that I couldn't hear; then he took the Bible out of the outlaw's hands, opened it, and put it back in his hands. And the outlaw said, I cain't read, you know. Lord, it's true I done it.

And just then, as Lawrence was lifting me off his shoulders, the floor of the gallows fell away, and the outlaw in the red shirt dropped toward the ground but jerked to a halt. The crowd gave off a loud noise, not a shout or a groan, exactly, but something made of many sounds. I never heard that sound again.

Oh, my dear, said Mrs. Jones. I'm amazed that you remember it so well.

I do, said Margaret, I do remember it now that I've dared to think about it. There are so many things that I should have dared before this.

And her tone was so bitter that the other ladies fell silent.

A Note About the Author

Jane Smiley is the author of numerous novels as well as four works of nonfiction. She is the recipient of a Pulitzer Prize, and in 2001 was inducted into the American Academy of Arts and Letters. She received the PEN USA Lifetime Achievement Award for Literature in 2006. She lives in northern California.

A Note on the Type

The text of this book was set in Simoncini Garamond, a modern version by Francesco Simoncini of the type attributed to the famous Parisian type cutter Claude Garamond (ca. 1480–1561).

Composed by Creative Graphics, Allentown, Pennsylvania

Printed and bound by Berryville Graphics, Berryville, Virginia

Designed by Maggie Hinders